# The Truth Lies Buried

Morton S. Gray

*Borteen Secrets series*

*Where heroes are like chocolate – irresistible!*

Published 2019 by Choc Lit Limited
Penrose House, Crawley Drive, Camberley, Surrey GU15 2AB, UK
www.choc-lit.com

A CIP catalogue record for this book is available
from the British Library

ISBN 978-1-78189-404-0

Printed and bound in Great Britain by Clays Ltd, Elcograf S.p.A.

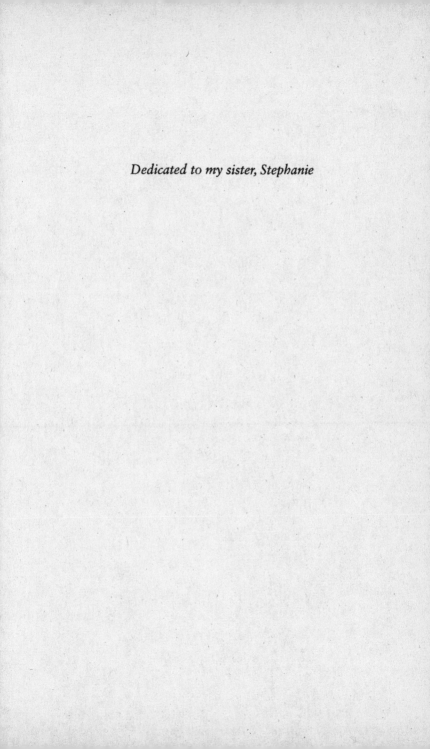

*Dedicated to my sister, Stephanie*

# Acknowledgements

This novel was conceived during a writing exercise run by author Linda Gillard at the 2011 Romantic Novelists' Association Conference. During the session, we had to choose a postcard and write a descriptive piece based on the image. My postcard was a wooden castle amongst trees. I gave the postcard back at the end of the class, but when I later told Linda it had formed the basis of a novel, she very kindly sent the postcard to me. It has been on my study wall ever since.

The first chapter of the fledgling novel, now actually the third chapter, was shortlisted for the Festival of Romance New Talent Award in 2013.

Thank you to the staff on the Makita stand at the Tool Show at Kempton Park Racecourse, who demonstrated the use of a chainsaw for carving sculptures and kindly marked up the equipment and clothing my hero would need in one of their brochures.

It has been lovely to bring my love of family history into the novel – and yes, I did once actually meet a lady researching her house ghost.

Particular thanks to Susan Wood for naming Owl Corner Crafts and thinking of a brilliant nickname for my hero, Carver Rodgers.

Appreciation must go to my lovely writing friends the ADC's, members of the Romantic Novelists' Association, especially the Birmingham Chapter. Margaret Ruess Newland read an early version of this book, Victoria Cornwall has been a constant support and helped me with some of the scenes. Thanks must also go to my family and my good friend Susan Wood for putting up with me during the writing and editing of the book.

My editor has been invaluable in helping me shape the novel into its final format. Thanks also to the Choc Lit tasting panel members who voted for my story: Rachel A, Jenny M, Cordy S, Hilary B, Lizzy D, Melissa C, Rosie F, Christine Y, Jenny K, Gill L, Katie P, Jo O and Alma H.

# Chapter One

Carver put his hands over his ears to cut out his brother-in-law's voice. The words were drilling into his brain and he wanted them to stop. There was only so much nagging he could take.

Kieron stood in the doorway of Carver's living room holding up the dishcloth from Carver's kitchen as if it were an exhibit at an auction. Even Carver, who didn't give a damn about such things, could see the fabric was green with mould.

'Look, I couldn't care less.'

Carver had to take his hands away from his ears to hear Kieron's reply.

'Well, you should. You're going to catch something awful and die.'

Carver saw the look of horrified embarrassment pass over his brother-in-law's features, as he realised the unfortunate phrasing of what he'd just said. Carver had seen that look too many times on too many faces since his wife had died.

A hazy vision of Bliss passed through his mind, causing a shiver to pass involuntarily through his body. *Why, oh why?* She should still be here, tossing her hair and telling her brother to butt out, but of course the dishcloth wouldn't be green if she were still alive and the house would be neat and tidy, not a complete tip. Kieron and Nina would be sitting in the lounge sipping wine after a wonderful Sunday lunch. They wouldn't be here trying to keep him alive ... or that was what they thought they were doing anyway.

Who gave a child a name like Bliss? Parents who realised their daughter was going to be lovely, ethereal and spiritual. The name had suited his late wife, with her long, silky blonde

1

hair and curvaceous figure. *Why was she dead, dammit? Why?*

Kieron recovered his composure, but continued his tirade. 'Nina says your kitchen should be condemned. There are so many different types of mould in there, it could be the topic of a PhD thesis on fungus and bacteria.' The words *Bliss would be upset* hung in the air unsaid, but Carver could hear them very clearly nonetheless.

'I've told you … I'm not interested. I don't eat in there anyway.'

'No, you just toss your takeaway cartons and beer cans in the sink, where they pile up and fester. That's when you bother to eat at all. Look how thin you've got, man. God knows what germs are on your plates and cutlery, if you can even find them underneath the rubbish.'

Carver shrugged. It was pointless to argue with someone who wasn't listening or even on the same wavelength. He didn't think his weight was any different to normal, and how could Kieron tell when he always wore overalls over his clothes? Did no one understand how he felt? How he continued to feel even after two, almost three years? Bliss dying had changed his world, like an asteroid striking the earth, like a tsunami, an earthquake …

He recognised that deep down his brother-in-law was hurting too. He'd lost his sister, after all. Appointing himself guardian of Carver's well-being appeared to be the role Kieron had adopted in his grief. Today, that role was particularly unwanted and irritating.

'You need a cleaner, mate – please.'

Carver shrugged again, annoyance starting to accumulate in his chest. He feared it was in danger of accelerating into anger.

'Can I at least arrange one for you?'

'Up to you.' He could feel his lips getting tight and his words clipped. This wasn't a good sign. He hoped Kieron didn't brandish the dishcloth at him again, he might just let rip with some choice words.

'If I do find a cleaner, will you at least pay them?' Kieron seemed oblivious to Carver's rapidly changing mood. 'Although, if we can find anyone willing to take on this hellhole, I'll be surprised.' He sniffed at the dishcloth, which he was still holding, and wrinkled his nose at the smell.

'Have you ever known me not to pay my way?'

Kieron looked at Carver askance, the penny dropping that he was getting mad.

At that point, Kieron's wife Nina appeared behind him to show her husband yet another specimen of interesting coloured mould, this time inside one of Carver's mugs. Her normally pretty face was set in an unattractive frown of disapproval. Kieron started flapping his hands to warn her to back off.

Carver couldn't stand any more. He took a deep breath and held it in tightly to contain the anger, together with the potentially damaging words that threatened to erupt from his mouth. He barged past the outraged couple. Nina squealed as the mug flew from her hand and smashed to pieces on the floorboards, but Carver didn't look back, couldn't look back, as he slammed out of the front door, nearly taking it off its hinges.

Reaching the bottom of the wooden steps in a couple of strides, he finally let out the breath he'd been holding and whistled. He would have preferred to scream, but a whistle would have to do for now.

A large grey dog lolloped out of the undergrowth. Carver ruffled pointed ears and affection for the animal became his overriding emotion, the anger lodged in a ball somewhere in his chest.

'Come on, Wilf, let's get out of here. I'm fed up with being treated like a naughty schoolboy. Let's run.'

The dog didn't need any further encouragement, matching his stride to run by Carver's side. Together they sprinted down the forest path, over the road, hesitating only a second to see if there were any passing cars, and onto the hillside overlooking the bay.

Carver ran along the rough turf until his lungs would take him no further. He sank to his knees gasping and Wilf, by now well used to this type of behaviour, plonked himself next to his master and settled down for a snooze. Carver marvelled at how well Wilf read his moods, knowing when to play, when to stay away and when to comfort. His chest felt tight after running, so he took a couple of precautionary puffs from the inhaler he kept in his back pocket.

The solid presence of the animal was what he needed today. To think he originally hadn't wanted the dog at all, had protested when his wife had arrived home with the tiny squirming puppy that made water marks on his polished oak floors. Wilf had been Bliss's dog really, but now he was most definitely Carver's. Two male souls united in their grief and loss.

Carver settled more comfortably on the grass, sitting with his knees bent, his hand on Wilf's warm flank, as he scanned Borteen Bay and the sea beyond for ships. There was a brisk wind, so there were several sails scudding across the waves.

The ball of anger and the breathlessness began to dissipate, and the thought of being able to sail away on one of the yachts started to become very appealing. *The white sail or the red? Choices, choices*. But, he sighed, even if he did go, he would still take himself on that journey and it would provide no escape from what had become his reality, more was the pity.

When his heart rate finally slowed after the run, he lay back, watching the clouds moving fast overhead and feeling his body almost ticking like a hot car engine that had just been turned off.

Then, despite the slightly chilly late September breeze, he fell asleep next to his faithful dog. Carver hadn't had an unbroken night's sleep since the day Bliss had died; he was plagued by nightmares full of recrimination and regret, and consequently was always exhausted.

He woke a while later stiff and cold. The afternoon was almost over, he could tell by the quality of the light as he sat up. The back of the blue overalls he habitually wore over his clothes were damp from the rain-soaked grass, his mind strained by dreams of Bliss, verging on nightmares. Wilf stirred and looked up at him expectantly.

*Who could resist that face?* Carver ruffled the grey fur with affection. There were times when he believed the one thing that kept him sane, kept him alive even, was caring for this beloved animal.

Carver lurched to his feet, scanning the view once more, stretching his calf muscles as he did so and noting that the tide was out to its fullest point. 'Don't think I'm up to running home, Wilf. We'll walk, shall we?'

The dog darted around, expectantly waiting for him to move. Carver laughed and did a couple of false starts to tease Wilf. Just for a moment he forgot himself – enjoyed himself – but then the shutters came down again and he could tell by the animal's stance that Wilf sensed it too.

He walked slowly across the rough grass, wondering what he would find at home.

Carver slowed his steps as they reached the road. The layby beside the path to his house was empty of cars, apart from his own pick-up.

*Hurray, Kieron and Nina have gone.*

After a momentary flush of guilt, because after all they were only trying to help, he was delighted that he could go back to his slovenly, grieving ways without fear of reprimand, at least until their next visit.

With a sigh of relief, he crossed the road, pausing to straighten the wooden carved and painted house sign, wobbly on its strut. It read *Tree Tops* and he'd smashed it over a year ago in an outpouring of frustration. He needed to mend it properly. Yet another thing he didn't feel like doing.

He made his way back through the forest, past all of the familiar trees that were like individual friends to him after living here for over twelve years and visiting the forest since he was a boy. Wilf followed without Carver having to give any command.

Putting his foot on the first step of the stairway up to the house, Carver changed his mind. He wasn't ready to return to the memory of his brother-in-law and Nina berating him for the state of the house, or to see what they had changed and moved in his absence in their desire to *help*.

Instead, he turned away and headed to the next clearing where a stump of wood stood in the middle of the space waiting for him. The perimeter of the gap in the trees was coated with wood shavings, evidence that he spent a lot of his time here. He unlocked the large waterproof metal box which housed his chainsaw.

His career as a specialist carpenter and his chainsaw hobby both enabled him to work out his anguish and frustration on wood, if indeed he ever could. The only time he felt truly alive was with a chisel or chainsaw in his hand; at least then he could forget reality and his grief for a while, or try to. It was getting more, not less difficult. *Time heals*, so people told him, but so far it had done nothing to take away the searing pain and gut-wrenching guilt.

In his day job he followed a prescribed pattern, often matching a worn or rotted cornice or panel for an old house, church or cathedral. He was a perfectionist in his professional world, renowned, and well paid for his skill. Conversely, his hobby working with the chainsaw gave him freedom of expression and it never ceased to amaze him what emerged from a newly cut log. It was as if he had divine communication, or could read the grain of the wood, instinctively knowing which parts to carve away and which to leave whole.

He paused to tie up his long hair in a band. A visit to the barber was yet another job he'd been putting off. His hand strayed to trace the scar on his face. He'd have a beard to match his long locks by now, but the hair didn't grow straight around the scar tissue and he looked ridiculous with a beard sticking out at odd angles, so he had to shave every morning. The mark was a constant physical reminder of what had happened to the love of his life ... why Bliss was no longer around.

Kieron and Nina may mean well, but what was the use of a tidy, clean home when he had no one to share it?

In the days after Bliss's death, he knew that Kieron had come to see him regularly to make sure that he hadn't turned the chainsaw on himself. His poor brother-in-law must have had nightmares about Carver lying in a pool of blood with severed limbs. Lord knew he'd been tempted. The only thing that had stopped him had been knowing that Bliss would want him to live to the full for her, to go to all of the places they had dreamed of and talked about. He still found it astounding that they'd been discussing that very subject, the issue of one of them leaving the world before the other, on the afternoon when she'd died. Their conversation had been a premonition of impending disaster maybe?

As yet, he hadn't had the heart to go anywhere far from where he'd scattered Bliss's ashes beneath her favourite tree. He couldn't understand why Kieron didn't blame him for the death of his sister, or even thump him. Maybe underneath all of his concern for Carver's well-being he did hold him responsible. No matter; Carver knew himself, knew that Bliss would still be alive if it weren't for his actions.

He started up the chainsaw and began to carve, harnessing the afternoon's frustration and annoyance at his in-laws' interference in his life, entering the only world where he could find any peace, cut off from his thoughts by the immediate need to control the saw.

The result of his fevered carving was a wooden mermaid, complete with scales on her tail and the face of his dead wife.

# Chapter Two

It was like a bizarre game show, one in which you had to name the inhabitants of the seaside town of Borteen and pair them with their respective businesses or addresses. Except that in her current state of mind Jenny wouldn't be scoring too highly. It would be almost funny, if the occasion throwing her up against all of these people wasn't her mother's funeral.

Sitting alone in the front pew, next to the dark wooden coffin with its sheath of lilies that seemed to loom over her, she was the sole Simpson in the congregation. As far as she was aware, she was the only surviving relative. Well, that wasn't strictly true; her father must be out there in the world somewhere, but who knew where ... she certainly didn't.

Her mother had refused to give her any information about her missing parent, even when Sheila had just a short time to live and was very well aware that was the case. The subject of her father had been taboo for as long as Jenny could remember and it seemed Sheila Simpson was determined to take her secrets to the grave, much to the frustration of her daughter.

Jenny glanced behind her to see that the church was packed; hers was the only empty pew. She had to look away quickly, because brimming tears threatened to overflow. How had so many people become aware that the service was being held today? She knew the answer really. Maeve, who ran the gift shop in Borteen, had been her mother's lifelong friend and, once Jenny had given her the funeral arrangements, she would have spread the word.

Mumbling her way through her mum's chosen hymns, the cloying scent of the lilies sticking in her throat, Jenny focussed on the stained-glass window in front of her in an attempt to keep herself together. The minister summed up her mother's life and the lump in her throat grew ever more painful.

Sheila Simpson had lived a simple life. Born in Borteen, she'd married a childhood friend and given birth to Jenny exactly nine months afterwards. When her husband, Timothy, had disappeared when Jenny was just seven, Sheila had gone to work at the local council office in the administration department to support herself and her daughter. She'd still been working there when she got her cancer diagnosis earlier in the year.

Jenny had often been frustrated by her mother's *little life*, but could see now that maybe it had been the only way Sheila could cope with the world, a comfort to keep things contained and simple. She'd always done her best for her daughter and delighted in her achievements. She'd encouraged Jenny to follow her dreams and introduced her to the hobby of quilting, which Jenny recognised had kept her sane when faced with some of the more challenging phases of her life.

Maybe she'd been too harsh in her opinions concerning how her mother conducted her time, with so little ambition or excitement. Her husband disappearing so mysteriously twenty-five years previously had defined her mother's existence and probably rocked her world from that day until the time of her death. What Jenny didn't understand, and probably never would, was her mother's reluctance to talk about this pivotal event of her life.

Crossing her legs tightly in an effort to maintain control over her emotions, Jenny smoothed her unfamiliar straight black skirt. She favoured bright colours normally, but as her mother hadn't specified in her otherwise detailed funeral plan how her mourners should dress, Jenny had opted for traditional black. The suit had been purchased on a hurried shopping trip to Sowden, the nearest city, and had probably, with hindsight, been a mistake.

Most of the other mourners were in brighter colours. Jenny wished in a way that she'd ignored tradition, but she'd felt so conscious that, apart from the coffin, she would be the centre of attention today. It was another reason why she was trying to contain her emotions, as she had no wish to speak to all of these people with mascara running down her face. Although she supposed they would all understand.

She'd held herself so tightly that she'd lost all feeling in her legs by the time the service ended and almost toppled headlong after the coffin when she stood up to follow it down the aisle. Reverend Hopkins hastily steadied her and continued to hold her arm supportively as they walked out of the church. Jenny clung to the poor man like a lifebelt in a stormy sea. She was sure he would have her fingerprints clearly visible on his arm afterwards.

The coffin bobbed ahead along the path into the churchyard, carried by the funeral director's men, as there were no relatives to perform the duty. The minister and Jenny stood by the church door shaking the hands of those who had attended the service. Not everyone would come to the graveside.

All of these individuals had made the effort to be here today for her mother. It was touching, unbelievable almost. She tried to dismiss the thought that Maeve might have bullied them into attending. Her mother had known full well that she was dying and so had planned this event in detail, right down to the donations bucket at the end of the aisle, proceeds to be split between Borteen Church and her mother's chosen charity of Cancer Research. The sound of coins being thrown into the bucket's depths reverberated in Jenny's heart.

As familiar faces grasped her hand or nodded at her as they passed by, she tried to get her befuddled brain to remember who they were and where in Borteen they belonged. At least she recognised Mr Wong from the Chinese takeaway. The totally unknown faces were mainly from the council office where Sheila had worked, but unlike the locals, these people tended to introduce themselves. Most of the faces she recognised, but many of their names annoyingly refused to attach themselves to the individuals in her mind. She became an expert at generic greetings that had no need to use names.

When everyone had filed out and stood milling around on the path outside the church, the minister put a guiding hand under Jenny's elbow and led her through the churchyard towards where her mother was to be buried. She didn't know how she felt about this either. She'd never been to a burial, only cremations, but Sheila had been insistent. She wanted to be reunited with her parents in the family plot. Jenny had been too young to remember those earlier funerals. Burial or cremation was a very personal choice. She started to wonder what she would choose. *No! Let's not go there.*

As they walked Jenny tried to catch a glimpse of the waves over the sea wall, hoping it would ground her in her normal reality that she felt a great distance from right now. The sounds of seagulls and families playing on the beach were incongruous and almost disrespectful given the situation she currently found herself trapped in.

She breathed great gulps of sea air as they caught up with the coffin bearers and the truth of the situation hit her full force, yet again. The gaping hole in the earth was for her mother. Jenny was scared of pitching headlong into the soil far below as she wobbled on jelly-like legs. The minister released her arm and went to stand at the head of the grave, making her feel even more unstable without his support.

While her imagination embroidered the details of her

12

potential fall into the earth, the coffin was lowered down gently. Was that really her mother in that oak box? The shiny brass plate proclaimed very clearly that it was: Sheila Simpson, 1958-2017 RIP.

She couldn't help the sob that escaped her tense body. No. She wanted to scream. *There's been a mistake. Bring her back up. She can't be dead. Can't be. Open the box. She won't be able to breathe in there.* But, of course, in her heart she knew it was true. Sheila Simpson was dead, taken in her fifty-eighth year by a hungry unmerciful cancer.

Jenny batted away the tears that had built up and now refused to be denied their exit. She unfolded the wad of tissues she'd put in her jacket pocket *just in case* and used one to dab at her brimming eyes.

She had to keep herself together, couldn't give in to self-pity. Her mother would expect her to keep a straight back. Everyone was looking at her. The minister said something she didn't catch. Surely she couldn't say pardon on such an occasion, so she just stared at him with what she hoped was a pleading expression.

Thankfully, Reverend Hopkins was used to the bereaved being distracted and repeated his request. 'Is there anything you would like to put into the grave, Jenny?'

She remembered the lily she'd taken from the edge of the sheath of coffin flowers just for this purpose. The poor bloom had been all but shredded between her agitated fingers.

*Sorry, Mum. Love you always.*

She flung the bedraggled flower towards the brass plate and the thunk of the heavy stem on the wood of the coffin sounded so final and forlorn. Jenny gulped and looked away, scanning the crowd, focussing her eyes anywhere but down that sad, deep hole.

Others were shedding tears too. Jenny could see Maeve scrubbing at her face with a lace handkerchief. Jenny had been at other funerals and knew the occasions tended to evoke memories of personal events, making memories of lost loved ones surface to produce repressed tears. This effect meant that not all of the grief being expressed was for the person in the coffin.

Reverend Hopkins closed his service book. The crowd began to disperse, no doubt eager to try the sandwich buffet, which Jenny had arranged from her mother's detailed instructions at The Ship Inn, a short walk away.

Again, Jenny's legs refused to move. A warm arm linked with hers. She jumped with shock at the sudden contact. 'Let me walk with you, Jenny. We haven't seen each other for years.'

The young woman next to her looked to be about the same age, dark curls cascading around her face. A search of her memory banks for a name jerked Jenny out of her maudlin state. Someone she'd been at school with, perhaps?

'Shall we walk together to The Ship?' The woman spoke as if she was sure Jenny hadn't heard the first time.

'Yes, thank you. I seem to have lost command of both my legs and my brain.' She put her soggy tissue in her pocket.

'It's an emotional day. My dad passed on a few months ago. Pippa, by the way, Pippa Freeman. I didn't expect you to recognise me after so long.'

Jenny stopped walking, pulled away a little and examined her companion more closely. 'Really? Pippa?'

'I've changed a bit.' Her laughter was like a tinkling bell. 'Filled out, grown big hair.' She fluffed up the curls on the side of her head with her free hand.

Jenny smiled for the first time that day and started walking again. 'You certainly look different ... but better different, I hasten to add. What was your nickname at school again?'

'Stick insect.'

'Oh, how awful we all were.' Jenny could hear the whole

class chanting the nickname, and remembered the thin, short-haired girl cowering in the middle of the circle.

'Scarred for life.' Again, the tinkly laugh. 'I'm joking, well sort of, I think it's why I keep my hair long. A reaction, I suppose.'

By now, they'd covered the short distance to the pub, and Pippa moved ahead to open the heavy door, with its inset stained-glass picture of a galleon with full sails.

'Deep breath, Jenny. It would be nice to have a coffee or wine together sometime.'

Pippa released her arm, but Jenny grasped hers back for a second. 'Thank you. I'd still be standing in the churchyard if you hadn't come along ... and yes to coffee, or indeed wine. Why not both?'

Pippa smiled. How could such a seemingly self-assured and attractive young woman ever have been bullied at school?

'It feels cheeky to ask, but could you stay nearby? I feel embarrassed that I can't remember a lot of these people's names or how they fit into Borteen and my mum's life. Could you help me out, do you think?'

'Sure, no problem at all. I just hope I can remember some of them myself.'

They both giggled and it sounded so wrong to Jenny on such an occasion.

She took the suggested deep breath and walked past Pippa into the warm familiarity of the pub. Her mother had always said that the gathering after a funeral was like a birthday party with the person whose birthday it was missing. Sheila would have loved catching up with all of her friends and acquaintances.

The function room thronged with people. Silence fell as she entered the room, the sight of the bereaved daughter seeming to drive away all of the conversation and laughter that had been in the pub before. No one had touched the buffet table, piled high with different types of sandwiches, pieces of pork pie and cheese with pineapple sticks.

Pippa again came to her rescue, leading Jenny to the buffet table and presenting her with a plate. Jenny didn't feel hungry at all, but half-heartedly loaded it with a couple of sandwiches and a cheese straw.

Conversation began to flow again and people formed an orderly queue to pile their plates with food. Pippa guided Jenny to an empty table. 'You need a sit down for a while to eat your sandwiches.'

Jenny didn't feel like eating, but she could see the sense in the sit down, as she was starting to feel exhausted.

She kept expecting her mother to appear from the crowd after a trip to the ladies', rushing over to adjust Jenny's collar or to retell some gossip about someone in the far reaches of the room, but of course she wouldn't. She was gone … forever.

Jenny took a half-hearted bite of a cheese sandwich and immediately regretted it. The food stuck in her throat and tasted like cardboard in her emotional state.

'Where did you go after you left Borteen High? I think that was the last time I saw you,' asked Pippa. She was rapidly turning into Jenny's guardian angel.

'I did my A-levels at Sowden College and then went to uni.'

'My education stopped after Borteen. I couldn't face any more bullying.'

It was a sobering thought that anyone's education would be affected by the behaviour of their peers.

'Pippa, I'm sorry if I played any part in all that business.'

'Don't worry, it was mostly the boys.' Pippa unconsciously played with the ends of her long hair. 'What did you study at university?'

'History and archaeology.'

Pippa looked puzzled. 'But didn't you go to work in London?'

'Yes, more's the pity. I gave up my passion for money and security. There was a company graduate scheme which didn't mind what your degree subject was. They fast tracked me into accountancy. Of course, by that point I'd decided to marry Ian and we wanted a decent mortgage for a house in Surrey, so I sort of got carried along by the tide.'

'Ian?'

'I met him at uni ... another big mistake.'

Pippa put her head on one side. 'Didn't work out?'

'I think we were kidding ourselves. I don't believe we were ever properly *in love*, rather both thought it was time we had someone to settle down with. We drifted apart. He began to drink heavily and then took off with the barmaid from the golf club.'

'I'm sorry.'

'Don't be. He saw more of her than me anyway. He played golf five times a week.'

Bewildered, but deep down relieved to be free again, Jenny had changed her name back to her maiden name of Simpson and rented a flat on the outskirts of London. But the city could be a lonely place. Serial dating had left her feeling frustrated that her perfect man appeared not to exist, or at least for no longer than five dates, by which time her beau's bad habits, expectations and hang-ups had usually surfaced. She guessed that this was mutual and her foibles became apparent in the same timescale too. She'd promised herself a period of celibacy to determine what she really wanted from both life and a relationship. However, she'd never met anyone who measured up to what she wanted.

At work she'd done well and gained promotions, but deep down she hated the job and was scared, but secretly relieved, when the company decided to relocate to Edinburgh. As she'd decided that she didn't want to go north, she was made redundant. She'd hardly had time to visit any employment agencies to look for another job before her mother had announced her illness and getting a new post became secondary to spending time caring for her mum for the last few months of her life.

As the only child, she'd returned home to the little seaside town of Borteen where she'd grown up and become a full-time carer for the eight months it took for her mother to die. It wasn't even supposed to be that long, but her mother had clung onto life for far longer than her doctors had expected.

'What about you?' she asked Pippa, dragging herself out of reliving her memories.

'Nothing as dramatic as you. I did a beauty therapy course and opened a nail bar in Borteen, in the alley near the newsagent, but it didn't work out really … fine in the summer when the tourists were about, but dead in the winter months.' She paused. 'Then Dad had his first stroke, so I let the shop go and helped Mum with the guest house; admin, cleaning, cooking and such. I've been there ever since.' She sighed.

Jenny began to feel guilty that she was just talking to Pippa. Almost as if she'd heard her, Maeve from the gift shop rushed over to envelop her in a hug, wiping away stray tears for the loss of her friend as she withdrew. Maeve gave Pippa a hug too, mumbling something about the loss of her father.

When Maeve went back to her table, Jenny told Pippa in secretive whispers about the game show quiz she'd imagined herself playing when she was in the church. It was hard not to giggle like schoolgirls. Together, they set about identifying as many of those at the pub as possible.

It truly was like a tour of the town, but then her mother

was Borteen born and had lived there all of her life. She had a lot of friends and acquaintances. The room was growing hot and the chattering loud. Jenny supposed she ought to circulate, even if it was the last thing she felt like doing.

*Back straight, head high, get on with it.* The voice in her head was her mother's.

She shook herself, fluffed up her spiky blonde hair and decided to treat this like a business gathering. She'd played a role at work for enough years. She'd detach from her emotions and get through the event. She'd done that so many times before in her corporate job, she just had to remember the state of mind and think herself into it.

Surprisingly, she began to almost enjoy it. Imagining herself a member of the royal family, with Pippa next to her as her aide, there to prompt her about names and roles, she began to work the room. Yes, she could do princess. She drew herself up and smiled, stopping just short of a royal wave.

Mr Wong was tucking into the sandwich buffet. Sheila Simpson had ordered a takeaway from him every Friday night for as long as Jenny could remember. He mumbled something through his full mouth. Jenny smiled and touched his arm.

A woman whose face she recognised was making a beeline for her. Jenny searched for a name, but looked back at Pippa with a plea for help in her eyes when nothing came to her.

Pippa laughed. 'Jenny, you must remember my mum, Ruth?'

Jenny felt her face colour. 'I remember your face, but as usual your name had deserted me.'

Ruth grasped her outstretched hand. 'I'm so sorry about your mother. I had no idea she was ill, or I would have visited.'

'Thank you. Once she was diagnosed the illness took hold

very quickly, I'm afraid. She hated people seeing her when she was poorly. Mercifully, she didn't suffer for too long … eight months. Some linger for years.'

Ruth nodded and then addressed her daughter. 'I've got to head back, Pippa. I could only get cover for a short while. Sorry, Jenny, we've new guests arriving this afternoon.' Jenny now knew that Ruth and Pippa ran the Rose Court Guest House opposite to the promenade.

As soon as Ruth had gone, Suzy Meadows from the Cancer Research Charity Shop approached to tell Jenny that her mother had often come to donate items and to choose new novels from the selection on the shop's shelves. A lump came into Jenny's throat, which prevented her saying what she actually wanted to say, that she'd donate her mother's clothing and the books that lined the shelves at the house to the shop, just as soon as she had the chance to sort them out. Instead, she smiled weakly at Suzy and squeezed her hand. The girl was very distinctive with her facial piercings, tattoos and goth-like black clothes.

Next came Mandy from the craft centre, Owl Corner Crafts, over the road from the pub. The name was quickly whispered in Jenny's ear by Pippa. 'So sorry for your loss,' said the buxom blonde.

'Thank you.'

'Your mum loved to wander around Owl Corner Crafts, but don't tell Maeve. I think Sheila always felt it a betrayal of her friend's gift shop to even come through my door, but then, we do stock very different items.'

'Now I have more free time, I'll have to come and have a wander myself.'

'You're welcome anytime.'

'Mandy's one of my best friends,' said Pippa. 'We'll all have to go for a night out soon.'

Jenny nodded and Mandy smiled.

'Sounds good, but more competition for the men, eh, Pippa?' Mandy winked.

Pippa's tinkly laugh rang out.

Mandy disappeared towards the exit. Borteen must be employing a lot of relief workers today, as so many local businesses and shops were represented here. Jenny reminded herself she was supposed to be playing princess and drew herself up straighter. *Imagine a string pulling you up from the top of your head.*

Fred from the butcher's shop solemnly came to stand in front of Jenny. He grabbed her hand and pumped it up and down. 'Lovely woman your mum. I had quite a crush on her when we were young. Loved it when she came into the shop, but had to be careful the missus didn't catch me flirting.'

Jenny could tell he was upset, but couldn't help a fascination with the vibrations of his belly fat as he vigorously shook her hand.

Fred was accompanied by a woman that Jenny recognised as belonging to the newsagent's shop. Her mum had a daily Sowden Gazette delivered. Since her death, they had piled up on the table ... unread.

Jenny shook yet more hands and realised that her princess act was slipping as she became increasingly more exhausted. It was a big relief when the last job was to thank the landlord of The Ship, Lally Kensington, for providing such good food and the space to celebrate and toast her mother's life.

She went to retrieve her handbag from the table where she'd first sat down.

'Thank you so much for your help, Pippa.'

'It was my pleasure. What will you do now?'

'After this?'

'No, I meant – will you stay in Borteen, or head back to London?'

'I think I've had my fill of London. Fill of accountancy

too. I'd like to have a go at running my own business, but I don't know why I say that as I've absolutely no idea what business I could run.'

'Small accounts?'

'No way.'

'Well, what do you spend most of your time doing?'

'For the last few months it's been cleaning.' She laughed, but the laughter was tinged with pain as she saw herself cleaning up around her mother's sick bed in the lounge.

'Cleaning then,' said Pippa, with a wink.

'Really? No! I don't think I've got the confidence.' She'd meant it as a joke, not something to be taken seriously.

They didn't finish the conversation, as a couple more guests – Jenny didn't know what other word to use to describe them – who had finished their sandwiches wanted to speak to her before they left.

Eventually, when everyone had gone, Pippa walked out of the pub and along the promenade alongside her.

Jenny felt wearier with each step and grimaced when Pippa reawakened the conversation about cleaning as a job.

'I do a lot of cleaning too, at the guest house.' She waved her hand at the building opposite. 'You can charge at least twelve pounds an hour, maybe more.'

'Hmmm, I'm not sure I'd want to—'

'Think about it. It's an easy business to start. Just the right insurances, dusters and a mop and you're off.'

'Maybe ...'

They exchanged mobile phone numbers and promised to meet very soon for a drink.

Jenny walked wearily up the hill towards her mother's home, musing about a possible career as a cleaner. She wasn't too sure, but then she needed to do something with her life.

# Chapter Three

Aliens landing on a newly discovered planet would know exactly how Jenny felt today. The light-blue business suit was a mistake, as were the high-heeled suede court shoes. She fought with each step to pull her feet from the thick mud, while trees formed hostile monsters around her, dripping moisture onto the shoulders of her jacket and hiding the way ahead. The smell of damp soil and dead leaves filled her nose. Heart thumping in response to her over-active imagination, her mind supplied potential attackers lurking behind each thick trunk, as she crept onwards.

It had all appeared so easy when Pippa had thought up the idea to earn money while Jenny was between jobs. Well, not between jobs exactly … more something to do while she decided what she wanted to do with her life.

The response to her card in the newsagent's window, within a couple of hours of paying two pounds to place it, had sent her confidence soaring. The small white square of cardboard had been taped to the grimy window between adverts for a plumber and a babysitter.

Her first caller had sounded desperate.

'I saw your card in the newsagent's window.' It was a deep male voice.

'Oh, wonderful. How can I help?'

'We're looking for someone to tackle a house which is out of control.'

'Out of control? What do you need me to do?' It sounded more than just a regular cleaning job.

'Everything on your list and more. A thorough clean and sort out to begin with and then possibly regular maintenance?'

When he'd said that the house was in a wood, she hadn't envisaged this. This wasn't a wood, it was a forest. A forest where the sound of a chainsaw tore through the air, setting her teeth on edge.

Parking in the layby, on the country lane up the hill on the way out of Borteen, as she had been instructed, she noted the lopsided *Tree Tops* sign and warily followed the narrow path into the dark trees. She'd assumed there'd be a driveway and the fact that there wasn't had her checking the directions she'd written in her new notebook for the tenth time.

How safe was this? She was going to an unknown address, after a phone call from a complete stranger and a male stranger too – madness! What was she thinking?

She moved cautiously past the never-ending trees, senses on full alert and, just as she seemed to be getting closer to the chainsaw blare, it stopped.

The silence left behind was complete for a moment, then birdsong, rustling leaves and a seagull cawing filled the void, as if she'd imagined the jarring machine noise.

At last, she spotted a building. She began to make her way towards it, squealing as an icy drop of water dripped from a branch down the back of her neck.

She stopped dead.

*My goodness. Am I in a dream?*

Jenny stood still, shocked at the wonder of the structure in front of her.

The building was a fairy-tale castle, made of wood, not stone. Nestled against two huge trees, it blended into its surroundings. There was a small clearing in front of the house, but the trees grew close around the other three sides. The bronze carpet of autumn leaves echoed the browns of the wood. She admired the symmetry of two turrets and two balconies. Glass in the upper arched windows sparkled

24

in the bright sunlight that had appeared after the earlier rainstorm. Once again, she had the feeling of having stepped into an alternate reality.

Who lived in a house like this?

Walking up the wide staircase towards the front door, Jenny's hand lingered on the silky-smooth banister. The smell of woodsmoke began to fill the air, drifting from further away into the trees. She admired an ornate heart, looking almost like lace rather than woodcarving and linking capital letters 'C' and 'B' above the doorway.

There was no response to her knock, but as the chainsaw had started up again and dominated the airwaves, she might have missed a shout from within. Her confidence began to wither away. She contemplated returning to her car and forgetting her new business venture altogether.

As the thought of running away surfaced, the memory of the anguish of the past few months hit her full force and she knew she couldn't give in now, not when she was at last making progress. She had to move on from her mother's death and make a new life for herself.

*Back straight, head high, get on with it.* The words, and the voice that echoed them in her head, were again her mother's. It was one of her mum's often used phrases. Her mother may physically be gone, but she lived on in Jenny's head and Jenny supposed she always would.

With renewed determination, she went back down the steps and across the clearing, weaving through the trees in the direction of the overwhelming sound of the saw.

Another clearing lay ahead and she noticed a man moving. As she got closer, she could see he wore faded blue overalls, huge ear defenders and goggles. With movements reminiscent of a boxer trying to decide when to strike, he appeared to be sizing up a tree trunk propped up on the ground. The chainsaw purred in his hands and his body braced as he moved in and connected with the wood. Shavings rained through the air.

The howl of the saw began to make her head thud and her pulse race. Watching the man carving was like observing an intimate scene between lovers, as he shaped the log. There was something fascinating about the undulations of his back and his deliberate movements, as his strong arms handled the heavy saw like a paintbrush. She watched mesmerised as the shape of a bird began to emerge from the wooden block. The man ducked and dived, wielding the saw with obvious skill. Jenny's best pair of smart shoes sank deeper into the muddy leaf mould as she waited patiently for him to notice her.

Suddenly, a huge grey dog leapt out of the undergrowth. The animal was as tall as Jenny when it jumped up, close enough for her to see flashes in his eyes. She backed against a tree, her heart in her mouth, stifling a scream. The dog circled around her, barking and snarling. Climbing out of harm's way was impossible in her tight skirt, even if she could climb a tree. Enormous teeth came close to her face and saliva dripped from the animal's jaws. Jenny clutched her handbag in front of her and stood as still as she could, given that she was shaking so violently. Scared of passing out, she closed her eyes and prayed for a miracle.

After what seemed a lifetime, during which she'd had plenty of time to imagine being eaten by the baying dog, the chainsaw silenced.

'Wilf, away. Come here, you mangy beast.'

Jenny chanced opening her eyes. The dog retreated instantly in response to the man's words. She sank down to the ground, her terror taking away all care for her suit.

The chainsaw man came towards her, removing his ear defenders as he walked. He took off his goggles, revealing slate grey eyes that showed concern, but maybe a hint of amusement too. Wood shavings coated his long curly hair.

'Are you all right? I wasn't expecting visitors.'

Jenny stuttered when she finally found her voice. 'You w-weren't ex-expecting me?'

'No.'

'But you rang me? Unless I have totally the wrong place.' Her voice sounded much higher in pitch than normal.

A look of puzzlement passed across his features and then his whole body tensed.

'You're the cleaning lady. My brother-in-law, Kieron, said he'd rung you. I'd completely forgotten.'

Jenny attempted a smile, while she contemplated how she felt about being called a *cleaning lady*.

He took off a thick glove and extended his hand. 'Carver.'

Was that his name? The 'C' from the heart above the house door?

Jenny couldn't decide if he intended for her to shake his hand or to use it to haul herself from the ground. She grabbed his palm and pulled. Her skirt made an ominous ripping sound as he lifted her to her feet. Meanwhile, she was puzzled by the tingles that ran up her fingers in response to his touch.

'Jenny Simpson.' She was annoyed at how weak and squeaky her voice sounded.

He nodded, the corners of his mouth turned up, but the smile didn't quite reach his eyes. On one side of his face there was a scar that went over his jawline and disappeared beneath his overalls. Trying not to stare, she dislodged her shoes once again from the mud. He had an unkempt look, definitely needed a haircut, but somehow all her eyes saw was the wound. How did you ask someone about such a thing? *How did you get your scar?* could be considered a rather personal question after only five minutes of acquaintance. The mark began on his bottom lip and that

27

part of the scar was silvered. Goodness, she was staring at his lips. Jenny began to feel hot with embarrassment.

Carver, thankfully, appeared unaware. 'Come up to the house and I'll show you around. You'll probably run a mile rather than take on the job, or that was my sister-in-law's opinion in any case.'

She trailed after his boot prints, keeping a wary eye on the dog, who now followed close on her heels, as if daring her to step out of line. She felt so far removed from the cool, calm, businesslike image she'd hoped to portray. She wished she could rewind to when she first rang the doorbell; this time Carver would open the door when she knocked.

They reached the building, he whistled twice and Wilf trotted obediently to a large kennel inside a fenced area beneath the wooden structure. Carver drew a latch across the gate to contain the dog.

He bounded lithely up the steps and pushed open the front door. It hadn't been locked, Jenny realised, but it only opened halfway and they had to squeeze through the gap into the house. A mountain of unopened post towered against the wall behind the door. She debated whether to remove her mud-caked shoes, but Carver didn't take off his boots and the floor looked little different to the forest floor anyway, so she didn't bother.

He led the way down the central hallway. Jenny spied a living room with every surface piled high with books, magazines and an assortment of stuff. The kitchen was full of dirty dishes, takeaway bags and plastic trays, liberally peppered with empty beer cans. It didn't smell particularly pleasant. She tried not to let Carver see her wrinkling her nose against the odour.

She'd never seen a house in such a state, even in her student days. It was almost scary. Was she really going to agree to clean up this mess, this ... total devastation?

Carver turned and she schooled her face so as not to reveal her shock. She wished she could stop her gaze travelling to his scar, as she was wondering what sort of accident or attack had caused his disfigurement. Pity, he was a good-looking man, when he wasn't scowling. She forced herself to meet his eyes.

'Can you do anything with this place? It was my in-laws' idea to get a cleaner. I'm not too bothered, to be honest, but they suggested a thorough sort out and then regular maintenance. What do you think?'

Jenny searched for a tactful reply. 'It will be … a … challenge.'

He sort of grinned, or was it a grimace?

All her senses were telling her to walk away, this was a big job, but she badly needed a new start and something about Carver intrigued her, not just his scar. 'Will you want me to do every room? Or are there *no go* areas?'

'If you are going to take on the job, I guess we may as well do it properly. My wife … died … I haven't been able to face sorting her things. Could you do that for me too, or rather help me to do it? I'm sure it might be easier with someone standing over me.'

'Oh, I'm so sorry. My condolences. How long ago did she die?' At least this gave a reason for the state of the house.

'Nearly three years now.' He looked away and rubbed at his eyes.

Her heart contracted at his so obvious pain.

He turned back. 'When can you start?' There was a definite crack in his voice.

'We haven't discussed my rates yet.'

'Kieron said twelve pounds an hour.'

'That's my normal rate for *simple* cleaning.' Wow, she was talking as if she did this all the time.

He frowned. 'I guess this isn't a *simple* cleaning job.'

'Not really, I'm afraid.' She thought quickly. 'To give you an idea, I would guess, and I haven't seen upstairs yet, that it will take a good, erm … ten mornings of four hours working to sort and clean, and then probably one morning a week to maintain.' Goodness, she sounded as if she knew what she was doing.

He looked down at his boots and she thought for a moment he was going to send her away.

'I would do it for fifteen pounds an hour, reverting back to my normal twelve when the house is clearer and cleaner. I will understand if you'd like to get another quote and there are companies that specialise in this sort of job.' *Oh no, what am I saying? This sort of job? He could be terribly offended.*

He didn't appear to have taken offence, but there was a flash in those grey eyes when he spoke. 'That's quite a bit more than I was expecting.'

'I realise that, but having seen the job …' Did she want to walk away? She couldn't read his expression. She was becoming fascinated by his face. Was it just the scar? No, it was his eyes too and the way he moved his mouth.

'How about we see how it goes? I was expecting twelve pounds an hour, which would be … eight mornings' work at your new rate. We'll review on day six and see how much is left.'

'Unless you want to get another quote.' Secretly, she admired his quick mental calculations. This was an intelligent man.

'No … I want you.'

His response took her by surprise, as did the strange flip in her stomach.

She held out her hand and Carver shook it, setting off those tingles again. 'Deal.'

'When would you start?'

'How about tomorrow morning?'

He nodded, but his expression was sad. 'You realise I'm going to find this whole process difficult … very difficult? I may be unbearably grumpy.'

'Let's see how it goes, shall we?'

He nodded. 'Until tomorrow, then.'

She tried to return to a businesslike tone, even though the emotional feelings permeating from this obviously unhappy man were beginning to get to her. 'I'll see you at nine-thirty in the morning.'

She had her first client. However difficult the job might be, she hugged herself in glee when she got back to her car. Even the mud on her car mats and the split in her skirt didn't seem to matter. She'd been carer for her mother for just eight months, but even those had made her fear she would never work outside of her mother's house again. She hadn't a clue what she wanted to do long term, but this job at least gave her a breathing space and it was liberating to be self-employed.

When Kieron had insisted on calling a cleaner to deal with the mess Tree Tops had become, Carver hadn't imagined a slim, elfin figure with spiky blonde hair. His stereotypical image of a cleaner was far removed from the reality of Jenny Simpson.

Watching her disappear into the trees as she made her way back to her car, trying to hold the split in her skirt together, he questioned whether he was happy about a woman being in his home at all, and this woman in particular. She was eye-catching, but he'd been trying not to notice. Who was he fooling, he'd noticed …

Meeting new people bothered him. He knew they always wondered about his scar. Some people blatantly asked him about it. Jenny hadn't and for that he was grateful. He did a good enough job of piling guilt upon his own head, without having to explain where his disfigurement had come from and to relive everything all over again. He didn't much care if his house was clean or dirty. It would never be the same without Bliss.

It did, however, somehow trouble him that he'd noticed Jenny Simpson in a way he hadn't noticed any other woman since Bliss had died. He'd even felt a stirring of arousal when she began to negotiate over her fee and he'd caught a glimpse of the spark in her eyes.

Maybe Nina and Kieron were right. It was time to move on. He'd been living in a frozen state for a long time, not allowing himself to enjoy the simple pleasures of life, except for his woodwork, and that he could do alone without the need for conversation.

He wandered back into the house, annoyed that the door didn't open properly because of his reluctance to tackle the post behind it. He picked up his drum. He hadn't played with the band since his loss, but lately he'd found himself beating out favourite tunes on the bodhran. After drumming along to a hummed reel, he sighed with a mixture of pleasure and disgust. Was he beginning to feel normal? Could he ever be 'normal' without Bliss?

Noticing Jenny as an attractive woman felt like another sign that things were changing and somehow it made him irrationally angry with himself, as if he was disrespecting Bliss's memory.

*Face it, Carver. She's dead. She's never coming back and it's all your fault.*

# Chapter Four

The following day was Wednesday and Jenny arrived at Tree Tops ready for action, dressed more appropriately this time, in jeans and T-shirt. Laughing at her image in the mirror that morning, she'd had an overwhelming desire to add a headscarf over her spiky, blonde hair, to make herself look like a stereotypical cleaner from a comedy film.

A rough plan for how to tackle the out of control house had formed in her mind as she watched television the previous evening. She'd decided that the priority must be to make things more hygienic.

She moved through the forest more confidently in her old trainers and casual clothes. The trees appeared much friendlier in the autumn sunshine. She paused for a moment to admire the wooden house, as it became visible through the trees. She'd honestly never seen another building quite like it before.

Carver answered her knock on the door this time, but his expression didn't make her feel very welcome. Thunderous was an understatement for the set of his face.

'Good morning.' She decided to ignore his mood and be bright and breezy. 'I wonder if we could start by discussing your priorities for the deep clean. Would you like me to start upstairs or down?'

'You're the cleaner. I'll leave it up to you.' He shrugged and, pushing past her, went outside. She heard him click open the bolt on the dog run, whistle Wilf and trudge off through the leaves with the dog.

*How rude!*

Carver didn't seem any more comfortable having a cleaner than she was being one.

In the absence of any clear guidance, she decided to put her provisional plan into operation and start in the hallway. She began to pick up the unopened mail that prevented the front door to Tree Tops opening properly.

Having put the envelopes in three carrier bags that she'd found discarded in the kitchen, she swept the corridor that went from the front door to the kitchen at the back of the wooden house. The floor was still dusty and would need a proper clean, but it made her feel better to know that she'd at least finished one job. She still had to fight a sick and overwhelmed feeling when she peered into the kitchen at the back, the lounge to the left and the downstairs loo, plus a study that was full of boxes on the right, or was it a dining room? It was difficult to tell.

Judging by Carver's reaction this morning, she was going to have to use her own initiative and leave him piles of things to sort out. So much for doing this together.

She sat cross-legged on the floor and began to sift through the post. There were so many leaves interspersed amongst the envelopes that her pride in having swept soon departed. She would now have to sweep again before she left.

Sorting obvious junk mail and flyers into one bag to throw out and the rest into envelopes addressed to Mr and Mrs, Mrs Rodgers and Mr Rodgers, she propped the three piles of post needing Carver's attention against the hall wall, but she didn't have much confidence he would even look at them.

She decided that Carver's name must be a nickname, as most of the envelopes were addressed to Mr D. Rodgers. She came across one to a Damien Rodgers. The name was familiar and it niggled at the back of her mind. Was he at school at the same time as her? Did he look about the same age? It was so difficult to tell.

She swept the hall floor again, then went in search of the dustbin, walking warily in case the dog was around. Thankfully, he didn't appear to be.

Going back into the house, she realised she hadn't even looked upstairs yet. She was almost scared to, as surely the wooden floors of this tree house were in danger of collapsing beneath the jumble of Carver's life. What had happened to make him neglect everything like this? Surely it must be more than the death of his wife, although she was well aware that grief was an emotion that people reacted to in different ways.

She swept the kitchen floor next and used a dustpan and brush, which she had discovered behind the door, to add the dirt to a bin bag.

By now it was already mid-morning and she spotted Carver sitting outside on a log bench. He had a piece of wood and a chisel in his hands. If this job was going to work she needed his input for the sorting and so she had to at least build a working relationship with the surly man.

She made two cups of coffee. She had to disinfect the mugs first, as mould was growing at the bottom of them. It gave her an *icky* feeling, but she told herself off and just got on with it.

It was a pleasant day with sunlight filtering through the leaves, already starting to thin as they changed colour and began to fall to the ground with the changing season. She walked gingerly over to the bench, trying not to spill the drinks.

'I've made you a coffee.'

'Thanks.' He didn't look up and his face remained pre-occupied.

She put his mug on the wide arm of the bench next to him and sat as far from Carver as she could on the seat. He was working on a wooden disc, carving the stylised head of a

35

man surrounded by leaves. She had a little inner giggle, as he was living up to his nickname.

'Is that what's called a Green Man?'

He looked up with a startled expression, as if he hadn't really registered her presence until then. 'Yes, a Green Man.'

'I've seen them for sale, but I don't fully understand the significance. Is it just a decoration?'

Carver put his work and the chisel on the bench between them, picked up the drink and cradled the mug in his hands. He fixed his grey eyes on her. Her insides did a strange cartwheel. Could he see into her soul? It sure felt like it.

*Don't look at his scar, Jenny.*

But, inevitably, her eyes were drawn to the red slash on his face and particularly the silvered bit on his lip. *You are staring at his lips. Stop it.*

Carver didn't seem to notice, as he was intent on answering her question.

'As always with such myths, there are lots of versions. The Green Man, to me, represents a woodland spirit. Displaying his image is symbolic to ask the ancient gods to renew the woodland after the autumn and winter die back.'

'Will you put him on the house wall?'

'We'll see. If you take a look over there you'll see that there are quite a few versions on the house already. I might sell him instead.'

'Oh, if you do please give me first refusal.'

He almost smiled. 'Will do.'

He was wearing an open-necked shirt under his blue overalls and she could see that his scar extended down onto his chest. The mark gave him a dangerous, almost piratical appearance, now that she'd got over the initial shock of it being there. She dragged her eyes away and gazed into the trees for a moment.

'You love trees, don't you?'

Again, that flash of grey eyes, as he glanced at her. 'Guess the house, its location and the carvings are a bit of a giveaway.'

'Did you build Tree Tops?'

'Every last plank, yes.'

His dog wandered out of the trees. Jenny tensed, leaning back into the bench and lifting her feet from the ground.

'Wilf won't hurt you – unless, of course, I ask him to.'

She didn't feel reassured. 'I've never been comfortable near dogs. I was bitten by a Jack Russell when I was five. Nothing serious, but it's left me feeling very uneasy near animals.'

'Wilf, here,' commanded Carver.

The dog walked straight to his master and Carver laid his hand on the grey head.

Jenny edged as far away as possible, her heartbeat galloping.

'He obeys without question, he was trained by a police dog handler. Wilf, kennel.'

The dog trotted away to his kennel under the wooden house. 'See, he's very obedient. Another time you can make friends with him.'

'Maybe,' she said, but she knew her tone didn't suggest any excitement at the prospect. 'Oh well, I'd better get back to work. I've done a first clean of the hall and kitchen floors. There are piles of envelopes for you to go through. I got rid of the obvious junk mail. I'll spend the rest of my hours today in the lounge.'

Carver didn't respond. The word *whatever* hovered in the air. He was already working the wood again, his face intent and concentrating, his attention far away from her.

She decided not to push her luck and retreated while he was at least speaking civilly to her.

Carver still didn't know what to think about this woman being here in his wood and even more so about her being in his house. She'd dressed more practically this time with jeans, a fleece over a T-shirt and old trainers. She was pretty, with her tousled short blonde hair and blue eyes. He was trying hard not to notice the colour of her eyes, or to allow himself to sink into conversation with her, but it was difficult, as for a change, he wanted to talk. She smelled good too, he'd picked out jasmine and rose in her flowery perfume.

He sipped the coffee that she'd made for him without being asked. Strong, just as he liked it. Running his free hand over the carved face by his side, he felt for rough patches and tried to decide which part to work on next. If Jenny liked it when it was finished, he was half-minded to let her have it, if such a gift wouldn't be misconstrued.

Why did things between men and women have to be so complicated?

*You shouldn't be looking at her at all. You don't deserve to.*

Jenny spent the rest of the morning attacking spiders' webs in the lounge. The spiders seemed to have decided to take over. It was fortunate she wasn't squeamish about the eight-legged insects. She didn't like killing them though and wherever possible she put them outside, dropping them gently over the wooden banister to the forest floor below. She hoped Carver didn't spot her doing it.

She questioned her audacity at demanding payment for cleaning, when she didn't seem to be making much progress. She salved her conscience by polishing the wooden shelf above the fireplace and cleaning the picture frames that were mysteriously all lying flat on the shelf, face down. The photographs in the frames all featured a beautiful woman with long straight blonde hair. It had to be Carver's wife, Mrs B Rodgers from the envelopes she'd sorted earlier.

Carver chose that very moment to appear in the doorway.

She hurriedly replaced the picture frame she had been studying and felt her cheeks flame with colour.

'Oh,' he said.

'Sorry, did you want them face down again?'

'No, they should be displayed. That's Bliss, my wife.'

'I guessed …'

There was definite evidence of moisture in his eyes. She polished to the end of the shelf to give him time to recover.

'Right, that's my time done for today. I'm afraid it doesn't feel as if I've done much.'

'There's a lot to do. You've made a start.'

'I'll be back in the morning. Did you see the envelope piles I left for you?' He could hardly miss them in their prominent place in the hall and it felt foolish to have said anything.

'I did. I can't promise to deal with things quickly. I've got into bad habits and it's – all so difficult and overwhelming somehow.'

'I understand, really I do, I've just—'

He interrupted her, suddenly changing back into a different mood. 'Do you want me to pay you each morning?' He began rummaging in his back pocket.

'No, no. The end of the initial clean will be fine. That is, as long as you're sure you want me to continue. I can see that this is very … challenging for you.'

He just stared at her for a moment and then spoke abruptly. 'I'll see you in the morning.' He turned away, disappeared down the steps and was halfway to the clearing where he did his carving by the time she had reached the front door.

Jenny felt washed out for the rest of the day. She'd had plans to start clearing her mother's house, but instead drank mug after mug of tea and watched property programmes on TV. The realisation that she had a lot to do here as well as at Tree Tops somehow made her feel stuck. The cleaning job, or attempt at it, hadn't been difficult, but the emotionally charged energy of Tree Tops, along with the hefty dose of her own grief, had drained her.

Carver himself fascinated her. His scar. His dead wife. His obvious misery. And the way her body reacted to him, even when he just glanced at her.

There were decisions to be made. Did she stay in Borteen or did she go to live somewhere else? If she stayed in Borteen, did she stay in this house or move? It all felt too much to think about and she pondered that Carver would be surprised if he realised her dilemmas were not that different to his own, or so she imagined.

She toyed with ringing Pippa to ask if she'd like to go out for a drink, but settled instead for a hot bath, cheese on toast and early bed with a book to distract her from her thoughts.

# Chapter Five

Her alarm sounded all too soon the next morning. Once more at Tree Tops, Jenny, armed with the gauntlet-like rubber gloves she'd bought in the tiny Borteen convenience store earlier that morning, busied herself with black bin bags. She tried not to examine too closely what she was doing, as many of the items she was picking up were far from pleasant. She kept her focus on moving forward an inch at a time through the mess of the kitchen.

She worked systematically along the surfaces, leaving anything she was unsure what to do with in piles for Carver to look through. She didn't hold out much hope that he would sort things out anytime soon though, as the letters she had so carefully categorised the day before were still on the floor in the hallway, apparently untouched.

Even after her first attempt at a clean, she knew that the kitchen cupboards would require further attention, but at least this way, she could make a drink more easily and the mugs, plates and cutlery were no longer a public health hazard. She would have found it difficult to disagree with Carver's sister-in-law about the mould problem.

There were more photographs on the kitchen wall of the beautiful angelic-looking woman she now knew was Carver's wife, Bliss. She itched to know more about their story, but felt that she was just being nosy, as their relationship history had no bearing on her cleaning job. Besides, Carver Rodgers appeared to be a man of moods and she had no desire to upset him again when she was this far from the road alone with him and his dog.

An hour and a half later, the kitchen was transformed and

she couldn't help a glow of pride. Maybe she could do this job after all.

'Blimey!' Carver's exclamation from behind her made her jump what felt like two feet in the air.

When she turned, he was staring around the room with wide eyes. 'Is this my kitchen or did you get a new one fitted while I was out?'

'It's yours.' She smiled. 'It was just ... hidden.'

There was something child-like about this tall man gazing around his own kitchen as if he had never seen it before. He ran a finger along the work surface, then examined it and his expression suggested amazement when it came away clean. He moved over to trace a man's face in a photograph framed on the wall. She'd wondered about it as she'd polished the glass at the front of it earlier.

'I don't know why, but that man looks very familiar. May I ask who he is?'

Carver turned and stared at her. He paused before replying, totally unaware of his effect on her insides, which felt jelly-like all of a sudden.

'My father, Michael Rodgers.'

'Does he live near here? Is that why I recognise him?'

'No ... well, he did once, but he ... disappeared twenty-five years ago, when I was eight.'

Jenny sank heavily onto the stool in the corner. She felt the colour drain from her face. Her heart had begun to beat erratically and faintness threatened to overwhelm her. She hoped she wasn't going to be sick on the floor she'd recently cleaned.

'Are you okay? Are you ill?' Carver's face and voice held panic and concern, his eyes wide open.

'I don't believe it! So ... so ... did my dad. Twenty-five years ago, almost to the day. I was seven. Wait a minute ... you must be *that* Damien Rodgers.'

'*That* Damien Rodgers?'

They stood in stunned silence for a little while, both lost in their own thoughts, eyes locked, while Jenny recovered herself.

'We played rock, paper, scissors,' she whispered.

'Did we? Have we met before then?' Carver looked so closely at her that she felt a blush rise to her cheeks as he scanned her face. He hadn't said anything about her knowing his real name was Damien.

'At the police station.'

He still looked blank, a frown now screwing up his features.

The strange boy in short trousers. He'd had a scowl back then too. It was a fragment of memory, but it was etched on her mind. Two children in the same waiting room. Two children with distressed mothers, both trying to keep out of their way. Now she thought about it, Jenny could remember her mother, Sheila Simpson's tear-stained face and feel her own bewilderment about what was going on ... where her dad had gone and if he was coming back. He never had.

'But how did you remember my name? You were only seven.'

'It was something my mother said. It stuck in my memory.'

'Let me guess, something about me being named after a character in a horror film?'

Her cheeks coloured yet again and she nodded.

'Yes, *The Omen* films. I remembered you years later when I was deemed old enough to watch them.'

Her mum had sat at the other end of the waiting room to the boy's mother and the women strangely hadn't spoken to each other beyond what was necessary, even though their children were playing together. There had been no sign of either of the women's husbands for several days. Both men had vanished, seemingly with no trace. No notes, no flight bookings, no bodies, no blood. They'd both just gone … disappeared. Yet, there wasn't any sense of the two women being united in their loss, rather the opposite. Why?

The young Damien had won most of the games of chance that, thinking back, her younger self had hardly understood, and Jenny had quickly lost interest in reciting *rock, paper, scissors*. She did, however, remember being fascinated by the colour of the boy's eyes, Carver's eyes. Those grey eyes with silver flashes were staring at her now, as he searched his own memory banks.

'You won every game,' she said.

He smiled and it seemed more genuine than before. Did she imagine that he looked somehow younger, with a hint of vulnerability? Maybe his seemingly normal moodiness hid something deeper?

'Did you ever find out anything about your father's disappearance?' he asked.

'Nothing at all. He seems to have evaporated into thin air and was never seen or heard from again.' She felt the familiar discomfort in her body, the feeling that she was discussing a taboo subject. 'Did you?'

'I can remember conversations at the dinner table with my mother. We even began to speculate about alien abduction, because my father's disappearance was so complete.'

'Do you think they could still possibly be alive – our fathers?' The question stole her breath and she had to concentrate on moving air in and out of her lungs to stop the light-headed sensation threatening to overwhelm her again.

'Who knows? I used to try to spot my dad in crowds. Even now, just occasionally, I catch my breath when I think I see him. He left a huge hole in my world.' Damien went back to stare at the picture on the wall. 'I have this on the wall to remind me that my father actually did exist. I can still remember him carrying me high on his shoulders … feeling on top of the world.'

'My life was never the same either. My mother was never the same.' Jenny rubbed her shoulders where the discomfort raised by discussing her father had lodged. Her mother had forbidden Jenny to ever speak about her dad's disappearance all those years ago and Sheila Simpson had stuck to her resolve never to air the topic even when she was close to death.

'I don't think my mum ever recovered either. It was as if Dad took a big piece of her with him, wherever he went.'

'We must have been at school together?'

'Probably not. I didn't go to Borteen schools. Mum had to work, so I had a childminder in Sowden and went to school there.'

'It's such a huge coincidence that your brother-in-law chose my card in the newsagent's window. Don't you think?'

'Just chance.'

'What if it's a sign?'

'A sign of what?' He was frowning now and looking increasingly uncomfortable.

'Maybe we're meant to finally solve the mystery.' A little petal of excitement began to unfurl inside of her.

He paused just longer than was comfortable before replying. She felt trepidation flooding over her enthusiasm.

'Look, Jenny, after all this time, I think it's probably better we let things lie. I'm not sure I'm that interested.' He put his hand on her sleeve. The warmth of him contrasted with his cool, warning tone.

'Is your mother still alive?' she asked.

'No, long gone. Yours?'

His hand remained on her arm. Now it felt like a caution, rather than a comfort.

'She died a month ago.' There was a familiar catch of

emotion in her words. Tears were never far away when she mentioned her late mother. They'd been so close, as there had only been the two of them for so many years.

'I'm so sorry. My condolences.' He paused, as if choosing his words carefully. 'As regards our fathers – I'd say the trail has gone cold, iced over in fact and ... we should leave it that way.'

He removed his hand and her whole body felt instantly cold. There was a thin veil of politeness over what sounded like anger in his tone. The earlier thaw in his face had frozen over again. His scar looked red and livid, as if it too had reacted to his mood. She felt disappointed that, once more, she'd upset him.

Carver turned on his heel. She watched him walk back up the hallway and outside. The front door banged against the wall now the post no longer acted as a doorstop.

That angry gleam in Carver's eyes when she'd suggested trying to find out what had happened to their fathers reminded her she knew very little about him. Anger scared her. She might have imagined his emotion, but she didn't think so. He may be an attractive man, but as her mother had often said, '*Handsome is as handsome does*'. The veneer of politeness and concern could veil something much darker.

She finished off the washing-up and went to find Carver before leaving to go home. She was a bit hesitant, but she had to get the relationship back to a working basis at least and submerge the possible links between their fathers, if that was what he wanted. She didn't feel she could leave without seeing him, or let a *bad taste* linger in the air.

She found him in his carving clearing, shovelling wood shavings and twigs into a wheelbarrow. He glanced up, but didn't stop working.

'I'll be back tomorrow to do more in the kitchen. Are you

46

still happy for me to leave piles for you to sort out?' The comment was a less than subtle hint that he appeared to have done nothing with anything she had left for him so far.

He stopped mid-shovel and curling bits of wood began to fall to the floor from the spade. He stared at her for a moment. 'Look, it may be better if I spend some time with you going through the stuff you want me to make decisions on. I'm not great at tackling things right now.' He half-laughed. 'But you've probably gathered that already.'

She smiled, but didn't say anything. She wondered if, despite his apparent moodiness, he enjoyed her being around, making him coffee and trying to engage him in small talk. However, he hadn't exactly given her that impression and the knowledge that their dads had disappeared around the same time appeared to have done little to improve their wary working relationship.

'The sorting will have to begin next week though, as I have to go and discuss a job at Sowden Cathedral tomorrow. Which reminds me, I'd better find a key for you.'

He crossed the clearing with his long strides and jogged to the house. She followed more slowly. The thought of being at Tree Tops on her own didn't fill her with much joy. Disconcertingly, Wilf was pacing around the clearing, but thankfully didn't show any interest in her at all.

Carver came down the house stairs and handed her a key. The fob attached to it was a woolly sheep. She decided not to comment. He noticed her warily eyeing the dog.

'Wilf is fine, you know.'

'I'm sure he is. I'm just not that keen and he's so huge.'

'I promise he'll be locked in his kennel when you're here tomorrow, but we should make time for you to make friends with him.'

It was Jenny's turn to half-smile.

The short drive home was a time for reflection. Jenny

drove down the hill towards Borteen, for once not taking any notice of the cloud formations over the sea, which was normally one of her favourite things to look for.

She drove along the seafront, past the high street and then back up the hill to Priory Avenue. She parked her car in the drive and looked up at the windows of the 1950s semi-detached house where her mother had lived ever since she'd married her father, and where Jenny had lived until she left for university. The woodwork badly needed painting, or else replacing altogether. It was home, except it wasn't really; it still felt like she was visiting her mother's house.

She'd hardly closed the front door with its coloured glass fanlight when heavy tears began to flow down her cheeks. Her mother's passing had been rather sudden in the end, because in typical style her mother didn't want to bother the doctor with yet another *little* ache. The ache had turned out to be secondary cancers in her bones. Since the funeral, Jenny had drifted through the days and visited a couple of university friends, but now she realised she hadn't properly allowed herself any time to grieve. She'd spent more time trying to distract herself from her feelings, rather than beginning the healing process.

The solitude of the house seemed to swallow her up and her thoughts returned to her conversation with Carver about their fathers.

Standing in the middle of the lounge, she closed her eyes and inhaled. Was there any vestige of her dad here? After all, this had been the family home before he'd disappeared and the place she'd lived as a child, but all she could smell was a trace of her mother's perfume and the potpourri with hints of lavender and hyacinth in a bowl on the old-fashioned sideboard. Surely, there must be some energetic imprint of her father, however long ago he'd lived here.

*Nothing.* She could feel nothing. *Zilch. Nada.* It made her very aware of the empty space inside her, where she imagined her father's love should live.

She opened her eyes and walked around the room scanning the furniture and the items decorating the walls. Was her father responsible for buying any of the ornaments or pictures? The one common theme was the old clocks dotted around the rooms of the house. None of them showed the correct time. She remembered her mother saying she couldn't stand the ticking if they were wound up. Were they anything to do with her father? Is that why her mother had kept them?

She realised that she'd missed the opportunity to ask her mother that question, but in any case, the mention of her father would have resulted in an argument or stony silence. Sheila Simpson was as traumatised by her father's disappearance as Jenny herself, from the moment he had gone missing to the day she had died.

There were photographs of Jenny at various stages of her schooling, culminating in a graduation shot. Jenny frowned at her hairstyle at that age. There were no photographs of her mother or father. On reflection, it struck Jenny as odd. Why was there nothing to remind her mother of her lost husband? No wedding photo, no images of Timothy at all. There surely had to be a memento, something her father had bought for her mother, but Jenny wasn't sure. It was frustrating not to know. If only her mother hadn't got so upset if he was mentioned. Sheila Simpson must have felt abandoned, maybe angry, but there had to be much more to all of this than she knew and she would never get any answers now that her mother had gone.

Sooner, rather than later, she would have to tackle the loft. If there was going to be any trace of her father in the house, it would more than likely be boxed away up there. Her mother had liked her boxes.

Jenny suddenly craved a photograph of her father on the wall, like the one in Carver's kitchen. She wanted to know what features to look for in a crowd. It had never occurred to her before just how completely her father had been shut out of her life, almost as if he'd never existed, or even had any part in her conception. Why?

A strange melancholic mood settled over her. She forced herself to unpack a patchwork quilt she had pieced together in London before her world had imploded. She hadn't touched the fabric since, apart from to box it up when she left her London rented flat. There had been no time to process being made redundant, as the loss of her job was followed so quickly by her mother's announcement of her cancer diagnosis.

Jenny sighed and began to top stitch the quilt by hand. Her heart wasn't really in it. The fabric had been perfect for her modern tiny loft style apartment, but she wasn't sure it would look right here in Borteen. The stitching felt like a veneer or plaster she was trying to put on top of her emotions. At some point, she would have to unpack her mother's house and her own feelings, but for now she just kept stitching. She reasoned that if it didn't look right when she'd finished it she would donate the quilt to a charity.

She lay in bed that night remembering all of the good and the emotional times she'd shared with her mother over the years and each one produced its own fresh batch of tears. It was distressing, but cathartic. Bereavement was a process and not an event, she reminded herself, as she soaked yet another tissue and struggled to breathe through her blocked nose.

In contrast, the memories of her father were few and fleeting, difficult to grasp, ghostlike, almost as if she'd erased any of the recordings that had included him.

# Chapter Six

Jenny was disgusted when she looked in the mirror and a puffy-eyed, sad monster looked back on Friday morning. She was glad after all that Carver wouldn't be at Tree Tops today.

Out of the blue, there was a friend request on her Facebook page from an old school friend – well, she'd never really been a close friend, more someone she knew in her class. The message revealed that Cindy was still living nearby in Sowden on the far side of Pink Moor. After exchanging a couple of messages, Jenny arranged to meet Cindy for coffee in Sowden on Saturday afternoon. At least it felt positive and she resolved to seek out more local old friends to kick-start her non-existent social life. She didn't have an excuse any longer.

She resolved to see Pippa again too. She had been so kind on the day of the funeral and would surely be able to answer a lot of her questions about those from school who had remained in the locality.

Jenny set off to clean at Carver's with memories of her schooldays surfacing every few minutes.

Working at Tree Tops knowing that Carver wasn't around was somewhat unnerving. Jenny was aware of every sound. Add in the fact that she was conscious of Wilf locked in and pacing his run beneath the house and Jenny felt on edge the whole time. She rationalised that the dog would surely bark if a stranger came near.

She cleaned out several kitchen cupboards, leaving out items she thought should be binned, like out of date half-empty flour bags and cereals. Did Carver actually eat anything here? The fridge had a definite odour of being unused, apart from fresh milk and a couple of eggs. Jenny washed the glass shelves. She cleaned steadily, but couldn't help wondering about the man and his state of mind as she worked.

She gave the downstairs loo, basin and floor a good disinfect. It desperately needed it!

After that, she moved into the lounge again. Apart from the mantelpiece and an attempt at cobweb and spider removal, she hadn't done anything else in this room. The pictures of Bliss stared at her as she worked. Jenny longed to ask her questions about Carver, but it seemed silly to talk to a photograph.

Having sorted magazines and newspapers into piles on the coffee table, binned the rubbish, moved the furniture and swept underneath and shaken the rugs outside over the banister, she was hot and sticky.

She set to rearranging the furniture neatly. One cushion on the second small sofa would not lie flat and Jenny had just lifted it to investigate why, when an angry voice cried out.

'Leave it!'

Clutching her chest where her heart thumped erratically, she turned to see a furious Carver in the doorway. The cushion had fallen to the floor, revealing a crumpled pink jumper on the sofa.

Carver recovered himself a little and rubbed his hands through his hair. 'I'm sorry. It was my late wife's.'

'Oh, okay.' Not daring to touch it, she picked up the fallen cushion and replaced it on the sofa on top of the jumper. The garment underneath meant the cushion still didn't lie flat, but she was too scared to mess with it again.

She straightened up and willed her voice not to shake even though she could feel a tremble in her body. 'I've actually finished my hours for today, so I'll leave you to it.'

She thought for a moment Carver wasn't going to let her out of the room; he stood looming in the doorway, but he moved aside after what appeared like a debate with himself over whether to say any more.

'Thank you, Jenny. The room looks great.'

She hadn't expected that tone or comment, but nonetheless, she didn't look back, or at him. Every instinct told her to get out of the building.

It took her the walking distance to the car through the trees to stop shaking; this state wasn't helped by Wilf letting out a loud bark as she reached the bottom of the house steps.

As soon as she was in her car and had firmly locked the doors, she sent a text to Pippa with an invitation to meet up. She'd received a positive response by the time she was parking her car at home and had an arrangement to see Pippa in The Ship at seven-thirty that evening.

'It's all your fault,' she said to Pippa as soon as they were sitting in a cosy alcove in The Ship with ice-cold glasses of wine in front of them. Jenny tried to maintain a straight face.

Pippa looked puzzled. Her hair curled around the collar of her flower-patterned blouse and she hugged her skinny jean clad legs.

Jenny paused for effect. 'Your idea for me to start a cleaning business.'

Pippa squealed, a little too loudly for Jenny's liking, as heads turned from the bar. 'You did it, didn't you? Wow, well done, you.'

'Don't be so hasty, I've only got one client.'

'That's okay, it sounds as if you've at least made a start. I can put the word out for you to get more jobs.'

'Hmm, hang fire on that. I'm not sure cleaning is for me. Oh, b—' Jenny ducked down over the table.

'Whatever's the matter?' Pippa sounded worried.

'The one cleaning client I talked about just walked in and we didn't have a particularly good parting this morning.'

To Jenny's horror, Pippa blatantly looked around inquisitively. 'You don't mean to say you've been allowed in Carver's castle?'

'Shhh.'

Thankfully, Carver disappeared over to the other side of the bar with his pint of beer. He didn't appear to have seen Jenny, or heard Pippa's loud voice. She sat up again and tried to change the subject.

'So, how many of our classmates from school are still living around here?'

Before Pippa could answer, the pub door opened again and Mandy walked in. Her face lit up when she saw Pippa and Jenny. She came over to them.

Jenny noted Mandy was wearing tight skinny jeans and a fluffy jumper that was cut low at the front, displaying her cleavage. Her eyelashes were too long not to be false and her make-up was immaculate. Jenny felt absurdly jealous of the little diamante stick on jewels on the corner of Mandy's eyes.

'Can I join you?'

'Sure. I was just asking Pippa how many of our school classmates are still in Borteen.'

'I'll go and get myself a drink while you answer that one. Either of you need another?'

They both shook their heads as their glasses were still full.

Pippa put her head on one side. 'Classmates still in Borteen? Quite a few actually and loads from the years above and below too. Not everyone has been as adventurous as you, you know.'

'I'm actually meeting Cindy Lewis tomorrow afternoon. We got back in touch via Facebook.'

Pippa pulled a face. 'Good luck with that one.'

'What on earth do you mean?'

'I won't say anything now. It wouldn't be fair. You make your own mind up. Full report when you get back.'

'You've made me nervous now.'

'No, sorry, don't be. My issues don't have to be yours, do they?' She smiled, but Jenny didn't feel reassured.

Pippa wouldn't be drawn on her *issues*, instead she changed the subject this time.

'There's a whole load of our class that left after GCSEs and went to work in their parents' businesses.'

'I guess that makes sense if the businesses need staff and maybe eventually they could inherit.'

'Like me I suppose.' She pulled another strange face.

Mandy hadn't come back to the table and as Jenny glanced across the room she realised that the buxom craft centre owner was batting her false eyelashes at Carver and no doubt ensuring he had a good view of her assets. Jenny felt unaccountably annoyed. Why? She wasn't interested in Carver in that way ... was she?

Eventually Mandy joined them, but not before Jenny's insides were wound like a spring.

'The dishy Carver tells me he's already met you, Jenny.'

'Yes. I've been working for him.'

Mandy glanced over to the bar, where Carver appeared to have pointedly turned his back to the girls. 'Mmm, I'd work for him anytime.'

Jenny didn't think she meant cleaning.

# Chapter Seven

Jenny slept in on Saturday morning. The wine she had shared with Pippa and Mandy had affected her head more than she realised. She hadn't drunk much alcohol since returning to Borteen because she had to always be alert for her mother's needs and, if necessary, be capable of driving to the hospital in Sowden.

She allowed herself a few moments snuggled up under her duvet to review the evening before. She liked both Mandy and Pippa and believed they could become good friends, but the way Mandy had sidled up to Carver had really irritated her. Was irritated the right word? Riled? Upset?

She had even begun to imagine him and Mandy leaving the pub arm in arm and she hadn't liked the image at all. Thankfully, when she'd glanced across at the bar again, Carver had gone, so she didn't have to find out how she would actually feel.

Mandy had made a few more suggestive comments about the widower, making it clear she was interested in him. Jenny had remained tight-lipped and refused to be drawn on any detail about Carver's home. Client confidentiality, she told Mandy.

Jenny showered and applied her make-up carefully over the dark rings beneath her eyes, trying to remember details about Cindy Lewis, who she was meeting that afternoon. Pippa's reaction to the mention of her name had been less than encouraging.

When she saw her old classmate at the café in the big department store where they had chosen to meet, Jenny had to mask her surprise. Cindy Lewis had been thin at school and disinterested in lessons. She was famous for messing up recipes in domestic science and being the cause of more than one fire alarm when she forgot to set her cooking timer. In those days, her short skirt had barely covered her underwear, which was probably why she had been so popular with the boys.

This Cindy was almost as wide as she was tall. Her blue eyes were like studs in the ample flesh of her face. Jenny was shocked, hardly recognising the girl from the past in the woman in front of her, but she tried not to let it show. They'd not really been friends at school, but had chatted on occasion. Jenny remembered, maybe too late, that Cindy had been a spiteful and teasing girl at school, which might explain Pippa's reaction, as she had been bullied.

'You look good, Jenny Simpson. Let me guess, no kids yet.'

'No, none and you?'

'Five. Why do you think I look like this? A body can only take so much stretching.' Cindy ran her pudgy hands down her ample hips.

'Do you have boys or girls?'

'Three girls and two boys. Little terrors the lot of them.'

'Have you brought pictures to show to me?' Jenny decided she'd better take an interest in what felt like a safe subject and she was curious anyway.

Cindy flipped the cover of her key ring and displayed a tribe of mini Cindy's in a photograph with pride. She regaled Jenny with all the faults, talents and virtues of each one. Maybe too much detail!

'And their dad?'

'Dads, actually. I've been married twice. Two from the first one and three from the second. Divorced again now, but I'm working on husband number three, been dating him a few months and I might yet get him to the registry office.' Cindy's smile was almost menacing. Jenny had a fleeting vision of a praying mantis, the strange insect renowned for eating its partner after mating.

'So, your current man isn't the father of any of your children?'

Cindy shook her head.

'Do you think he'll want children too?'

'He does want kids, but I'm not sure I can face any more. I mean I forget the little darlings' names now! I'll just have to carry on taking the pill in secret.'

Jenny tried not to judge Cindy, but secretly thought that this level of deceit could easily cause a relationship to flounder, if it was discovered at a later date. She wondered, irreverently, if Cindy's cooking skills had improved.

She'd had some disastrous relationships herself and her marriage had ended in a mess, but she hadn't managed to produce anything as precious as a child. The little dart of jealously she felt inside took her completely by surprise. Maybe it was because she wasn't getting any younger. At thirty-one, children were still a distant dream. She felt tears pricking her eyes at the sudden thought that if she did ever manage to have a baby, her mother wouldn't be around to share the joy.

Cindy, seemingly oblivious to Jenny's rush of emotion, took great delight in gossiping about their old school friends and especially in recounting any tales of disasters or misfortune. She didn't think to check first if Jenny was still in touch with any of these people. Cindy was particularly scathing about Pippa's failed attempt at running a nail bar in Borteen. It made Jenny feel very uncomfortable and her initial delight at reconnecting with another friend soon disappeared completely. Pippa's review of their former schoolmates had been much more positive and her less enthusiastic opinion of Cindy was obviously valid.

There were some individuals that Cindy hadn't mentioned,

but Jenny decided to leave well alone and not to remind her of omissions. She wasn't sure she could take any more information delivered in Cindy's malicious tone, even if she might be curious what she would say about them. Cindy hardly paused for breath.

The pair lapsed into silence. Jenny realised she was studying the back of her teaspoon. She put it back onto her saucer with a clatter.

'Sorry to hear about your mum passing on. Are you going to stay in Borteen for good?'

Jenny felt her neck prickle with disquiet, as she realised that anything she said was more than likely to be repeated by Cindy to someone else.

'Thank you and good question. I'm not sure. I've started a little cleaning business and I'll see how that goes.' *No, you silly girl. You shouldn't have mentioned that.*

'Why cleaning? I thought you were doing something high-flying in the city before.'

'Somehow I can't face the corporate world at the moment.'

'Wish I could afford a cleaner, my house is a right tip. Got any clients yet?'

'One so far.' Jenny shrugged with slight embarrassment. 'Maybe you know him, Carver Rodgers. Lives in the wood at the edge of Borteen.' *Jenny, have you lost your marbles? Why did you say that?* It was almost as if she had lost control of her tongue.

Cindy's reaction to her news surprised her.

'Oh no, you don't want to have anything to do with him.' A shiver passed visibly down Cindy's body. 'Right strange. Something very dodgy about how his wife died.'

'Really?'

'Yes, you google it. The case was all over the newspapers at the time. You wouldn't catch me going near that place on my own. He could be dangerous.'

'Dangerous?'

Jenny was pleased when sufficient time had elapsed for her to make her getaway. She was vague when Cindy suggested meeting up again. The phrase *over my dead body* was playing over and over in her head. Even that phrase caused her to wince over the loss of her mother.

As she walked from the café it truly felt like an escape. Jenny had a horrid feeling that Cindy would have filed away information about her to pass on to someone else. She began to regret saying anything about her new business.

Cindy's words echoed around and around Jenny's head on her way back to Borteen. When she got home, a quick search on the internet didn't reveal any information about Carver's wife's death, just some glowing testimonials about his carving. It somehow felt like a betrayal to be looking at all. Carver was her client and, she reasoned with herself, she was just cleaning for him, not applying to be the next Mrs Rodgers.

Why did that statement produce a strange sensation in her stomach?

She didn't know how to find out any more about Carver's wife's death without contacting Cindy again and she was somehow reluctant to do that. She could ask in the library for local newspaper back copies, but that felt even more of an intrusion into Carver's privacy and, besides, the librarian might know him. Maybe she could make discreet enquiries the next time she saw Pippa, but not Mandy.

Her desire to run away from Cindy made the house in Priory Avenue feel like sanctuary for the first time. When she had closed the curtains against the rainy, prematurely dark early evening, put on her fleecy pyjamas and set the television to her favoured property programmes, she picked up her quilting and sighed with relief. Maybe this could become home after all.

There were worse places to live. Priory Avenue was a quiet street and it was only a short stroll downhill to the seafront. The whole of Borteen was built on a hill. One thing you could guarantee if you lived here was having well-toned calf muscles.

Jenny toyed with getting in touch with Pippa to suggest Sunday lunch, so that she could tap her for information about Carver and tell her about her encounter with Cindy, but after her experience today, she decided she would have some time to herself the next day.

She got up early and walked to the beach. She had tossed and turned all night. Images of Carver and Wilf, mixed up with little videos of her mother.

The tide was newly out, so she amused herself beachcombing near the water's edge. Using a stick to turn over seaweed, she collected sea glass and interesting stones in her pockets. She had an idea to replace her mother's tired potpourri with her beach finds. Yet another small way of making the house her own.

The slight breeze and salty air felt as if they were cleansing both her mind and her spirit. She must do this more often. The beach was divided almost in two at one end by a stream that meandered across the sand. The piece of the beach furthest from the town was designated a dog beach and Jenny realised that on that side, Carver was running along with Wilf. She stood near the stream mesmerised by the playfulness in the man and dog's movements.

It was inevitable that Carver would recognise her. He paused mid-stride, almost tripping over his own feet, as he waved and then ran on. Jenny turned to walk back up the beach towards the town, thinking that she was pleased Carver could find some release from his normally tormented state of mind by playing with the dog.

In a replay of her memory game at the funeral, she walked

along the promenade, high street and into the various alleys off those streets and tried to remember as many of the shopkeepers as she could. Pippa had helped to fill in some gaps. She almost needed to mark everyone on a map or plan so that she didn't forget again. Of course, the best way to memorise the names was to use them.

She spotted Fred the butcher, arm in arm with Olivia from the newsagents. Were they married or just friends? She made a mental note to ask Pippa. 'Hi, Fred, Olivia.'

'Hello, yourself,' answered Fred. 'Are you window shopping? Not many shops open on Sundays in winter.'

'Yes, I find it's cheaper to look when the shops are shut.'

Fred and Olivia laughed and passed by her.

As she walked, reciting names, she made a vow to shop locally from now on whenever she could. When her mother was ill, she had shopped mainly online. Her mother's favoured way of shopping was time consuming, as Sheila had always gone from shop to shop in Borteen, chatting with the shopkeepers along the way. During her mother's illness, Jenny often had just one afternoon to spend away from the house while Maeve came to sit with her mum, so shopping had to be efficient and quick.

Maeve was the one person who was aware of her mother's diagnosis. It still surprised Jenny that Maeve had been able to keep it quiet as she wasn't the most discreet of people.

Jenny mostly hadn't been able to face going into Borteen, in case another of her mother's acquaintances asked any awkward questions about her mother's whereabouts, so she generally escaped Borteen for a coffee in an anonymous café in Sowden. Jenny began to refer to it as the *Sowden dash*, as she only had the limited time window.

Now all that could change and Jenny could patronise the local businesses again, particularly as so many of the shopkeepers had come to her mother's funeral.

She couldn't resist looking over the sea wall to see if Carver and Wilf were still on the beach. They'd gone and the tide was coming in.

She sat on a bench on the promenade to mull over once again something that had happened on one of those *Sowden dash* occasions. She'd forgotten to put some essential shopping items on her online order from the supermarket, as she'd been in such a rush. So she'd decided to have her coffee in the supermarket café before getting the things she needed. The café was above the huge store and had a good view over the city to the cathedral.

Jenny had queued up behind a long line of people, marvelling that the supermarket café was so busy. She resisted the cakes and pastries, opting for a sensible cheese sandwich for her lunch. When she reached the head of the queue, she'd asked for a skinny latte. The girl serving had taken her time making the coffee and Jenny then understood why the queue was so long. The girl placed the cup and saucer on Jenny's tray next to her sandwich and then made a strange sound in her throat.

'Look, you have a sign in your coffee.'

'A sign in my coffee?' Jenny had been confused.

'I can see a castle and a heart in your future.'

'Really?' Jenny had examined the drink and wasn't sure she could see anything at all.

Just then a man in a suit had come up behind the girl. 'Miss Finch, can I see you in my office as soon as possible please?'

Jenny saw that her name badge said *Becky*.

'Oops, he's caught me at it again. I guess I'm in trouble.'

At the time, Jenny had had no reason or desire to prolong the conversation. She'd spent her time in the café staring at the patterns in the froth of the milk on top of the latte, trying to see what Becky Finch had seen.

Sitting overlooking Borteen beach remembering the encounter with Becky, the girl's words now seemed possibly prophetic. Or at least, and Jenny reddened even though she was alone, she'd been right about the castle in Jenny's future; that was if you counted Tree Tops as a castle. Could she also be right about the heart? The whole subject of Carver Rodgers produced strange mixed emotions in both her body and her mind. She wished Cindy hadn't set up yet another layer of doubt about the intriguing man.

# Chapter Eight

Monday dawned all too soon. Jenny dressed in her cleaning garb and set off for Tree Tops. After Cindy's accusations, she had an uneasy feeling in the pit of her stomach. Parking in the layby, she dodged the raindrops that had started to fall from a leaden sky as she picked her way along the forest path. She understood completely Carver's decision to live in a house here, even though she thought it would be too isolated for her on her own. She loved the sound of the rain making its way through the leaf canopy in this place she had begun to recognise as special.

Carver opened the front door when she knocked, as if he'd been standing waiting for her. His stony reaction to her cheerful 'good morning' left her feeling rather flat. The man appeared tormented by his own demons, but Jenny felt guilty today, as if it was written on her forehead what she had been searching for on the internet behind his back.

Why didn't she just ask him about his wife? Somehow, he didn't seem that approachable, particularly not today. And he didn't strike her as someone who would be happy about people gossiping about his marriage.

As soon as she'd squeezed past him into the hallway, he went down the steps and strode off into the trees, pausing as a coughing fit overtook him for a moment. No backward glance or farewell, not even a grunt to acknowledge her presence. He didn't even respond to Wilf's hopeful bark. He'd started to lock the dog in his kennel run when she came to clean and she was grateful for it.

A new batch of unopened mail lay behind the front door and a weekend's worth of dirty dishes lay in the sink. He had continued to walk into the house with his boots on despite Jenny's efforts to sweep and the wooden floorboards were once again liberally coated with forest floor.

Dismayed at this lapse into old habits, she shrugged off her coat, placed Carver's spare keys on the work surface and switched on the kettle. She needed a cup of tea to salve her conscience and put her in the right frame of mind to clean. The familiar chainsaw purr started up in the background. The kitchen, always a dark room due to the tree branches close outside the window, was today gloomy, as a storm closed in.

A thunderclap boomed overhead. Jenny slopped milk over the side of her mug. She stood still, alert, like a frightened animal. The air felt thick and silent, the wind had dropped and the chainsaw had stopped too.

The hairs on the back of her neck stood to attention and a sixth sense told her to go to the front door. She peered out into sheets of rain, which made the trees on the opposite side of the clearing almost invisible. A flash of lightning illuminated the ground and a dark silhouette loomed against the trees. Jenny squealed as Carver staggered out of the woodland, coughing. Wilf began to bark in his kennel below.

Carver lurched up the steps and sat down in the doorway, wheezing and coughing. Soaked from the rain, he dripped water on the muddy floorboards. Rushing towards him, crouching down to check for injuries, her first thought was that maybe he'd been struck by lightning. His normally clear eyes were red-rimmed, as he concentrated on drawing air into his lungs.

Thankfully, there was no sign of the blood she had feared she might see. Jenny had a sudden vision of an inhaler on the work surface in the kitchen and ran down the corridor to fetch it. When she returned, Carver lay slumped against the wall coughing. She sank to her knees beside him, feeling cold rainwater seeping into her jeans.

'Carver?'

No response.

She tried again.

'Carver, please, you need to use your inhaler. Come on, you can do it.'

Her mind leapt ahead. She saw her fingers dialling 999 and flashing lights arriving outside, although almost at once she realised that an ambulance wouldn't be able to penetrate this far into the forest. A wave of fear swept in, restricting her own breathing. A cold sweat breaking out on her forehead, she took a deep shuddering breath and told herself firmly that she had to keep calm. It seemed ironic that she could breathe so fully when he was coughing.

She removed the cap and he finally took the inhaler from her hand, putting the nozzle to his mouth. He pressed to release the medication and took a deep breath. Once, twice. The effect was almost instantaneous. He took another couple of shuddering breaths, put his head back against the wall and opened his eyes.

Jenny sighed in relief, her face close to his. 'You scared me half to death.' She realised belatedly what she had said. 'Oops, sorry, that comment feels totally inappropriate in the circumstances.'

'Did you think I was ... dying? Inhaler should have ... been in my pocket. This was just a mild attack, you should see me ... when I really get going.' His grey eyes fixed on hers, exhaustion written beneath them.

'Will you be all right now or do you want me to call a doctor? An ambulance?'

'I'll be fine.' He smiled weakly. 'Just need to let my body recover.' He coughed again. 'Thank you, Jenny.'

To hide her growing embarrassment at their closeness,

she asked, 'Tea or coffee?' Kicking herself that she appeared to have caught her mother's disease of thinking a hot drink could solve any problem in the world.

'Strong tea, I think.' His voice was sounding more normal now his breathing was under control.

She stood up and closed the front door to shut out the storm that continued to rage outside. She had a sudden thought. 'Do I need to fetch your saw? Surely the rain won't do it any good.'

'There's a waterproof box in the clearing. I dropped it in there. More concern for my saw than myself.' He grinned.

'You did give me a terrible fright.'

'Your trousers are soaked.'

She looked down at her legs and then across at his. 'So are yours.'

'I'll go change and find something dry for you to wear.'

Carver disappeared upstairs. He moved much more slowly than usual.

Jenny had made two mugs of strong tea by the time he returned. He looked very different wearing soft faded jeans and a checked shirt and she realised that she had only ever seen him wearing his blue overalls. His damp hair curled tightly on his head. It was a relief to see colour returned to his face and the light in his eyes virtually back to normal, apart from the shadow of exhaustion.

He thrust a pair of grey jogging bottoms at her. 'They'll be too long, but the waist's adjustable and at least they're dry.'

He was sipping his tea when she came back into the kitchen after changing. It seemed strangely intimate to be wearing his trousers and she felt tied up like a bag, as she'd had to pull in the drawstring tightly and roll up the legs. She warily scanned his facial expression, trying to judge his mood. Had he returned to the sullen attitude of earlier?

His words, however, suggested that he hadn't. 'Jenny, I'm sorry, I owe you several apologies.'

'How long have you been asthmatic?'

'Since I was seven.'

'And do you just use the Ventolin? My friend at uni had another inhaler too.'

'I've got one of those. Look, you probably noticed I've gone back to old habits over the weekend? It's been a difficult couple of days for me and, stupidly, I haven't been taking my regular asthma medication either.

'I shouldn't have been using my saw with the thunderstorm approaching, but I was just in one of my self-destructive moods. The atmosphere was stifling, the thunderbolt shocked me into realising what I was doing and I started to cough and wheeze badly ... then I realised I hadn't got my Ventolin with me. I don't need it often, if – and I stress – if I take the preventative medication as prescribed, but I usually carry it just in case.

'So, all of this was self-inflicted, I'm afraid. Also and I'll continue before I change my mind again ... you already know I don't say much, I've not been fair to you since you have been working here.'

'What? Why?'

'I've hardly been civil to you since you started to work for me. Hardly treated you like a human being. I'm sorry, it's me, not you. I can assure you of that.'

'I just get on with my work.'

'You've made such a difference to my home already. Even if I've tried to sabotage it since you were last here. You see ... I don't really feel that I deserve a nice home. Don't feel I deserve much of anything these days.' He started coughing again.

Jenny waited for him to say more, but he didn't. It was more than he'd ever said to her in one go.

She sipped her tea slowly, watching his face and body slowly recovering.

'You get off home. I think I need to go to sleep for a while.'

'Okay, I'll be back tomorrow. As long as you are sure you'll be okay.'

'I'll be fine – well, as fine as I ever am these days.'

Exhausted herself after all of the tension and worry, Jenny craved a long soak in the bath and a simple meal in front of the television. She knew she should take a long walk on the beach to clear her head, but couldn't face going out again today and, besides, it was still drizzling.

The cleaning business had seemed like a reasonable idea, but now the doubts had multiplied. Only one client, Carver, had so far materialised from her advert in the newsagent's window and her experiences of trying to clean his house had made her question this as a future direction. She'd even begun to think wistfully of her office days in London and she never thought she would ever do that. Did she make a go of things in Borteen or return to the city? The early starts, stuffy tube journeys and seas of anonymous faces didn't hold much appeal now that she had made her escape, but still …

Her mind kept replaying the events during the storm. She was well aware that the morning could have ended so differently if he'd had a full-blown asthma attack. In particular, Carver's words about not deserving anything kept haunting her. She feared she was getting too involved with thinking about the man instead of treating him impartially as a client. She was cleaning his house and nothing more, right? Had he left his inhaler in the kitchen on purpose? Was he a danger to himself?

*Not your problem, Jenny.* She shook herself, walked into the kitchen and made yet another healing cup of tea. Trouble was, despite his manner most of the time, she had begun to see Carver Rodgers in her dreams. *Stop it, stop it. Change the subject, mind!*

She reasoned aloud. '*The world is your oyster. You can be whoever you want to be, Jenny.*' It was another of her mother's well-worn phrases. Why did they automatically appear in her head? It was inevitable using the phrases upset her, as they reminded her of her mother too much.

She had been left comfortably off when she inherited her mother's house and savings. Her mother had worked since Jenny started school in an administration job at the council and had always lived modestly, so she'd accumulated a decent amount of savings. Jenny also had her redundancy settlement, which although not huge, meant that there was no immediate need to rush at a new future without due consideration. Somehow, not having any urgency for deciding how to make a living made it even more difficult for her to make a choice about her way forward, but she couldn't just vegetate. She had to do something.

Her appetite seemed to have deserted her. She knotted the cord of her dressing gown tighter and sat on the kitchen stool by the old-fashioned breakfast bar. '*Make a list, Jenny.*' Her mother's voice was strong in her head yet again. It was almost as if her spirit was still here in this room, as if her mum had actually spoken aloud. Sheila Simpson had always advocated writing a list to get through difficult times.

Jenny picked up yesterday's daily calendar sheet. The calendar had been a present from Rosie, her friend from London, the previous Christmas. She glanced at the saying: 'Today all of your dreams can come true.' Oh well, that hadn't happened. She turned it over and began to write on the blank side.

*Home – Make Mum's house my own. Decorate in my style. Buy lamps. Order conservatory?*

*Job – What do I want to do? Do I really want to clean for a living?*

*Interests – Join social groups – possibles are family history, rambling club, craft group?*

*Man – Too complicated – avoid (especially Carver Rodgers).*

She looked at what she had written. Maybe her mother's wisdom could help her after all. A memory of her mum's voice echoed through the ether: '*Write a list and then tackle some easy things to get you moving forward.*' Her mother always insisted that the written statement of intent would start the ball rolling and that some things would begin to happen without any effort. '*Ordering from the universe*' was how Sheila had described it.

Jenny went into the lounge, intending to switch on the television, but instead just stood looking around the room. Things covered every surface. Her mother's things. The myriad of reminders that her mother had gone were like quicksand. Jenny submerged daily into lethargy and grief, despite wanting to start her life afresh.

Another of her mum's precepts for life reared up unbidden from the midst of what her mother must have seen as homely and Jenny viewed as a mess: '*If you don't know what to do with things, put them in a box until you do.*' She hadn't yet dared to look in the loft to see just how often her mother had followed her own advice.

She needed boxes and she needed them now.

Well, she had plenty of those in the garage from her own move. Her belongings were sandwiched next to her mother's, adding to the chaos and the sinking feeling that hit Jenny every time she came back to the house. She was almost tempted to call in a house clearance company. It struck her that the display of too many belongings made her stop short of calling the house her home.

She knew exactly what she had to do, but her tears made the cardboard soggy as she boxed up her mother's half-finished needlework projects and a novel with a flowery bookmark still in the page her mum had last read. The end had been mercifully quick, but hadn't allowed her mother any time to finish off loose ends.

The lounge looked so bare when she'd finished. She almost opened up the boxes and put everything back. The sideboard looked particularly weird, with just one of the clocks and a pair of glass candlesticks Jenny had played with as a child on top of it. She polished the wood surface and wound the clock, immediately regretting it as a loud ticking noise invaded the space.

She took the boxes into the garage for now. As she returned to the lounge she jumped and clutched her chest as the clock she'd brought back to life began to chime the hour, loud and insistently. Now she understood why her mother had lived with clocks not showing the right time.

Jenny recognised that she either had to sell the house or change it to make it her own. Up until now, all through her mother's illness and since her death, it felt as if she had been camping in the house. She desperately craved a sense of belonging, as feeling displaced was beginning to get to her.

# Chapter Nine

Jenny somehow expected to continue the friendly relationship she had reached with Carver the day before, but it was not to be. When she got to Tree Tops the next day, Carver's scowl left her feeling bewildered. Every time she thought she had made her way through some of his barriers, he would do something to prove they were back to square one. It didn't matter if she told herself it probably wasn't personal, it still felt like it. Why couldn't he just be friendly towards her?

It was time to tackle the upstairs of the house. She crept up the staircase, even though she knew Carver wasn't in the building. She supposed a *normal* cleaner wouldn't have thought anything of it, but going into someone's bedroom, such a private space, felt invasive, even though she had permission.

Despite her reticence, she also felt guilty about her enormous curiosity. *I'm just human,* she told herself.

There were three bedrooms and a bathroom on the top floor. On the face of it, upstairs didn't appear as difficult to tackle as downstairs. It was dusty, but not quite as much clutter and rubbish had accumulated up here. The bathroom was in need of a good going over, but she'd expected that.

The main bedroom had a large wooden bed, bedside tables with stainless steel lamps with simple shades. There were two wooden wardrobes; one had a heart shaped decoration tied around one of the handles. Underneath the window was a dressing table and stool. The dust was particularly thick on a hairbrush, hand mirror and a couple of perfume bottles. At the end of the surface was a red leather jewellery box. These must all have belonged to Bliss. In the middle of the dust was a large handprint, where Carver must have rested his palm to reach across and open the window.

Jenny was just smoothing the covers of the bed and wondering if she should ask Carver where he kept the spare sheets so she could change it, when he wandered into the room and began to rummage around in a drawer.

He looked over. 'You really didn't need to make the bed. I don't usually bother.'

'*A bed should be made to look inviting, so you want to get into it.*' She was quoting her mother, but suddenly realised what she had said and the possible misinterpretation of her words. She blushed to the roots of her hair, mainly because of the unexpected tingle the thought of getting into bed with Carver had created in her body.

He grunted something unintelligible and rushed from the room.

*Oops.* She laughed. Belatedly, she hoped he hadn't heard her giggle.

When she'd finished her superficial tidy and assessment of what needed to be done upstairs, she went back down to the lower floor. Carver had some music playing and was tapping on a round drum with a beater. Jenny stood in the hallway, just out of his eyeline and marvelled at how man, drum and beater became one in time to the music. It was a similar experience to watching Carver wield his chainsaw. A song came on which she recognised and without thinking she began to sing, only to halt in sudden embarrassment. Carver looked over, but didn't miss a beat.

'Come on, that sounded good. Keep going.'

With his encouragement, she put down her duster and gave herself over fully to singing along. He seemed to become even more enthusiastic about his strumming and she realised that before she'd appeared he had been making as little noise as possible probably because he was aware that she was upstairs. At the end of the piece, they both collapsed onto the chairs, laughing.

'You like folk music then?' Carver was, for once, smiling widely.

'Love it! I used to sing with a band at uni.'

'I used to play with a band until …'

'Well, maybe we should both get back to it.' The idea suddenly felt so right to Jenny and the sparkle in Carver's eyes suggested he thought the same. How fast his moods changed.

'Okay. How about I get in touch with some of the lads and see if they are still doing nights at the pub? I'll let you know.'

'Great. I need to pep up my social life.'

'I don't have one, so me too.'

Her list making seemed to work its magic; she had already rung a decorator and started to make enquiries to get a quote for a conservatory. This last purchase felt a great indulgence, but it would definitely add value to the house if she did choose to sell and would significantly change the way she used the space in the house and garden. It was a big step forward in making 18 Priory Avenue into her own home, rather than her mother's house.

The new conservatory would radically change the back garden. Jenny felt guilty for what felt like trying to eradicate her mother's presence in the area Sheila had tended with love. On the other hand, things had to change, or Jenny couldn't stay here. She believed her mother would want her to stay, so the changes had to be made.

It was both exciting and daunting to think about choosing paint colours and wallpaper for all of the rooms. When she had finished, the house would look very different. She scanned the lounge as if expecting the ghost of her mother to pay her a visit and tell her off for moving her things.

Determined not to get maudlin again, she put on her raincoat, grabbed her umbrella and set off into Borteen in search of lamps.

The drizzle meant that the seafront was quite empty. Jenny enjoyed the feel of the damp air on her face. The sea was hidden in a mist and she marvelled at how the view from the promenade was never the same from one day to the next.

She explored some of the little alleyways off the high street. In one gift shop window, she saw a wooden Green Man plaque. Compared to the one Carver had been working, it was very crude and she couldn't believe the hefty price tag.

She came across an art gallery that also sold pottery and wrought iron work. Two twisted metal lamps with orange shades took her eye, but the price tag made her eyes water. Venturing further into the shop, she found a floor-standing lamp with the same design and shade.

It was too much for all three, she'd convinced herself, and almost made it out of the door before the shop assistant spoke.

'You know, if you have all three I could do a deal.'

It would use up most of the proceeds from her deep clean at Tree Tops, but she decided to buy them. The owner even agreed to deliver them to her door later. She deserved some nice things. The lamps felt like a step in the right direction.

On the way home, walking rapidly and trying to control her umbrella, she had the distinct feeling that someone was following her. Every time she looked back, there was no one there, but she couldn't shake the uncomfortable feeling.

# Chapter Ten

There was another car parked in the layby when she arrived to clean on Wednesday. She pulled up behind it feeling slightly peeved that she couldn't park in her usual place. Was she becoming a boring creature of habit?

The path to the house was muddy and she wondered what state the floors of the tree house would be in today. Carver still walked into his home with dirty boots on. She supposed that she should be grateful that the flooring was polished wooden boards and not carpet. How did you retrain a grown man?

She inhaled deeply. There was no other smell like this place: leaf mould, pine resin and wood smoke. She'd grown to like it.

When she approached the house, the sound of raised voices made her hesitate. One voice was Carver's; he sounded exasperated and the other male voice had a distinctly angry tone. But, before she could decide whether to knock on the door, or go away until later, Carver erupted from the building and sent her flying. Her head collided painfully with the wooden balustrade around the walkway. She saw stars.

'Jenny, Jenny. Oh, no. Are you all right?'

She was surprised to find her head and upper body supported in Carver's arms. Putting a hand to her head, she felt a lump swelling up near her temple. Carver was kneeling awkwardly above her.

Stunned into silence, she couldn't think of how to reply to his concerned look. As she tried to collect her thoughts, the door opened again and another man nearly fell over the two of them.

'Yikes, Carver, what on earth are you playing at?'

'I just knocked Jenny over when I dashed out of the door. I think she's a bit concussed.'

Jenny found her voice at last. 'I'm just a little shaken. I'll recover in a moment.'

'Ah, is this the lady who has performed miracles in your home?'

'Yes, yes. She has worked wonders and now I've hurt her.'

'Let's get her inside. I'll make some tea. That will revive her, or so my mother always used to claim.'

Jenny would have laughed, if she didn't feel quite so disorientated. She found herself manhandled into the lounge and deposited gently on the squishy sofa. Her head felt clearer, but a throbbing had set up a rhythm in the bump. She extended a hand to the other man.

'Jenny, Mrs Mop,' she cursed inwardly. Why had she referred to herself as *Mrs* anything?

He grasped her hand. 'Kieron, Carver's brother-in-law and I'm sure he would say his main tormentor. I was the one who rang you in the first place.'

Carver reappeared with some frozen peas wrapped in a tea towel. He placed the cold compress gently against her head. When she grasped it, he left the room again and returned with three mugs of tea.

He pulled a chair up close to Jenny and sat staring at her. It was rather disconcerting.

'Are you feeling better? I'm so sorry for being a clumsy oaf.'

'You weren't to know I was outside the door. I could hear loud voices and I didn't like to knock and interrupt. I was just about to go away again.'

'We always argue. We always have and I suspect we always will,' said Kieron.

'It's just that everyone seems to think they know what's best for me since Bliss died,' grunted Carver. 'My brother-in-law tries to run my life and tell me how I should feel.'

'Hey, that's a bit below the belt. Nina and I worry about you, that's all. Bliss would have wanted us to keep an eye on you.'

'Bliss,' Jenny repeated and the name slipped off her tongue like a particularly delicious dessert. 'She looks beautiful in the photographs.' Jenny pointed to the large frame on the sideboard. She felt wary, but recognised if she was going to continue working here, she needed to know more, if possible.

Carver scowled at Kieron and then turned to Jenny. 'Yes, that's Bliss. We'd been married for ten years when she ... died.'

'Have you any biscuits? I think Jenny might benefit from some sugar.'

'Sure, I'll fetch some.'

Jenny quickly began to improve. Was tea magically healing, or was it just that the years of expectation about feeling better after a cup of tea, from being brainwashed by her mother, made her associate recovery from accident, illness or bad news with the drink? She pondered the thought while she devoured a couple of sugary biscuits and tried not to notice that Carver was staring at her again.

They talked about Borteen, the weather and the tourists, who, now the seasons were turning, were dwindling in number.

Kieron cleared up the empty tea mugs and left the room. He hadn't spoken a word to Carver since her employer had complained about his behaviour.

'I'm sure he just cares about you,' ventured Jenny, when Kieron was out of the room.

Carver's tone changed abruptly. 'Please don't pretend to know anything about my life.' He got up and slammed the door as he left. The sound of the chainsaw soon rent the air.

Kieron apologised profusely when he came back into the room.

'I'm so sorry. He's a bit touchy today. It's the third anniversary of his wife's death, you see.'

She picked up the last biscuit with shaking fingers.

'The sugar will help the shock.'

Jenny wasn't sure if he meant from her blow to the head or Carver's outburst.

'I'm really fine now. Honestly, but I think I'll go home. I won't clean today.'

'Well, I'm coming with you to your car and if I see any sign of wobbliness, you're not driving.'

Jenny fingered the bump; the swelling was going down. She would have a bruise, but after the short rest she was recovering.

Kieron looked very different in appearance to Bliss, but nonetheless there were echoes to show the family link in his jawline and hair. They were halfway down the track when he stopped her. 'How are you feeling?'

She turned and smiled. 'I'm fine.' She fingered the sensitive spot on the side of her head as she spoke.

'I'm glad I've met you in person, it gives me the chance to tell you what a difference you've made to Carver.'

'Really?' She was instantly wary and felt her heart rate speed up.

'His house is starting to look like a home again and, even if it might not seem like it, I think that has vastly improved his mood. He was almost civil when we came around to see him on Sunday.'

'As jobs go, it's been a bit of a challenge, especially to begin with, but I don't see much of Carver at all.' Jenny was annoyed to feel a blush rising on her cheeks.

Kieron sighed. 'No, I don't suppose you do. He's too busy taking out his anger and bereavement on pieces of wood.'

'He does some lovely carvings.' Jenny didn't really want to prolong the conversation, she was keen to get home, but her curiosity about Carver kept her talking.

'Oh, yes, I'll grant you he's very skilled, but I wish he worked in joy instead of torment.'

'Does he blame himself for his wife's death?' Her heart started thudding at the audacity of the question.

'Undoubtedly. Even though in my opinion there was absolutely nothing he could have done differently.'

'Sorry, it's really none of my business. So ... sad. Bliss looks beautiful in the photographs at the house.' She hoped Kieron might say more, as she didn't dare to ask another direct question. Unfortunately, he just smiled sadly and made his farewells.

Jenny went on her way, still not knowing what to think about Carver and his wife's death.

She spent the remainder of the morning resting. Both the painter and the conservatory company were coming that afternoon to give her quotes for the work at the house. It felt as if she'd waited ages to make a start and now everything was happening at once.

# Chapter Eleven

When she went to the turret house the next day, Carver seemed in a much friendlier mood. He enquired after her health following her bump and lingered in the kitchen as she made them both a mug of tea.

'Have you ever thought of selling your Green Man plaques?' she asked.

'Not those in particular. I do set up in the layby every now and then to sell some of my sculptures. We'd be overrun with them otherwise. Mandy sells smaller things for me at Owl Corner Crafts too.'

He appeared to wince, when he said 'we' as if his wife still lived at Tree Tops. Probably, he'd not got out of the habit of including Bliss, even though he was now alone.

'I only asked because I saw a far inferior version of a Green Man in Borteen the day before yesterday, selling for fifty-eight pounds.'

He dropped his jaw to mimic surprise. 'Wow, maybe I should go into mass production. Then again, I'm afraid it would bore me carving the same thing time after time. Each one of my pieces is different. It's the individuality that excites me. I love the way a shape appears out of the wood. It's like magic, as if I am following some divine plan. When I'm working in a church or cathedral doing repair work, I like the challenge of recreating the original craftsman's pattern, but it's the original stuff I like best.' His eyes were alight as he described his craft, his arms moving as if wielding an imaginary saw or chisel. She felt her breath shorten and her heart quicken; she focused on the silvered scar on his lip and then the spark in his eyes.

Carver looked suddenly embarrassed as if he'd said too much or maybe realised he was getting too familiar. He put down his mug. 'Anyway, I'd better get back to it.'

Jenny felt bewildered by how his face had abruptly closed down. The chainsaw started up before it was humanly possible for him to reach it. Still, the conversation had been an improvement on Carver's usual silence or grunts. Maybe he was getting used to her.

There was something about the way he moved his lips when he talked that intrigued her. She kept replaying videos in her head. The red part of his scar didn't seem to be the first thing she noticed any more.

*Stop it, Jenny. No men, remember.*

Rocked to his core, Carver had enjoyed talking to Jenny, until he suddenly realised that he was admiring her curves. It felt like a horrible betrayal of Bliss. The sharpness of it dug into his heart and gut. He had to get out of the house to save Jenny from seeing him doubled up in real pain.

Pain produced by the thought that he might be beginning to forget Bliss.

Pain that he might be considering risking his heart again.

Pain that he might be leaving the identity and refuge of his widowerhood.

He was scared that he no longer knew who he was, if he didn't have that familiar identity to cling to.

The house, Tree Tops, had been a labour of love. Carver had slaved over its construction, with the occasional help of his friends and brother-in-law.

Bliss had once joked that she wanted to live in a castle with turrets. Carver had been so besotted with her that he wanted to fulfil her dream. He'd known, of course, that it was unrealistic to try to build a stone castle, as the cost would be too high and he didn't have the necessary skills.

Instead, he had fallen back on resources already available to him – wood.

His grandmother had left the forest to Carver in her will. It had taken many months to persuade the council to give him planning permission, but eventually it had been granted. The councillors had stipulated that the house had to be hidden from the road, that no driveway could be put into the woodland and access had to remain the muddy path it was today. This had both advantages and disadvantages. It was very difficult to get furniture to the site and deliveries had to be made to the layby. He wondered if they'd thought he would give up on his project with these restrictions, but Carver had become even more determined.

He'd designed the house to have two turrets at the front, to give the impression of a castle. These turrets were then joined to a two-storey square building. The whole structure was set on stilts, with the dog kennel and run beneath, plus a workshop for Carver.

As the wood used in the building had mellowed and silvered, the whole house had merged with its surroundings. Gothic shaped windows and conical wood shingled roofs had added to the image of a fairy-tale castle, which was Carver's original inspiration. The main rooms having a rounded front wall had made furnishing them difficult, but Carver had made most of the furniture himself anyway, so it hadn't really been a problem.

Bliss had loved the house. Carver had worried that it was too isolated when she was there on her own, but she had embraced the way of living, becoming more like the wood spirit she had reminded him of when he first met her.

He'd been playing with the band, Borteen Celts, and had lost the beat entirely when he caught sight of the ethereal girl with blonde hair and floaty dress. She'd caught his eye, laughed and from that moment, he was lost. Bewitched.

He could still clearly remember the day he had led his lovely girlfriend into the wood with a scarf tied over her eyes; see Bliss's wide eyes when he took off the blindfold he had made her wear on the way to the clearing. She'd been so surprised and so touched that Carver had built such a perfect home just for her.

She'd walked around in wonderment, touching each piece of wood, marvelling at its smoothness, exclaiming over the stairway that could be lifted like a drawbridge to maroon them in their own private world. He couldn't remember a time when he'd felt so proud, so ecstatic, so at peace with his existence.

He'd gone down on one knee on the balcony, proclaiming his love and she'd accepted his marriage proposal with an excited squeal. How could that world have disappeared? How could Bliss have gone and all because of him? If he could turn back time, he would sacrifice anything for things to be different.

He spoke to her sometimes, willing the very essence of her to be here, to speak to him from the afterlife. As yet, there had been no reply.

After her funeral, he'd pulled up the stairway, hibernated in his wooden castle with his dog and memories of Bliss. He'd even debated whether to set light to Tree Tops with him inside, so that he could join her in the afterlife she believed in, and leave the pain of her loss behind. He felt almost a coward that he hadn't been able to do it.

When the funeral director rang to say Bliss's ashes were ready for collection, he'd known exactly what to do with her remains. She'd been part of the wood. She'd believed in the old ways of magic, runes and fairies. He'd spread her ashes around the roots of the tree she'd called her Wishing Tree. It seemed appropriate.

The Wishing Tree was the place she went when she needed

to think something through or to ask for help from the ancient spirits she believed in. The tree was near to a sacred well and many others also hung tokens in its branches to remember loved ones or to ask for assistance with their troubles.

Carver prayed that some magic spell would take her ashes and reconstruct her in front of his eyes. Instead, her ashes had remained on the ground, silvery grey and lifeless, nothing like his lovely wife, who had been full of energy, love and laughter. He'd cried until he thought he might wash away her remains, watering Bliss into the sacred ground.

A daily pilgrimage to the Wishing Tree saw time allow green shoots to grow, until he could just imagine what he'd scattered there. He knew that Bliss had been returned to the forest and there she would always remain for him.

Now, Jenny had appeared in his life and he didn't know what to do. She was so different to Bliss. Could he allow himself to pursue a fledgling attraction? Could he ever consider a relationship again ... love again? If this woman would ever consider getting close to him, and he doubted it after how he had been acting. The see-saw moods that echoed his troubled mind must make him seem grumpy and irrational. Could he contemplate a future where he might have to face the possibility of scattering another's remains at the Wishing Tree too?

Yet, could he face a future without a companion? He hadn't made a very good job of that for the last three years, existing rather than living.

Was he destined to spend the rest of his life alone?

Carver sat cross-legged in front of the Wishing Tree and spoke aloud, to tell Bliss about Jenny and his confusion over his feelings. He'd noticed Jenny, was aware of the way she moved, the way she spoke. He'd never done that with any woman apart from Bliss.

For the first time, he felt as if she was trying to communicate. The breeze appeared to carry tinkling laughter and when he stood, he felt she was telling him to move on. It wasn't healthy staying stuck in this limbo land. He had to be open to new possibilities, and hadn't Bliss told him she'd want him to live fully if anything happened to her?

He believed that the chances of Jenny, or anyone else for that matter, being interested in him, with his strange lifestyle and changing temper, were remote, but still …

'Part of my heart will always have "Bliss" engraved on it. You know that, my darling,' he said to the sky.

Carver turned away from the Wishing Tree, wiping a tear from his cheek, and strode off with new purpose in his step. He had to try to begin to live again.

# Chapter Twelve

Carver was... these days and even have, she looked for woodwork that he might have carved. Had n't he had a meeting to discuss a commission for the cathedral?

Jenny treated herself to a tour of Sowden Cathedral for an afternoon treat. She couldn't explain what it was about these large religious buildings that attracted her. She loved the space, the light, the windows, the stone, even the strange incense smell. The intricate vaulting of the cloister roof and the circular chapter house were fascinating, but the crypt was by far her favourite part of the building, somehow made even more special by the fact that it wasn't always open to the public.

She had paid for extra parking to allow herself plenty of time to look around. The choir was practising in the nave and the huge space reverberated with sound that reached Jenny's soul. She sat for a moment listening, thinking of some of her favourite abbeys and cathedrals: Worcester, Malvern, Tewkesbury, Gloucester, Ely and Durham. She also loved the ruins of Lindisfarne, Fountains and Riveaulx.

The stained glass here was amazing, particularly with the sun trying to make its way through the rainbow glass. When the angelic singing finished she wandered past her favourite tombs, especially the one depicting a knight and his lady in marble, with a greyhound at their feet so lifelike she could imagine the animal running off down the nave. She paid a pound to light a tea light in remembrance of her mother, picked up a leaflet about a tour of the fossils in the stonework of the cathedral and then took the curved stairs down to the crypt.

The level of sound changed down here, much quieter, with dust motes drifting around in the dim light and the air several degrees cooler than in the main cathedral. She sat down on a stone bench and drank in the atmosphere.

Carver was never far from her thoughts these days and, even here, she looked for woodwork that he might have carved. Hadn't he had a meeting to discuss a commission for the cathedral?

When some ladies appeared, reading aloud from the cathedral history pamphlet, it destroyed the atmosphere in the crypt. Jenny grew restless and went to view the children's art exhibits in the cloisters. Local schools had provided the displays and Jenny saw signs of real talent amongst them. She searched for the art from Borteen High School, her old school, and was delighted with their display of pictures of faces depicted with painted tiny balls of screwed up paper. She wondered if Mr Mortimer was still in charge of the art department. He'd always judged Jenny's work as mediocre, but she'd loved the lessons.

She giggled as she remembered another snippet about Cindy Lewis. The girl had once stood up to Mr Mortimer after he criticised a piece of her art. She'd stuck out her tongue, ripped the offending paper into small pieces in front of him and earned herself a lengthy detention.

Jenny was still laughing at the memory when she recognised a familiar figure coming towards her. She felt her face colour red and hoped it would fade before Carver noticed her. When she thought about it she didn't know why she was surprised to see him here, after all he made his main living as a specialist carpenter in such buildings. But she couldn't help the irrational feeling that she'd somehow conjured him to appear with her thoughts about him in the crypt. She watched recognition flood his face and he gave her one of his rare smiles.

They exchanged a few pleasantries about the artwork on display and Carver asked if she would join him for a coffee in the cathedral café. Away from Tree Tops, they were both shy with each other and sipped their coffee almost in silence.

Jenny thought of lots of things she would like to say, but worried that Carver would view them as trivial. Eventually she ventured, 'Are you working here?'

'Yes, I got the commission I came to discuss last week. They have their own resident carpenter, but sometimes they ask me to help with something detailed. I'm known for my intricate carving.'

She glanced at his fingers and, aware of her scrutiny, he flexed them.

'Can you go around the cathedral and point to the bits you've worked on?'

'Yes, I can, but I wouldn't want to bore you.'

'I think it's fascinating, actually. I've always loved cathedrals, abbeys and castles.'

'Religious or a romantic then?'

'Well and truly romantic. That's why I end up getting hurt.' The words were out before she had censored them. She blushed yet again and looked into the dregs of her coffee as if the secret of life was written there.

They fell silent again. Carver began doodling on a napkin with a pencil. His drawing formed an intricate lacy pattern.

'Is that something you're working on?'

'No, no, just doodling. Inspiration strikes at the weirdest times.'

'How did you come to be a carpenter?'

'One of my father's friends was one and having watched him at work as a small boy, I was hooked. It was all I wanted to do.'

'What qualities do you need to be one?'

'This is starting to sound like a job interview.'

'Sorry. I have too much curiosity for my own good.'

He shrugged. 'Staying power, perfectionism and pride.'

'Pride?'

'Yep. If you are not proud of your work, you probably

wouldn't have the staying power to complete a detailed piece. It's painstaking work.'

'Very skilled.'

'It takes a particular type of person and a long apprenticeship.'

'Could I do it?'

'You tell me.' He smiled.

Just as she had begun to enjoy their conversation, he stood up abruptly.

'I'd better get back to work.'

She wasn't sure if she'd upset him, but he didn't give her a chance to say anything else. After a curt nod, he was gone.

As she left the cathedral, she bumped into another man she recognised. It took a few moments to place who he was ... *Andrew Jenkins*. Andrew had been the sixth form heart-throb. Spotty, gangly, teenage Jenny, complete with braces, had known that she had no chance of ever being his girlfriend, but like many of the other girls she admired him from afar and fantasised.

'Jenny Simpson, isn't it?'

Amazed that he recognised her, let alone remembered her name, she felt colour flood her cheeks for the umpteenth time that day. Why did she blush so much?

Andrew's hair still hung over one eye and curled up over his shirt collar as she remembered. He wore a grey pinstriped suit, white shirt and red tie and had a laptop bag slung over one shoulder.

'Andrew, hello. Do you work here in Sowden?'

'Yes, I'm an estate agent. Just popping in to see my daughter's artwork in the cathedral.'

'Oh, the children's art is lovely. I went to see it earlier. How old is your daughter?'

'Eight going on twenty-eight.'

'Been married long?'

'Married and divorced. On my own now, but see Katie every other weekend. She's a darling. Are you married?'

Did she imagine the strange look in his eye?

'Same as you, been there, done that, got the T-shirt.' She laughed, very aware that his eyes were roving over her in an assessing manner. She hadn't imagined the strange look.

'Hey, do you fancy dinner, Friday – tomorrow even? We could compare notes on our old classmates.'

She hesitated for a fraction of a second, but wasn't sure why. Her intuition seemed to be trying to tell her something, but she ignored it and replied, 'Why not. That might be fun.'

'Let's make it seven, when I finish work. See you at the pizza restaurant over there.' He pointed at the red-painted restaurant across the road from the cathedral.

She walked away with a strange sense of foreboding. What was she doing, little Jenny Simpson going out with Andrew Jenkins? It wasn't really a date though, was it? She shrugged off the weird feelings, giggled like a born-again schoolgirl and went off to buy something to wear.

By the time she got home, Jenny felt tired. She looked out of the kitchen window. Since the conservatory salesman had been and marked out the shape, she could now guess at the space that the conservatory would give her. Wandering back into the lounge made her feel satisfied that she had made the right decision to employ the decorator; the room would look so much bigger and brighter without her mother's busy floral wallpaper. Her new lamps stood out like beacons of hope for her future in the house. She had a few moments dreaming about the sort of curtains to put at the bay window. She was tempted to make them herself, but thought it might take her too long.

She settled down to read her book and had almost fallen asleep, when she was startled out of her reverie by a banging on the door. Such was the nature of the hammering that she didn't want to answer it. She peered through the spyhole in the door and was surprised to see Carver outside.

Opening the door, she was met by a barrage of questions.

'Did you move it? Or take it? Where have you put it?'

Jenny felt scared by his demeanour. 'What exactly are we talking about?'

'Bliss's jewellery box. It's missing.'

'Well, I hope you are not accusing me of taking it.'

'No one else comes to the house.' He had a menacing tone of voice.

'Carver, you know I would never take anything from your home. I am not a thief.'

'Well, it has gone and I'm not happy.'

'I can see that, but let's be calm about this. What does it look like and when did you last see it?' She had a vision of the red leather box on the end of the dressing table even as she asked.

'It is a red leather box about this big.' He mapped the dimensions with his hands. 'It's normally in our bedroom and I opened it only last Saturday. It's gone. When I got back from Sowden it had gone.'

'Well, there you are. It couldn't have been me.' Jenny sighed with relief. 'I did dust a red leather box on the dressing table, but you saw me walk out of your house this morning and I wasn't carrying a jewellery box, was I?'

'No.' Carver calmed down a little, although he was obviously very upset.

'Look, I'll come over now and help you search.'

She refused the lift he offered and drove her own car to Tree Tops. The afternoon light was already beginning to fade.

When they arrived at the turret house, it was clear that Carver had ransacked the place in his quest to find the jewellery box. His face when he turned to her was full of anguish.

'Now did you make this mess, or have you had burglars while you were in Sowden?'

'I made the mess. I can't find it anywhere. I've looked and looked.'

'I can see that,' said Jenny, taking in the rooms that had been taken apart.

'Someone moved it to upset me.'

It seemed a very strange thing to say. 'Who would want to do that?'

'I don't know, but I have suspected it for a few weeks now.'

'I'm confused. Do you mean this has happened before? And yet, you accused me?'

'I'm sorry, I was terribly upset.'

'Well, it looks as if you've searched thoroughly inside. Have you tried outside around the house?'

Jenny didn't think searching through woodland undergrowth was in her job remit, but still she went outside with Carver and began the hunt nevertheless. She wanted to clear her name, if nothing else.

It took a surprisingly short time to find the jewellery box. It was hidden in the hollow of a tree trunk, quite close to the steps. Carver took it back into the house, cradling it in his arms and after a look through its contents, which were jumbled due to the box being upside down in the tree, he pronounced that everything appeared to be there.

Jenny made a coffee for them both and sat down opposite to Carver.

He looked uncomfortable and kept stroking the leather of Bliss's jewellery box.

'Right then, now tell me about this person or persons trying to unnerve you. I can't believe you've let me work here on my own if you thought someone was up to mischief around here.'

'I don't know who it is.' He hung his head.

'I know you don't know who it is, but between you and me, give me your suspect list. Who that you know has a vested interest in upsetting you about Bliss?'

'The trouble is when things like this happen you begin to suspect everyone. I'm sorry about storming round to your house and being abusive. I was out of order.'

'Apology accepted. So, come on, who would want to upset you.'

'I don't know. Kieron? Nina?'

'Why would Kieron want to upset you? Why would Nina? From the little I've seen of Kieron, he's on your side and trying to support you through this difficult time. Come on, you need to analyse this rationally.'

'Maybe I'm imagining it all.'

'You didn't imagine a jewellery box hidden in a hole in a tree, did you?'

'No, I guess not.'

Jenny had a sudden, if disturbing, thought. 'Carver, you are not having blackouts or anything, are you? I mean you couldn't have hidden the box yourself?'

'I don't think so. In the early days after Bliss's death, I was on quite heavy medication, but I haven't taken any for ages; as you know I haven't been very good at taking even essential stuff for my asthma.'

'Do you drink or smoke pot?' Jenny was aware that she might be treading on dangerous ground.

'No, I *do not*. Not to excess or a puff.' His indignant posture told her he was telling the truth. 'I tried drink and even marijuana in the early days too. They didn't help. You know I have a couple of beers, but never enough alcohol to be insensible.'

'So, is there anyone else? Bliss's parents? Siblings? Old boyfriends? Your old girlfriends? Anyone you owe money to or who might have a grudge against you?'

'No one I can think of.' Carver rubbed his head, making his long hair stand up like a sculpture.

'What other things have happened?'

'Nothing serious, just things moving – most of the time I tell myself I've imagined it, because they haven't moved far, but just far enough to unnerve me. As if ... as if ... someone has been systematically searching the house.'

'When did all this start?'

'When I think about it, about a month ago. This last one is the most serious though.'

'Come on, Carver, this could be important. I'll make a list.' She was starting to sound like her mother again. 'Start by telling me all the people you've ever given a key to.'

'I rarely lock up.'

'Well, maybe now would be a good time to start.'

'Jesus, Jenny, you've really got on this case.'

'Well, maybe I don't like being accused of theft.'

'I'll say sorry yet again.'

By the time they had drunk their coffee they still hadn't really identified any suspects, or motives. Jenny made an internal note that if she met Kieron again she would need to ask him if Carver suffered from any mental health problems. She didn't like to contemplate it, but she couldn't rule it out.

'I think it's about time we put your house back to rights. You sure have a way of making a mess. Let's make a start now and finish off when I come to clean tomorrow.'

'I'll pay you extra tomorrow, of course.'

'Actually, my hours are up tomorrow – the ones you agreed – so my money would be good. We never did have that review. Have you given any thought to whether you want me to carry on?'

'Yes, absolutely. We still need to sort some things together – and those are the things I'm going to need help with.'

'Bliss's clothes … right? We can do that tomorrow morning, if you are around.'

He nodded dismally. His whole demeanour was dejected and depressed. 'I'm going to do a few minutes' carving to clear my head.'

As she put things back onto shelves and into cupboards, Jenny tried to memorise the position of everything. She took a few photos of things she thought were valuable or sentimental, just in case. She knew that she wouldn't remember exactly, but she hoped she would notice if anything significant had been moved before she cleaned again. Of course, Carver could move things too.

The chainsaw was wailing non-stop in the forest, despite the rapidly fading light. When she had finished as much as she could, she made her way along the path to tell Carver that she was leaving.

He was engrossed in his work under a spotlight and the hairs stood up on the back of her neck when she realised that the figure he was carving looked a lot like her. She decided not to disturb him after all and made her way back to her car wondering what was happening to her world.

# Chapter Thirteen

It was a very different Carver who greeted Jenny at Tree Tops the next day. She nearly passed out to see his working boots in a tray near to the door and him wearing slippers of all things. She followed him into the kitchen, not daring to comment, to find a cup of tea ready and waiting for her and, not only that, but evidence he had been opening post. She was struck dumb.

She couldn't help but raise a questioning eyebrow when he smiled at her.

'I've been up since five wondering about the jewellery box being hidden in the trees and psyching myself up for today.'

'Carver, I do understand. I've been trying to tackle my mother's belongings too.'

He turned away for a moment. Did she imagine the tremor that shook his shoulders?

She tried to diffuse the situation. 'By the way, I calculated that if I work a long morning today, then I've fulfilled our initial contract for cleaning.'

He turned back. There seemed to be panic in his eyes. 'But you will come back?'

'I thought I would come every Wednesday morning. If that would suit you, of course.'

'Yes ... yes. That sounds good. Twelve pounds an hour, wasn't it?'

'Yes.'

'Just so that I know and can have the money ready for you.'

She could feel the tension growing in him again. Her eyes couldn't help straying to the two inhalers on the work surface.

'Yes, I'm taking my medication like a good boy.'

'Sorry. It's really none of my business. Shall we get going?'

'You can sense my reluctance?'

She nodded.

'Come on then.'

They trooped upstairs, Carver allowing her to go first.

Once again, it felt extremely weird being in his bedroom, especially alongside him. It made her movements clumsy.

Carver had evidently thought about how to tackle this, as there was a roll of rubbish bags on the dressing table and a couple of empty boxes on the bed.

He opened the wardrobe with the heart ornament on the door handle. She heard his shuddering breath and was enveloped by a cloud of unfamiliar perfume, which must have been ingrained in the clothes within. Bliss's style of dress was floaty and colourful.

Carver took out a couple of hangers. His shoulders were shaking and he looked at Jenny with dewy eyes. 'This is so hard.'

'Let me.' She pushed past him. 'Is there anything you want to keep?'

'I've already taken a few favourite things out, so ... no. It all needs to be bagged up. Things you think suitable for the charity shop in the boxes, anything worn for the bin.'

'Do you mind which charity shop?'

'No preference.'

'It's just my mother supported the Cancer Research shop in Borteen. The one run by Suzi Meadows.'

'Don't know her, but sounds like a good one.'

He looked so awful, his skin grey, his eyes lifeless.

'Look, do you really need to do this with me? Shall I just get on with it?'

'Would you?'

'Of course.'

'Can you check pockets, please?'

'Sure.'

He seemed desperate to go and reluctant at the same time. When he'd left the room, she took a deep breath and began to work systematically down the rail. She took each item off its hanger, checked any pockets and put it in a bag or folded it into a box. The hangers she returned to the rail, rather than making another mess that would need to be cleared. She found a few bank notes, coins and a small locket, but mostly the pockets just contained tissues and receipts.

It was heart-rending to think that the beautiful young woman in the photographs around the house had worn these clothes and that she was dead. Each of these outfits had been chosen and worn by her. Her energy and scent surrounded Jenny as she worked. The lump in her throat grew until it was extremely painful.

After dealing with the clothes hanging up, she tackled the shoes beneath and then moved on to the drawers in the dressing table. Sorting Bliss's underwear felt even more difficult, but she recognised that Carver would never have been able to do this job, so she just got on with it.

It seemed to take forever. She finally went downstairs to ask Carver to help her to transport the now anonymous black bags to the bin and the boxes covering the emotional contents to her car, so that she could drop them off at the charity shop on her way home.

Carver was sitting in the lounge, leafing through magazines. He looked up. 'Done?'

'Ye-es.' The emotion of it all overwhelmed her and she burst into noisy tears.

'Jenny?'

He was over to her in seconds and, after a moment's hesitation that she glimpsed through her tear-filled eyes, he pulled her into his arms. She sobbed into his warm, solid chest.

'I'm ... sorry. That was one of the most difficult things I've ever had to do. I kept thinking about Bliss and how she died so young. Such lovely clothes.'

'I should have done it myself ... not made you go through that.'

'No. I can see that it would have been even harder for you. It was right that I did it for you.'

She pulled away from him, embarrassed now that the emotion was spent. 'Can I show you the bags and boxes, and explain what needs to go where? We can put the charity stuff straight into my car.'

The house felt somehow lighter without Bliss's clothes in it, but Jenny did wonder if Carver felt as if he'd cleared his wife out of Tree Tops. She'd changed the beds, vacuumed and tidied the rooms upstairs. Meanwhile, the *new* Carver had washed up and wiped the kitchen surfaces. Maybe there was hope.

'Your money is in the lounge in an envelope. I'll just fetch it,' he said.

'I've still got an hour to work.'

'Well, in that case, I have a suggestion.'

He came back with the envelope and she put it into her bag, which she'd left on one of the kitchen stools before she went upstairs.

'You don't want to count it?'

'I trust you.' She smiled.

'If that's the case, then it's time.'

'Oh dear. What are you thinking?'

'It's time you made friends with Wilf.'

Her heart rate shot up. 'No, no.'

'Yes, yes. But if you really don't want to, I'll understand.'

'I'm just so scared.'

'I can understand that if you were bitten ... by a Jack Russell, did you say?'

102

'Yes, vicious little thing.' She found she was hugging her arms around herself defensively.

'Every dog can be vicious if it feels threatened or unhappy. If they are trained well, they learn to control their aggression … most of the time.'

'You are not filling me with any confidence.'

'Let's just give it a go.'

They walked down the hallway and paused for Jenny to put on her trainers and Carver his boots.

'Have you had any other strange occurrences?'

'Not since the jewellery box, but that is one of the reasons I'd like you and Wilf to be friends, so that I can leave him out when you are here – just in case. He'd soon alert you to anything strange.'

Jenny gulped at the thought. 'Okay, that makes more sense and gives me an incentive to be his friend.'

Carver unlatched the gate to the dog's run and Wilf came to him for some fuss. Jenny giggled in delight as the huge dog rolled on his back to have his tummy rubbed. She edged closer to watch the animal's *blissed out* expression. In this position, he looked harmless, but still huge.

Carver smiled up at her. 'See what a big softie he is?'

'Maybe, but he looked very different when I first met him.' A vision of snarling teeth and dripping jaws made her pull back to the safety of the bench.

'He thought you were an intruder then.'

'And now?'

'You haven't made any moves to befriend him, but already he knows that you are someone I *allow* to be here.'

Wilf rolled over and stood up. Just as if he'd understood their conversation, he came over to Jenny and sniffed at her leg.

It was hard not to flinch and put her legs up onto the bench, but she resisted … just.

'Put out your hand … slowly and let him sniff it.'

Her hand was shaking when she extended it towards Wilf. He sniffed it thoroughly and put out his tongue to lick her finger. It was all she could do not to pull away.

'Well done. You could easily have jumped back when he licked you. His tongue feels strange, doesn't it?'

'Yes. Warm, moist and almost like Velcro.' She giggled.

'Now, let's see if we can get you going with a couple of commands. Try *Sit, Wilf.*'

The dog sat immediately. Jenny and Carver laughed. Wilf got up and wandered around again, when he realised he wasn't expected to stay in that position.

'Call him.' This time Carver whispered close to her ear. '*Here, Wilf.*'

There was a pause whilst she processed the tingles Carver whispering in her ear had caused. '*Here, Wilf.*'

The dog trotted dutifully over to her. She glanced at Carver and he nodded.

'*Sit, Wilf.*'

The dog sat and Jenny was delighted.

'See. It's fine. You can be friends.'

'I'm just terrified that he'll jump up at me again.'

'Well, if he does, just say, *Down, Wilf.*'

Wilf lay down on the ground. They both laughed. 'See, he's too obedient for his own good.'

Jenny reached out a tentative hand to pat the animal. 'Poor thing is getting pushed around with all of these commands in the air.'

'I'm going back to the house so that you can spend some time alone with him. Experiment with the commands and yell for me if you feel uncomfortable. I'll come running … I promise.'

She liked this new edition, *easy to be with*, Carver, but didn't trust his mood to last. Her heart rate accelerated, as he left her alone with the dog. She knew it made sense to do this, but actually doing it was a different matter.

Wilf had wandered off and was scratching at the base of a tree.

'Here, Wilf.'

The grey head shot up and Wilf came over. He had obviously come to terms with the fact that Carver had given her permission to give him commands and was playing along.

'Sit, Wilf.'

He sat.

'Roll over, Wilf.'

She laughed aloud when the dog complied. She reached out a hand and rubbed his warm tummy.

Applause came from the direction of the house. Carver was beaming with approval and she felt an inner glow ignite. She wished Carver could be like this all of the time. She would want to spend time with him then. What was she saying?

It took two journeys, with them both carrying bags and boxes, to load her car boot and back seat with the things for the charity shop. She smiled and waved as she drove away and was pleased to see that Carver was smiling and waving back at her. For once she didn't really want to leave.

As she dressed that evening, choosing the high-necked jumper with tiny seed pearls embroidered all over the front of it, which she'd bought for the occasion the other day, some navy thick leggings and boots, she couldn't help feeling that it had been a mistake to arrange her *date* with Andrew. Although he had been the heart-throb at school, she had never really liked his arrogant ways.

She drove back over Pink Moor, trying to still her uncomfortable feelings.

Sowden felt a very different place in the evenings and as she walked through the streets, she wished she had parked closer to the restaurant. There was something about walking past closed and shuttered shops that set her heart racing with fear. The alleyways all seemed menacing and dark shop windows looked as if they had eyes. She spooked herself by remembering her feeling of being followed in Borteen and walked faster just in case.

Andrew wasn't at the restaurant when she arrived, so she asked for a table in the window and sat down to wait for him, sipping a sparkling mineral water, watching the traffic and pedestrians outside.

He arrived fifteen minutes late, made no apology and proceeded to order his food first. Jenny declared herself to have feminist tendencies, but still liked her men to act in a courteous fashion; no, she liked people in general to be polite. It had nothing to do with gender.

Yes, this had been a mistake, she was now quite sure of it, after just five minutes in Andrew's company.

He told her all about his troubles, gave her his life history, ran down his ex-wife and praised his daughter. He failed to ask Jenny one single question about herself and she made a decision to volunteer as little information as possible.

At the end of the meal, Andrew said, 'We'll go halves then, shall we?'

She had a job not to exclaim aloud in disgust, but dutifully paid her half, even though Andrew had eaten twice as much and had drunk several beers, when she'd only had water.

She just wanted the evening to be over.

Andrew walked up the street with her, mumbling something about how pleasant it had been to spend the evening with her and how they would have to do it again very soon. Jenny became evasive and didn't commit to anything more. Thinking quietly, *no way on this earth* and *over my dead body.*

Suddenly, he took her completely by surprise by grabbing her hand and whisking her into a shop doorway. Before she had time to take a breath to exclaim, his mouth was on hers and his hands underneath her jumper and on her breasts, his fingers digging into her skin. She pushed him away and batted at him with her handbag until he let go.

'I thought that's what you wanted.' He sounded surprised.

'No way! Bye, Andrew.' She went to move past him.

'Come on, Jenny. Don't be like that, you know you want me, you always have.' He grabbed her arm tightly and her shock morphed into fear at the expression on his face.

'Let me go.'

'I don't think so,' said Andrew, grabbing her other arm too and manoeuvring her back into the shadows of the doorway. Her bag fell to the ground in the struggle.

She wanted to scream, but fear clutched at her throat. Andrew moved closer, his breath rancid, his hands like manacles.

'Is there a problem here, Jenny?' The nearby voice was loud and familiar.

Carver appeared illuminated in the light beyond the doorway. He stood quietly, but his tone and posture dared Andrew to make another move. Andrew let go of Jenny's arms and shrugged. She edged past him, instinctively towards Carver. He didn't hesitate and without another word or glance at Andrew, he linked his arm with hers, scooped up her bag and they began to walk up the high street together.

Jenny felt relief rushing through her. She turned to see Andrew heading off in the opposite direction and was not at all sorry to see him go.

As they walked along, Carver continued to hold her arm. However, with her heightened senses, what had felt like a rescue began to have different connotations to her. How had Carver appeared at that very moment? Had he been watching her with Andrew? Was he stalking her? Had he been the person following her the other day?

He asked where she had parked her car and she reluctantly told him. By the time they reached her Mini, she had worked herself into a real state. She had spent the last part of the walk trying to remember sketchy details of a self-defence class she had attended years ago in London. Was she better off with Andrew the sleaze or Carver the stalker?

She had decided not to say any more than she had to, rather to make her getaway as quickly as possible, but as she unlocked her car, her growing suspicions got the better of her.

Carver looked completely bewildered when she turned on him, her rage barely contained.

'Have you been following me?'

'I'm sorry?' He scratched his head, but took a step backwards. 'I just came with you to your car to make sure you were safe. I didn't want that lecher following you ... hitting on you.'

'Not now. I mean earlier. How come you were right there when sleazy Andrew grabbed me?'

'Excuse me for wanting to protect you. When I left the cathedral, where I've been working, as you well know, I saw you coming out of the pizza restaurant. I'll admit to being curious about the man you were with. I thought I recognised him as someone Mandy from the craft centre had trouble with a few months back – so, yes, I followed at a distance and when I realised that he ... wasn't a ... a gentleman, I decided to step in. He's lucky I don't believe in violence or I might have decked him with one of my tools or at least a right hook.'

Jenny didn't know what to think about Carver's story, but he did have a tool bag slung over his shoulder, so that part of his explanation was true.

Carver stood watching her, his head slightly on one side. 'Look, Jenny, I think I've totally misread this situation. If I've caused any offence, albeit unintentionally, I'm sorry. Now can you please get into your car and lock the doors, so I know you are safe and I can make my retreat before you bite my head off again?'

She got into her car and watched him walk away. The slope of his shoulders spoke of dejection. A lump appeared in her throat. Coupled with the shock of Andrew attacking her, she had a horrible feeling she'd misjudged and upset Carver. It suddenly mattered that she'd hurt him with her words, but it was too late to take them back.

What an evening!

# Chapter Fourteen

By the time Jenny got home, she blamed herself entirely for the disastrous evening. She'd known deep down that the meeting with Andrew was a bad idea, her intuition had been screaming at her, but she'd ignored it and paid the price.

*Fool! Prize idiot!*

Added to all that, there was the whirlpool of emotions associated with Carver and how she had reacted to his *rescue*. She was sure now that it was the shock of Andrew's attack that had made her turn on Carver.

Her mind kept working over the pickle she'd got herself into with Andrew and debating whether, if Carver hadn't stepped in, she would have been able to handle the situation herself. Would she have been able to get away? The evening could have ended very differently. Andrew had felt so threatening and determined.

Whatever conclusions she drew, the experience had totally spooked her. She put her car into the garage, something she didn't often do. It was a tight squeeze, but felt necessary.

Once inside the house, she closed all of the curtains and checked the windows and doors twice over. If she'd had a drawbridge like Carver's, she would have raised it tonight.

When she was sure that she was safely locked in, she tore off her clothes and dived into the shower. No amount of scrubbing or hot water could erase the energetic imprint of Andrew's hands on her body. She felt sick.

*Fool, stupid fool.*

She went through the evening again and again, examining the motivations of Andrew and Carver. She was still unsure. Hot salty tears joined the too hot water of the shower, as she tried to scour away her thoughts, recriminations and the feel of Andrew's horrible probing hands. Carver had acted like a gentleman, but had he been stalking her?

Dressed in her pyjamas, the cord on her dressing gown firmly knotted against the chilly evening air, she flicked through the channels on the television, but she failed to find a programme to absorb her; even her normally beloved property programmes didn't distract her. The lustful look on Andrew's face illuminated by a street light kept returning to her mind, making her cold and shivery. Giving up, she went to bed, where she kept reading the same paragraph of her book over and over, as she replayed how ungracious and doubting she had been of Carver's attempt to rescue and protect her.

*Aggghhh …*

Unable to sleep, her bedclothes in a tangle and a sheen of sweat on her skin, she came downstairs in the middle of the night, half-scared Andrew might be lurking somewhere in the shadows, even though she knew the thought was illogical.

*Don't be ridiculous Jenny, Andrew Jenkins isn't a threat. He's a prat. Get over it.*

Andrew wasn't really interested in her, he had just fancied his chances last night. After all, he must have known all of the girls fancied him at school. Maybe he'd imagined that Jenny was a sure thing after she'd stared at him so many times in her teens.

When she wasn't thinking about Andrew, she thought about how she had messed things up completely with Carver. It became a never-ending circle of thoughts and self-blame.

She kept coming back to the same conclusion … that she would have to ring Carver to tell him she wouldn't be cleaning at Tree Tops ever again. It would be just too embarrassing to go back there after last night's events, her outburst and allegations about his behaviour.

It wasn't as if she'd had any further enquiries about her cleaning services anyway and, although she knew she could advertise more widely, she wasn't sure her heart was in her new business any more. So, she resolved to put all her efforts into finding a job. It seemed better to make a clean break and put her half-hearted attempt at self-employment and her surly, but intriguing client behind her. But was that the right decision ...

Maybe she needed to talk it over with someone.

She sat on the sofa, warming her hands on yet another coffee mug and browsed job websites, in an attempt to occupy her troubled mind.

There were lots of jobs she had the qualifications for, but she had reached a stage in her life when she didn't want to do just anything. Her next job had to be worthwhile, to fit the new imprint of Jenny, if, of course, she could decide what that was.

The endless list of care assistant and recruitment agency posts bored her. Any job that did attract her seemed to have a horrifyingly low wage. She knew that the salary wasn't the point and she did have her savings and inheritance to top her up, but even so, after her well-paid job in London, even her battered self-worth demanded more.

She shivered and closed down her laptop to return to the warmth of her bed.

The next morning, she messaged Pippa to ask if they could meet for coffee, forgetting that Saturdays were one of the busiest days for the guesthouse.

Pippa said that she would be finished with cleaning and washing by three that afternoon and would leave her mother to greet any late arriving guests. Jenny gratefully made arrangements to meet her at the café on Borteen Promenade.

Jenny spent her morning removing non-essential items from the lounge, as the painter had said he would be starting on Monday morning. She tried not to think about the Carver and Andrew situation, but inevitably her thoughts strayed back to it all of the time.

Pippa arrived at the café late. Jenny had begun to wonder if she had the right meeting place. Pippa's hair was tied back from her face. She looked hot and dishevelled.

'Sorry, sorry. A last-minute panic when we discovered a guest had ... erm ... had an accident on the mattress in Room Four. I do wish he'd told us.'

'Yuck.'

'I know. Most guests are lovely. In fact, this guest was lovely. I just wish he had said something. Just finding it meant we had little time to do anything before the next Room Four guest arrived. It's when Mum and I really miss Dad, when we have to manhandle things such as mattresses. It was like something out of a comedy film, manoeuvring the soiled mattress downstairs and another one from the attic room. I'm worn out. Anyway, can I get you another drink?'

Jenny wasn't sure another coffee was a good idea, but the caffeine felt necessary for her sleep-deprived brain. 'A skinny latte, please.'

While Pippa was at the counter, Jenny debated how much she could trust her friend and what she would share about the events of the previous evening.

Pippa took the drinks off the tray and removed the tie from her hair. 'You okay? You look a bit peaky, as if you haven't slept.' Her curls cascaded around her shoulders.

'Gee thanks! But, you're right, I have a lot on my mind.'

Then, despite her hesitation, she told Pippa all about what had happened on Friday night, including her thoughts about it. She just needed to offload.

Pippa steepled her fingers together, her elbows on the table, as she listened patiently. She waited until Jenny had told her everything on her mind before speaking. 'Hmm ...

Andrew Jenkins is a sleaze. I could have told you that. All that teenage adoration must have gone to his head. I'm sure Mandy had a nasty encounter with him recently.'

'Carver said much the same thing.'

'So, what's the problem with Carver rescuing you? I don't understand that bit. Surely you were relieved he intervened?'

'I was. I guess I didn't get the chance to shout at Andrew for the way he acted, I was just so shocked, so I think part of my outburst was letting off steam. But it was something that Cindy Lewis said about Carver's wife's death being suspicious and the feeling I've had sometimes that someone might be ... watching me ... following me ... that made the rest come out.' She ran her hands through her hair.

'Yikes! So, you think Carver might have developed *a thing* for you while you've been cleaning for him?'

'Maybe ... no ... oh, I don't know. I probably totally over-reacted and made myself look a complete idiot. In any case, the *fit* I had at him, accusing him of following me, makes it far too embarrassing to go back and clean at Tree Tops on Wednesday.'

'Well, it's only Saturday. I'd let the matter lie a while ... maybe think about it.'

'You're probably right, but I've done little else but think about it. Do you remember anything about his wife's death, by any chance?'

Pippa shook her head. 'Just that it was a horrible accident. I don't remember anyone talking about it being suspicious.'

Jenny decided she'd said enough. She changed the subject and asked Pippa about running the guest house with her mother. Pippa made her laugh with more tales about the misdemeanours and strange requests of guests. She felt the tension that had built up inside her begin to fade away. Living on her own somehow made issues fester and grow to much larger proportions than were probably necessary.

This was the very reason she needed to widen her social circle.

As they left the café, the skin-crawling sensation she'd had several times lately re-appeared. She stopped and looked around her.

'You okay?' asked Pippa.

'Yeah, just got that feeling of being watched again.'

Pippa scanned around too. 'Well, I can see no sign of Carver hereabouts. Is there anyone else who might watch you?'

'Not that I'm aware of. I'm probably being paranoid and spending far too much time on my own.'

'Why don't you come to us for your evening meal?'

'Oh, no, I wasn't hinting ... honest.'

'We would be pleased to have you.'

Jenny enjoyed her meal with Pippa and Ruth and was grateful that Pippa didn't mention anything about her Friday night misadventures or her possible stalker to her mother. Jenny spent Sunday sewing and sorting for the decorator. As soon as she went to bed, however, her worries resurfaced and she tossed and turned, sleepless, for hours. She even watched a property programme in the middle of the night.

As a consequence of her nocturnal wanderings and anxieties, she slept through her alarm and woke to the painter hammering on her front door.

After making him a cup of tea, embarrassed that she had greeted him for his first day of work at her house in her dressing gown, she scurried to get dressed. His radio, set to the local radio station, began to blare over his constant whistling. She fervently hoped the rooms wouldn't take him too long to paint, as she wasn't sure how much of the increased noise levels she could take. Yet another consequence of living alone, she was used to peace and quiet.

However, the pay-off for standing the noise would hopefully be clean fresh rooms and a new sense of belonging.

She picked up her mobile several times to ring Carver, but each time she chickened out and switched it off. Finally, fiercely annoyed with herself, she grabbed the handset and forced herself to select his number.

Still undecided whether to resign as his cleaner or try to make peace with him, when the call went to answerphone, the choice somehow seemed clearer. It felt cowardly, but she left a short message apologising and telling him she had given up her cleaning business, so she wouldn't be seeing him on Wednesday as arranged after all.

She surprised herself by bursting into tears and even sobbing aloud when she ended the call, the dam of tension in her body finally overflowing. She was glad that the painter's radio and whistling were far too loud for him to overhear the call, or her subsequent crying.

Carver didn't feel any better after a vigorous bout of chainsawing. His arms ached, but he hadn't even been able to produce anything saleable. He'd reduced a huge tree trunk to shavings and splinters. The resulting sculpture was a mushroom that looked more like part of the male anatomy and a puny specimen at that. He started up the chainsaw again and reduced it to wood chips. The waste of a good sculpting log annoyed him, but the remains would at least be used in his wood burner.

He must have done something terribly wrong on Friday evening. No matter how often he replayed his words and actions, he couldn't recall what he'd said or done that might have upset Jenny this much. He'd rescued her from that lecher, hadn't he? As far as he could see, she had been in great danger of molestation, or even rape. He hadn't expected to be hailed a hero, but neither had he expected this. It must have been his concern for her safety that had been misconstrued.

*Women*! How to fathom them? Her message, telling him that she wouldn't be cleaning for him ever again, had stabbed at him with each word. He'd wrongly imagined that they'd begun to find common ground, especially when she'd sorted Bliss's things and he'd held her as she cried. How wrong could he be?

The thought that Jenny wouldn't be coming back to Tree Tops upset him deeply. He'd started to enjoy the tidiness of the house, having a clean bathroom and kitchen. He reasoned that he could just employ another cleaner, but no, he'd grown comfortable with Jenny herself. He'd looked forward to her visits, even if he found it difficult to show it, felt guilty to even feel it.

He particularly liked that he could openly talk about Bliss with her. His brother and sister-in-law seemed to think his dead wife should be a forbidden subject, only mentioned if absolutely necessary.

He'd actually believed that Jenny could begin to help him move on from his grief.

Whatever he'd begun to feel for her, and it had only been a fledgling attraction, it was obvious to him now that it was in no way reciprocated.

*Fool!*

# Chapter Fifteen

The days began to meld into one for Jenny. She sorted more of her mother's things (and there were a lot of them), looked for jobs on the internet and in the local newspaper, made cups of tea for the decorator and tried not to have regrets about burning her bridges with Carver.

Despite her vow to patronise the local stores, she'd gone back to shopping in the anonymous supermarket in Sowden, as she had no wish to run into Carver by accident. At least in the big supermarket, she might be able to spot him coming the other way down an aisle and hide.

She felt despondent trawling job websites on the internet. The job agencies she'd rung, for all their promises, didn't seem to be finding any work for her fast. Maybe it was her insistence on a job with some meaning. She might not be desperate for the money, but she was desperate for something to occupy her mind and also for companionship. Living on her own in Borteen was not healthy for her state of mind.

About to give up for the day, she spotted a job post asking for family history researchers and tutors. She sat up straight in her chair, disbelieving what she'd read, with goosebumps on her arms. She read it again.

Could this job advert be true? But, yes, it appeared to be.

The record office in Sowden intended to offer a new service of individual and group genealogy tutoring to people wishing to trace their ancestry. Perfect!

So perfect, she was almost scared. What if she didn't get the job?

Within fifteen minutes, she'd filled in the application form. She tried to reassure herself that she was a strong candidate. Her degree was in history and archaeology, plus she'd traced her own genealogy and helped many friends to get started with their research too.

Not having an envelope to kiss, as she would have done in the years of postal applications, she fervently kissed her computer mouse before pressing send and whisking her hopes off into cyberspace.

Her close friend in London, Rosie, rang out of the blue. They'd sent texts to each other nearly every day after she had come back to Borteen and Rosie had sent her condolences and flowers when Jenny's mother died. The pair had tried to maintain their relationship, but when it became clear that she wouldn't be returning to her city life, the contact had dwindled and become sporadic. They now inhabited different worlds.

'Hi, Jenny. How goes it?'

'Still feeling a bit of a fish out of water up here.'

'It's someone's birthday in a few weeks, isn't it?'

Her first birthday without her mother. Jenny took a deep breath before replying. 'Yes, I suppose I can't postpone it. Thirty-two. I can't believe it.'

'I was hoping you'd say I could come up and stay. We can catch up and celebrate. Is that weekend okay?'

'Perfect.'

Arrangements were made and it put a spring in Jenny's step to think of showing Rosie around the area. Something to look forward to …

Carver had made a promise to himself. He would keep his house tidy by himself and for himself. It seemed more important, because if nothing had moved, it was easier to convince himself that no one had been in the house again whenever he'd been out. The incident with Bliss's jewellery box had unnerved him more than he cared to admit, even to himself. Before that, he'd almost persuaded himself that he'd imagined that things had been moved. He now religiously locked his front door, even when he just popped to the clearing to carve.

He'd decided he didn't want to find another cleaner, someone who might destroy his fragile equilibrium, such as it was, all over again. He now took off his boots when he went through the front door, putting them on the tray behind it and was forcing himself to open his post every day. Most of it went straight into the recycling bin anyway. Not as scary as he'd once feared.

Washing-up, he found, was almost therapeutic; a time to allow his mind to wheel around the issues of his life, to plan carving projects and decide who to approach to ask for the detailed, skilled carving commissions that were his first love.

It became almost a game to keep things in order in the house. He was embarrassed, even though alone, when he found himself talking aloud to an imaginary Jenny as he cleaned.

*See, I can do it. No post behind the door. No mud on the floor. Clean sheets on the bed. I can do it without you ... almost.*

Why did talking aloud to Jenny feel different to talking aloud to Bliss? He couldn't answer that question. Was it because Bliss had ... gone and Jenny was very much alive? He often thought about their awkwardness in the bedroom together as they prepared to tackle Bliss's clothes and then afterwards when Jenny was upset and he'd hugged her to his chest as she cried. At least the short spell of Jenny cleaning at Tree Tops seemed to have jerked him out of the unreal state he'd lived in for so long.

No matter why, he was starting to feel better, as if the darkness that had descended when Bliss had died was lifting. And, just as if the world saw his mood had changed too, he began to get more commissions for carving again and that made him feel even better.

If only Jenny hadn't taken against him, he believed he would feel more at peace than since that fateful day three years before when his life had changed forever.

# Chapter Sixteen

An interview! She'd got an interview for a job she would love. Jenny did a happy dance around the lounge.

History had always been her thing, that's why she'd studied it at university. She'd also traced family trees for both her mother and father's families. She'd originally started work on her father's side of the family in the hope of finding relatives who might know where her father had gone, but she'd drawn a blank. Both parents had been only children and her grandparents had been too. There were no long-lost relatives who might be able to give her information about her missing parent after all.

Her father's family tree, which she'd taken care to hide away from her mother, had several lines that stretched back to Ireland. Her mother's appeared predominantly from the Borteen and Sowden area, as far back as she had managed to trace. Her mother had been very proud of her local heritage. Jenny had heard Sheila boasting to Maeve about it one day.

Why had they never framed a copy of her tree for the wall? Her mother had asked Jenny for it, but she'd never made time to have a nice copy printed. Yet another thing to beat herself up for with regards to her mother.

When someone became ill unexpectedly, all of those things you'd meant to do with them and for them came into sharp focus. Jenny had to be careful she didn't chastise herself too much. There would always be regrets, but she must try to focus on the positives.

She spent the next few days revisiting her family tree to remind herself of the techniques for searching. She also had a happy afternoon at the archives in Sowden to familiarise herself with the procedures for obtaining original documents and to browse the shelves. She couldn't help but watch the library assistants and wonder if these would be the people she would be working with in the future. She observed them moving around the archives and tried to judge the way they approached customer service.

Just in the short time since she'd last studied her ancestry, so many more historical records had been deposited and digitised. It didn't necessarily mean she could trace any further back in time, but the new information she discovered gave more depth to her knowledge of the story of her family.

Jenny was delighted to come across a reference to one of her mother's ancestors running a fruit shop in Borteen. She set about trying to identify where in the town it had been located, revelling in the old maps of the town and how the shape of the streets wasn't far different to the present day, whilst battling down the sadness of the knowledge that she wouldn't be able to share the find with her mother.

She concluded that the fruit shop must have been the present-day bakery and pie shop on the corner of the alley in which Maeve's shop was situated. She made a mental note to speak to John Hutchinson who ran the shop the next time she was in Borteen. She had no difficulty remembering John's name, as for a while when she was in her teens the man had paid a lot of attention to her mother.

When she returned home, the painter had nearly finished what would soon become her bedroom. It looked very different to when her mother had slept there and Jenny was glad of it. A fresh coat of primrose paint and a gold patterned wallpaper feature wall made her feel much more reassured that she could settle into the room without too many memories invading her nights.

She looked forward to trawling the shops in Borteen and Sowden for finishing touches. She'd promised herself a faux fur throw on the bed, as it was one thing that her mother had never allowed her to have in her teens. A tiny rebellion!

Spending the evening clearing out the wardrobe and bagging up her mother's clothes for the charity shop was even more painful than clearing Bliss's things, but it had to be done. She put the bags at the bottom of the stairs ready to take to the charity shop the next day. With a heavy heart, she went to watch one of her favourite late-night programmes where an adopted child was in search of her birth mother. The show always made Jenny cry and tonight she needed a good sob.

The days seemed to be zooming by, almost as if she was on a rapidly tilting slide towards her interview. No matter how often she told herself there would be other jobs if she didn't get this one, her stomach turned over as she realised how much she wanted this post.

When the interview day arrived, she tried to keep her thoughts buoyant. Today was a day to smile and to show off her skills. Somehow, her business suit didn't seem appropriate for this role ... too severe. She covered her bed with rejected garments, before settling on a long skirt, boots, long-sleeved cream T-shirt and her cream woollen coat. She adorned the top with a long, beaded pendant.

Strangely, she couldn't remember ever being this nervous for any interview before, almost shaking as she climbed the steps to the grand Victorian building where the archives were housed. However, it turned out not to be a conventional interview after all. The two women who greeted her, Lani and Sandra, explained that they thought that actually having a go at the job would be the best test for the applicants, allowing them to assess the knowledge of the candidates and also how they would approach the role. Lani was to observe, while Sandra pretended to be just starting on her family history research.

All of Jenny's nerves disappeared instantly. She could

do this. She'd done it so many times before when helping friends to research over the years.

Soon, she'd asked Sandra questions and begun to help her to draw up a rudimentary family tree. Jenny was genuinely interested in the family that began to emerge. She didn't do the work for Sandra, rather guided her to look in the right places, so that if she had been a client, she would have the joy of discovery that Jenny herself loved so much. As she spoke, she glimpsed the observer, Lani, smiling her approval.

*Yes.*

Jenny took her test researcher to one of the computer terminals to explain how Sandra could look up the details of births, marriages and deaths, stressing that those records started from 1837 onwards. She explained how to order any appropriate certificates and what these would potentially tell her about her family. She showed Sandra a range of useful websites, talked about census records, being careful to describe the differences between the 1841 census, the 1911 census and all of those ten years apart in between.

Then, she took the trouble to describe the layout of the archives office itself and where Sandra would find church records in the books on the shelves and on the microfilms stored in numbered boxes. She'd spent enough time in the archives over the years to not even hesitate and her visit the previous week had helped to refresh her memory. She made a list of further records, including wills and poor law information, plus other websites and publications that might be useful for Sandra to progress her family tree. Jenny became so absorbed that she'd almost forgotten that Sandra wasn't a real client.

When Lani told her that her time was up, the next candidate, waiting for her interview near the reception desk, sat shaking her head. She had obviously seen and heard an enthusiastic, confident Jenny in action.

Lani told Jenny that the final decision on the post was to

be made on Friday of the following week. Jenny crossed her fingers on the way out and said a little prayer for good news.

She left the building on a complete high, knowing that she could not have improved her performance and had done her best. Hopefully it was enough, but it was now in the lap of the gods.

She treated herself to a coffee in The Crimson Sheep café in one of the back streets of Sowden by the cathedral. Her head felt floaty and her ego, for once, buoyant. That was until Carver opened the door. He stopped still in the doorway, as he caught sight of her sitting at a nearby table, probably deciding whether to retreat, but instead he came over smiling, his silver-grey eyes full of uncertainty. She was genuinely pleased to see him.

'Hello, Jenny. You are looking very nice. Hope everything is going well for you.'

'Fingers crossed. I've just had an interview.'

He nodded and made as if to walk to another table and Jenny suffered a moment's indecision before saying, 'Join me?'

He turned back. 'Are you sure?'

'Yes.'

Carver took off his heavy waxed coat. He looked thinner, or did she imagine it? Was it just because he wasn't wearing his customary overalls? He struggled to insert his tall frame into the chair opposite to her, so she pulled the table towards her to make more room, being careful not to spill her drink.

'Where was your interview?' he asked, when he was finally settled.

She found herself wanting to smile at him. It was good to see him again. She'd spent long enough pondering over the events of the evening when he'd rescued her from Andrew to decide to give him the benefit of the doubt. She'd more than likely over-reacted.

'At Sowden archives.'

He ordered a coffee from the waitress, who was hovering nearby with her notepad.

'So, you've given up cleaning completely?'

She smiled ruefully. 'In truth, you were my one client. My business never really took off and, if I'm honest, I'm not sure cleaning is the right career for me.'

He sort of grimaced. 'You were good at it though, but never mind. Did the interview go well today?'

'I do hope so. It felt good. It will never make me rich, but I do believe it could be my ideal job.'

'What would you be doing day to day if you got it?'

'Helping people to draw up their family trees. I'd love it.'

He moved to one side as the waitress put his coffee on the table. He thanked her and picked up the spoon. 'In that case, I'll put a charm on the Wishing Tree for you.'

'Pardon me?'

He looked instantly embarrassed. 'Sorry, family joke. I forget other people won't understand the reference.'

'Sounds intriguing though. Please tell me more about the Wishing Tree.'

He shifted in his seat, repositioning his coat on the back of the chair, and then fixed his extraordinary grey eyes on her. Her insides did the familiar loop-de-loop in response to his full attention. She stared down into the froth remnants of her coffee to regain her composure.

'There's an old tree not far from Tree Tops, next to an ancient well on the edge of Pink Moor. For generations people have made offerings to the *supposedly* sacred water and hung things ... charms ... in the tree to ask for help and luck. My late wife loved the tradition.'

'Sounds wonderful and, yes, please put a charm on the Wishing Tree for me. I would really love this job.'

'I've often thought about having a go at my family tree, but I haven't really got a clue where to start.'

'Let me know if you would like some help. I won't

charge you.' She winked and then felt her skin redden with embarrassment.

They carried on talking, about Jenny's decorating and conservatory, about Carver's potential commissions, neither mentioning the event that had caused the parting of their ways, although Jenny found herself on the point of apologising for her behaviour on that night several times.

She glanced at her watch. It was time to go home and see what her decorator had done today. She gathered her things together. 'I shall have to make a move.' As she stood, Carver put his hand lightly on her sleeve.

'I'm so glad I've seen you. I've missed having you around Tree Tops. I was a moody *B* to begin with … well, most of the time … and for that I apologise.'

Her stomach swirled with confusion. Should she say anything more? 'Take care of yourself, Carver.'

She walked away from the café, her euphoria after the interview diminished. She wanted to turn back and apologise to him for her behaviour that night. It felt good to have spoken to him, but cowardly not to have cleared the air properly. She reached the Guildhall gates and paused to cool her face on the metal railings.

'You all right, love?' A man standing next to her asked. He looked concerned.

Jenny flashed him a huge smile. 'Sorry, just a moment of indecision. I'm fine now.'

She walked back in the direction of the café, her pace increasing as she got closer, the crimson sheep on the swinging café sign seeming to wink at her.

A warm gust of cooking smells and coffee hit her as she opened the door. Chattering voices swirled around the small space.

An elderly couple now sipped tea at the table where she'd sat with Carver. She'd missed her chance.

# Chapter Seventeen

The transformation of Jenny's home was gathering pace. Now the decorator had completed the main bedroom, it made sense for Jenny to move in there. With her friend Rosie coming up to Borteen in a couple of weeks, the race was on for Jenny to get settled in the main bedroom and freshen up the room that up until now she had called her own. It would be a difficult transition to get used to. At least her friend's visit had forced her into swapping into the bigger room.

As she still hadn't finished moving her things in and her mother's things out, the contents of both rooms were piled around the rest of the house. Today, to add to the upheaval, the contractor would arrive to begin digging the foundations for the new conservatory. Jenny had agreed to all of this activity, but it almost felt as if she was under attack from all sides.

When she'd been drinking her morning cup of tea, she stared out of the window and said a farewell to the garden her mother had loved and tended. It had been a difficult decision to change things so radically, but she believed that if she didn't, she would never be able to live here long term. She'd wrestled one bush into a pot in the hope of being able to replant it elsewhere later, but the rest would have to be sacrificed. Her car was parked on the road, as a large skip now occupied the drive, in readiness for the dig.

She watched anxiously as a mini digger manoeuvred down the side of the house and past the garage. She couldn't look as it began to excavate. Halfway through the morning she had to go to the local shop for supplies of tea, milk and sugar, as all of the men working on her property seemed to drink copious amounts of milky tea with at least three sugars. Her new job appeared to be tea lady, not genealogist.

She had toyed with ringing Carver to ask if he would like her to help with his family tree following their conversation the other day, but she decided to let things lie for a while. Soon all thoughts of contacting him were eclipsed by a phone call.

'Hello, Jenny? It's Lani from Sowden Archive Department.'

Jenny's heart began to race. 'Hi. I didn't expect to hear from you yet.'

'We made our decision early. If you'd like it, you have the job.'

'Really? That's wonderful. I'd really like the post.'

'You do realise that it's four days a week? We're closed on Tuesdays. There will be occasional Saturday working too when you run a course.'

'Yes, that suits me well.'

'I'm so pleased. You were head and shoulders above the other candidates. There only remains the question of when you can start?'

'When would you like me to start? I'm totally flexible.'

'Is Monday too soon?'

'Not at all. I could do with getting some structure back into my life. I'll see you on Monday then.'

'Super news. We open at nine.'

Jenny put down her phone and did a circuit of her home yelling in joy to celebrate. It was a surprise, as she hadn't been expecting to hear anything about the job for another two days. She got very strange looks from the decorator until she explained. Maybe she should tell Carver his Wishing Tree charm had worked.

Maybe tomorrow …

'Miss, could you come out here a minute?'

Jenny, lost in the world of paint charts and eating the last of the *trick or treat* sweets she had bought for Halloween the day before, was trying to decide the colour for the hall, stairs and landing walls. She looked up at the builder's face peering through the kitchen window. He had a different expression to his normal cocky one. Jenny felt her body tense, as she immediately suspected some problem with the conservatory foundations that would cost yet more money.

Her wellingtons wrestled onto her feet, she jumped down from the back door into the muddy wilderness that used to be her garden.

The workmen, all wearing identical woolly hats, were standing in a circle, staring into the trench they had dug. Jenny's heart sank.

'Is there a problem?' She addressed Ivan, the foreman.

'Not exactly. We've been digging the foundation trench as you can see, but we've found buried treasure.'

'Buried treasure?' Jenny's voice sounded unusually high pitched and squeaky to her own ears. She squelched in the mud to the edge of the hole and peered down. A rectangular metal box lay at the bottom of the trench. The workmen had carefully removed the earth around it.

'How did that get there?' She stepped back so that she didn't fall into the hole.

'Have you lived here long, miss?'

'My family have been here for at least thirty-two years.'

'We thought for a minute we'd found a wartime bomb; thankfully it's only a box. Just thought you should see where we found it, before we lift it out. Where would you want us to put it?'

'Have you looked inside? Is there anything in it?'

A sheepish expression passed over Ivan's face. 'We tried to get it open, but it's locked. It's covered in rust, but doesn't seem too heavy.'

Jenny laughed. 'I'm relieved it's a box. For a moment, I thought you'd discovered an expensive problem or else a body.'

Her own words seemed to bounce around her head and a cold sweat crept over her. She'd wondered more than once over the years if her father had been murdered twenty-five years ago and his body buried somewhere. How awful would it have been if her mother had done the deed and buried him in the garden?

Her imagination was too active. A brief scenario of a police forensics team descending on her garden and erecting a white investigation tent over the hole flashed before her eyes. Phew. Thank goodness, they hadn't found a body, and one body in particular. Although come to think of it, the discovery of anyone's body would have been awful. She would definitely have moved away from here then.

But the question remained – who had buried this box here and why? Had her mother known about it? She had questioned over the last few years the nature of the relationship between her parents. It wasn't something you thought, or asked about as a small child. As far as she was aware they had played very traditional roles, her mother staying at home to look after Jenny and the house and her father going to work, until he disappeared that was, and then her mother had no choice but to go out to work to support them both.

Jenny smiled at Ivan. 'If you put it in the shed I'll have a better look at it later. I wonder if the key to the lock is in the house maybe? I'll have a search through my mother's things. Is there anything else down there?'

'Not that we can see, but I think I'll borrow my mate's metal detector and give this area a good going over before we pour any concrete. You will tell us what's in the box, won't you, miss?'

Jenny agreed with a smile and fetched the shed door key. The workmen hauled the box out of the hole, manhandled it to the shed and up onto the workbench. It had an outward sheen of rust, but seemed intact and still securely fastened – after all it had resisted the builders' attempts to open it.

She decided to leave the box alone until the builders were out of the way, even though she knew they were curious about its contents. Part of her wanted to keep anything inside to herself, after all it must have been buried in the garden for a reason and she had a distant spark of hope in her stomach that this might hold a clue to her father's disappearance. She didn't fancy trying to open it with the builders crowded around her, just in case.

Concentrating on paint colours proved difficult when she returned to the kitchen. What was in the box? She forced herself to focus back on colours.

On the stairwell walls, there were a series of brightly painted Spanish-looking landscape oil paintings. They didn't look like anything her mother would have bought, but Jenny liked them. She decided to centre the décor around the colours from these.

'We'll be off for today, miss,' declared Ivan, a while later. 'Be back tomorrow with the metal detector.' The other three men grunted and nodded, the bobbles on their matching woollen hats bobbing in unison, which made Jenny want to laugh.

She watched them trudge down the side of the house, before putting on her muddy wellies once more and making her way to the shed to examine the intriguing box more closely.

Brushing off the remaining soil, she noticed some etched letters on the metal surface. 'MJR'. She didn't think those initials belonged to anyone in her family or referred to any business she knew.

Her attempts to open the box with a hammer and chisel only resulted in damage to her thumb. As she sucked away the blood from the surface wound, she contemplated who could help her open it. One name leapt straight to the forefront of her mind. Dare she?

She went back to the house, carefully locking the shed behind her. It was starting to grow gloomy, more evidence that the nights were drawing closer in, and she shivered as much from the cooling air as a little wariness of being in the garden on her own in the dusk. She struggled to get her wellingtons off her feet, washed the rust from her hands and held a tissue against her bleeding cut.

She thought about asking the painter, who was just packing up for the day, for help, but she still felt quite secretive about what the box might contain. Secretive and hopeful. Before her doubts about the wisdom of the action overwhelmed her, she rang Carver's number, holding her breath to stop herself from chickening out.

'Jenny, what a nice surprise.'

'I'm ringing to beg for some help, actually.'

'What do you need?'

She laughed. 'Some brute strength and maybe a bit of lock know how.'

'*Lock* know how? You haven't locked yourself out?'

'No, no. My builders have found an intriguing locked box while they were digging a trench in my garden.'

'And couldn't *they* open it?'

She paused. 'They probably could have and they were interested to see if there is anything inside, but somehow I didn't want *them* to open it.'

'So, I should be honoured that you don't mind sharing it with me?'

He readily agreed to help her and arrived in less than half an hour with his tool bag slung over his shoulder. He looked unusually tidy and was, once again, not wearing overalls. She particularly noticed that he'd brushed his hair, his curls falling uniformly around his face, instead of rising up into the knotted bush she'd often seen on top of his head.

Their joint purpose seemed to smooth over any potential

lingering awkwardness between them. She led him straight to the shed and he put his tools on the old battered stool.

'No key?'

'I had a look in the tin of keys my mother kept in the pantry, but nothing looks like a fit.'

Carver ran his hand lightly over the surface of the metal box, tracing the initials with his fingers, then wiping the rust off his hand on the back of his jeans. He'd obviously forgotten he wasn't wearing his overalls.

He looked up at Jenny, a strange expression on his face. 'You do realise that these are my father's initials?'

'Really? Never!'

Had this box possibly belonged to Carver's father? Could this perhaps be a link between the two men?

'So, your father had a middle name?' She realised her mistake the instant she uttered the words. She'd spoken of Carver's father in the past tense, as if he were dead.

'He was, or rather, as far as I am aware anyway, still is, Michael *John* Rodgers. Tell me again where you found this.'

'The builders dug it up when they were preparing the foundations for my new conservatory.' Jenny waved her hand at the muddy mess near the house. 'Ivan, the builder, is going to use a metal detector tomorrow to make sure nothing else is buried down there, before they pour any concrete.'

'I wonder if this really could have been my father's? We did question if there was a link between our dads and their disappearance. This could be a clue? Although, I still think it's probably a long shot.'

Jenny didn't like to point out that when she'd wanted to talk about any link between their dads while she was working at Tree Tops, Carver had been unwilling to even discuss it.

'I must admit to being worried they'd found a dead body

buried in my garden.' She looked at him, her eyebrows raised.

'You mean, your dad or even mine?'

She nodded. 'Apparently, they thought to begin with they'd found a wartime bomb.'

Carver didn't say anything in reply. He was too busy staring at the box. His face had a strange wistful expression. Jenny had to fight the urge to put her arms around him for the comfort he so obviously needed. He must have been as badly affected by his father's disappearance in his childhood as she had. To hide her thoughts and desire to console him, she assumed a businesslike manner.

'There's only one way to find out if this is anything to do with our fathers. We need to open the box. I did have a go ...'

She held up her damaged thumb; the cut had stopped bleeding now, but it was still sore. To her surprise, Carver took hold of her hand and examined the cut closely.

His skin felt firm and warm. A quiver of arousal ran down her spine.

She thought for one moment he was going to kiss the wound, but instead he released her hand suddenly, as if he'd just registered what he'd done, or even, heaven forbid, what she'd been thinking.

She took a deep calming breath, her senses operating on overdrive.

'I hope you've put some antiseptic on that. When did you last have a tetanus jab?'

His concern seemed genuine, but she found it a disappointment that he was being so practical, when she'd imagined a kiss. She reminded herself that Carver worked with his hands. He was bound to be ultra-careful to avoid infection. She pondered asking him if the scar on his face was the result of a work injury, but she decided not to voice her question in case it destroyed their fragile friendly peace.

'Brute strength it is then.'

Carver appeared totally unaware of his effect on her. He set to work on the box with an old chisel. The lock stubbornly refused to budge and he had wounds to match Jenny's by the time it broke. Only the fact that he had greater strength and persistence made the difference in getting the box open.

He glanced up at her, face triumphant. Their eyes met briefly. Then he began to rub away the mud around the edge of the box lid.

Her heart felt as if it stopped as the lid moved.

'It's weird. I want to know what's inside, but at the same time I don't.'

'Be prepared that it might be a total anti-climax,' he said.

'True, but we have to open it now.'

They stood side by side looking into the metal container. It contained a large rectangular object in layers of wrapping.

The child in Jenny felt disappointed that the box didn't contain some sort of obvious treasure.

'Looks intriguing,' said Carver.

'Scary and exciting all at the same time. No gold or diamonds though.'

Carver looked at her askance.

'Well a girl can dream, can't she?'

'Whatever is it?' Carver said, looking inside the box again.

'No idea, except that the back of my neck is tingling.'

Carver stared at the object. 'At least it appears clean and dry. No sign of insect infestation either.'

Jenny shivered. The evening darkness and chill had begun to envelop them, the bare light bulb in the shed the only source of light. 'Can we unwrap it in the house? I'm getting cold.'

'Good idea. I feel in need of coffee … if you are willing to make me one that is.'

'Can you carry it, whatever *it* is?'

'*It* being the word.'

Carver carefully lifted the object in its wrappings out of the box. 'It's not heavy, just an awkward shape.'

'I'll carry your tools.'

As she picked them up, Jenny decided that the tools were probably heavier than the object. Carver walked slowly and carefully down the path, thankfully partly illuminated by one of the street lights on Priory Avenue. She locked the shed. He managed to find the plank across the trench in the gloom, just as she arrived behind him with her mobile phone flashlight on.

Carver kicked off his boots outside the door, before elbowing the door handle to open it and stepping up into the kitchen. He came back to the door to take his tool bag from her and watched patiently while she peeled her wellingtons off. The object was on the kitchen table when she went in. It seemed to dominate the space with its unknown identity.

'Can I wash my hands?'

'Sure, I need to do mine as well.' She wriggled her rust-encrusted fingers in the air.

Without thinking, she turned on the sink tap, squirted soap on her own and then Carver's hands. They took it in turns to rub their palms beneath the water flow. It felt strangely intimate, even though they weren't actually touching. She used one end of the nearby towel and offered him the other end. He laughed and dried his hands as they performed a sort of tug of war.

'My heart is thudding with anticipation about what *it* is,' she said as she filled the kettle and chose mugs from the cupboard. 'Coffee, did you say?'

'Yes, please. Nice and strong, but you already know that's how I like it.' He was scanning curiously around her kitchen. She was pleased it was clean and tidy, but was well aware it must appear rather old-fashioned.

When the drinks were made, Jenny led the way into the lounge. Carver followed with the bulky object. She noticed he was being very careful not to knock it into the newly painted doorframes. She switched on her three new lamps with their orange shades and allowed herself a moment's pride in her new purchases.

The lounge smelt of fresh paint and the furniture still looked somehow uneasy in the room. Carver put the parcel on the worn coffee table.

'This was your mother's house?'

'Yes. I've got decorators in at the moment, so sorry about the paint smell. Haven't got around to putting pictures back up yet.' Why was she apologising for her home? 'I'm updating and changing things to make it my own, but it is so hard ... as if I'm taking her out of the house.'

'I know all about that ...'

She smiled at him. 'Shall I get some scissors?'

'No need.' He took a penknife out of his pocket, unfolded the blade and began to tear tentatively at the first layer of wrapping. He glanced up at her. 'I know I've always been reluctant to have the *dad* conversation, but I suspect it's time for us to discuss their disappearance.'

'Even if this find has nothing to do with our fathers?'

'Yes. It's time. How we first met all those years ago is too much of a coincidence to ignore the discussion any longer.'

'Okay. It's fine by me.'

Underneath the first layer of wrapping was another, then a bag and what looked like the final covering, a soft material bag. She heard his breathing deepen, as he loosened the fastening.

He looked over at Jenny. 'I think this is it.'

She felt the colour drain from her face and her eyes widen in anticipation.

Focussing back on the object, Carver pulled at the

drawstring of the bag and eased the material back. Inside was an old clock, mounted in a tall, dark wooden case.

He stood it upright on the cloth bag and sat back. 'Well, I wasn't expecting that.'

'No, not what I imagined at all.'

They both sat in silence for a while, just staring at the clock.

Jenny reached out a finger and ran it along the curve of wood at the top of the clock case. She needed to feel that it was real. She was so aware of Carver's presence a few feet away from her, her body responding as if she had touched him instead. He spoke and broke the spell.

'Why would someone bury a clock in a garden? It seems very strange.' He picked up his coffee mug and cradled it in his hands.

'No idea. I agree, it's bizarre.'

'I notice you have quite a few clocks.'

'Yes.' Jenny scanned the room. 'You're right. There were even more in here before I packed some away. I suppose they have always been part of my life, so I don't really notice them most of the time. They were never wound up when I was a child, as it's far too noisy if they are all ticking away together out of sync. I made the mistake of winding up a particularly loud one the other day. I thought about packing them all away, but they are part of this place.'

'Did someone in your family collect them?'

'I haven't a clue, I'm afraid. I've never thought of them as a collection, but now you've said it, there are old clocks in most rooms of the house. I suppose it's possible it was my dad's collection …'

'You've remembered something?'

'Just wondering … my father used to work at the auction house in Sowden, as far as I know.'

'So not difficult to build up a collection of clocks, then.'

'Hmm … but it still doesn't explain this clock being buried in the garden. Why go to so much trouble to bury a clock?'

'So, in conclusion, it seems likely that this buried clock is something to do with your dad, but the link to mine, apart from the possible initials on the case, is questionable.'

'Maybe we should try to find links between our fathers anyway.'

'I do think it's time for us to brainstorm their disappearance. In any case, my mind has been working on the mystery ever since you first mentioned it, however reluctant I sounded when you first raised the subject.'

'Well, we both have fathers who disappeared twenty-five years ago. That's more than coincidence, I'd say. I'll get some paper and a pen. Things make more sense when you write them down.'

*Now I'm starting to sound like my mother. Great!*

'I'd like us to think of reasons why the dads would have gone at that point in time and why they would bury a clock in the garden, if indeed they did. It could have been your mother, of course.'

'I can't imagine my mother doing such a thing.'

'But remember she would have been much younger when the clock was hidden.'

'*Hidden*. Interesting thought. Why would you need to *hide* a clock? … I think we should work on possible links between our families too.'

She searched through a drawer in the old-fashioned sideboard. She had the feeling that Carver was watching her. She was pleased she was wearing skinny jeans and that her back was turned, as she was sure her face was bright red.

She sat down opposite him with her pen poised over the pad of lined paper. 'How do you want to play this?' She hoped the colour had faded from her cheeks.

'Just throw out ideas however silly and then we'll discuss them. I'll kick off with "abducted by aliens".' He laughed. 'That's the favourite explanation my mother and I had for the disappearance of Dad, by the way.'

'Russian spies who had to leave the country.'

'Good one. How about intelligence service operatives?'

Jenny wrote the ideas in neat columns on the page.

'You mean like James Bond?'

'Possibly. Your turn, let's keep the thoughts coming. Don't think too much, or you'll dismiss ideas.'

Jenny sipped the strong coffee and watched the expressions flashing across Carver's face. She was enjoying this and the thought made her go quiet while she questioned why.

'Come on, don't censor your thoughts, just throw them out.'

'Okay, some sort of crime, bank robbery, murder, fire, fraud.'

'So, they could have got away with *it* and been living abroad, South America, perhaps?'

She wrote South America in capital letters on the page, followed by a large question mark.

'Or they might not have … maybe they've been in prison for twenty-five years.'

'Surely we'd have known if there had been a trial?'

'Not necessarily, we were both quite young.'

'True, but I can't think news wouldn't have got out. We'd have been teased at school, surely?'

She rubbed the side of her nose with the pen as she thought. 'Maybe our dads were witnesses in a trial and had to be whisked away to a safe house somewhere.'

'But wouldn't they have taken us too?'

'Not sure. I don't know how these things work.'

He sat looking miles away for a while and then his face

became animated again. 'Horrid thought, but maybe they murdered someone and fled.'

'Don't joke. I was convinced the builders had found a body when they called me out to show me the box. I can still feel the ice-cold feeling between my shoulder blades.'

'Hmmm … I can see how that must have been a scary moment.'

'Between you and me, at that very instant when Ivan pointed to the hole, I had a dreadful thought that Mum might have killed Dad and buried him in the garden.'

They sat quietly again in mutual contemplation.

Jenny broke the silence. 'The way my mum clammed up whenever my father was mentioned, I always imagined he'd gone off with another woman, but then, if that was the case, why would she involve the police?'

'That doesn't suggest a link between the two men either.'

'Maybe they were both murdered by a serial killer.'

'One that murdered two men in the same week?'

'Hmmm … our mothers *were* at the police station at the same time.'

'True. Did they know each other? Or did our fathers? It seems too co-incidental that they were both there reporting missing husbands independently, but at the same time, if you know what I mean.'

'So, we have possibilities where they were either victims of crime or committed a crime. We do need to look at family links too.' Jenny ripped off the sheet detailing possible reasons for disappearance and headed up a new one with the word 'Links'.

'My family have always lived in the Sowden or Borteen area. What about yours?' Carver asked.

'Same as you, at least back into the early eighteen hundreds. I've traced the family tree, remember?'

'As I said the other day, I've always meant to look at our family history.'

Jenny made notes and then glanced up at him. 'Maybe I can help you with that.'

He smiled. 'What did you say your dad did for work?'

'He worked at an auction house in Sowden. I don't know exactly what he did there.'

'Mine was a car mechanic, as far as I am aware. Hmm ... I guess your dad could have had his car mended by mine, or mine could have bought antiques from yours.'

'It sounds plausible, but probably far from the truth.'

'Borteen isn't that big. They might just have met in the pub.' He pulled his hair back from his face. 'That's assuming any link between their disappearances, or between them at all.'

'Yes, but if they went missing at the same time, it would make more sense, I suppose, if they disappeared together, or went away because of some link to each other.'

'Maybe.' Carver reached over to touch the clock.

'Hobbies?'

'I really don't know.'

Jenny wrote 'Mutual hobbies?' She put the pen down and rested her chin on her hand. 'I'm sure the real reasons can't be as fantastical as the stories we are weaving.'

'You never know.' Their eyes met across the table. Jenny felt comfortable here with him, but that little nagging doubt still scrabbled around in the back of her mind. She tried to dismiss it.

Carver shifted in the seat, as if he was aware of her thoughts. 'Can you start another list about the clock?'

They turned as one to the wooden case on the table.

'Good thinking.'

'I still can't come up with a good reason why anyone would bury it in a garden.'

'It must have been there a while. There was paving on top of the place where it was found before the digging began. It was hidden, as you suggested before. But, why?' She turned to a new sheet of paper and wrote clock at the top.

'Stolen?'

'Hmm ... such hot property that it needed to be hidden so as not to incriminate the thief?' Jenny began doodling a clock at the bottom of the page as she thought. 'I don't like thinking of my dad as some sort of criminal.'

'I know exactly what you mean. It's better to have nice thoughts, although we've both probably romanticised our missing parents over the years.'

'True. Mine has become almost a hero figure, because the reality isn't there to confront or contradict me.'

He nodded. 'Mine too.'

She was sure he probably did the same thing with his late wife, only remembering the good and submerging anything negative to the far recesses of his mind.

He touched the clock again. 'Some sort of time capsule, perhaps?'

'I thought the idea of time capsules was that they had objects inside to link them to an era or date.'

'Not that then.'

She drained her coffee cup and put it on the table next to the clock. As she did so she calculated it was about five mugs tall and two mugs wide. 'Is there anything remarkable about this clock? What sort of wood is it made of?'

Carver pulled the clock onto his lap. He examined the case and the clock face. 'It's oak. I'm no expert, but I would guess this is an antique, though it doesn't look particularly valuable.'

'A definite mystery, but the answer is probably something simple. I bet my mum and dad had an argument because of the clock's loud tick and my father buried it in protest.'

They both laughed.

He offered the clock to Jenny and she took it carefully. As she put it on her lap a drawer appeared to glide like magic from the back of the case. 'Whoa. A secret drawer.'

'Anything in it?' Carver looked so excited, he reached out his hands towards her.

Instinctively she pulled the clock closer and ran her finger around the inside of the drawer. It was cleverly disguised by the wooden moulding and fitted neatly inside most of the lower part of the clock case.

'No, nothing.'

She passed the clock back to him and he examined the empty drawer again. He pushed it gently shut. Then, he couldn't get it to open again, no matter what he tried and frustration etched in his face. 'Definitely a secret drawer. You must have somehow touched the magic button to open it.'

'So, is the mystery to do with the clock or whatever was once inside that drawer?'

'That would seem to be the million-dollar question. Unfortunately, I don't suppose we'll ever know.' He put the clock back onto the table and took the lists from Jenny's hand. He scanned the sheets and then wrote in capital letters, *What was inside the clock?* on the clock page.

Jenny stifled a yawn.

'I'd better leave you to your evening.'

She shook her head, forcing her eyes wide again. 'Sorry, I'm fine. Everything just seemed to catch up with me for a second. How can we move this forward?'

'We need to keep adding to our lists to see if we can solve the mystery.'

She felt satisfied that agreeing to add to the lists meant she'd have to see Carver again.

'I'll make sure I go up into the loft,' she said. 'I've been avoiding it – couldn't face it somehow – but Mum might have kept some press cuttings about my dad's disappearance or something. She always stuck things in scrapbooks.'

'I wonder if it's worth getting the clock looked at by an expert?'

Jenny didn't respond. She didn't like the thought of letting the clock out of her sight just yet.

'Are you okay with all this?' Carver asked.

Jenny stroked the wood of the clock case again, to try and hide the emotion that was threatening to spill tears. 'Just trying to decide where the door to fairyland might be and when I stepped through it.' She wiped a hand over her eyes.

'I'm finding discussing all this difficult too, if it's any help.'

'Everything feels surreal at the moment, brainstorming the disappearance of our fathers, moving back here, Mum dying. I keep thinking I'll wake up and things will be back to normal, but of course they never will go back to *normal*.'

'You've had a lot to cope with, Jenny.'

'So have you.'

'I guess. It might be nice to be whisked away to the land of the fairies. Hey, we didn't put that on our list of possible fates for our fathers!'

'Ha, ha, not amusing.'

'I'd better go.' He stood up.

Did she imagine the lurch inside her? 'By the way, I got my job. I start next week.'

'Wow, well done. In that case, we need to celebrate. Come on, let's do something fun. The band I used to play with, Borteen Celts, have a gig at The Ship Inn tonight. Why don't you come with me? Unless you are too tired, of course.'

She didn't hesitate. 'I'd love to.'

'Shall I come back and collect you in about forty minutes?'

'No need. I'll meet you there.'

He got up. 'Would you like me to put the clock anywhere for you?'

'On the shelf above the fireplace maybe.' She moved the smaller clock that was there and Carver lifted the new find into position. He went to retrieve his tool bag from the kitchen. 'Do you mind if I have the box?'

'What, that old rusty thing?'

'It's got my dad's initials on it. I can clean it up and paint it. Boxes are always useful in my workshop.'

'Be my guest. I'll come out to the shed with you. I'll just put these wrappings in the bin on the way.' She started to pick up the wrappings from the clock. A piece of paper dropped out from the folds. Carver bent to retrieve it.

'Well. I'll take that as proof of a link between our fathers.'

He showed her the advertising flyer for a motor repair workshop.

'Is that where your dad worked?' She felt a gurgle of excitement growing in her stomach.

He nodded.

'There's something written on the back.'

Carver turned it over. Scrawled on the back in spidery writing was *We owe you, Arthur*. 'Arthur? Does that name mean anything to you? I don't think it does to me.'

'No, I don't think so. My dad's name is Timothy Simpson. He doesn't have a middle name and his father's name was Frederick.'

'Intriguing, but yet another mystery to add to the pot. Let's ponder on it another time. I've just got to pop home to feed Wilf. You sure you don't want to come with me and then on to the pub?'

'No, I'll meet you there, if that's okay.' She realised from her response that she still had a vestige of suspicion about Carver.

When he smiled, however, the world seemed to tip on its axis a little. She wanted to make him smile more often and preferably at her.

# Chapter Eighteen

Jenny couldn't believe she'd just said yes to spending the rest of the evening with Carver at the pub, but she was completely fed up with sitting alone at home watching old films and property programmes in the evenings; a night out might do her good.

The treasure-trove clock looked odd on the shelf above the fireplace, too tall somehow, but it had seemed the safest place to put it. Jenny kept staring at it when Carver had gone, willing the inanimate object to tell her its story and secrets.

The thorny subject of what to wear reared its head. She went to look through her wardrobe. While she sorted clothes, a thought kept nagging at her, an idea that had begun when she and Carver were discussing the fate of their fathers. It harried her so loudly that she threw down the skirt she'd been considering wearing and went into the tiny box room, which she'd designated an office, to open up her laptop.

Before she had time to think too deeply, she registered her father's details on three missing persons' websites. She had no photograph to include with her posts, but somehow it seemed important to reach out to her father without delay. He must be out there somewhere in the world, if he wasn't already dead and buried, of course. She didn't know why she had never done this before. Her mother had just been so anti any mention of her other parent. Now her mother was gone, however, there was nothing to stop her.

Finding the box in the garden had made her father seem more real, as if he'd gone from being flat in her imagination to 3D, someone who buried things in the garden. If indeed he had buried it. It was frustrating not to know and upsetting to have no one to ask.

She began to read some of the other entries on the missing persons' websites and the tales of joyful reconciliation, which echoed the television programme about lost families she sometimes watched. Tears streamed down her face.

When she looked up from her laptop, she only had fifteen minutes before she needed to leave to meet Carver at The Ship. She washed her face in cold water, willing the red blotchiness caused by crying to subside. The lack of time somehow made the decision about what to wear easier. She pulled on plum-coloured jeans and a white shirt. Draping a matching plum silk scarf in the neckline of the shirt, she grabbed her black jacket and bag, and arrived at the front door just as the taxi she had ordered beeped its horn.

Carver looked at the shiny new keys in his hands. They didn't feel like his yet. He'd changed all of the locks earlier in the day and installed window locks on the ground floor. If the strange happenings in his house continued now, he would definitely have to blame something paranormal. Maybe Jenny was right and they'd passed through some invisible fairy door. He didn't think so, but he would have been happy to believe it, if it provided a solution to the strange goings on. Nevertheless, he locked Wilf securely in his kennel.

He was amazed he'd been brave enough to ask Jenny to come to the pub. It wasn't quite a date, but he'd still been surprised that she'd agreed. She always seemed to look at him with a slightly suspicious expression on her face.

Carver took a detour on the way to The Ship so that he passed the Wishing Tree that Bliss had regarded as so special. There were still a few things hung from its branches that he recognised she had put there herself: a beach shell suspended from a ribbon; a plastic heart key ring from a cracker; and a little plaster owl wedged against the trunk.

Carver searched out the familiar items with the torch on his phone. It had become almost a ritual of remembrance.

'Here's thinking about you, Bliss. What do I do about Jenny?'

He didn't elaborate about what aspect of Jenny that Bliss might have an opinion about. He took a blue ribbon out of his pocket. He had taken it from Bliss's drawer earlier. It looked new and shiny compared to the other weather-worn scraps tied to the branches. He threaded his old front door keys on to the ribbon and tied it on the highest branch he could reach. They began straight away to tinkle in the evening breeze.

'Here's thinking about you, Bliss. You would have known what to do about the happenings in the house and Jenny. Although, I wouldn't have to think about another woman at all if you were still here.'

Having made his offering to the sacred tree, he trudged down the road towards the seafront and the pub, leaping in the hedgerow once or twice out of the way of speeding vehicles, as there was no pavement on this route into Borteen.

He hesitated outside the heavy pub door with its window of dark stained glass, a ship in full sail depicted crudely in the panes. The burble of noise from inside the bar sounded alien; he came here for a pint at least once a week, but was more used to being alone with the forest sounds. Taking a deep breath, he pushed open the door. The noise of voices and clinking glasses immediately became loud and almost too real. The smell of hops and aftershave enveloped him. His heart was thudding loudly, he was sure everyone would hear it. It was too easy to get out of practice at being with other people socially.

He scanned the crowd to see if Jenny had already arrived. She hadn't, but familiar faces rushed towards him. He hadn't seen some of the band members for a long time and had made a habit of avoiding coming to the pub if they were playing ... until now. His hand was shaken vigorously and his shoulders patted, as band members came to greet him with genuine affection and warmth. He had to wipe an arm across his eyes to remove the moisture that sprang there.

He'd just gained control of his emotions and ordered a pint, when Jenny peered around the door. Her eyes were wide like a fawn's, as if she too had found entry into the pub on her own daunting. She saw Carver, smiled and came over. He hid a new set of emotions by asking her what she would like to drink and began to introduce her to his friends.

There was lots of suggestive banter and Carver cringed, incredibly uncomfortable for both himself and Jenny. He introduced her as a potential singer for the band, which she strongly denied, and found himself promising to drum.

Jenny caught Carver's uncomfortable look. It must be hard, if you had lost the love of your life, to have yourself associated with another woman as a couple ... especially if it wasn't true. A betraying voice in her head piped up that it could be true, if she'd just relax and trust him. She liked Carver a lot, despite his moods, but something was stopping her from relaxing or pursuing the idea ... was it just Cindy's gossip?

She sipped at a large glass of white wine and chatted with the group about the songs that she remembered from her days singing with her band at university, even though the thought of singing with the Borteen Celts filled her with horror. Was it because Carver was here? She noticed that he'd been given a spare bodhran and held a beater in his hand. He was soon strumming along to the tune the band began to play.

Jenny once again found it fascinating to watch his

practised drumming movements. She'd never seen him as relaxed and happy. He winked at her when he caught her eye.

There were several singers, so the spotlight wasn't just on Jenny as she had at first imagined. She soared to an emotional high, singing along with the others to the intoxicating folk music. She was surprised at how many of the words and tunes she remembered, once she got going.

When the band took a break, Carver asked her if she'd like to take her drink outside. They sat on a bench at the front of the pub under the bright moon. The moonlight shimmering across the sea provided a fantastic view and the waves moving over the sand made a hypnotic soundtrack. She'd left her jacket inside the pub and the night air was chilly. Carver moved closer and she shivered then with anticipation rather than cold as his jean-clad leg rested against hers.

'I'm sure I can see the man in the moon this evening,' she said, to cover the tingles that ran up and down her spine at his closeness.

'It is a very expressive moon tonight, probably because the air is so clear.'

'Do you believe in anything, Carver?'

'You mean … a god?' He raised his hand and she wondered for a moment if he would hold her hand or put his arm around her shoulders.

'Well, I suppose I mean spirit, a force outside yourself?'

'I never used to, but Bliss was convinced about a spiritual world, magic, healing, all sorts of things like that.'

Speaking the name of his dead wife seemed to blow a cold wind between them and Carver moved away slightly, putting his hand back on his leg. Up until that point, she'd thought that he might even kiss her, but just as suddenly as the thought had occurred, the moment appeared to have passed and she felt her spirits plummet.

A band member came out to find them, as the Celts were about to start playing again. They went back into the pub, but even though the singing was fun and the music stirring, Jenny perceived that something had subtly changed. A strange sadness enveloped her and she sat down to watch for a while.

A few songs later when she went to the back of the pub to find the toilet, she recognised two people she knew sharing a table and a kiss; Cindy Lewis and Andrew Jenkins. Goodness, was Andrew the man Cindy had referred to as potential husband number three? She sincerely hoped not, after what she had learned about him from her disastrous pizza night meeting, but she had a horrible feeling he was the man Cindy had talked about.

Jenny skirted past the couple, hoping they wouldn't notice her. Thankfully, they didn't.

However, she wasn't so lucky on the way back. Andrew put out his hand to stop her progress between the tables and she had to acknowledge the pair.

'Hello, Cindy, Andrew. I didn't know you two still saw each other.'

'We met up again a few months ago.' Cindy's emphasis on the word *met* suggested intimacy.

'Your singing's good, Jenny. Pity you're still with that *toe rag* Rodgers though.' The sarcastic tone of Andrew's words jarred.

'You didn't heed my warning, did you?' added Cindy.

Annoyed that she felt the need to even listen to them, let alone reply, Jenny said, 'Carver and I are just friends.'

'Yeah, right,' Andrew sneered, with a smirk on his face. Jenny wondered if he was daring her to say something about the events of the last time they had met. She was tempted, but decided not to stoop to his level.

'Your mother would have been so upset,' added Cindy.

Jenny froze, all intentions of not rising to the bait forgotten. 'What has my mother got to do with it?'

Andrew now had a horrible grin on his face, matched by Cindy's. They looked alike, Jenny realised. *Two peas in a pod*, her mother would have said. More like matching gargoyles, thought Jenny unhappily.

'She wouldn't be very pleased about you having anything to do with the son of the man who murdered your father.'

Jenny felt the blow of the energy of Cindy's statement go straight to her stomach. She gasped, looking from Andrew to Cindy in disbelief.

The obnoxious pair seemed gleeful at getting a reaction. Cindy put her hand over Andrew's on the table and her eyes seemed to bulge as she continued. 'It's true, Jenny. I told you to look him up. Carver Rodgers killed his wife. Like father, like son. My mum always said his father killed your dad. The rumours were all around Borteen at the time he disappeared.'

Jenny didn't give them the satisfaction of any reply, she just stumbled away towards the chair where she'd left her coat. The sounds in the pub seemed muffled, including the music from the band, and she realised with horror that she was in danger of passing out. She slumped on her seat and downed the rest of her wine, desperate to stop the weird sensations coursing through her body and mind.

*Could it be true? Could it?*

Jenny felt hot, then cold. She fought to control her thoughts and battled the wave of faintness. She'd played right into Cindy and Andrew's vindictiveness. She could tell they had intended and wanted to hurt her. They had enjoyed baiting her and meant for her to feel doubts about Carver.

Her rational mind knew she couldn't take what they said at face value, but their words were like poison darts, spreading confusion and uncertainty. She recognised that it was just what they wanted, but she couldn't help her feelings.

Their laughter seemed to follow her flight across the pub. She looked over to the band, saw Carver pause in his drumming. His mouth seemed to be saying her name aloud, but she couldn't stay in the room with the maelstrom of her thoughts for a moment longer. She grabbed her coat and bag, turned and barged out of the heavy bar door.

The tears flowed freely down her face as she set off at a fast pace down the promenade and up the hill towards home. She should have challenged them. She should have asked for proof, but the shock made her want to run away into the night.

Halfway home, the feeling that she was yet again being followed kept her footsteps brisk. She breathlessly slammed her front door against the darkness, Carver and her possible shadow. Much peering from behind her curtains into the street convinced her that she'd imagined being followed; pity she hadn't imagined the evening's events too.

# Chapter Nineteen

Early the next morning, Carver woke up in a panic. He was convinced that he could hear someone downstairs. As soon as he had rubbed his eyes, he realised that he must have woken mid-troubled dream. He took a couple of puffs from his inhaler, just in case the panic heralded an asthma attack.

Padding barefoot to the stairs, he made himself examine every inch of the ground floor rooms for intruders, or indeed anything out of the ordinary. He still hadn't completely convinced himself his *happenings* weren't paranormal. Then he put on his boots and went outside to check on Wilf. The dog was so pleased to see him, he allowed the animal to follow him up the stairs and into the house.

He shared some toast absentmindedly with the dog, as memories slowly replayed in his mind of sitting at the front of the pub in the moonlight with Jenny.

Watching the moon on the waves.

Hypnotised by the sound of the sea and the beat of his heart, the warmth of Jenny's leg.

Feeling close to her. Feeling hopeful.

He'd even contemplated pressing his lips against hers, but at the last second the mention of Bliss had changed the mood, reminded him of his loyalties, his vows, his guilt.

Then to top it all, despite what he felt had been a great evening with the band, she'd gone, disappeared, without even saying goodnight to him. He'd watched her go. Her face looked strange, like a kitten that had been kicked, but by the time the band had finished playing the song and he'd gone outside, she'd vanished into the night. He was annoyed with himself that he hadn't just walked off the stage when he'd noticed her stricken face. She had looked disturbed by something, but what? Or by whom?

It hurt that she'd just gone, but was it his fault? Had she expected more of the evening? What had he done wrong ... again? He'd stood on the pavement outside the pub and felt hopeless, yet again. Unsure whether to go to her home, or whether to text. He checked his phone, but there had been no message from her. There still was no message this morning.

She'd left. She'd made it pretty clear that she didn't want to be with him. She hadn't even said goodnight to his friends who'd made her so welcome. It hurt.

Could he ever allow himself to love again? At only thirty-two years old, the thought of the lonely years stretching ahead were not always pleasant. Sometimes they were ... Things were simpler on your own. Your own timetable, pleasing yourself ... but a cold, lonely bed.

He'd loved Bliss heart and soul, which meant part of him had died when she did. He wasn't sure there was enough of his heart left after that heartache to share with another. He'd never been very good at courting and wooing, the games of love.

What had spooked Jenny last night? He'd thought that they could at least be friends. Where did this leave the unanswered questions about the clock, the possible connection of the disappearance of their fathers and working together to solve the mystery of the past?

Last night he'd gone back inside The Ship, finished his beer, made his excuses and walked back up the hill to Tree Tops with a heavy heart. His mood felt even worse this morning after a night of tossing and turning, mulling over the evening that had seemed full of so much potential, but ended in dashed hopes and dreams.

* * *

Jenny woke with a thudding head. She hadn't drunk a lot, but then it didn't seem to take much alcohol these days to affect her. An emotional hangover, perhaps?

She just hoped that she hadn't made too much of a fool of herself with Carver, the band, the pub. What must they have thought of her leaving like that after they had shown her nothing but genuine welcome, warmth and friendship?

She sat staring at herself in the mirror of her dressing table. Her eyes were dark and the rings beneath them did not make for a pretty sight. She shook her finger at herself in the glass.

*No men, remember. No men! You put yourself in dangerous waters, my girl. Carver is far too attractive and you still don't know the truth about his past. You need to know more about him before you allow yourself to feel ... to relax. And you must never listen to Cindy or Andrew ever again. They are most definitely not on your side. Fool!*

Carver. She'd looked up the meaning of his real name, Damien, yesterday. It meant *to tame*. She had resisted allowing him to tame her, but she knew that he had the potential to do so, if, and only if, Cindy and Andrew's malicious revelations were not true. She couldn't believe she'd allowed that awful couple to set the seeds of doubt in her head, but she had and those horrible doubts refused to let go.

Time to venture into the loft. Could her mother possibly provide the answers to the mysteries that plagued her life, after all?

She had resisted setting foot in the loft so far, but now she needed to find the legacy of boxes her mother had almost certainly left for her. She had to read her mother's scrapbooks to see if they cast any light on the disappearance of her father and any possible link to Carver's family.

It was going to be dusty, so she changed into old clothes.

She'd just opened the loft hatch when her phone began to ring. Carver's name flashed on the screen of her mobile when she retrieved it from her back pocket, balancing precariously on the chair she was using to reach the loft ladder. Even if she didn't want to answer it, she knew it would be a relief to get this conversation over and done with.

'Are you okay? I was worried last night when I couldn't find you in the pub.' He sounded wary and his clipped tone suggested he was maybe more than a little annoyed.

'Yes, I'm fine. I'm terribly sorry about last night. I just suddenly felt the need to get away ... overwhelmed, I guess.' She blushed, even though he wasn't there to see her embarrassment.

'It would have been good if you'd sent me a text, so that I knew you were safe.' She could tell he was trying to tone down his clipped words.

'Sorry, sorry. I was completely out of order.'

'Was it something I did or said?' He paused and she didn't answer for what she realised was a telling moment too long. The tone of his voice twisted her gut.

'No, of course not.'

The line went quiet again.

'Well ... if you're quite sure it's nothing I did. Shall I ring you when the band is playing again?'

He was testing her reaction for sure. She paused again, not knowing what to say. 'Erm, yes ... that would be nice.' She knew that her fake politeness would be obvious to his ears. She looked down at her hand, she'd dug her nails into her palm and drawn blood.

Carver said goodbye and she screamed in frustration when he'd gone. It was all she could do not to launch the phone to the landing below her. She wanted to smash something so badly.

It was time to end the speculation and find out what

she could about her father, Carver's father and the whole sorry connection, or not, between their families. Her senses reeling, she returned to her loft mission.

She banged her shins on the rungs of the loft ladder and grazed her back going through the narrow hatch. Finding the switch for the lights, she sat on the edge of the hatch rubbing her leg with one hand and her tears away with the other.

The loft space was bigger than she'd imagined, but her mother's legacy of boxes far, far exceeded her expectations. How had the ceiling taken the weight of all this stuff and where on earth did she start looking?

Moving anything set up dust clouds, which made her cough. If the mission hadn't been so vital to her peace of mind, she might have given up before she'd even started.

Her attention homed in on a large pink box, the box her mother had designated years ago as her memory box. A vague vision surfaced of her mother showing her this container, calling it the memory box, and promising to fill it with things Jenny might value in the future. It looked rather forlorn, wedged between the rafters on the decaying insulation that she ought to replace as part of her renovations. Something else to add to the list.

The pictures that her mother had glued on the sides of the pink box were of teddy bears and penguins, but they were rather faded and peeling now. She gulped against the emotion that surfaced at the thought of her mother doing this for her all those years before.

She had such mixed feelings. On one hand, eagerness to open the box to see what it contained was growing, but so was her fear. She was scared of the feelings, the avalanche of emotions which might be released. She wanted to know the truth, but was scared to know the truth at the same time. She felt stripped raw by the depth of her confusion.

Cradling the pink container, she descended the precariously steep ladder, all thoughts of document searching and reorganisation of the loft gone. This seemed the most likely and most important box of them all.

The pink box lay taunting her in the middle of the kitchen table and when she could stand the tension no longer, she flipped open the lid. There were photographs, but they were only of Jenny and her mum, absolutely none of her father. Disappointment mounting, she scrabbled through the box, but to no avail. There just weren't any pictures of her dad. Somehow, this upset her even more, as if her mother had sought to erase him from their lives completely.

It took a while for her tear-filled eyes to clear enough to focus on anything other than the photographs inside the box.

A lock of hair curled inside a baby shoe.

Jenny laid aside numerous birthday and Christmas cards and came across a poem she had written at junior school. The poem entitled, *Where are you, Dad?* tore at her heart strings.

Damp tissues soaked with tears began to form a mountain on the kitchen table.

She couldn't face going up to the loft again today. She pushed the loft ladder back into place and went for a long walk by the sea, not caring if she was soaked by the spray. She had to find at least one photograph of her father. There must be at least one in the house … surely.

# Chapter Twenty

Carver wasn't sleeping well again, not helped by this being a weekend when everyone was setting off fireworks. His only concession to Bonfire Night had been to take Wilf for a walk on the headland, so he could watch the rockets lighting up the sky in Borteen. Thankfully the dog wasn't bothered by the loud bangs, but he knew some people had a real problem with their pets at this time of year.

He'd spent all of Saturday carving wood to try to escape his inner torment and by dawn light on Sunday, he was back at the Wishing Tree. The misty drizzle, which had blown in with his mood, disorientated him. There were new offerings in the tree's branches. Other people believed the tree to be magical. The dawn light sparkled on something hung way up high, no doubt yet another offering.

Bliss's ashes were invisible after the passing of the three years since he'd scattered them around the base of the tree trunk, but he knew that they were there, that she was there ...

If her essence would be anywhere, despite her apparent failure to communicate with him from the afterlife, it would be here in her favourite place. He reached his hand behind the trunk of the tree, finding the place where she had insisted that he carve their initials. Carver had protested at the time. He hated anything that defaced his beloved trees whilst they were growing, but Bliss had been convinced that the affirmation of their love carved into this tree would keep them true to each other. The stylised initials entwined their names on this sacred bark. He'd told her it was unnecessary, as since he'd met her, he'd had eyes for no other woman. They all paled into insignificance. But she had been insistent and he found it difficult to deny her anything.

Even as he traced the carving with his fingers, he believed that he stood at a crossroads. Did it betray Bliss's memory to be caring so much about what Jenny thought of him? Bliss was dead, Jenny very much alive.

Why should he feel like a naughty schoolboy? He had been faithful to and besotted by Bliss, but she was gone. Should he honour her memory by living like a monk for the rest of his days? He had a horrible feeling that he'd upset Jenny yet again on Friday when the band had played at the pub, goodness only knew how. He hadn't been anywhere near her when she had appeared to get upset, but he desperately wanted to make things right again between them. He should have kissed her that night under the moonlight, then maybe the evening would have ended differently and he'd know if his fledgling feelings were returned or completely dead in the water. Was she playing hard to get, or just confused in the same way he was? He suspected the latter.

On impulse, he reached down and took off his boots and socks, as if this would help him to get closer to Bliss and maybe glean her opinion on his dilemma. He placed his feet on the ground where he knew her ashes lay. Despite this, he could only hear silence, stillness, the mere rustle of the leaves in the mist, as Bliss stubbornly refused to give him any guidance.

Hang on in there or butt out? Which?

An emotion he tried to refuse to recognise as anger began to bubble to the surface and an oath rose to his throat. If he didn't love this tree so much, he feared that he would tear off the branches and beat them on the ground until they were unrecognisable as living things. The image of Jenny singing with the band refused to let go. Conversely, he now had difficulty recalling Bliss's facial features, unless he looked at one of the many photographs at Tree Tops.

At last, he imagined he sensed Bliss's voice in the air. 'Live, Carver, live.'

It somehow seemed little consolation as he stumbled through the leaf mould towards home. He carried his boots and socks and stubbed his bare toe on a protruding root unnoticed, as the tears blinded his sight more than the mist.

Jenny got up early to start her working week. She hadn't had much sleep for days. Fireworks for Bonfire Night the evening before had been matched by the same loud bangs and explosions on Friday and Saturday too. She'd stood in the back garden watching the fireworks for a while on Friday evening, but by Sunday she'd had enough and just closed the curtains against the noise.

*New job, new start*, she told herself, desperately trying to improve her state of mind.

As she ate breakfast, she looked again at the items from the memory box, still spread across the kitchen table, and wondered if her father could really be dead. Surely, she would know, would feel it in her bones, wouldn't she?

In the way that the mind embroiders things, she imagined his body buried somewhere in the woodland near Tree Tops after he'd been murdered by Carver's father. But the story still didn't feel right somehow.

The thought made her question why Carver's dad would even want to kill her own. What dispute could have ended that way? What was the significance of the clock? Had there once been something important in that secret drawer? The damned thing probably had nothing to do with her father.

She decided that when she got home that evening she must wind the clock to see if it had a particularly annoying tick or chime. But even then, why would her mother bury an antique that could be sold to raise funds for them to live on? None of it made any sense.

For most of her life, her father had been *just missing* in her mind.

'He can't be dead. He just can't be. Not yet,' she yelled to her newly painted lounge ceiling. She'd given the decorator a key and he was finishing the spare room today, before working on the hall, stairs and landing for the rest of the week.

Her emotional mind told her to have nothing more to do with Carver, despite her attraction to him, but her rational mind told her that he couldn't be held responsible for the actions of his father and besides, she needed to stay in touch with him to try to discover the truth – if that was even possible. There was just that worrying niggling thought that Carver might have killed his wife, as Cindy and Andrew had suggested. Her head hurt with all of the circular, unresolved thinking.

It came down to a straight choice: stay away from Carver for now and maybe try to research the death of his wife herself, or challenge him directly. Another of her mother's sayings washed into her mind … *Don't let things fester, better to challenge them head on* … but how did you accuse someone of murdering their spouse? Somehow she couldn't just google the case again. The outcome felt too vital to risk possible misinformation from the internet.

She finished getting ready for her first day at work in the archives. She'd chosen wide-legged black trousers and a patterned tunic top, teamed with a long cardigan in slate blue. It was wonderful to look forward to going to work for a change. She hoped her mind-chatter would calm down as she became embroiled in the family stories and the joy of the people she imagined she would help with their research. It would make working worthwhile and today would provide a much needed distraction from the things swirling around in her head.

Why had she not allowed herself to do a job she enjoyed before? Why had she suffered years of working in a role that neither inspired nor fulfilled her? The fear of not earning enough to pay your way was a strange motivator, but one she knew was shared by a large proportion of the population. How different would the world be if everyone was free to follow their hearts in what they did for a living?

Her heart lurched as she walked up the stone steps to the archive building. Was she up to the job? After all, it was very different to what she'd done before. Sandra and Lani greeted her excitedly. There had already been a healthy interest in the new archives service as soon as it was announced and Jenny's appointment diary was filling up. People who wanted family history help could book one, two, or three hours with Jenny at a standard rate.

By lunchtime on her first day, she knew that her new job suited her down to the ground. She loved the complexity of the two family trees she'd already helped clients to begin.

Sandra was eating her sandwiches in the tiny staff room when Jenny went in.

'Well? Enjoying it?'

'Loving it.'

'Yay! Lani and I were saying earlier that we definitely made the right choice in appointing you.'

'Thank you. It means a lot to know that you both think that.'

Over the course of the afternoon, despite her dedication to the job, her thoughts kept straying to how to start her difficult conversation with Carver and whether her father had read her missing person appeals, or if he had long since been dead.

However, the second case of the afternoon, presented by a woman called Zoe, took all other thoughts out of her head.

Zoe initially said that she wanted to trace the previous

occupants of her home. She had recently moved to the property with her family. Jenny began to turn up census entries and maps for the address.

As she began to uncover details, Zoe looked at Jenny in a strange way, as if a mental debate raged in her head.

'Can I tell you something about this research? You are going to think me totally mad.'

'I'm sure I won't,' replied Jenny. She crossed her fingers under the desk.

'Since we moved to our lovely house there have been strange happenings.'

Jenny nodded encouragingly.

'Then my daughter saw a young woman in a blue dress on the landing. Since then she's seen her three times and I've seen her twice. That's who I'm trying to identify ... our ... ghost.'

Zoe paused and turned fearful eyes towards Jenny. Jenny couldn't decide if she was scared of the ghost or Jenny's opinion of her.

'You see, we thought if we had her name, we might be able to communicate properly with her.'

'That makes perfect sense to me. It must be rather scary ... but intriguing at the same time. You say a young woman? Are there any clues in the way she is dressed to show when she might have lived in the house?'

From what Zoe described and although it was merely guess work, the girl appeared to belong to the late Victorian era and luckily, the family who had lived in the house had been there for many years and appeared to have had seven sons and one daughter.

'You do realise that there's absolutely no guarantee that this is your ghost?'

'I do, but at least we could try using the name if we see her again.'

Jenny looked back at the screen. 'Well, if this is her, she's called Rosalind Masters.'

A little further digging revealed that Rosalind died in 1882, when she was seventeen. Jenny told Zoe how to go about ordering the girl's birth and death certificates if she wanted to.

Little tingles went up and down Jenny's spine. 'I've found this so fascinating, please let me know what happens next.'

Zoe promised and scurried off with the name *Rosalind Masters* written on a piece of paper. Jenny doubted she would hear from her again, but was intrigued. She told Sandra and Lani about the case, before she packed up and drove back over Pink Moor to home. It was weird to work one day and then have the next day off, but the archives office closed on Tuesdays.

The case set Jenny's mind wondering about the possibilities of ghosts, life after death and what form that might take. She stood silently, if a little self-consciously, in her lounge trying to see if she could pick up any ghostly resonance of either her father or her mother.

Carver had spoken about talking aloud to Bliss all of the time. Did his dead wife's spirit roam around Tree Tops? Jenny had heard that an unquiet spirit was more likely to remain on earth. Maybe a murdered one would be more inclined to linger? Was that why Carver thought someone was moving things in the house? Was it Bliss's unquiet spirit, or maybe even Jenny's father's?

The constant thinking began to get to her and she recognised she had to either continue the search of the attic for her mother's scrapbooks, use the library in her break on Wednesday to research newspapers or confront Carver. Come to think of it, she had something else she wanted to ask him too. Unfortunately the something else would mean she might have to hold off from challenging him about his wife's death for a little while longer.

She changed and drove to Tree Tops, remembering to put a small torch in her bag, as it was now getting dark so early. The path to the house through the woodland put her senses on full alert as usual, her unease somehow magnified by the torch beam picking out large branches. She couldn't quite get over the fear that someone or something might be lurking behind the tree trunks.

She could hear Carver's chainsaw blaring and saw his floodlight through the trees, so she sat on the chair on the balcony of the house to wait for his return and, before long, drifted off to sleep.

# Chapter Twenty-One

A lion's head had emerged from the stump of wood. It never ceased to surprise Carver where his imagination and chainsaw took him. He wandered back up the path towards the house, carrying the saw, his tool bag slung over his shoulder and Wilf at his heels. He was immediately on alert when he saw someone sitting on the balcony waiting for him.

It took him a few moments to register that it was Jenny and that she was fast asleep. Wilf hadn't reacted to her presence, but then he'd trained the dog to ignore her as she had been so fearful of the animal when she'd started cleaning for him. He motioned Wilf to his kennel, locked him in and stowed his tools in the workshop under the house.

He approached up the steps as quietly as he could and had a rare opportunity to observe Jenny in repose. Her eyelashes swept gently on her cheeks and there were dark smudges under her eyes suggesting that she hadn't been getting enough sleep. She wore no make-up, but her cheeks had a natural glow. He had to resist a sudden urge to kiss her lips, as he believed that would take them into uncharted territory and, of course, he couldn't be sure of her reaction to such a move after the last time they'd met. Why was she here, especially after the events of the band night?

He went to the front door, remembering too late that it had begun to squeak when he opened it. He had been meaning to put some oil on the hinge, but hadn't yet got around to it, like so many other things. Jenny jerked awake. He felt guilty to startle her. She looked bewildered until her eyes focussed and then she smiled at Carver. The smile reawakened the wish to kiss her, as desire unfurled in his body.

'Sorry, I must have dropped off. It's been a busy day.'

'How anyone can drop off to the sound of my chainsaw is beyond me.'

'Goes to show I must be tired.'

'Are you coming in?' He felt wary, as he'd been convinced he'd upset her terribly the last time they met. Maybe she would explain what he'd done.

He led the way inside, proud that there was no unopened post to kick out of the way. He paused to put his boots in their tray and Jenny removed her trainers and put them next to them. It felt like something a proper couple would do. A little spark of hope ignited deep in his stomach.

Carver found a kind of peace from tidying his house these days. He recognised that he'd let things slip badly before Jenny came into his life. Alone in the house after she'd resigned as his cleaner, there didn't seem to be any more excuses for piles of post or rubbish, so he'd been keeping on top of things, much to his brother-in-law's delight.

Maybe, he now admitted to himself, he'd been keeping on top of things in the hope that Jenny would visit Tree Tops again one day. He wondered if she would notice the changes he had made as she came into his home.

He'd begun to make pieces of wood sculpture, both with the chainsaw and more delicate items with his chisel, to display in the rooms of the house. Something Jenny had said about making her mother's house her own had struck a chord. He'd decided that it was time to reclaim Tree Tops for himself. Instead of feeling bad about Bliss's loss every time he walked into a room, he now needed the comfort and security of a true home. He'd even debated whether to sell the tree house, so that he could start again, but the horrible feelings that thought produced made him know he could never do that, however bad he felt, so he was working to change his impressions of the house.

When he had put an intricately carved obelisk on the mantelpiece, it had amazed him how the energy of the lounge had changed. He'd always poo-pooed Bliss's claims of energetic feelings in spaces, but now he was a firm believer.

What would Jenny think of his efforts? Would she even notice?

He turned around and caught a strange look on her face. *Hmm, not good news by the looks of things, mate.*

She didn't sit down and appeared oblivious of the things he'd hoped she would notice. He felt both disappointed and concerned.

'Is there a problem, Jenny?'

She'd rehearsed what she'd say so many times that she was scared it would come out like a script. Carver seemed so pleased to see her that she'd begun to lose her nerve. Instead, she decided to talk to him about her other suggestion and save the big confrontation for another time; maybe she could even combine the two if she could just be patient. Yes, patience was the key, otherwise she would never find out the information about the things that were bothering her.

'Carver, I've been wondering …'

'Sounds dangerous.' He smiled and looked relieved, almost as if he'd read her earlier thoughts and now sensed her change of heart and direction.

She'd noticed that the house was clean and tidy, but it seemed rude to compliment him. He'd probably got a new cleaner. Why did that thought disturb her?

'I realise it's all based on conjecture, but if our fathers – or one of them anyway – buried that box of *treasure* in my garden, do you think it's possible that they might have buried something here too?' She knew her voice sounded squeaky and tense.

Carver went over to the fireplace. He ran his finger over

an intricately carved wooden obelisk she didn't remember seeing there before.

'Interesting theory, but my father never actually lived here.'

Of course, Carver had built Tree Tops. 'Where did your parents live?' Jenny was disappointed, her spirits plummeting.

'All over the place. My grandparents owned this land before I built the house. Although, I suppose it's still possible my father would choose here if he did need to bury something. It is family land after all.'

Jenny couldn't help the thought, *but hopefully not my father's body*, coming into her head. 'I was going to suggest borrowing a metal detector.'

'Now that I can help you with. Bliss toyed with metal detecting as a hobby for a while, so there's one upstairs. It probably needs new batteries though.'

In the lull in the conversation Jenny's practised questions about Bliss's death kept rising to her lips, but she managed to swallow them down again. If there were more clues to her father's disappearance here at Tree Tops, she couldn't jeopardise finding them by challenging Carver right now. Not yet, in any case.

It felt horrible to be having these thoughts, she hated the duplicity. If she did think there was something to Cindy's allegations, why didn't she fear for her own safety alone here with Carver?

Instinctively she felt him to be a good man. The bottom line was that she didn't really believe there was any substance to Cindy's words, but they did stop her relaxing completely, worming doubts through her mind. She felt safe with Carver, liked Carver, but if there was ever to be any more between them, then she would have to have that difficult conversation regardless, to put her mind completely at rest. Otherwise Cindy's words would always stand as a barrier between them.

'Are you working full time now?'

She nodded. 'Almost. It's generally Monday to Friday with Tuesday off as the archives are closed, plus the occasional Saturday if they want me to run a course.'

'Enjoying it?'

'Yes, I love it.'

'I'm so glad it's working out for you.' His smile was warm and genuine. 'Would Saturday morning be any good, then?'

They made arrangements for Saturday morning. Carver walked her back to her car in the layby through the dark trees. Jenny left him with her accusations stuck in her throat, but with an excited feeling about having a go with the metal detector.

It became increasingly spooky that the cases Jenny dealt with at work were echoing the issues playing on her mind.

There had been the lady tracing her house ghost, when Jenny pondered life after death and the existence of spirits. Today, her client, an elderly lady, burst into tears as she began to explain to Jenny what she wanted from the research.

'We lost my father.' Tears escaped from Dorothy's eyes and teetered on her wrinkles.

Jenny gulped back her own tears as she watched the emotions playing across the old woman's face.

Dorothy dabbed at her eyes with a lace handkerchief.

'I'm sorry, my dear. It happened such a long time ago, but it still upsets me as if it were yesterday. He went off to war and never came home.'

'That must have been horrible for you.' Jenny paused, but suddenly she needed Dorothy to know she truly understood. 'My dad did the same. I mean, not because of the war, but he went out one day and was never heard of again.'

Dorothy grasped Jenny's wrist and Jenny had to concentrate hard so that her own tears didn't overwhelm her.

'Our poor mothers.'

'Poor us too. You never get over such a thing.'

'My mum wouldn't talk about it. I think she was angry, you see. I've got the telegram announcing that he'd died and his medals, but I still don't know what happened to his body.'

Dorothy's face portrayed the extent of her anguish.

Jenny took the details of Dorothy's father and began to look for relevant records. It took a long time for the ache in her chest to subside as she searched the military files. She was sad, but then again pleased to be able to tell Dorothy where her father enlisted, details of where he had been posted in Britain and Europe and even the story of a time when he'd got drunk and was reprimanded for it. The last piece of information was the detail of the war memorial in France where his name was commemorated. Jenny didn't add that it was probably likely that his body had never actually been found or buried.

The elderly lady hugged her tightly before she left, holding photocopies of the documents Jenny had found like a lifeline. Jenny hoped that she had helped to put some of Dorothy's demons finally to rest.

Conversely, she found her own demons haunting her dreams and her sleep continued to be disturbed by the maelstrom of thoughts in her head. She stared despairingly at the dark rings under her eyes as she got ready to visit Carver again on Saturday, her duplicity at not revealing her other questions making her feel rather sick. The sun had begun to warm the earth as she made her way through the trees to Tree Tops.

Carver was sitting on the bench near to the house, with Wilf at his feet, waiting for her. He too looked pale and dark eyed, his scar showing up red in contrast to the rest of his pale skin. She hardly noticed it these days, as it was so much a part of him, but today the scar looked particularly livid.

Jenny glanced warily at the dog, as Wilf lifted his head when she approached, even though she could see the animal regarded her as a friend. She forced herself to reach out a hand and lightly touch his grey ears.

'Wilf, stay,' said Carver, putting a hand on the dog's collar before he greeted Jenny himself. He raised the metal detector in the air. There were headphones hanging around his neck and a shiny trowel on the bench. 'Batteries charged and ready to go.'

'Exciting. I feel strangely nervous.'

'I know exactly what you mean. I've managed to resist detecting before you arrived. I was so tempted, but it didn't seem fair to have a go without you. It feels like something we should do together, even though, if I'm honest, I think it is a total long shot.'

She smiled at him. 'I know, but at least the niggling possibility will be exorcised.'

They walked towards Carver's woodworking clearing.

'You say the metal detector belonged to Bliss? Wouldn't she already have scanned this close to the house?' His dead wife's name felt strange on her lips.

'I'm not sure. I seem to remember her grumbling about tree roots here at Tree Tops and going to see the local farmer to get permission to detect in his fields.'

'Did she ever find anything exciting?'

'There's a plastic box somewhere full of bolts and a ploughshare. She once told me she'd found a piece of jewellery, but I'm not sure what happened to it. I feel guilty now that I didn't show more interest, but I think at the time I was under pressure as I had a big church commission for a new pulpit and screen.'

Jenny's enthusiasm nosedived. Surely Bliss would have found anything that was buried near here.

Carver appeared to sense her change in mood. 'Let's have a go anyway. It will be fun and I promise you bacon sandwiches for lunch.'

'How can a girl resist the offer of a bacon sandwich?' Her spirits rose again, although the questions she still burned to ask Carver seemed to form a cloud shadow above them. It stopped her fully relaxing, as she hated feeling deceitful.

They took it in turns. One of them wielded the metal detector, whist wearing the headphones and the other held the trowel, poised to dig down into the earth if the other gave the sign. Jenny found the detector cumbersome, but was determined to persevere. If Bliss could do it, so could she.

They soon had a growing collection of nails and bolts.

Carver began laughing and Jenny took off the headphones, so that she could hear what he was saying. 'I think we're detecting over the rubbish pile from when we built Tree Tops. We should try further away.'

He led her to the far end of his land. The trees were dense and dark, but on the boundary to the next property, they had been cleared and a long corridor of grass and undergrowth stretched before them.

'If I were going to bury something, then this is where I would choose to do it.'

After another forty minutes, Jenny's arms were heavy and aching. It wasn't the weight of the detector, more the unaccustomed motion of scanning the ground.

'Have you had enough?' asked Carver. He seemed very tuned into her feelings and moods. It made her even more guilty, thinking of the possibility of her suspicions being tattooed on her forehead for him to clearly read.

'I must admit to looking forward to my bacon sandwich,

but this is addictive. I'm nearing exhaustion, but I don't really want to stop. The next *beep* might be an exciting find.'

'Come on, we'll have our lunch and try again later, or maybe next Saturday.'

'Can't do next week, I'm afraid. I've a friend from London coming to stay. We're going out for my birthday.' *Why did I say that? Too much information.*

'Happy birthday for next week. Big party?'

'No, no. More likely the wine bar with Pippa, Mandy and Rosie, the friend who's coming to stay.'

As the day was relatively warm for the time of year, they sat on the bench below the house, with bacon sandwiches and large mugs of coffee. The bacon was warm and delicious, cooked just the way she liked it with crispy rind, but somehow it stuck in her throat. It was as if she was here under false pretences, her thoughts leading up to today whirling around in her head and building up the barrier between them.

Carver leaned towards her, appearing to study her mouth. For one awful moment, she thought that he was going to kiss her and although she would love to know what it felt like to have his lips meet hers, the words she had been practising before her arrival made it so wrong to even think of kissing him. He wiped a dab of tomato sauce off her lip with his napkin and smiled.

Jenny gulped and finally spat out some of the words that had been haunting her. She really couldn't keep them inside any longer; it wasn't healthy for her, or fair to Carver.

'There's something I found out that I haven't shared with you.' She felt her cheeks flush scarlet.

'Whatever do you mean?'

Jenny felt the full weight of his attention. The flecks in his silver-grey eyes seemed to light up.

'Apparently, there was gossip in Borteen at the time our fathers disappeared ...'

'Gossip?'

She nodded. 'Yes, a story that your father ... finished off mine.' She felt lighter now the accusation lay out in the open. The relief was short lived.

'Finished off?' He said the words slowly as if testing their significance, his half-eaten sandwich clasped in his hand.

'Murdered.'

'Murdered?' He repeated the word slowly.

'Yes.' The hairs began to rise on the back of her hands.

'I don't believe it.' The furrow between his eyebrows deepened.

'So, you didn't know anything ... about the gossip, I mean?'

'No. Absolutely not.'

'I was going to try to find my mother's scrapbooks from the time, but there are so many boxes in the loft to sort through, I haven't managed it yet.'

Her heart thudded again, although Carver appeared to be calmly absorbing what she'd said, rather than reacting in any way. The lack of reaction was almost more unnerving than the expression of some emotion.

'And exactly who told you of such an accusation? Have you always known?' There was a hint of steel in his tone.

'No. It was news to me too. I do wish my mother had felt able to speak to me about all this before she died, but Dad became one of those taboo subjects over the years.'

'It's one of the greatest sorrows of someone dying. There is ... always, in my experience anyway, something you wish you'd asked, known or said.'

Jenny felt she couldn't hold back any longer. Her other question was festering like a volcano about to erupt from her mouth.

'Carver, this isn't an easy thing to say, but the same person who told me about the tale circulating that your father killed mine, made another accusation ...'

'Another accusation?'

'About your involvement in your wife's death ...'

She held her breath and immediately wished she could take back what she had said.

A look of pure pain crossed Carver's face. He dropped his sandwich and Wilf moved in to devour it unnoticed.

'What on earth did this ... *person* ... say? Who was it, anyway?' His words were now tight and clipped.

She took a deep breath. 'She said that you were responsible for the death of your wife ... of Bliss.'

Jenny edged along the bench further away from Carver. Too late, she wondered how wise she had been to be deep in a wood with a potential murderer, or even a murderer's son, alone.

He put his hands to his face. His voice, when he finally spoke, was muffled by his fingers. 'Her death *was* my fault.'

Carver looked up at Jenny, his eyes dark saucers, his skin pale and his scar bright red.

'I mistakenly thought we were friends, Jenny, but you seem to have such a low opinion of me and my family that you've listened to malicious gossipmongers. I think it might be better if you left ...'

He turned away from her, his arms held tightly around his body.

Jenny lurched to her feet. She was shaking from head to toe. 'I just thought you should know what someone is saying about you, and ... yes ... I'll admit, for us to be truly friends, I do feel I needed answers to the questions her accusations raised.'

He slumped back on the bench. 'I guess you want to know what happened when Bliss died?'

Her heart clenched. She wanted to know, but then she didn't. He looked so wretched that she wanted to take back all she had said, wanted to rewind to the happier time earlier in the day, but then she also knew for certain that the doubts she had would eventually eat away at her peace of mind and their friendship, so had needed to be voiced for better or worse.

He got up and began to pace the clearing. Jenny perched on the edge of the bench, but not relaxed, as she wondered if she might need to make a run for it through the trees. Had she been stupid accusing someone who could be a murderer? And so far, he hadn't denied it after all.

He avoided her eyes, acting almost as if she wasn't there and he was talking to the trees.

'We were happy that day. Laughing. We'd had a great time visiting the secret cove at Locran down the coast south of here. You can only reach it by hiking miles across farmland from the Sowden road. We'd taken a picnic down there and looked in all the rock pools. I particularly wanted to go to the cove, because driftwood sometimes washes up there. I had sand in my boots and love in my heart. Bliss had just told me we were going to be parents. That was her reason for wanting a day out somewhere special to us, so ... so that she could tell me the news.'

Jenny's breath caught in her throat. If hearing this felt painful for her, what was he going through re-living that day?

'I drove back through Sowden and over Pink Moor. We were singing along to the radio, enjoying the twisty roads with the fantastic views of Borteen Bay and the sea beyond. I kept making Bliss squeal by turning the wheel more sharply than I needed to. We were so ... so happy.'

He stopped and sighed, then continued with a different tone in his voice.

'We came around a tight corner and there was a dustbin lorry, huge thing, right there in the middle of the road. I swerved to try to avoid it, but I over compensated, turning the wheel and mounting a rock opposite. We went off the road.'

There were tears pouring down his cheeks now and Jenny couldn't help but begin to cry too. She wanted to comfort him, but feared he would push her away if she tried to put her arms around him.

'Then, we were rolling ... rolling ... over and over ... down and down the hillside ... totally out of control. We were both wearing seatbelts, but the car ... hit a tree.' Carver shuddered and moaned. 'Amazing really when you think about it ... it isn't as if there *are* many trees on Pink Moor. But we somehow managed to hit one. The windscreen shattered. The airbags went off ...'

He sobbed until he gained enough control to continue speaking.

'I must have passed out. I came round to the refuse collectors trying to help me, staunching the blood that was pouring from the cut on my face and chest with their jackets.' He pointed to his scar. 'It took me a little while to realise that Bliss was beyond any help ... then the pain in my face and my body took over my heart as well.'

He pulled his hands viciously through his curls. His face was full of anguish and pain.

'I wish I'd died too. It would have been much kinder. I've railed against God, spirit, life. I killed my wife and my unborn child. So, yes, Jenny, in answer to your question ... it was my fault. I did kill my wife. I killed Bliss and our baby.'

She hadn't anticipated this sort of confession. She didn't quite know what to say. She just felt mortified that she'd made him go through all this again.

Carver looked at her with haunted eyes and then

crumpled in front of her. His breathing became noisy and laboured. She recognised the signs of the onset of one of his asthma episodes.

'Carver, where's your inhaler?'

He seemed to be deliberately ignoring her. He closed his eyes, but didn't stop her rummaging through his pockets. Her frantic fingers closed on the inhaler and she offered up a quick prayer of thanks, as she removed the cap and placed the mouthpiece to his lips. He didn't inhale.

'Carver, breathe, please. I'm sorry … I'm sorry I doubted you.' She wanted to cry again, but knew that she had to keep her wits sharp. 'You didn't kill them. It was an accident. A tragic accident. Please breathe. If you don't, you'll leave me feeling responsible, just like you do about Bliss.'

Still no response.

'Carver, please, I think I'm falling in love with you. That's why I had to be so hard on you. I needed to know. Needed to be sure. You have to breathe.' Her heart clenched along with her fingers, as she held her own breath without realising it.

His eyes flickered open. His pupils were dark pools that at another time she would delight in looking at, but the fear that he wouldn't use the inhaler, that the asthma would take hold, made her hands shake. He put his hands over hers, stilling the tremors, and took two big puffs of medication. His breathing still rattled in his chest and he coughed, but Jenny could see his colour returning.

'Say that again.' His voice was like gravel.

'What?' She blushed.

'Have you just told me a lie to bring me back from the edge of oblivion?'

'I think I'm falling in love with you, Carver Rodgers. Whatever the dodgy link between our families.'

He cupped her face and briefly put his lips to hers, then he pulled away and stood up.

'Thank you for your help just now, Jenny, but at the moment, however much I'd like to, I can't get past the fact that you thought me capable of ... of murder. Think my father capable of murder too. And now ... I'd like you to go.'

There wasn't any appropriate reply. She grabbed her bag and made for the path to the road. Tears filled her eyes as she stumbled back through the trees to her car.

What a mess.

What had she done?

Could he ever forgive her and could she ever forgive herself?

Carver watched Jenny disappear into the trees with very mixed feelings. He had so badly wanted her to give him a sign that she was attracted to him in the same way he was to her, but to couple that with the accusation about Bliss had near to crucified him.

Recounting the tale of the accident had left him mentally and physically exhausted, and with his chest tightening up on top of that, he was completely washed out.

How could she have thought him capable of killing Bliss on purpose? For him it cast doubt on the authenticity of the rest of her words. It was just as if she'd stabbed him with a knife.

He whistled Wilf. The grey shape of the animal appeared instantly out of the trees and Carver motioned for the dog to follow him up the steps into the house. He pulled up the steps, reminiscent of pulling up a castle drawbridge to maroon him inside the house. He went through the familiar motions of lighting the wood burner and tried not to think until he had prepared a bowl of food for Wilf. He put two remaining bacon rashers from his lunch with Jenny on a plate for himself, but he didn't eat them. Instead, he sat staring into the stirring flames. Wilf helped himself to the bacon from his plate without Carver even noticing.

His dream of a possible new start with Jenny had almost come true; just for one tantalising moment, he had tasted it, tasted her delicious lips, only for it to be snatched away from him. It was the first time he'd cried out loud for a long time. Wilf crouched nearby on full alert, with concerned eyes fixed on his master.

Carver sat in front of the roaring wood burner, rocking himself in his misery and vowing that never again would he put himself and his heart in this position.

# Chapter Twenty-Two

Jenny somehow fumbled her way through the next working week. She threw herself into her clients' research queries, trying not to allow her thoughts to stray far and most definitely not to Carver Rodgers.

She knew that she needed to make an effort to get out more, to join groups in the local area and make new friends beyond Pippa and Mandy, but somehow after a day at the archives, followed by clearing up after the decorator and rearranging for Rosie's visit, she didn't feel up to socialising.

One exciting thing that happened during the week was Ivan pronouncing the conservatory finished. He waited for her to come home on Thursday evening and proudly showed her the space beyond the dining room and kitchen.

'I'll miss coming here, love, and we had the excitement of finding that box too.'

Ivan had been very disappointed that he hadn't made any more finds when he'd metal detected the rest of the area around the house wall. Conversely, Jenny was pleased he hadn't found anything more. She still secretly feared her father's body might be buried outside.

She'd shown Ivan the clock. One, because he had asked what was in the box and two, to gauge his reaction to a clock being buried. For all she knew, it could be a local Borteen tradition to bury a timepiece in one's garden; after all, she'd heard of shoes being placed up chimneys to ward off evil spirits. Ivan, however, was as perplexed as she was about the find.

When she opened the patio doors in the dining room, she now stepped out into a bright room. It wasn't huge, but she could already imagine it looking lovely. She relished the new space and the different dimension it gave to the house. When Ivan first showed the conservatory to her it had been dark, but in the daylight it was even nicer, with the clouds scudding overhead.

She would need to decide on flooring, furniture and lamps. The ravaged garden craved attention and she couldn't wait until the weather improved, so that she could remodel the space outside the new structure. She looked forward to poring over garden planning books to fill her winter evenings, but all that would have to wait until after her birthday weekend.

Despite her best intentions, her thoughts often strayed to Carver. The machinations usually began with the memory of his chaste kiss and then the heat would fill her cheeks as she remembered the clumsy way she had repeated Cindy's gossip, in effect accusing him of killing his wife. Anguished guilt would then rush in to fill her mind, coupled with a vision of the absolute mask of pain on his face.

By Friday evening, she was desperate to talk it all through with Rosie. Rosie wasn't involved in Borteen life and would be going back to London on Sunday, so Jenny thought she would be able to share all of her thoughts, even the ones about her attraction to the owner of the wooden castle in the trees. She didn't feel she could open up to Pippa completely about it all, especially her debacle with Carver, because of Pippa's local connections. Also, she didn't know Pippa well enough yet to be totally candid, whereas Jenny and Rosie had already shared times of happiness and pain in London.

Carver had thought about ringing Jenny ten thousand times a day since he had last seen her.

Maybe he'd overreacted. After all she was only acting on misinformation from someone else.

No, he'd blown it.

She'd blown it.

But there was that niggling doubt.

Still, he had to put it behind him and settle back into a singleton life.

Didn't he?

He was working this week on a commission at Borteen Church. When he took a break, he found his breath catching in his throat when he saw a young woman sitting on a bench in the churchyard. He really imagined it to be Jenny, until she turned her head and he saw from the woman's profile that it wasn't her.

'Hi, Carver. Are you working in the church?' asked a voice from behind him. 'Nice and local for you.'

He jumped out of his skin. Pippa stood behind him, a bunch of flowers in her hand.

'Sorry, didn't mean to startle you. My dad's birthday!' She shook the flowers meaningfully and a few petals floated onto the path.

'Must be a difficult day.'

'Yes, it just brings everything into sharp focus, but Mum and I are doing okay, thankfully.'

Pippa walked past him a little way down the path and he trailed after her to the carved stone commemorating her father's life and death. There were already two bunches of fresh flowers there.

Pippa bent down to read the labels on the other flowers and then put her own bunch alongside them. She stood up and grinned at him, wiping away a tear. 'Anyway, how are things going with ... Jenny?'

'She's not cleaning for me any more.'

'She said. I kind of hoped you two might get together.'

'No. Any chances of that are over and done, crashed and burned.'

'I'm sorry to hear that.'

'Yes, well, sometimes the past prevents the future.'

Pippa put her hand on his arm. 'Don't say that, Carver. Bliss would want you to move on, to enjoy life.'

It was on the tip of his tongue to tell her to mind her own business and what did she know, but he had to agree with her thoughts.

'Thanks, Pippa. I'd better get going, wood to carve.'

'It's her birthday on Saturday.'

'Whose?'

'Jenny's. We're meeting up at the wine bar to celebrate. You could join us.'

'Have fun.'

Pippa winked and Carver turned away, not trusting himself to reply.

Jenny hung around in Sowden after work to wait for Rosie's train on Friday evening. She took the opportunity to get some shopping from the big supermarket and had a coffee in the café, hoping to see the clairvoyant coffee maker again. A little guidance would have been welcome in her lost state, but unfortunately the girl she had seen before was not serving behind the counter this time.

Sipping her coffee, Jenny felt unaccountably nervous about seeing Rosie again. Why, she wondered? This was the person she'd spent a lot of time with in London, but that was it, wasn't it? London seemed like a different world now … a different lifetime. Somehow more sophisticated than life in sleepy Borteen.

As the train came in, Jenny waited at the end of the platform, scanning the people who emerged from its doors. Rosie appeared out of the crowd, wearing the 'uniform' of a woman working in business in the City, a tailored suit and expensive high-heeled court shoes. Despite the professional *veneer*, however, Rosie's face cracked into a wide smile, as she enveloped Jenny in a perfumed hug.

Most of Jenny's anxieties fell away. The pair were back to their normal banter in seconds. However, Jenny was aware of a great big cloud of ... of what? ... sadness maybe? ... hanging over her head.

Rosie towed a small overnight bag behind her, her voluminous handbag over her arm. The handbag looked way too heavy to be supported on Rosie's forearm. Jenny led the way to her car, fingering her sensible cross-body bag and realising she no longer displayed the traits of a city business girl. It was weird how the metamorphosis had happened without her conscious intention, but happen it had.

'By the way, I've moved jobs.' Rosie looked rather sheepish, as if she needed to confess.

'Goodness, when? You never said.' A wave of hurt invaded Jenny's chest.

'It was about the same time as your mother died. I figured you had enough going on to listen to my career change.'

Jenny secretly thought listening to Rosie's news might have been a light relief at such a time of anguish, but she held her tongue and instead showed bright enthusiasm. 'And how is it going? Do you like it? Don't you miss creepy Morris and Abdul the security guard?'

Rosie laughed. 'I've come to the conclusion that no matter where you work, there are always the same categories of people. They just have different names, backgrounds and body shapes. Look, I'm sorry I didn't say anything about my career move. You had a lot on your plate.'

Jenny tried to dismiss the worrying tremor of uncertainty inside of her. 'So, who do you work for now?'

'I was headhunted.' Here Rosie smiled with obvious pride. 'A glass manufacturer, Borden Glass. The London operation makes glass for the drinks and food industry.'

'Wow, that's different.'

'Yes, whisky bottles, jam jars, that type of thing.' Rosie grinned. 'You will never guess where their other factory is?'

'No idea.'

'Sowden, of all places.'

'Wow!'

'I mentioned to my new boss that I was coming up here this weekend and he suggested I should take a look, if we've time, of course.'

'What does the other factory produce then?'

'Decorative glass ... they do tours. Presumably touristy tours, but it might be fun.'

'Sure, why not.'

'I mean I wouldn't announce I worked for the London operation or anything, just do a tour like a tourist, so I have a feel for the place.'

'Sounds fun, sure.' Jenny nodded. 'It might help you to know more about the business and I'm always up for finding out more about this area.'

She drove over Pink Moor to Borteen. Unfortunately it was already dark, so Jenny described the views Rosie would see in the light and told her friend about local landmarks. The lights of Borteen showed where the town ended and the sea began.

'No wonder you are not in a rush to return to London.'

'It is lovely, isn't it?' Jenny's glow of pride was as much for a confirmation in her own heart that she had made the right decision, as an acknowledgement of her friend's approval. Her tension increased, however, as they approached Priory Avenue. What would Rosie make of the old-fashioned house? But why should it matter?

'You've grown up.' That was Rosie's pronouncement as she walked through the downstairs rooms of the house.

'Pardon?'

191

'This is a grown-up house.'

'What an odd thing to say.'

'Just an observation.' Rosie giggled.

Jenny showed her to what was now the spare room. She still had a momentary pang about the changes she'd made to her childhood bedroom. Rosie was suitably enthusiastic about the newly decorated space, but Jenny couldn't help but wonder if she really meant it, or was just being kind. This was a far cry from the elegant, but tiny loft apartment, almost a carbon copy of the one Jenny herself had lived in, that Rosie rented in London.

What was happening here? Why was she feeling so insecure? And, particularly, why insecure about Rosie?

They shared a supper of salad, meats and cheese.

'Can we go to the beach?' asked Rosie.

'It's dark.'

'Aww. Don't you ever go to the beach in the dark?'

'In the summer, yes, but I think you'd find it rather chilly tonight.'

Instead they opened a bottle of wine and sat in the lounge, reminiscing.

'Why do I get the impression that there is something big you are not telling me about,' said Rosie, eventually.

In reaction to her friend's statement, Jenny slurped a little too much wine and choked.

'See, guilty choking, a sure sign.'

Jenny pulled a face at Rosie. 'I didn't want to depress you with the murkier parts of my life.'

'Ooo, do tell. I like murky life parts.'

Jenny burst into tears. The tension of the last few weeks, indeed months, surfaced and refused to be denied. Through the wall of teardrops, she saw Rosie put down her glass, alarm written all over her face. She came and sat on the settee next to Jenny and put her arms around her.

'Hey, I'm so sorry, I had no intention of upsetting you this much.'

'You ... di-dn't, have-n't ... it's just been ... so hard.'

She gave in to the sobs for a while, later becoming aware that she'd thoroughly soaked the shoulder of Rosie's blouse. When she pulled away, Rosie presented her with her wine glass and she took a thirsty glug of the pale liquid.

Rosie sat back and looked at her. 'Right, that's it. I want a full account of what has been going on and I'm not going to bed until you've told me everything.'

Jenny emptied it all out in a continuous stream, the time of her mother's illness, her death, the funeral, the house changes, her flirtation with self-employment. She saw Rosie's eyebrows raise when she began to talk about Carver. Jenny didn't hold back, there was no point. It all poured out of her like a waterfall of words, what had happened, including the discovery of the clock, her feelings about everything, and lastly her confusion over how she felt about Carver, especially now she had irretrievably, in her mind, blown any chance of them ever being close again.

Unusually, Rosie didn't utter a word of reply, she just stood up and went to look at the clock on the mantelpiece, as Jenny dried her tear-stained face with tissues and drank another inch of wine from her glass.

Rosie turned and picked up her own drink. 'Goodness, it's all been going on. This Carver must be some guy. I've never known you to cry over a man, not even your ex-husband.'

'It isn't all about Carver.'

Rosie put her head on one side. 'Yeah, right.'

The next day dawned bright and clear. The crisp air held a promise of frosty mornings to come.

Rosie looked somehow less intimidating when she came downstairs wearing jeans and a fluffy blue jumper. She presented Jenny with a pretty carrier bag and a card. 'Happy Birthday!' She kissed Jenny on both cheeks.

The bag contained a gorgeous gossamer-light scarf. It had a swathe of butterflies along its length, the two biggest butterflies at each end embellished with gold paint. The card matched the theme, as it too was adorned with gold embellished butterflies.

Jenny was overwhelmed by the lovely gift. 'It's absolutely beautiful. I shall wear it this evening.'

They ate toast and jam for breakfast. Jenny's nose felt snuffly after all her crying the previous evening, but her heart definitely felt lighter for having unburdened her thoughts and told Rosie about all that had been going on in her life. It seemed better to have everything out in the open between them.

'Rosie, you're going to meet some of my Borteen friends tonight … it's just I haven't told Pippa and Mandy all that I've told you.'

'In that case I'm flattered you trust me and my lips are sealed, promise.'

'Great. Now, how about that walk on the beach? It will be blowy and cold.'

'Sounds lovely, beaches are good for the soul and I don't get much chance to spend time on them.'

'I think our beach walk might be over quite quickly if it's as bracing out there as I suspect.'

'Spoilsport.' Rosie stuck her tongue out.

'Well, there are several cafés for a warm up coffee and we can have a mooch around the shops.'

Following lunch, Jenny was taking her friend to Borden Glass Discovery Centre for a tour of the glassworks – they'd already googled the location and prices for the tour. In the evening, they were meeting Pippa and maybe Mandy at the wine bar on the seafront for Jenny's birthday celebrations.

It was going to be a very full day and Jenny suspected she might feel she needed another weekend to recover from all of the activity when she was now used to a quieter life.

The friends seemed to shed years in age as they walked down the hill towards the seafront.

'It reminds me of being on holiday,' said Rosie. 'Rushing towards the beach, with my mum telling me off for running ahead, because she was carrying all the stuff.'

'I suppose it was different for me, as we lived here, but I still feel the pull of the beach, nonetheless. It's like a magnet for everyone.'

As if in silent agreement, they both began to jog and then to run, giggling and laughing, until their feet were on the sand. Both were breathless and happy. Despite the chill, Rosie insisted on taking off her trainers and socks.

'You just have to feel the sand between your toes,' she said.

They spent a happy half hour walking on the beach and picking over the shells and pebbles washed up on the tide. Jenny, as always, collected any sea glass in her pockets. She was fascinated by how the waves transformed something clear and sharp into opaque jewels.

Rosie turned; her nose was becoming bright red in the cool breeze. 'I'm loving this, but I think I need a coffee and a warm place to sit and drink it, so that I can thaw out. My toes are going to drop off.'

'Race you to the café then.' Jenny pointed to the café on the promenade and set off with Rosie close on her heels. They had to pause at the bottom of the beach steps for Rosie to put her shoes and socks back on.

When they had warmed up and drunk their coffee, Jenny began a walking tour for Rosie of the retail side of Borteen. They walked along the promenade to Owl Corner Crafts. Mandy Vanes wasn't there, but someone Jenny vaguely recognised was behind the counter. Rosie admired the art for sale on the walls and, for the first time, Jenny realised that some of the wood carvings on display were Carver's work. She was rather taken with a small figurine of a woman with an intricate lacy carved dress.

After she had gone back to look at it five times, Rosie exclaimed in an irritated voice, 'Buy it! Treat yourself for your birthday.'

So she did. A piece of Carver in her house. She liked the thought. It was just such a pity that they had parted badly the last time she had seen him.

Borteen Church was next door to the craft centre and Jenny took Rosie into the churchyard to see where her mother was buried. At the moment there was a simple marker with her mother's name, year of birth and death. She regretted not bringing any flowers with her, but to her surprise, there was a lovely arrangement of chrysanthemums already placed near to the graveside.

'I wonder who left those for Mum? Probably Mum's friend Maeve.'

Jenny could feel tears threatening and didn't want to spoil the light-hearted feel of the morning, so she led Rosie quickly back to the promenade, pointing out The Ship Inn on the other side of the road and Rose Court Guest House next to it, which Pippa ran with her mother. The shops closer to the steps onto the beach were those typical of a seaside town, inflatable boats and surfboards, vying with all colours and shapes of buckets and spades, windmills and kites, as the stock spilled over onto the pavement – maybe optimistically given the winter season.

'Shall we walk up one side of the high street and down the other? I'm getting much better at remembering the names of the shopkeepers. It's almost a personal mission to fix them all in my memory.'

Rosie appeared to find this very amusing and entered into the spirit of the game, asking Jenny to name the owner of each shop as they walked.

Rosie got totally distracted by the little vintage shop, Polka Dot Paradise, and Jenny had to put her memory game on hold whilst her friend explored the three floors of vintage clothes. Rosie bought a cute little black jacket and exclaimed with glee when it was put into one of the shop's trademark pink polka dot carrier bags.

Jenny was now recalling about seventy per cent of the owners' names. She was pleased with her memory game progress, but vowed to get to know one hundred per cent before very much longer.

She hailed Fred the butcher, as he was standing in the doorway of his shop, and waved to Suzie Meadows, who was putting the finishing touches to a winter themed window display at the charity shop.

After a sandwich lunch, Jenny drove over Pink Moor to Sowden and the Borden Glass Discovery Centre. The building was sleek and modern with a large showroom displaying the different types of decorative, mainly cut glass, made at the factory. It was a cleverly designed space, where tourists waited for the tours and where the tours also ended, presumably to maximise sales. The tour itself was interesting. They watched workers preparing glass blanks for sports awards, the hot molten glass glowing orange as it was swung and blown to shape the trophies. Later in the tour they saw some of these blanks being engraved on lathes to produce intricate cut glass trophies.

'It's very different to the London operation,' said Rosie.

'Different good or different bad?' asked Jenny.

'Just different. The London factory is more about mass production and keeping cost down, this seems more relaxed. Useful to have seen it though, because now when someone at work talks about this factory I will understand a bit more of what they are talking about.'

This time when they drove back across Pink Moor, Rosie could see the views of the bay for herself. Jenny chose the route that went past Tree Tops, so that she could show Rosie where she had been working, even though the house itself wasn't visible from the road.

It was a mistake, of course.

'You are pretty smitten by this Carver guy,' Rosie commented.

Jenny didn't reply, but felt her skin redden in response.

They went back to Priory Avenue for a couple of hours' rest before Jenny's birthday celebrations began.

Jenny was enjoying Rosie's visit, but it was unsettling her at the same time, making her question yet again the possibility of a return to a London job. It was difficult not to be a tiny bit jealous of her friend's fast-paced existence. Jenny even missed dressing up in expensive suits. However, there were pros and cons to both ways of living. She would love to have known exactly what Rosie was thinking about Jenny's new location.

Before they went out of the house later, Jenny reminded Rosie that she didn't really want Pippa to know the complete *ins* and *outs* of her debacle with Carver, as she was wary of any gossip reaching his ears. Rosie promised to be discreet.

The girls walked down to the seafront, shivering in the cooling air, but both not wanting to lug a big coat around with them on a night out. Jenny was wearing a thin cream blouse with her plum jeans, black jacket and the beautiful scarf Rosie had bought her for her birthday. Rosie wore a sequined mini dress, topped with the vintage jacket she had bought earlier and wedge heels. Jenny did hope that Rosie's expectations of an evening out in Borteen weren't too high.

When they got to the wine bar Jenny was pleased to see that her favourite window seats were free. Pippa arrived with Mandy in tow. Mandy apologised for having no birthday card to give to Jenny, as she hadn't known it was her birthday before Pippa had persuaded her to come out with them. Pippa gave Jenny a small wrapped box and a card. Inside the box was a sheep brooch. It had a black wooden body and strands of brightly coloured wool had been wrapped around the wood to form its torso. Jenny loved it and pronounced she would call her sheep *Woolly*.

The girls insisted on singing *Happy Birthday* to a red-faced Jenny, who was glad not too many locals were out this early in the evening. The other occupants of the bar joined in with the singing, which heightened her embarrassment.

Surprisingly, it soon became apparent that Pippa had taken a dislike to Rosie. Jenny did wonder if Pippa was resentful of Rosie's easy closeness with herself. Mandy, seemingly oblivious, asked Rosie lots of questions about London life. The answers to these solicited further frowns from Pippa's corner.

Just when Jenny had decided that she couldn't take any more of Pippa's disparaging remarks about city dwellers, the evening took yet another unexpected turn. She spied a familiar face outside the large windows of the wine bar. Rosie also caught sight of the figure, although of course she had no way of knowing that the man who had caught her eye was Carver.

'Dishy man alert,' mouthed Rosie in Jenny's ear, rather too loudly.

'Too true, dishy man alert,' echoed Mandy.

Pippa replied sarcastically. 'That's not a dishy man, that's Carver.' She turned to Jenny. 'Hope you don't mind, I mentioned we were having drinks here for your birthday.'

Rosie's eyes were now glued to Jenny's. Jenny shook her

head, willing Rosie not to say anything incriminating or embarrassing, especially in front of Mandy.

Jenny was surprised that Carver would come anywhere near her after their last meeting and uncertainty and confusion warred in her mind with panic.

Carver looked smart and handsome illuminated in the street light outside. He wore tight fitting jeans and a navy long-sleeved shirt underneath a navy padded gilet. Did she imagine it, or had he had his hair cut? There was uncertainty playing across his features too, as he caught sight of the girls sitting by the window and came into the wine bar.

He politely asked if anyone needed another drink, but before he went off to the bar to get them, he presented Jenny with a tissue paper wrapped object. She could tell that he would rather have spoken to her without three other girls listening, as he glanced from one to the other of them, as if trying to decide what to say.

'I understand that it's your birthday. This little gift comes with an apology for my behaviour the last time we met.'

'I think it's probably me who should apologise.'

'Mutual apology then?' He smiled and put out his hand.

She grasped his palm and smiled back at him, as tingles set up residence in her stomach. When he let go of her hand, he turned on his heel and headed for the bar to get the drinks.

Three sets of eyes settled on Jenny with questions apparent in the set of their eyebrows.

Jenny shrugged and turned over the object Carver had given to her to unwrap. Inside the crisp tissue paper was the Green Man Jenny had watched Carver working on at Tree Tops. It was much nicer than she remembered it, the surface tactile and smooth. She examined it closely so that the other girls didn't see the sudden arrival of tears in her eyes. It was a big deal that Carver had come here, apologised and given her something so lovely. It really mattered to her. Rosie held out her hand to take the present from her to have a look at it, but Jenny was reluctant to let it out of her grasp.

When he returned, Carver seemed eager to drink his glass of wine as quickly as possible. Knowing what she did about him, she was certain that drinking wine with four women must be his idea of hell, especially as Mandy was flirting outrageously with him yet again. Jenny could swear that Mandy had positioned herself so that Carver had a good view of both her legs and cleavage. She had her eyes fixed firmly on his face and her false eyelashes looked in danger of taking off as she was batting them so much.

It made Jenny appreciate all the more the effort Carver had gone to and his bravery in wanting to clear the air between them. She thanked him wholeheartedly for the Green Man. She would have liked to kiss his cheek, but decided it might be a step too far.

Carver made polite conversation with Rosie, whom Jenny had introduced to him, but soon made his excuses and was gone back out into the night. It felt as if part of her went with him or, at least, wanted to go with him. By the set of her face, Mandy felt the same.

Jenny didn't quite know what to make of his visit, but was pleased that they had broken the ice after their falling out. At least it meant that they could say a pleasant *hello* to each other if they did happen to meet in the future in Borteen or Sowden.

'I think someone has made a conquest,' said Mandy sarcastically.

The other girls were all laughing and nodding.

'No, no. I just admired the carving when he was working it and we had a slight disagreement the last time we met. I'm sure he just wanted to clear the air.'

'Yeah, right,' said Pippa.

Thankfully, Carver's visit seemed to have diffused the

animosity between Pippa and Rosie. For the rest of the evening, Pippa spoke mainly to Mandy and Jenny to Rosie. Jenny decided she was getting old, because an evening in a wine bar didn't seem to be her favourite thing any more. She felt a tiny bit displaced, as if she had arrived somewhere she wasn't meant to be and her mind kept drifting back to Carver as she ran her finger over the Green Man's smooth surface.

It was cold on the way back up the hill, so Jenny and Rosie walked as fast as Rosie's high wedge heels would allow.

As they went through the door of 18 Priory Avenue, the landline telephone rang out, despite the late hour. Its loud ringtone jerked Jenny out of her thoughts of being cold and shivery. For an instant, she hopefully imagined it to be Carver, but an unknown male voice asked if he was speaking to Jenny Simpson.

Her anti-telephone salesman hackles had risen. Jenny often regaled her friends with her winding up of a conservatory salesman when she lived in London. She could tell that he'd anticipated a sale until she delivered her punchline, 'But do you usually install conservatories on first floor flats?'

'Who wants to know?'

'My name is Timothy Simpson.'

Jenny reeled backwards, catching her shin on the corner of the coffee table. Whilst juggling the phone and rubbing her leg, she didn't quite know what to say. Her heart was beating so strongly, she thought it might break through her ribs. Rosie was looking at her with alarm on her face.

'Are you still there, Jenny?'

'Dad?' The word felt unfamiliar to her lips. Tears threatened to spill over.

'Yes, love. Happy birthday! I hear your mum has passed away.'

Jenny's senses were immediately on alert.

202

Did this call explain why she had felt that she was being watched lately?

Had her father been following her this evening? How else would he know they had just this minute arrived home?

Why was he making an appearance now? Had he read her missing person's advert, perhaps?

Her fingers were hurting because she was clutching the telephone so tightly. The realisation of the physical sensations her father was evoking made her suppressed, long-held feelings, and a surprising amount of rage at what felt like his betrayal, surface. She had always thought that she wanted to find her father, had fond images of them embracing, being friends, but right now the overwhelming emotion was anger.

'What is it to you? You disappeared. How long has it been? Twenty-five years?'

'I understand that you will be upset, Jenny.'

'Too right I'm upset.' She almost threw the phone down, but kicked the table instead, stubbing her toe painfully.

'I'll ring another time.'

Panic rushed in. She didn't want to speak to him, but she didn't want him to go either, not at least until he'd answered her questions. She rubbed her painful foot.

'Hang on. Don't you dare go. Why have you rung now? What do you want?'

The line had already gone dead.

Jenny burst into tears and Rosie hugged her tightly.

'Your dad?'

'Ye-s-s.'

A wall of misery hit her. She sat down and examined her damaged shin and toe. When she had recovered enough to talk to Rosie and tell her what Timothy had said, Rosie grabbed the handset and tried to see if she could retrieve the number from which the call had been made, but the caller had withheld their number.

'He'll call back, I'm sure.'

'Maybe not. You heard how I reacted. I went into shock and then this huge ball of anger burst out of me.'

'It's completely understandable. I'm sure even your dad realises that it won't be an easy reunion after all this time.'

Jenny burst into tears again.

'I want to see him, but I don't want to see him. OMG, Carver!'

'What about the intriguing, delectable Carver?'

'I need to tell him my dad is still living. Not dead.'

'It's rather late now. Why don't you go and see him when you've dropped me off at the station tomorrow?'

'You don't think I should ring now?'

'Up to you, but some things are better face to face. I mean maybe your dad might ring back. He might be able to shed some light on what happened to Carver's father too.'

'If I haven't scared him away. Oh, why was I so stupid?'

Jenny took the Green Man from her bag and took off the tissue paper wrapping. She'd put Carver's figurine of the woman in a lacy dress, which she'd bought as a birthday present to herself, on one end of her fireplace earlier, now she put the Green Man at the other side, but not before she'd kissed his wooden face, hoping that maybe Carver would pick up the affectionate vibration through the airways.

# Chapter Twenty-Three

Carver was tidying up his carving clearing. He did this every now and then, usually when he was mulling over thoughts in his mind. In effect, tidying the clearing meant that he had troubled thoughts.

There was something remarkably cleansing about building a fire with all of the scraps, twigs and wood shavings. Of course, he had to manage any fire carefully, due to the close proximity to the trees. He sat on an upturned log with a long stick as a poker, feeling almost primeval. He imagined this scene to be timeless. Man and the power, warmth and light of a fire.

Jenny had looked lovely on the previous evening at the wine bar. Her hair was spikier than normal, her blouse and jeans figure-hugging. He realised now that he'd blustered into the lion's den. What had made him think she would be pleased to see him on her birthday, especially when she was celebrating with her girlfriends? Initially she'd looked scared, as if she feared he might say something awful. He believed he'd got off lightly and at least broken the ice. The encounter, especially as she wasn't expecting him to be there, could have gone very differently.

Yet again, he couldn't help but be confused over Jenny's previous accusation about the death of Bliss and her declaration of interest in him. With hindsight he could see that she had needed to be sure about one, before she could be sure of the other. Well, no matter now, he'd blown any chances of a relationship or even a true friendship with her, he was sure. He'd been so hurt by her words and the remembered guilt about his part in his wife's death, that he had closed the door on Jenny's feelings and uncertainty.

He poked the fire viciously in regret and annoyance with himself. If he'd been more understanding, Jenny could be sitting here with him right now.

He almost fell off the log he was sitting on when a figure stumbled into the firelight, clasping a torch. Initially, Carver didn't recognise Jenny. He had never seen her with her hair combed severely back, instead of raised in spikes. She wore shapeless clothes, jogging bottoms and an oversized sweatshirt. Her face was devoid of make-up and parchment pale, and it seemed as if he had conjured up her spirit with his thoughts, so he half expected her to be a mirage, not a real person.

Wilf hadn't reacted to Jenny's approach, but why was he surprised when he'd trained the dog to ignore her? Wilf had no doubt recognised her scent and Carver had probably missed the dog raising his head in curiosity as he was so absorbed in his own thoughts.

'Jenny, you scared me half to death.' He felt a wave of joy at seeing her and maybe having the chance to explain himself more clearly. Getting up, he dragged another log beside him for her to sit on. He didn't trust himself to speak just yet, in case he said the wrong thing or everything came out in a muddled rush.

'Thank you for my birthday present. I truly love it. Sorry, I know we parted badly last time I was here, I was awful and you must hate me. But I needed someone to talk to about something only you will understand. I would have come earlier but we slept in this morning and I had to take Rosie to catch her train back to London this afternoon. I've been very unsettled since last night.' She sat down on the log and picked up the sister stick of Carver's to have a prod at the fire. 'It's lovely and warm sitting here.'

'Have you looked up there?' He pointed skywards with his fire stick.

Above them, through the gap in the tree canopy, the stars

twinkled like jewels. Carver laughed at her open–mouthed wonderment.

'Wow. You live in another world.'

'Strange you should say that. I've been thinking how this scene – man, fire, forest, stars – is timeless. We could be back in the Bronze Age.'

'Before we go any further, Carver, can I apologise wholeheartedly for my awful behaviour towards you the last time I came here? I'd mistakenly listened to someone who was malicious and gossip–mongering. She sowed the seeds of doubt in my mind, but I shouldn't have listened to her, shouldn't have rated her opinion.' She turned her head away to prod the fire, so he couldn't see her expression. 'I should just have asked you about Bliss and not made silly accusations. I was out of order and I'm sorry.'

'Look, we made our peace yesterday evening. You don't need to say any more. It's been a strange time for both of us. I guess the space of a few days has mellowed my reaction to your words and ... far from hating you, I've *hated* you not being here. I've missed you more than I care to admit.'

She smiled at him then and they sat in silent contemplation of the flames for a while. Her face looked vulnerable in its porcelain paleness and he noticed the arch of her eyebrows and the curl of her eyelashes. The temptation to cup her chin and bring his lips to hers threatened to overwhelm him.

'You mentioned a problem. From the look on your face it's a serious one.'

'You could say that, with bells on.'

'When you're ready, I'm all ears.'

'You know I said that the local gossip was that your father murdered mine?'

Carver nodded and gritted his teeth against yet another accusation.

'Well, it wasn't true.'

'How can you be sure?'

'My father is *alive*.'

Carver nearly fell off his log for the second time. 'How do you know that?'

'He rang me.'

'That must have been a shock.'

'It was ... a complete shock. I couldn't bring myself to speak nicely to him. I was so taken aback and for some reason full of anger.'

'Heavens.'

'I feel so stupid now. I should have listened to what he had to say, instead I've robbed us of the chance to get answers to our questions.'

Carver reached his hand across to still her fingers that were grasping distractedly at her trousers. 'I'm sure he will get in contact again.'

'Maybe, but I was hardly encouraging or receptive. It was something about him ringing as soon as I walked through my front door last night – as if he was outside and watching me. I've had the feeling that I've been being watched ... followed for a while.'

Carver squeezed her fingers gently; her hand was cold. 'I can see why you reacted like that. I'm sure when he's had time to reflect, your dad will too.'

'Rosie said the same when I dropped her at the station in Sowden. It's just ... my mind started working on our secret agent scenario. I mean, my father must have followed me at least yesterday, maybe for longer – and I have had the feeling of being shadowed, just never caught anyone behind me. I imagined my house bugged, that he was listening to me and maybe even watching me and I had to get out. Even on the way over here, I wondered if he was following me. I'm very confused. I thought I wanted to know, thought I wanted to find him, but now ...'

'Hey.' The response seemed totally inadequate. He squeezed her hand again. He hoped that the gesture would feel reassuring. He turned back to the fire to prod a falling cluster of sticks. Jenny's hand felt small and cool in his. She made no move to disentangle herself, so he held on. Her fingers began to warm up until the mingled heat of their hands almost burned his skin.

'Do you think I was mean reacting like that to him? I've managed without him for twenty-five years and even though I have loads of questions, even started to try and find him, I kind of feel he's given up the right to expect anything from me.'

'Perhaps, but ... don't you want to know why? Why he went missing? Why he stayed away so long?'

'Sure I do, but I've begun to wonder if I could even believe him? Would he tell me the truth? After all, Mum isn't here now to tell me any different. He can make up whatever story he likes. The other thing I've been worrying about is ... whether it was the other way around and he murdered your dad? There are so many unanswered questions flying around that my head hurts. And I sent him away without getting the answers to any of them.'

Jenny prodded the fire a little too ferociously and Carver had to stand up to sort out the resulting movement in the logs.

'Sorry.' She sort of sighed, or was it a sob? Carver could tell she was fighting back tears.

'Don't worry about it for now, but if he does ring again would you ask if he knows anything about my dad?' It troubled him that he'd had to release her hand to sort out the fire and he wasn't sure if he should pick it up again as she'd put it back on her leg. 'There can be no right or wrong with what you think about your dad. Only your feelings and wishes are important. As you say, he's forfeited any right to expect anything. Anything at all, but you haven't.'

'So why do I feel I'm in the wrong?'

'What do you think your mother would say about all this?' Carver had come to realise when she was working for him that Jenny was still heavily influenced by her mother, used a lot of her mother's sayings and then apologised for doing so.

'That's just it, I don't know. She never talked about Dad and wouldn't be drawn on the matter even if I tried. She was full of shed-loads of anger too.'

He watched Jenny shiver, even though the early evening was mild.

'Can you hold my hand again, please? It made me feel safe and I haven't felt very safe since I got that phone call last night.'

Carver smiled, took her hand and squeezed it again gently. 'Would you like a hot drink?'

'I'd love one, but I don't want you to leave me here by myself.'

'No need.' He grinned again. 'I brought a picnic.' He released her hand just long enough to set up another log as a table in front of them, and then poured hot tea from a flask into the flask cups. He took muffins and biscuits out of a bag beside his log. He'd meant to share the picnic with Wilf, who had been his constant companion since he'd lost Jenny's friendship. He vowed to make it up to the dog tomorrow.

He suddenly realised that he felt happy. It seemed mean to think such a thing when Jenny was so troubled beside him, but he couldn't remember the last time he had used that word about himself. That's what he felt ... happy.

The fire began to die down and Carver knew they would be able to leave it soon. What now? Jenny looked tired and vulnerable. He stood and pulled her gently to her feet. After a moment's resistance, she allowed him to draw her close to him. He wrapped her in the folds of his coat. She smelled of flowers. He hugged her and noticed that her head was a perfect fit just under his chin. They stood still for a few timeless moments, until he reluctantly released her to cover the fire with damp earth. When he looked back, her face was raised up looking at the stars.

He placed his lips gently against hers and sank into her dewy warmness. Her hands came up around his neck to pull him closer.

A twig snapped loudly nearby. Wilf growled. A low, warning growl. Carver knew his dog well. He sprang away from Jenny, his senses on full alert.

'Let's go to the house.' He tried to keep his voice light and calm, but Jenny already looked like a startled fawn. He grabbed his flask, bag and her hand. Motioning to Wilf to be quiet and follow, he set off at a brisk pace across the clearing. He thought, momentarily, about picking up a stout stick as a weapon, but decided to go for cover instead. He didn't know if the sound had been made by an animal or human and he couldn't hear any sound of pursuit. He reasoned that it could be a fox or a badger, but all of his senses were screaming that it was a human presence. Someone had been watching them. Was it Jenny's father?

They reached the tree house and Carver checked that the door was still locked. He turned the key, flung the door wide and thrust the picnic remains at Jenny. 'Inside,' he commanded. Wilf took the order to include him and bounded up the steps.

He hauled at the rope at the side of the door and the steps to the house folded up, making access to the house without a ladder impossible. Steps secured, Carver bolted the front door behind them.

'Probably nothing.' He smiled at Jenny, he hoped reassuringly, but he felt wary; maybe it was all the talk about being followed. 'Let's open the window and listen. No lights for a while. Okay?' He squeezed her shoulder.

They listened for twenty minutes, but only heard the sounds of the forest.

'Do you think we imagined it?' she asked.

'Possibly. I suppose we are both jumpy at the moment. Even if there was someone or something there, they were probably just attracted by the fire. The chances of something hostile is quite remote. I sometimes get people fly-tipping on my land ... could be that.'

'Come on, Carver, you're only saying this for my benefit. Trying to play it down. I saw how you reacted, you felt threatened too.'

'I will admit I did, but from some sort of sixth sense. Wilf doesn't often growl like that.'

'You don't think it's my dad, do you?'

He allowed himself a moment's contemplation before he spoke. 'If it is, I suspect he's just looking for a way to get close to you.'

'You're probably right. I didn't give him much of a chance, did I?' She yawned.

'Hey, you're tired. Why don't you get some sleep and I'll keep watch for a little while?'

'Do you think that's really necessary?'

'Not sure, but I'm going to do it anyway. You know where the spare bedroom is and you know there are clean sheets on the bed, because you put them there.' He laughed, but it sounded unsure even to his own ears.

He watched as she felt her way up the stairs and out of sight in the gloom. He realised when she'd gone that he hadn't kissed her goodnight.

# Chapter Twenty-Four

Jenny felt her way up the stairs and, only pausing to remove her jogging bottoms, she snuggled down on the squishy mattress of the spare bed. Its patchwork quilt was faded but warm and it didn't take her more than a few seconds to drift off to sleep.

She awoke smelling smoke and began to panic, until she realised the smell was on her hair and her clothes from the fire in the clearing. It wasn't light, but something had woken her. She shrugged off the covers and listened, shivering at the cold air of the room.

Pulling on her jogging bottoms, she strained her ears to see if she could hear the sound again. A peep around the curtain confirmed the dawn was breaking.

She tiptoed onto the landing. She could tell even in the poor light that the door to Carver's room was open, his curtains not drawn and his bed sheet smooth and unslept on. Another wave of panic hit her. Where was he? Should she have gone to sleep before she had made sure he was safely in bed too?

Heart beating wildly, she crept down the stairs. She heard the noise again and stuffed her fist against her mouth to stop herself from laughing as she realised what it was. Carver was curled up on the sofa with Wilf, both snoring loudly in unison. She tried to gulp down her laughter, but she must have made a noise as Carver stirred and stretched. Wilf got off the sofa, came over to sniff Jenny's hand and then moved away to settle on the floor.

Carver smiled at her, his eyes sleepy.

'Morning.'

'Sorry. It's very early and I woke you with my laugh.'

'What were you laughing at?'

'You.'

'Me?' He sat up.

'You were cuddling the dog and both of you were snoring. Very amusing.'

'I don't snore.'

'Oh, yes you do and so does Wilf – with almost the same tone.' She ducked as he threw a cushion at her.

Carver rolled his neck around. 'Ow. I've cricked my neck sleeping here.'

'You've been there all night?'

'Seems that way.'

Without thinking she sat down beside him and began to work at the knotted muscles of his shoulders. Carver groaned. 'That's so good.'

She continued until she became self-conscious about what she was doing. When she stopped, he turned his head and gave her a light kiss on her lips.

'Thank you. Would you like coffee?'

'Great.' She was pleased he'd kissed her and that his attitude towards her didn't appear to have changed overnight. Massaging his shoulders had ignited desire inside of her.

She followed him into the kitchen, trying to damp down her feelings. 'You know, something occurred to me last night when I was drifting off to sleep. I'm sure I can remember coming to this clearing before. I remember another bonfire and people sitting around it.'

'It could have been anywhere though. Woods do tend to look the same.'

'Perhaps.' She thought quietly for a little while, remembering. It was one of the rare occasions she could recall being with her father on her own. She couldn't prove where she was, but she had a strange inner knowing that it was the same place.

214

They sipped coffee and nibbled toast. The silence was companionable. When they'd finished, Carver stood and went to find his coat. 'I'm going to have a look around. See if there are any signs of anything happening in the wood last night after what we heard.'

'Then I'm coming too.'

'Okay, but I'm bringing Wilf. He's as soft as butter most of the time, but he does a good line in growling if necessary and, as I think I mentioned before, he was trained by a police dog handler, so he has a few extra moves if ever I need them.'

After Carver had lowered the steps, they retraced their route to the fire clearing. Jenny felt a warm glow as she remembered sitting next to him by the flames, holding hands. He'd made no attempt to hold her hand this morning, but then she reminded herself that he had other things on his mind.

Wilf walked close by his master and it struck her again how well trained the dog must be. She was still a little wary, but now she knew the dog wouldn't jump up at her and would follow her basic commands, she'd relaxed a bit.

They all walked silently by unspoken agreement, including the dog. Carver stood still in the clearing, listening. She pointed in the direction she remembered the crack coming from the previous evening. Carver nodded. This time he did take her hand, helping her over the tree roots. She didn't want him to let go. She smiled to herself as he towed her down the path behind him.

It didn't take long to find the source of the noise they had heard. In the strip of land where they had attempted to metal detect themselves, there were signs of digging in several locations. The first few holes were careful and rectangular, the holes away from these were almost half-hearted insertions of a spade into the soil.

Carver released her hand and dropped into a crouch by one of the bigger holes.

'Well, whoever they were, they were definitely trying to *find* something, rather than trying to *bury* something.'

'Looks like our hunch was right. Someone else thought things might have been buried here.'

'I wonder if they found anything? Unlike us, whoever it is might know what they are looking for.'

'I may be wrong, but these shallow holes suggest they didn't know for sure.'

'Tend to agree.'

'Are you going to report this to the police?'

'I don't really see the point. I can back-fill the holes quite quickly and there is no actual damage. If I'm honest, I'm happier with holes than finding rubbish dumped and, believe me, that's happened before. Wilf isn't giving me any signs that anyone is still around this morning.'

The dog was wandering about, sniffing among the roots of a nearby tree and then he sat down.

'Thank goodness they've gone. I hope they don't come back.'

'I suppose that is a possibility. I'm also asking myself if the hole digging is connected in any way to the things being moved around my house. Maybe I need to get security cameras.'

'You don't think these happenings have anything to do with my dad, do you? The thought has just occurred to me.'

'Who knows. Maybe something else to add to the list of questions if you do ever sit down to talk to him.'

'Oh well, after all this excitement, I guess I'd better get my things and go home.'

Carver's face changed. He looked crestfallen. 'Pity, I was wondering if you, erm …'

'Erm …?'

Now he was looking extremely embarrassed.

'I need a shower and ... just wondered if you'd ... erm ... like to join me?'

'I've got to be at work in Sowden at nine.' She smiled at him, her body's reaction tempting her.

His face fell. 'Jenny, look, I'm not very good at this and I'll make no secret of the fact I like you a lot. But I've no wish to destroy our *friendship* again. I need a clear sign from you here.'

In answer, she grabbed the front of his T-shirt and pulled him in for a lingering kiss. She pulled back and giggled. 'We'd better get a move on then ...'

Wilf stirred when Jenny squealed, as hand in hand they raced across the tree roots, the clearing and up the steps to the house. He put the keys in her hand.

'You unlock, I'll raise the drawbridge. Wilf, kennel,' he yelled over the balcony.

Their exuberance lasted until they reached the shower room. Then self-consciousness and uncertainty hit both of them.

'Anyone would think we're teenagers,' commented Carver as he pulled her closer to him and looked deep into her eyes.

'Guess we are both out of practice and talking about that, I'm not ... not using any contraception at the moment.' She blushed.

'And I haven't got any condoms ...' His face was now as red as hers felt.

'Can I make a suggestion?'

He nodded.

'We don't need to rush things, do we? Why don't we take a little time to *get to know each other* first?'

'So, no shower?' He looked disappointed.

'I didn't say that, did I?' She clasped the bottom of his T-shirt and pulled it up over his head and off his body. Instantly they were back to laughing and kissing each other.

It was strange to be in the large shower cubicle she'd previously cleaned, but with a naked Carver washing her body in a caring, sensual way.

This was the first time she'd seen the extent of his scar, as it reached from his face and down over his chest. She was wary of mentioning anything about it, in case it broke the spell they both seemed to be under.

She nibbled his shoulder playfully as he soaped her breasts, pulling her closer so that her wet torso slid up and down his own body. Their kisses became more urgent, the strokes of their hands firmer and more insistent. When they were both as satisfied as they could be without actually joining together, they snuggled on the floor wrapped in warm fluffy towels from the heated towel rail, and began to caress each other all over again.

Reluctantly, Jenny had to eventually pull away. 'I've got to go to work,' she protested, her voice husky with desire.

'Okay, but now we've *got to know each other*, I demand a replay very soon. You also need to understand that I'm not a one night stand kind of guy.'

# Chapter Twenty-Five

Jenny floated through the archives front door, feeling blissfully relaxed and contented.

'You look happy,' commented Lani. 'The cat that got the cream?' She winked and for once Jenny didn't blush, she just smiled and remembered the sensations that had coursed through her body.

It somehow made it more special that she and Carver hadn't *gone all the way* with their encounter. They had both concentrated on giving each other pleasure and discovered sensitive parts of each other's bodies that they may not have found if they had been busy rushing to an inevitable climax. Her euphoric state lasted for most of the morning.

After lunch, Sandra introduced her to Robert, a stout man in a camel-coloured woollen coat. He reminded her of a stereotypical second-hand car salesman, with his dark hair slicked back.

Jenny went into her usual banter about the facilities in the record office and led him over to the cluster of tables where she worked with her clients. A nagging feeling about this person invaded her mind, something she couldn't quite put her finger on. Did she know him? Recognise his voice?

Once they were seated, Jenny asked Robert what he wanted to achieve with his family tree. His aftershave was cheap and had been applied liberally. The sickly smell stuck in her throat.

'I want something to pass on to my family when I'm gone.'

'That's often why people begin to trace their ancestors. Now if you can give me the names of your mother and father, we'll make a start.'

The hairs began to stand up on her neck as he proceeded to name Jenny's own grandparents. She stopped writing and looked more closely at him.

He didn't say a word. He just stared back at her.

'You're my father, aren't you?'

'Yes, love. I'm Timothy Simpson, not Robert.'

Jenny wondered what love had to do with it. She felt uneasy being cornered at work. Her instant emotion was once again anger.

Did Timothy imagine she'd launch herself into his arms, all the lost years forgotten and everything forgiven?

'I don't think it is very fair of you to come to my place of work. You must have known that this would be an emotional reunion for me.'

'I couldn't think of another way to guarantee you would speak to me after your reaction to my telephone call.'

She sat back and stared at him.

'I still don't think that this is fair and I'm afraid I am feeling rather angry at the moment.' Jenny used terminology from an assertiveness course she had once attended. 'I'd really like you to leave. If you want to speak to me, we need to arrange to meet at a more appropriate time and place, but this, most definitely, is not it.'

Lani had noticed the unusual tone and pitch of her voice. She wandered past. 'Is everything all right, Jenny?'

Her reply was squeezed out between gritted teeth, as she was determined not to cry in front of Timothy. 'Yes, thank you, Lani. We have decided that I can't help Mr Simpson at the moment, so I won't be charging him today.'

She stood up and her father did too. She didn't want to look directly at him any more.

'Jenny, please.'

'I would ask you not to make a scene at my place of work, if you ring me again we can arrange a suitable meeting.

Good afternoon.' She turned and virtually ran for the ladies' toilet.

Lani came in moments later. 'Jenny, did that man upset you?'

'He did, I'm afraid, but not for any of the reasons you are probably imagining. Has he left?'

'Yes, I made sure he'd gone out of the door before I came in here.'

Jenny breathed out heavily and splashed water onto her face.

Lani was still hovering near the door.

Jenny turned and gave her a shaky smile. 'I'll go and make tea for everyone. Goodness knows I could do with a cup. If you do notice that man coming in here again, would you be kind enough to warn me?'

'Of course, Jenny. I'll alert Sandra too. Do you want to talk about it?'

'Maybe when I've made that tea and calmed down. Thank you for being concerned.'

Lani tried to give her a hug, but Jenny sidestepped. Her emotions were in danger of spilling over.

Even though Lani had assured her that Timothy had left, Jenny still poked her head tentatively out of the toilet door and scanned the research room. She scurried to the staff office to boil the kettle. It wasn't until she had poured boiling water into the mugs that the tears began to flow and the tension to ebb away.

The more Jenny thought about it, the more her father's audacity upset her. What had he imagined? That she would fling her arms around him after twenty-five years?

Twenty-five years of not knowing his whereabouts.

Twenty-five years of believing that he didn't care.

Twenty-five years of mourning for someone who turned out not to be dead.

Did he think that their brief antagonistic phone conversation would have warmed her up to his reappearance? How dare he feel he could just take up where he left off? He knew nothing about her life, after all, he hadn't been there for most of it.

She recognised that she was almost like a toddler having a temper tantrum, but underneath all of the emotion and hurt, a steely resolve began to form in her chest that if she'd done without him this long, she didn't really need him any more.

However, yet again she felt wrong-footed. There were two questions that she wanted answers to: where had he been and why had he left in the first place?

She was certain that the phone would ring as soon as she got home that afternoon. In fact, she hadn't even taken off her coat. She almost began to believe her own tales that her father had been a spy, as he appeared to be doing a good job of spying on her. She felt her breathing speed up and her heart beginning to thud as she answered the call.

'Why now, Dad?'

'Your mum is gone.'

'I know that, but why did you have to wait? I don't understand.'

'There's a lot I need to explain.'

'Too right there is.'

'I'm sorry I upset you today, Jenny.'

'Really? Is that apology just for this afternoon or for the last twenty-five years?'

'Don't be like that, love. I just want the chance to explain.' His voice sounded loaded with his own set of emotions.

'Go on then, explain.' Jenny didn't feel in the mood to give him any leeway.

'Not on the phone, love.'

'Yes, on the phone, right now.'

'I'm not willing to do that.'

'Very well. Please go away and leave me alone. I don't need you and I don't want to hear your pathetic excuses.'

'Jenny, be reasonable. Let's go out for a meal together, so we can talk. You can choose where and then you can leave at any time you wish, but please give me this chance.'

Jenny wanted to say goodbye, her younger self wanted to throw the phone across the room, but her rational self returned just in time for her to remember the questions to which she wanted answers. One meeting. That's all she would give him.

'Tomorrow night. The Ship Inn.' Maybe The Ship wasn't the right place; she might come across someone she knew and it could be embarrassing if the meeting became difficult. 'No, make that The Blue Ball at the top of Borteen High Street.'

'I know The Blue Ball, but can we make it Friday night at seven? I'm away until then.'

'Friday, seven, The Blue Ball.' With that, Jenny ended the call and burst into tears. She moved through lots of different emotions. She regressed back to being a fatherless child and rocked herself remembering how that had felt. She ranted and raved about the man who thought he could disappear from her life and then just waltz back in twenty-five years later. It felt like a betrayal of her mother's memory even speaking to him.

Yet, at the same time, this reaction felt irrational. She'd put the postings on the missing persons' websites, she'd longingly dreamed of a reunion with her father, but she'd done all of that calmly and dispassionately without accounting for her reaction to his actual reappearance. There was something else she couldn't quite put her finger on too; something was odd, something was itching away at the back of her subconscious.

She was aware that her father might still be watching her, so she closed the curtains to protect herself from prying eyes. Another thought came to her: if her father was a spy, had he bugged her house? She spent the next fifteen minutes looking under tables and in light shades, as she'd seen people doing in spy films, trying to identify anything strange. She became so paranoid that she knew she had to get out of the house.

She rang Carver. 'Am I okay to come over tonight?'

'You bet.'

She giggled as he'd said the words in what he obviously hoped was a sexy tone.

'I've got news to share with you. Shall I call for a takeaway en route? And, erm … essential supplies?'

She caught sight of herself in the mirror. *You hussy*.

Carver must have been embarrassed too, as he almost stuttered over his next sentence. 'I've already been out for … es-sen-tial supplies, but food would be good too.'

'Chinese?'

'Sure. I like most things on Mr Wong's menu. Maybe get a selection?'

'I will and, Carver, would you mind if I stay over? I'm not working tomorrow, as it's Tuesday and the archives don't open on Tuesdays.'

'Sounds perfect. Unfortunately, I've got to work tomorrow. I've got a commission in Borteen Church, but maybe we could meet up for lunch.'

'Right, I'll pack a bag and pick up the takeaway on the way over. See you in about thirty minutes. I badly need a hug.'

'Me too.'

She could feel his grin in his words.

Even driving in the car, she kept checking her mirrors to see if anyone was following her. Anyone being her father.

The table was laid when she arrived at Tree Tops and

Carver was dressed in a smarter shirt than normal with his black jeans, his hair combed and a certain look in his eye.

By the time he'd taken the takeaway bags from her and pecked her on the lips, however, he'd picked up on her mood.

'What's wrong?'

'I had a visit from my father at work.'

'Goodness, are you okay?'

'And another phone call tonight too.'

Carver rubbed her shoulder. 'Okay?'

'I guess. You know what it's like – a blummin' emotional rollercoaster. I've arranged to meet him on Friday evening for dinner. I decided that you were right and I should at least hear him out. We'd better start on this food before it goes cold.'

They paused in the conversation to take the foil cartons out of the bags and put them onto the table. Jenny removed lids and Carver poured her a glass of wine. When they were settled and helping themselves to rice and the various dishes, Carver said, 'I'm glad you are giving your dad a chance. I'd offer to come with you as back-up, but coincidentally, I've got news too.'

'Really?'

'Well, after I told Kieron briefly about our discussion about our fathers a while back, he tried to contact my father through social media and … it worked.'

'You've found your father too?' She put her fork down on the table for a moment.

Carver nodded.

'Thank goodness. I'm so pleased for you.' She reached a hand across the table to run across his forearm. 'At least our theory about one dad murdering the other wasn't true. Have you met him yet?'

'I'm having dinner with him in Sowden on Friday evening.'

'Friday is obviously Dad day! Well, I hope we both get on well then.'

'So do I.'

'How do you feel about it all?' Jenny grabbed a napkin to staunch the trail of sweet and sour sauce that was running down her chin.

'About the same as you, I suppose. Nervous, not quite trusting it to be true, wondering about ulterior motives, full of questions and childhood upset.'

'That about sums it up.'

They finished the bottle of wine and as much of the takeaway as they could manage. Carver had lit the wood burner in the lounge, so they sat on either side of it with a coffee.

'Is it still okay to stay over?'

'Of course.'

Somehow seducing each other didn't seem top of the agenda any more; their thoughts about their fathers had taken over. Carver had gone into protective, caring mode and Jenny was glad of it.

*This is a good man*, she said to herself. *A keeper if he wants me.*

# Chapter Twenty-Six

Later in bed, they snuggled up to each other, held hands and kissed goodnight, but neither made any move to do anything more than provide comfort.

'You okay?' mumbled Carver sleepily.

'Yes, very much so. I like being here with you. I feel safe.'

'I'm glad.'

They both drifted into sleep.

The next thing she was aware of was Carver cupping her face with his hand and whispering in her ear. 'You awake?'

'I am now,' she said teasingly. 'What time is it?'

'Dawn's breaking, but I woke up with you snuggled up to me and I just wanted to make sure you were ready, willing and able.'

'Mmmm ...'

His hand had left her face and was sliding up under her nightdress. He rolled closer towards her, feathering kisses across her eyes, her nose, her cheeks and finally capturing her lips at the same time as he found her nipple and squeezed gently.

For a few seconds, she allowed herself to savour the sensations in her body, before deepening the kiss and gently exploring his mouth with her tongue. Making sure she left his hand and arm plenty of room to continue exploring her body, she began her own explorations.

His chest was firm and almost hairless, his buttocks nicely rounded and good to squeeze. She gasped as his hand travelled down her stomach and between her thighs, as if he couldn't wait to reach the warmth of her.

He pulled back slightly from her lips. 'You are sure this is what you want?'

'Absolutely sure.' She pulled his head back down and left him in no doubt, with her hungry kisses and urgent pressing of her body against his, that she was ready to take this step.

They matched each other's movements, as if they had been made for each other. All too soon, they were lying hot and perspiring, but both with big smiles on their faces as they lay back against the pillows.

'That was my first time in a long while,' he murmured. The words *since my wife's death* hung in the air.

'Mine too. Can we do it again?'

'Hey, you'll wear me out and I'll have to go out for more *supplies*,' he joked, pulling her over on top of him.

When they eventually were up and showered, with yet another excursion to bed occasioned by caresses in the shower, Carver told her his plans for the day.

'I'm working at Borteen Church this morning. I've been replacing a piece of wood on the pulpit and it's ready to fix in place. What do you say to meeting me there later? We could have a bite of lunch and maybe a walk on the beach. It looks as if it will be a nice day, if we can believe the weather forecast.'

'That sounds lovely. How about I bring you a picnic lunch around twelve-thirty?'

Carver's grin was wide and genuine. He kissed her neck.

'It's a date!' They were both smiling at each other, but Jenny's mind was doing cartwheels about his choice of words and his affectionate caress. It somehow meant a lot that they'd slept together all night before making love.

She took great care over the picnic. Bite-sized sandwiches with lots of different fillings, crisps, tiny cupcakes, a box of fresh fruit, fruit juice in cartons and bottled water to drink. Her heart was racing as she walked into the churchyard at Borteen, clutching a bag containing the food.

Why was she still so nervous? They'd made love several times now and Carver had made it clear he wanted a relationship with her. She came to the conclusion it was the fear that it could all go horribly wrong ... that she'd imagined it. She had been trying to protect her heart in all this, but was failing rapidly with each kiss, touch and affectionate look from those steel-grey eyes.

Jenny visited her mother's grave for a few moments. 'Afternoon, Mum.' The flowers she'd noticed at the weekend were still there and, of course, their placement now made sense. She supposed her father had left them for his estranged wife. It was all she could do not to hurl the flowers over the sea wall. Instead, she forced herself to breathe away the emotions, because she wanted a nice lunch with Carver, not for the meeting to be poisoned by her negative thoughts about her dad.

She walked across to a memorial bench that faced the sea. The church was set on a slight hill, so sitting on the bench you couldn't see the beach below at all, just the place where the sea met the sky at the horizon.

Jenny sat on the bench, balancing the picnic bag carefully on the wooden slats.

The weather forecast had been correct. It was one of those days that felt it should belong to a different season. Jenny sat and stretched out slender jean-clad legs across the gravel, the warmth of the sun soothing her mind. She noted the interesting shapes and colours amongst the stones and tried to resist her kleptomaniac tendencies when it came to pebbles.

She waited patiently on the bench as she didn't want to disturb Carver at work, but also, she hadn't been inside Borteen Church since her mother's funeral service and had no desire for anything else to upset her before she met Carver.

Carver, her new lover. Boyfriend or man-friend? She giggled and hugged her legs in glee.

He emerged from the church doorway at exactly twelve-thirty, as if he'd set a timer so as not to be late for their rendezvous. She watched him scan the churchyard. When he caught sight of her, a huge smile lit up his features. The highlights in his hair glinted in the sun. Wilf was close on his heels.

*Oh dear, girl, you are in real danger of falling hard for this man.*

Wood shavings coated the front of his blue overalls. He brushed them off as he walked towards her, clasped her hand in greeting and bent to kiss her cheek.

He sat down, still holding her hand. She marvelled at how a man who spent so much time using his hands for his work could have such well-manicured nails.

'How do you keep your hands so clean and undamaged?'

'Remember they are my livelihood. I can't afford to injure them, so I always wear gloves when I'm using sharp tools.'

'Sorry, I was being nosy. Are you hungry?'

'Not nosy, just curious and yes, I'm starving.'

'I hope I've brought enough food then.'

He motioned for Wilf to sit on the path. Belatedly she realised that she'd put the picnic bag between them, so Carver was unable to sit very close to her.

She busied herself unpacking the bag, laying out the dainty bites on a cloth between them. She began to panic, as everything looked so small for a lunch for a man.

'It looks delicious. You really shouldn't have gone to so much trouble.'

His voice was muffled as he was busy trying out the different flavours of sandwich.

'I haven't got anything for Wilf.'

'I'll give him a few bits of mine, shouldn't really though.

He only gets fed morning and evening and I don't want him to get fat. The vet will insist I take him to doggy weight watchers next time we go for his annual check-up if I'm not careful.'

'Is there really such a thing as doggy weight watchers?'

'Oh yes. Not good for his joints to carry weight.'

They were quiet for a while, chewing in joint contemplative silence. It felt like a natural silence though, comfortable and relaxed. The dog lay in a sunny spot on the grass.

Carver bent to unlace his boots. As he took them off, she noticed there was a hole in one sock, but she didn't say anything. He looked up at her. 'They feel tight today. It must be because it's warmer than it has been and I've been standing up all morning.' Straightening, he turned to face her, getting distracted for a moment by a stray tuna and mayonnaise bite, before saying, 'So have you given any more thought to what you are going to do about your dad?'

Jenny was feeling pleased that he had enjoyed her picnic, but the question brought her back to earth with a bump.

'I'm going to try not to react to my historic feelings, rather to see who he is now and listen to what he has to say and why he's suddenly reappeared in my life.'

'Sounds like good advice. I know what you mean about the historic feelings. We've both had twenty-five years to worry, fear, be upset, hate …'

The sun went behind a cloud dowsing the scene in front of them and dropping the temperature by several degrees. Jenny shivered. The churchyard was quiet, but she could hear children playing on the beach below.

'I think it was my shock that stopped it feeling right before. Hopefully, I've got it all straight in my head now and can listen to what he has to say. I need to set aside any judgements and, of course, all of the things I've imagined over the years.'

A sudden thought crossed her mind and she sat up straighter.

'What is it?'

She giggled. 'Mum's buried over there.' She pointed in the direction of her mother's grave. 'I just suddenly felt like a naughty child talking about Dad in her hearing, she always forbade it when she was alive. And I have a feeling Dad might have left those flowers for her.' She pointed at the chrysanthemums.

'Look, I don't profess to be religious or anything, but Bliss always said that your earthly concerns disappear when you die. Even if your mum is listening, or watching your dad lay flowers, she will think about the situation very differently by now.'

Jenny didn't like to contradict him, but she knew how stubbornly her mother had refused to discuss her father. She couldn't believe that even dying would have changed her mother's set opinion. She felt the need to change the subject.

'Have you finished working in the church?'

As if in answer, he began to remove his overalls, revealing faded jeans and a well-worn blue T-shirt. 'Yes, all done. The pulpit is as good as new and, hopefully, Reverend Hopkins will be pleased. Have you time for a walk on the beach?'

'Yes, that would be lovely.' She started to pack away the leftover food. Carver picked up a couple of carrot sticks and threw them to Wilf. Then he grabbed a final cupcake for himself from the bag. It was a simple gesture, but highlighted how much more relaxed he was with her now.

'Thanks for the lovely lunch. Maybe we could do it again sometime.' He put on his boots and laced them up.

'Maybe ... if you are good.' She smiled. The innuendo wasn't lost on either of them.

The sun had emerged again from its shrouding cloud. She put the picnic bag in her car and he stowed his tools and overalls in his. He put on a fleece, took out a ball and whistled Wilf.

Carver was satisfied with the way his day was going. He'd had a morning awakening beyond his wildest dreams with Jenny and she was still smiling at him at lunchtime. He'd repaired the church pulpit so that it was difficult to see the new piece of wood. He knew that most people going into the church wouldn't even notice, but he had his professional pride.

Lunch had been very pleasant, although he wished Jenny had made bigger sandwiches, instead of bite-sized ones. He could tell she still wasn't totally comfortable with Wilf's presence, but he had felt nervous to leave the dog in his kennel at Tree Tops in case the hole-digging person, or persons, returned while he was away. He had no reason to believe they would hurt his dog, but he didn't want to take any chances.

The fog that had descended on his life when Bliss died appeared to be lifting. He had begun to notice things again that had been invisible for so long. Take the lunch, for instance. He had taken great delight in appreciating the subtle tastes of the delicate food that Jenny had provided. Food for a long time had just been a necessity that he had thrown down his gullet to keep him going, without much enjoyment or finesse.

He'd also begun to enjoy looking at Jenny and was trying to shrug off the guilt for doing so. He particularly liked the way she spoke from behind her hand when she was embarrassed or shy. And the way her body felt against his was something else … If he was honest with himself, he knew he was showing signs of coming out of his all-consuming bereavement.

Carver saw a different side of Jenny as soon as they got onto the beach. Having said that, he felt his own mood lighten too as soon as his boots touched the sand. They whirled, ran, and laughed. Jenny even began to throw the ball for Wilf, although she baulked at picking it up again covered in the dog's saliva. That made him laugh too.

The wind ruffled her hair. The tide was out and they ran full pelt towards the surf. They stopped just short of the waves and Jenny yelped as the water lapped right up to the toes of her boots. Carver leant down and sent a few icy drops of seawater in her direction. She retaliated and then ran further up the beach.

'There's something about the smell of the sea, the wind in your hair and the sand,' Jenny said as she came to a halt again.

'It brings back all of my childhood memories.'

'Donkey rides.'

'Ice cream topped with sand.'

'Mum changing under a towel.'

'The windbreak falling down.' He put his arm around her shoulders and she put her arm around his waist. It felt good.

'Annoying people with loud radios camping next to you.'

'Exploring caves.'

'Collecting pebbles and shells.'

'Scaring the girls with crabs.' He squeezed her waist.

'Building dams and then flooding people out further down the beach.'

They were both laughing and then kissing.

Wilf ran out of the surf and made them squeal and break apart as he shook the water from his fur all over them.

Jenny jumped to one side as she almost trod on an elaborate swirl design on the sand. It appeared to be made of two different coloured sands and it was so exquisite it would have been a crime to spoil it.

'How beautiful,' she exclaimed.

'A fitting end.'

'End?' Jenny looked confused.

'Unless I'm very much mistaken, someone made this with their loved one's ashes,' said Carver.

'Really? I never thought of that. As you say, what a lovely thing to do.'

Carver could almost hear the unspoken question on Jenny's mind.

'I scattered Bliss's ashes under her favourite tree in the forest.'

'That's lovely too. The Wishing Tree you told me about?'

'Yes. It felt like the right decision and it means I have somewhere to go when I need to speak to her.'

They continued to walk along the shore, but their mood had become more thoughtful.

Carver stopped and called Wilf to his side and attached a lead.

'Are you okay?' Jenny asked.

'Yes, it's just that dogs aren't allowed any further along the beach.'

'Ah, I hadn't thought of that.'

'Come on, I'll race you two to the café. Last one there buys the coffee.'

They were instantly childlike again. Jenny surprised him by getting a head start. In fact, despite his long legs, she got to the café easily in front of him, even though he was being towed by Wilf. He was touched to notice that Jenny put her hand on Wilf's collar when they puffed up to where she stood.

'You take a seat and I'll get the drinks, but you're paying remember? You lost,' she said.

He handed her a bank note with a smile.

It was nice that she didn't have to ask him what he wanted. She knew his preference for strong coffee. He loosened his hold on the lead and allowed the dog to drink

235

from the water bowl by the wall. Then he made his way over to one of the bench seats overlooking the sand. He looped Wilf's lead around the chair leg.

Jenny returned with coffees and two cakes.

'More cake?' he teased.

'I'm hungry. It must be the sea air.'

They sat watching the beach activity, mainly dog walkers and families with children determined to enjoy the beach despite the season.

'Are you up to another race across the sand?'

'Actually, I was thinking of buying a couple of buckets and spades and challenging you to a sandcastle building competition,' she said.

'I'll bury you in the sand, if you like.'

'Ooo no, too cold at this time of year.'

Jenny produced a traditional castle with four towers and curtain walls joining them up. Carver built one of his favourite images, a mermaid with long curling hair and scales on her tail. He used his ever-present penknife to form the small details.

'Wow,' said Jenny.

'What's my prize then?'

'Excuse me?'

'You said it was a competition.'

'Well, you definitely won. What would you like?'

'Dangerous question. How about a kiss and yet another coffee after a race?'

'You're on,' said Jenny and before she registered what he was doing, he was off across the sand with Wilf at his heels.

She hightailed it after him yelling, 'Cheat!'

Carver had a warm glow inside. It felt good to feel so free and childlike. He stopped before he got to the promenade and pointed across to the dog free side of the beach. 'Look, Buzz has drawn a labyrinth.'

'A labyrinth? Who's Buzz?'

'He's the guy who runs the crystal shop in Borteen High Street. He designs a labyrinth every now and then and invites people to walk the path if they make a donation to his chosen charity.'

'Yay, I can tick off another shop owner on my list.'

Carver knew all about Jenny's memory challenge.

They watched several children running around the intricate path in the sand.

'Ooo, I want a go.'

'Unfortunately, I can't take Wilf over on that part of the beach, but you go.'

Her disappointment showed openly on her face.

'I tell you what, I'll ask Mandy at Owl Corner Crafts if she'll watch Wilf for a minute.'

He sprinted up the slipway and Jenny followed him to the old building that looked as if it had once been a school. There was a bench next to the entrance and Mandy was sitting on it.

'Afternoon, Mandy.'

'You're looking brighter.' She smiled and looked pointedly at Jenny. 'Hi, Jenny.'

Mandy agreed to hold Wilf's lead for a while, with a big suggestive wink at Carver and the two of them headed back down onto the sand. Carver grabbed Jenny's hand as they walked.

'Feel rather guilty dumping Wilf with Mandy.' He turned to look back. Wilf had his big head resting in Mandy's lap and she appeared to be talking to him. 'Having said that they look pretty happy together.'

'She fancies you, you know?'

'Nah, we're just old mates.'

'Believe me, she has the hots for you.'

'When you get to know Mandy a little better, you'll realise

she flirts with all the guys. Shame, I think she must have some deep insecurities. Anyway, I'm taken.' Carver grinned at Jenny. 'Come on, I'll race you.'

Jenny sped after Carver across the beach, her heart warmed by his words.

Before her on the sand was an elaborate pattern of paths, delineated by ridges of sand. A few people wove in and out of the trackways. Some took it slowly and others ran, bypassing the slow ones by leaping in and out of the lanes. Carver led her up to the beginning of the maze and introduced her to Buzz. She didn't mention that she'd bought incense sticks from him in the past and a brightly coloured bag for a friend's birthday years ago.

Buzz held a pink, heart-shaped bucket, which seemed incongruous as he was a tall, grey-haired man, probably in his sixties. 'I merely ask a donation. This time the money will go to buy some new toys for the children in the cancer ward at Sowden Hospital.'

You couldn't help but smile at this man. Jenny couldn't decide what it was about him that made a broad grin appear on her face. She began to fish around in the little leather bag she was wearing across her body, but Carver said, 'I'll get this.' He put a note into the bucket and led the way into the labyrinth.

Jenny smiled again at Buzz and followed, carefully allowing Carver space to walk at his own pace. To begin with, she felt self-conscious and wobbly, but then she began to just focus on each step, amazed at the calm feeling that swept over her. By the time they'd walked all the paths, which took longer than she'd imagined, she was so relaxed that she thought she could fall asleep standing up.

As she emerged from the end of the path, Carver was waiting for her. Buzz finished talking to a family about his charity and the labyrinth, then turned to ask them about their experience.

'I can't believe how relaxed I feel.'

'Your first time?'

She laughed. 'Walking a labyrinth? Yes.'

Buzz surprised her by grabbing her hand. He looked intently into her palm. It somehow felt as if he was searching her soul, but she didn't pull away. He let go of her hand almost as quickly as he'd grasped it.

'Be wary. All is not as it seems, but others you doubted are true and part of your destiny.'

'What on earth does that mean?' She looked between Buzz and Carver.

'Sorry, I can't interpret the message. Only that you will know in your heart what it refers to.'

He nodded at them and turned away.

'Bizarre,' said Jenny.

'A lot of people swear by his messages. He would have charged you for that in the shop, although I believe he gives far more money to charity than he keeps himself. He seems a lonely old guy, but Bliss would have said *a wise spirit*.'

Jenny felt rather disturbed by the strange message. *Be wary. All is not as it seems, but others you doubted are true and part of your destiny.* She kept repeating it like a mantra to remember what Buzz had said.

'I've got to go and retrieve Wilf.'

They started to walk back to collect the dog. Carver took her hand and she leaned in towards him. Was he the one who was true and part of her destiny? Or the one of whom she should be wary?

When she got home and looked at her mobile, which she'd switched off before lunch, there were several messages from Rosie. Jenny rang her back and told her what had been going on since her friend had returned to London.

'Goodness you've been busy. I did wonder if your dad returning would lead to you being friendly with dishy Carver again. Make sure you keep me up to date with developments.'

Jenny ended the call and sighed. It had been a lovely interlude with Carver, but the words of the strange man on the beach kept revolving around her head, making her feel uncertain yet again.

*Be wary. All is not as it seems, but others you doubted are true and part of your destiny.*

# Chapter Twenty-Seven

Jenny had to walk down the hill to the bottom of the high street and back up the hill again along the high street to reach The Blue Ball, as there was no linking road across the hillside.

As she walked she reflected that she couldn't understand her feelings at all. She'd spent so many years wanting to find her father, so why did she feel so strange about being finally reunited? It was almost as if she was going to meet the hangman.

The Blue Ball was not normally a pub she frequented, so that made her slightly nervous too. She was cold and out of breath by the time she walked up the steps, through the door and into the bar.

It had a very different feel to Jenny's favoured pub The Ship Inn. Whereas The Ship had large open rooms, The Blue Ball had several, tiny cramped rooms leading into a conservatory. Jenny wrinkled her nose, as the cooking smells were not particularly pleasant and didn't bode well for her enjoyment of her evening meal.

She walked down the corridor, scanning the tiny bars for Robert. Then she realised she was still thinking of him as Robert and not Timothy Simpson. Her nerves were galloping.

He rose from a table in the corner of the conservatory as she entered the room. The same camel coat he had worn at the library was draped around the back of his chair.

'Jenny, love. Come and sit down.'

He pulled out the chair opposite to his own for Jenny to sit down. As she sat, he planted a kiss on her cheek. It took all of her will power not to wipe it off in front of him. She made an effort to take a deep breath; she'd promised Carver she would be open minded this evening. The deep breath didn't do much to change her mood and the hackles at the back of her neck were still raised.

'I'm so glad you agreed to give me a chance ...'

Waves of confusion coursed through her. Surely she should feel affection for her father, not all this animosity and suspicion? It was a far cry from the reunion she had always imagined which went something along the lines of her rushing along a road and into her dad's arms.

She didn't trust herself to say much. 'Talk to me.'

'What would you like to know?'

'Everything.'

Did she imagine the alarm in his eyes, eyes that were so unlike her own? Did he have any features that resembled hers? Jenny didn't think so, but was she just biased because of their bad start?

The waitress picked up on the atmosphere that was developing between the two. The girl looked at them uncertainly and pointed at the menu board almost apologetically.

It was a relief to focus on the blackboard and try to work out which dish was the source of the horrid smell lingering in the air so that she could avoid it. She opted for fish and chips. Her father obviously didn't object to the smell as much as she did, because he chose the roast dish which included cabbage as a vegetable.

She repeated her request when they were alone again. 'Talk ...'

'I'm more interested in talking about you. My life is boring.'

'What!' Jenny was stunned. Did the man think she had no right to know what he'd been up to, where he'd hidden all these years and why?

Timothy picked up on her tone and sat up straighter in his seat. 'Go on then, ask me some questions and I'll do my best to answer them.'

It was a strange thing to say.

'Did Mum know where you went?'

'No. We never had contact again.'

'Where did you go?'

'Spain.'

The food arrived and Timothy made a fuss about having black pepper and extra gravy brought to the table. Jenny had the strangest feeling he was playing for time.

She struggled to open the little packet of mayonnaise and applied it to the side of her plate. At least it gave her some respite from looking at her father.

'So did your mum keep my things?'

'Your things?' Her senses were on full alert.

'My clocks?'

'Did you collect clocks?'

'Not exactly. My boss used to give them to me.'

'Your boss at the ... auction house?'

'Yes. There was one in particular. It was my favourite.'

Jenny experienced a weird earthquaky sensation inside of her. She decided not to tell her dad they had found the clock that he was obviously referring to. There was something decidedly strange going on here. Unless her mother had buried the clock, surely her dad would know that it had been buried in the garden ... or had he been watching her after all?

She was vague in her reply. 'There are lots of clocks at home.'

They ate and just about managed to keep a conversation going about the pub, the food, the waitress, anything other than personal stuff. Jenny was in no mood to volunteer any details about herself, but somehow she had to establish a rapport with this man.

'By the way, did you by any chance see my missing persons' ads?'

'Yes, that's why I'm here.'

At least something made sense at last.

'Have you been following me around, Dad?'

'No.'

Why didn't she believe him? She was beginning to realise there was something about the set of his eyes when he made a reply that didn't sound like the truth.

'What about Michael Rodgers?'

'Who?'

She was back to being suspicious again. The strange feeling inside her body was becoming unbearable.

They returned to safer subjects. Jenny was dying to ask more questions, but her overwhelming need right now was to get out of the situation.

'Can we do this again?'

'Sure, I'd love to. The sooner the better.' He smiled what looked like a genuine smile and didn't show signs of picking up on her uncertainty.

Was she misjudging him? Was he just nervous? Maybe if they met a couple more times she would warm to him. Maybe ...

'I have a few things to sort out, then maybe I could ring you to arrange another meeting?'

'You've got my number now. Don't leave it too long though, love.'

Jenny took out her purse to pay for her share of the meal.

'I'll get this,' said Timothy.

'That's kind. I'll pay next time.'

She put on her coat, eager to get away from the pub, her father, everything ... Giving a little wave, she rushed from the room and walked as fast as she could back down the high street and then up the hill to home.

Her clothes smelled like cabbage even away from the pub and although she hadn't made any physical contact with Timothy, she felt the need for a hot shower when she had locked up. Why would being with her own father make her feel so awful?

Carver had probably as many misgivings about meeting his father as Jenny had about meeting hers. He'd chosen the pizza parlour opposite the cathedral in Sowden as the meeting point, as Jenny had said that the pizza was good.

He didn't normally pay much attention to his clothes or hair. As far as he was concerned, people had to accept him as he was. This meeting, however, felt very different. His vague memories of his father included feeling inadequate in his presence. Carver somehow wanted to appear adequate today, although he was having difficulty knowing what that comprised. He'd chosen beige chinos, a cream woollen jumper and his better waxed jacket. He felt that his boots were his trademark, part of who he was, so he wore those anyway; he'd just given them a brush and a rub with a duster.

The man waiting for him at a table in the window looked much smaller than he remembered, but then he'd been a child the last time he'd seen his dad.

Amusingly, Michael Rodgers was dressed in very similar clothes to Carver himself, as if they had shopped together. Michael got up as he approached the table and Carver thought for one horrid moment that the man was going to try to embrace him. Michael obviously read his thoughts, or maybe the expression on his face, and the possible hug morphed into a polite handshake.

Carver sat down quickly and the waiter zoomed over to take a drinks order and give them the restaurant menus.

The two men sat hiding behind the oversized laminated

lists and didn't speak properly until the waiter had taken their order.

'I know this feels a bit awkward, son, but even if I never get the chance to say anything else, I just want to say that I'm sorry I wasn't there for you.'

Carver was dismayed by tears appearing in his eyes. 'Was ... was it because of me you went away? I need to know because I've always thought it was.' He blurted out the words and batted the hot tears with the back of his hand.

'Of course it wasn't because of you.' Michael leaned across the table and tried to take Carver's hand. Instinctively, Carver recoiled and tucked his hands safely on his lap. Michael sat back. 'Why on earth would it have been because of you?'

'Because of my asthma?'

It was Carver's father who now needed to use the napkin to mop his eyes. 'Did your mother never tell you anything?'

'Nothing at all. She never mentioned you unless I did and then she changed the subject as quickly as possible.'

The men sat uncomfortably in silence trying to get their emotions under control. Just as Carver was beginning to feel better, the pizzas were brought to the table and the flurry of organising cutlery and using the pizza cutters meant the two men didn't need to make any effort to talk for a while.

By some sort of mutual understanding, they kept their conversation carefully neutral. It was more a getting to know you chat, talking about likes and dislikes. Each of them kept away from the emotionally charged subjects of why Michael went away and Carver's childhood. Carver saw his father looking at his scar, but he didn't ask him about that. He glossed over Bliss's death, but didn't go into any detail.

When Carver looked back on the evening, he realised that they had spent more time in silence than talking and he still hadn't asked some of the important questions he needed to voice. The main thing was that they had broken the ice and, however Carver felt about his father and the intervening years since he had last seen him, the family link was still there.

Their time in the restaurant ended with amusement when father and son discovered that they had folded their napkins in an identical way. 'I didn't realise that napkin folding was genetic,' commented Carver.

They had agreed to take things slowly and arranged to meet for a drink the following week; the details could be arranged later now that they had exchanged mobile numbers. Carver breathed a sigh of relief that the evening hadn't been too difficult apart from his childish tears. His father had also been emotional and that fact had stopped Carver getting angry, as he had thought prior to the meeting that he might have a tendency to do.

There was no need for genetic tests to prove their kinship. The two men could tell instantly that they were related; from the dress sense, through long limbs and fingers, to the napkin folding, there was no doubting that they were closely related. In fact, when Carver caught sight of the two of them in the mirrors on the wall of the restaurant, they looked so alike, despite the fact Carver had long curls and Michael was almost bald.

As they walked out of the door, Michael turned back. 'Oh, I nearly forgot. I believe that you are in touch with Jenny Simpson?'

'Yes, I am.' The hairs on the back of Carver's neck prickled.

'Her father, Timothy, would like to see her again too.'

'I don't understand.' The prickles had become ice-cold and were rapidly multiplying.

'What do you mean? I'm only passing on a message for

Timothy Simpson, Jenny's father, that he would like to meet up with her again.'

'But Jenny's seeing her father this evening. We were discussing it this afternoon.'

Michael looked perplexed. 'Well, whoever she's meeting, it isn't Timothy. He's still in Spain.'

It was on the tip of Carver's tongue to ask how he knew, but that knowledge was subordinate to the sudden lurch of fear for Jenny's safety. Who exactly was she meeting this evening?

'I think I'd better go and find her and quickly.'

'Damien?'

Carver winced at his father's use of his given name.

'There are things I need to tell you about why I went away, why *we* went away. Now is obviously not the right time. I think you should get to Jenny as quickly as you can.'

Carver nodded and ran to the car park.

# Chapter Twenty-Eight

Carver paused when he was sitting in the driving seat of his pick-up to dial Jenny's mobile number. The call went straight to voicemail. 'Ring me, Jenny. It's urgent. Very urgent.'

He desperately tried to remember what she'd said about meeting her father. He thought she'd mentioned a pub in Borteen, but which one?

Reversing his pick-up, he paused again at the entrance to the car park as he redialled her number. Again, her familiar voice on her answerphone message.

He drove over Pink Moor, fast, but not too fast – he knew how speed could lead to disaster. He was so intent on reaching Jenny that for the first time since the accident that had killed Bliss, he didn't remember to pay a silent tribute to his dead wife as he went around the fateful bend where their crash had happened.

Of course, he realised a little further down the road that he'd forgotten and a stab of guilt hit his gut. He shook himself and returned to his mission. He had to find Jenny, she could be in danger. That was the priority.

He mentally listed the pubs in Borteen: The Ship Inn was on the promenade. The Blue Ball was at the very top of the high street, the wine bar at the bottom on the other side of the road and The Smugglers' Chest on the road towards the cliffs and quarry. Had he forgotten any?

After a frantic sprint around the pubs trying to spot her, his breathing was laboured and he stopped for a precautionary puff of his inhaler on the promenade. He couldn't afford to feel ill now. He realised it wasn't going to be that easy to find Jenny.

He tried her mobile yet again, but once more got Jenny's

answerphone. He scanned the beach below in the darkness. A few people were walking by the light of torches on the far side where dogs were allowed, but it would be very difficult to spot Jenny in the dark even if she was there, and why would she be anyway?

*Think, Carver, think.*

He had driven to Sowden and eaten a meal with his father and then driven back over the moor; chances were that in that time Jenny might have already eaten with the man she thought was her dad and returned home.

Crossing his fingers with hope and reminding himself to breathe, he made his way back to the pick-up, untidily dumped in two car parking spaces at The Ship Inn in his earlier rush.

He drove to Priory Avenue, scanning the pavements on the way. Nothing.

The relief at finding her car in her drive made him grin, although it was short lived as he remembered she would probably have walked into Borteen. He ran up the path and banged on the door. There was silence for quite a while and his heart rate increased again. He was just thinking of making his way to the back of the house, when he heard a muffled voice.

'Who's there?'

He sighed with the joy of hearing her voice.

'It's me, Carver.'

She opened the door a crack; the security chain was in place, her face white, peering through the gap.

'Carver, what the heck?'

'Sorry, sorry. I just had to know you were okay.'

She opened the door fully after a few moments of wrestling with the security chain. She was wearing a fluffy dressing gown and her bare feet poked out of the bottom of her flowery pyjamas. Carver shut the door behind him, before enveloping her in a bear hug. He realised he was squeezing her too tightly and let her go.

'Sorry, sorry ... again. I was so worried for your safety.'

'Why on earth? You'd better tell me what this is all about. I'm fine as you can see.'

'You haven't been looking at your phone.'

'Oh, no, sorry. I switched it off when I got back from meeting my father – needed some thinking time.'

He followed her into the lounge, trying not to blurt out what he had come to say, even though the words threatened to erupt from him. His eyes were automatically drawn to the wooden clock on the mantelpiece as they sat down.

'Did you have a good evening with *your* dad?' she asked.

'It's early days. We're a little uncomfortable with each other at the moment. It will take time, I guess. How was your evening?'

'It was okayish. I'm still not comfortable. Something doesn't feel quite right.'

'Thank goodness you've said that.' He raked a hand through his hair.

'Why? What do you mean?'

'The man you met tonight – I don't quite know how to say this – he isn't your father.'

'What! How on earth could you know that?' Her hands automatically moved to clasp her face and then she crossed her arms firmly around the fluffy dressing gown.

'My dad mentioned that your father lives in Spain. He'd apparently requested that my dad ask if you would be willing to meet up with him if he flies over.'

If Jenny had been white when he'd hammered on her door, she was ashen now.

'So ... who exactly did I meet this evening?'

'That is *the* question. Does this guy look like your father?'

'That's just it, I don't know. I only have hazy childhood

251

memories and I haven't been able to find any photos here, as yet.'

'That's a little strange. Surely your mum would have kept one for you, no matter what she thought of the man.'

The colour was returning slowly to Jenny's face. Her eyes sparkled as she turned to him. 'You know, now it all makes sense. The uncomfortable feeling, the awkwardness, the way this *Timothy Simpson* didn't seem to remember much about Mum or me and refused to say much about what he's been doing all of these years.'

She stood up, a determined look on her face. 'Will you help me search the loft?'

Carver stood up too. 'Right now?' He saw the firm set of her mouth.

'Yes, right now. I have to know.'

'Sure. We're looking for a photograph, right?'

'Yes. I refuse to believe that Mum didn't keep any. She was a hoarder after all.'

He smiled grimly. 'Lead the way to the loft.'

Carver moved the loft hatch, standing on the chair from the spare bedroom, and pulled down the loft ladder, while Jenny went to put some clothes on. He pulled himself up the steep metal steps. Jenny had told him where the light switch was. He flicked the switch and had to stifle a groan as his heart sank to his boots. The roof space was rammed full of boxes.

He went back down the rungs and waited for Jenny to emerge from her bedroom wearing old jeans and a sweatshirt.

'Your mum certainly *was* a hoarder.'

'I take it you've looked up there? *"If you don't know what to do with something, put it in a box."* That's me quoting Mum, by the way.'

'Hmm … a maxim she took to heart by the looks of it.'

'I think we need to search in some of the older boxes. We'll have to move some of these more recent ones out of the way.'

They made a channel through the cardboard mountain, Carver lifting the heavier boxes out of the way so that they could focus on boxes at the far end of the loft with faded lettering.

'Some of these boxes could be classed as antiques.'

'Cheeky!'

Despite the circumstances and the motivation for searching this dusty, gloomy space, it was nice to be doing something with Jenny. Now that he'd had time to absorb his panic from earlier in the evening, he realised that he'd been very worried, even scared about her safety. A warm glow kindled inside him. He was falling for Jenny, in a way he thought he'd never fall for a woman again after losing Bliss.

Her hands were getting dusty, at this rate she'd need a shower after this search. They both would. He tried to shake the image of Jenny in the shower out of his head.

She stopped rummaging in the box she'd just opened and yelled, 'Eureka!'

He peered over her shoulder in the restricted space. It seemed to have taken ages, but she had finally found a box containing small clocks and watches and some envelopes, one with photographs. Carver had to half-lift, half-drag the box into the only bit of space they had, as it was too cumbersome for her to manage. She took out the envelopes and showed Carver the rest of the contents.

'Let's take these envelopes downstairs. After all that, I find myself almost scared to look at an image of my dad. My back aches and I need a cup of tea.'

'Are you sure you can wait to make tea, before having a better look at these?'

Carver was itching to know if the man Jenny had met this

evening was actually her father. Or was it that, almost more importantly, he couldn't wait to know whether his own father had told the truth?

'I've waited this long, another five minutes won't hurt and you're here to keep me safe.' She smiled at him, squeezed his arm and planted a dusty kiss on his cheek as she descended the last rung of the loft ladder.

He wanted to kiss her properly, make love to her, but with everything else on their minds it seemed totally inappropriate, so he restrained himself.

They sat sipping tea with the two big envelopes Jenny had found in the loft on the coffee table between them.

'I need to work up to opening these.' Her expression was fearful. 'That quick look in the loft, despite the poor light, convinced me these envelopes contain the photographs I've been looking for.'

'Are you ever going to open them?' Carver's impatient expression brought her out of her trance-like state.

'Will you do it? Now it's come to it, I feel rather sick.'

He picked up the first envelope and pulled the contents out onto the table.

These weren't photographs and it took a while to register what the documents were.

'Auction house receipts?'

'What?' Jenny moved to look at what Carver was holding in his hands.

Carver grabbed a couple more and examined them more closely. 'Interestingly, they all seem to be for purchases of clocks or watches.'

'The ones in the box, perhaps?'

'And the one we found buried, maybe? We'll have to look more closely later.'

He picked up the second envelope, looking at Jenny before he shook the contents on top of the other papers.

They both stared in silence at the images.

Carver began to sort them out, lining them up facing towards Jenny. There were wedding photographs, other group photographs and a single portrait of a man. Neither of them spoke until he'd checked the envelope was empty and the photographs were arranged across the table.

Carver picked up the photograph of the man on his own and, after a brief look at it, placed it into Jenny's shaking hands. 'Well?'

'This most definitely isn't the man I met tonight.'

Carver sat back in the chair and huffed out a long breath. 'You are convinced, even given the passage of all this time?'

'One hundred per cent sure.'

'So, who the hell was the man you met and why would he be impersonating your father?'

Adding to the emotion of confusion was the relief that his own father had spoken the truth.

'I've no idea. If I felt sick before I opened the envelopes, I feel even worse now.'

'I can fully understand that. I think we might need a trip to the police station.'

'But what can we say? What can we prove? As far as we are aware no crime has been committed.'

'Maybe not yet, but you've got to admit this is all very weird and that guy *was* impersonating your father.'

'What could he hope to gain from me?'

'I can't help thinking this is related in some way to things being moved at Tree Tops – to those holes we found.'

'Maybe.'

'I think we at least need to alert the police that something odd is happening around here.'

'Not tonight. I can't face it tonight.' Jenny was back to looking ashen again.

'Tomorrow, then. And ... I'm not leaving you here on your own. Pack a bag, you're coming home with me.'

She didn't argue. By the time she'd gathered a few essentials, he'd packed the photographs and papers back into the envelopes, washed up the mugs and put the loft ladder and hatch back into place.

They didn't say much as she locked the house. She looked warily around them all the time until they were in his truck and continually scanned behind them as he drove to Tree Tops.

Carver carried her bag and held her arm firmly as they walked through the trees to the house. 'Where's Wilf?' she asked.

'I'm still a bit nervous to leave him here on his own after that digging incident the other day, so he's staying with Kieron and Nina. Nina is quite happy to have a guard dog, given what's been going on here. I think it's made her nervous too.'

He scanned the area surrounding the house and checked the door was still locked, before opening it. He motioned Jenny to go through into the house and then hauled up the stepladder, so that they were marooned in their own wooden island.

'Hot chocolate before bed?'

'Yes, please, yummy.'

She took the photograph of her real father out of the envelope she had brought with her and stared at it. She was still staring at it when he returned with two steaming mugs.

'This is just the photograph I was hoping for. Ever since I saw yours in the kitchen, I've wanted one of my own framed on the wall at home.'

Given what she'd just said, Carver didn't dare tell Jenny how he had used the photograph in his kitchen over the years. Whereas he still asked Bliss for the answers to questions and advice, as he had done when she was alive, he used his father's image in the picture as someone to blame when things went wrong and as a focus for his anger. Maybe all that could change now his dad had reappeared and he could get to know an actual person rather than a static image.

'I've put a hot water bottle in your side of the bed.'

'That's kind.'

He could tell she was totally caught up in her thoughts about her father.

'I noticed some patchwork quilts around your house,' he said, to distract her. 'Did your mother make them?'

'No, that's my hobby. I love sewing.'

'Ah, great. I hoped that might be the case. Maybe you can help me out then.'

She looked at him curiously, before responding. 'Yes. I've done it for years. I find it very relaxing and it's in a way like your woodwork in that the combination of materials is almost alchemical.'

'Well, I've been given a special commission to carve the characters for a nativity scene outside Borteen Church. As you know, I repaired the pulpit recently. Well, a while back there was a notice appealing for items for a raffle. I gave them a figure I'd carved and I guess the vicar got the idea from that.'

'How is the nativity scene going?'

'It's actually quite strange. I'm finding it hard carving the male characters. I have no problem with females, but the men are a different matter. But I have an idea.'

'The way you are looking at me I have a horrible feeling it involves me.'

'How about a joint effort?'

'But I can't carve wood, although I've always fancied a go.'

'Well, I'm sure I can arrange for you to do that, but what I mean is, how about I carve the figures and you dress them? You could have great fun with cloaks for the kings.'

'A lot of work though, but go on. You give me a wood carving lesson and I'll sew some cloaks.'

Carver smiled happily at her, before remembering why she was in his home in the first place.

'Come on, let's get some sleep. In the morning we need to decide what to do about this man impersonating your father.'

'Can we ask your dad about him?'

'I was thinking that would be a good idea, so we can get our story straight before we approach the police.'

# Chapter Twenty-Nine

Jenny tossed and turned. Carver was fast asleep, breathing evenly, so she tried not to yank at the quilt. Every time she fell asleep she was plagued by dreams about her father and then he became the imposter, his face morphing into a garish mask, as he threatened her. She never quite managed to get to the bottom of what he wanted, but the look in his eyes jerked her awake every time.

Carver's voice whispered in the darkness, 'Jenny, are you awake?'

She groaned in answer.

'You okay? You cried out.'

'Did I? I'm having nightmares ... about fathers.'

He switched on the bedside lamp on his side of the bed, shielding her eyes with his hand.

'Understandable, I guess. Can I get you a drink?'

'I'm sorry I've woken you. A tea would be absolutely lovely.'

He must think she was made of tea. She always seemed to be drinking it when they were together. The room was freezing. She shrugged down in the duvet, while she listened to the sounds of him making the drinks in the kitchen below.

'Are you cold?' he asked, when he came back into the room.

'It is rather chilly.'

'I think we've got our first frost of the year. Come and have a look out of the window.'

She pulled on her dressing gown, tried to tidy her hair with her fingers and went with him onto the landing. It was a clear night and the scene outside the window was illuminated in the moonlight.

The branches of the trees, now virtually devoid of leaves, were coated in heavy frost. It was a magical sight.

Carver pulled her back against his chest and she delighted in the warmth of him.

'Shall we go and get warm in bed?'

'Yes, we mustn't let the drinks go cold now you've bothered to make them.'

She thought maybe drinking the tea wasn't quite what he was referring to. He put on her bedside lamp and propped up the pillows for her to sit against. It suddenly felt rather odd and a little uncomfortable to be about to get back into his former marital bed. The way his face suddenly changed in the lamplight made her think the same thought had just occurred to him.

Leaving her dressing gown on, she sat back against the pillows. She'd never encountered a widower before. The men she'd dated had been single, separated or divorced. It struck her that he was very different, as he'd never stopped loving Bliss, rather had her snatched away from him. It was uncharted territory for Jenny.

As if he'd read her thoughts yet again, Carver almost continued the debate she'd been having in her head.

'I never imagined I would meet anyone else after losing Bliss.' He paused. 'I just don't want you to think that *this* is all about sex. I can't deny that part of my heart will always have *Bliss* engraved on it, but I'm starting to care for you ... a lot.'

She could tell by his expression that the feelings had been awkward for him to articulate and that made her appreciate them all the more. 'It's mutual.'

'I'm glad.' He put down his cup and grasped her hand, rubbing it lightly to warm it up. 'We have no way of knowing what is to come over the next few days, as we unravel this mystery surrounding our fathers, but whatever it is, I hope we are strong enough to weather the storm together.' He squeezed her hand again.

Somehow, his last words blew an ice-cold sensation over her body. Was it a premonition, a sign? Had Bliss's ghost just got into bed with them or was she just being silly?

'Look, I hope you don't think I'm making overtures ... erm, trying to take advantage of you. Would you prefer to go downstairs and I'll light the wood burner?'

She giggled and pulled the covers up to her chin. 'It's fine, and I never imagined you were making ... overtures! Just being nice and trying to explain your feelings.'

He laughed too. 'I'm still half asleep.'

'Sorry about waking you.'

She sipped the hot soothing liquid. They sat side by side with a gap between them. It didn't feel right to be apart.

'Do you want to talk about the nightmares?'

'Not really, I'm sure you can guess what they are about.'

'Fathers, blasted fathers. We've neither of us been lucky on that score.'

Jenny woke the next morning snuggled up to a warm chest. Lying still, she felt Carver's body rise and fall with each breath and worried that she might have dribbled on his T-shirt.

She couldn't remember finishing her tea, or going to sleep. They hadn't made love, or 'overtures' as he referred to it. The memory of him using that word unfortunately led to uncontrollable giggles. She rolled onto the other side of the bed and tried to stifle them with the duvet, but the bed was vibrating despite her best efforts.

A concerned voice from beside her made her realise she'd failed.

'Jenny, Jenny. Are you crying?'

She rolled onto her back and allowed her laughter to come out.

'What on earth are you laughing about at this time in the morning?' He was leaning up on one elbow now and began laughing too.

'Sorry, something just tickled me.' She didn't dare tell him what for fear of denting his male ego.

'What day is it?'

'Saturday, I believe.'

'Great. Breakfast and then a wood carving lesson?'

'Sounds perfect.'

By mutual unspoken agreement, neither of them mentioned the fact they had shared a bed for the night without any *overtures*.

Fuelled by bacon and eggs, Jenny felt quite perky considering her broken night and the worries about who her real father was. They went across to the wood carving clearing. Carver insisted on her wearing ear defenders, a mask, heavy gloves and a thick apron for protection.

'Isn't this a bit over the top,' she mumbled through the mask.

'Maybe, but I don't want to be responsible for you being injured.'

He set up a log in front of her. 'Now, have a good look at the log first. I always find the piece speaks to me and I can read where to make the cuts. Let me know when you have some ideas.'

Jenny skirted the log in her unfamiliar garb and could see nothing at all to suggest a pattern in the piece of wood.

It looked like a log.

Just a log.

It didn't speak to her and she began to think this was a bad idea. She had a horrible feeling she was about to make a fool of herself.

'Well, anything?'

'Nothing, I'm afraid. How about you?'

'Yes, but this is your piece. I can see several possibilities, but you are going to be the one doing the cutting. Take a deep breath, relax and look. You are probably feeling too much under pressure and that's stopping you *reading* the wood.'

Unconvinced, Jenny did as she was told and suddenly noticed a grain in the wood she hadn't seen before. 'Yes! I can see an owl.'

'Great. Now take it slowly, you can always cut a little more off, but you can't stick it back on once you've sliced it off.'

That statement made her feel even more nervous, but oblivious Carver put the heavy chainsaw in her hands. She sliced tentatively at one side and then lost the plot entirely. She couldn't see the owl any more, just the dangerous, sharp blade. The unfamiliar weight and vibrations unnerved her. She moved the saw away from the wood and Carver, sensing that something was wrong, took it from her and switched it off.

'What's the matter?'

'I can't do it. I'm so scared of making a mess that I've lost sight of the owl.'

'I can see it. Come here.'

He fired up the saw again and put it into Jenny's hands. Then he stood behind her and guided her arms. The crude shape of an owl began to appear and then the bird's ears, nose, and feathers. Carver was a real master of the saw, she realised. There was something surprisingly sensual about allowing him to guide her arms with his body close up behind hers, his warmth reaching her even through the layers of their clothing. They were producing something artistic together despite her hesitancy. Her heart was thudding with exhilaration.

By the time the owl had a very wise, life-like expression, Jenny's arms ached terribly. Carver finally switched off the saw.

She removed her mask and ear defenders. 'That was amazing. I wish I had half your skill. Can we do that again sometime?'

'If you like.' He was laughing, but she knew it was with excitement and happiness too. 'Now, what are you going to call him?'

'How do you know it's a he?' She put a hand out to touch the carving. 'I'll call him Wisel, I think.'

'And would you like to take Wisel home to put in your garden?'

'Oh, yes, please. Can I really?' She kissed him tentatively, the first time they'd made any loving contact since their serious conversation in the night. It was weird that declaring they were beginning to feel something for each other had appeared to drive a wedge between them. She sincerely hoped it was temporary.

'Come on, you can help me to load him into my truck.'

'How will we get him to where your pick-up is parked? He's too heavy, surely?'

'I have a trolley.'

Cue much grunting and laughter as they worked together to get the owl onto the trolley.

'We're a good team,' said Carver, before turning to trundle the trolley through the wood.

When they got to Jenny's house, Carver manhandled the heavy owl from his truck onto the trolley again and round to the back garden. Jenny ran around opening the gate and moving things out of the way. There was a stepping stone halfway up the rockery that formed a perfect perch for the wooden bird. Carver was out of breath when he'd finished positioning it.

'Have you been doing some gardening?'

'No, why?'

Carver pointed to two patches of disturbed earth just below the rockery.

'Goodness, someone has been digging in my garden.'

'Trying to find the box we've already found, would be my guess.'

'But how brazen to dig here in daylight.'

'It might have been overnight, remember. May be worth

264

asking if the neighbours saw anything, but my guess is it will have been done while everyone was out or asleep.'

'And we have no way of knowing if they found anything else.' Jenny felt a shaky feeling in her body again, the joviality and companionship of the last few hours forgotten.

'I'm not happy leaving you here on your own, given someone has been exploring your garden.'

'I'm not that happy myself, but I have to live my life, Carver. You can check no one is in the house and then I'll lock myself in.'

'You sure it wouldn't be better if you stayed with me for a while?'

The offer was tempting given the feeling of vulnerability spreading through her.

'No. I promise to keep my phone close by and to ring you if I'm worried. You take care too.'

'I think we need to have that meeting with at least my dad as soon as possible, yours too if he's flown here already. I'll ring my father and set something up. Then, we're going to the police.'

Carver insisted on checking Jenny's house thoroughly. She tried not to show just how nervous she was about him leaving.

The house felt very empty when he'd driven away and she jumped at every sound. She rang her close neighbours, but neither side had been aware of any unusual activity in Jenny's garden.

She curled up in her favourite chair and thought through the events of the last couple of days. The rerun of the conversation with the man who had claimed to be her father kept being interrupted by memories of waking up snuggled close to Carver's body. A sigh escaped her lips. She was terribly afraid she was falling heavily for the handsome, sometimes surly, carpenter.

# Chapter Thirty

Things moved fast. By Monday afternoon, Jenny was walking to The Crimson Sheep café in Sowden with some reluctance. After her recent experiences, she had almost not co-operated, as she didn't trust anything to do with her father. How on earth could she ever be sure exactly what the truth was?

Carver had arranged for her to finally meet her supposed real father, Timothy Simpson, in advance of a gathering when Carver and his father would join them, hopefully to discuss what had happened in the past and why someone would bother to pretend to be Jenny's dad.

The man they now called 'The Imposter' had rung her on Sunday evening, wanting to meet up with her again. Jenny had found it difficult not to challenge him there and then, but she and Carver had discussed the importance of not revealing they were aware of any deception to avoid scaring him off, until they had at least some answers.

How could someone be so cruel as to play with her emotions in this way, and to what purpose? She'd been polite and put 'The Imposter' off until Wednesday evening, claiming to be busy. When she had put the phone down she had screamed and shouted her annoyance and frustration to her lounge wall.

Carver had chosen Sowden for the meeting of the families in case 'The Imposter' was lurking around in Borteen. Jenny hated all this sneaking around, but she knew it was necessary.

They had discussed a strategy for the meeting at The Crimson Sheep and decided not to tell their dads about finding the clock in Jenny's garden, or indeed to volunteer much information about anything, until the two men had told their own story. But could they actually trust what their fathers would say?

Jenny had been very careful to ensure that she wasn't being followed as she left the archives after work and had taken a very circuitous route to get to the café. It wasn't beyond the bounds of possibility that 'The Imposter' was still following her.

As she got close to the café door, her heart began to pound.

Could she trust this?

Who was her real father?

Would she ever believe now that anyone was her genuine dad after what had happened?

Maybe she needed to insist on a DNA test, but goodness only knew how long that would take to process.

She'd been instinctively aware that something was strange about the man who had turned up at the archives proclaiming to be Timothy Simpson, so she'd just have to trust her gut instinct this time too. *Stay alert, Jenny*.

As it was, she needn't have worried. The man sitting at the table in the corner of the café waiting for her looked familiar and had the dimples she'd noticed on the photographs she now had displayed in the lounge at home. The dimples were indeed replicas of the ones in her own reflection in the mirror. However, the recognition that this was actually her father didn't make her feel any warmer towards the man.

Timothy Simpson grasped her hands and squeezed almost painfully in his enthusiasm.

'Jenny. I always knew you would turn out to be beautiful.' His accent was a strange mix of Borteen vowel sounds with foreign accents she couldn't quite identify. Was it Italian? Portuguese?

'I'm sorry if this seems cruel, but I need you to prove that you are my father and not another imposter,' challenged Jenny.

His face crumpled. 'I understand, love. Michael told me someone had turned up pretending to be me. It must have been very scary.'

'It was and I need to know why on earth someone would do that.' She sat down heavily on the chair opposite to the man.

'First things first, let me help make you feel sure of me. You have a mole next to your belly button that looks like a dolphin.'

Jenny felt colour flush her cheeks. 'Not exclusive enough.'

'Your mother's favourite perfume was lavender.'

Jenny shook her head.

'Okay, how about your doll when you were four? She was called Suki.'

'Dad? How can I ever trust that it's you?'

'Did you find my letters to your mother?'

'Letters? No, nothing.' Jenny was stunned. 'Are you saying that you've been writing to Mum all this time?'

'We weren't in touch for many years after I … left, but in the last few years I made contact again. I sent her some of my paintings and she told me she was ill.'

Jenny knew straight away that the colourful pictures in the hallway must be the ones he was referring to.

'Did you still love her, Dad?'

'I never stopped loving either of you.'

'Then why did you go? I don't understand any of this.' She felt tears threatening and shook her head to try to drive away the emotion. She would need a clear head to discover the truth, if she ever could.

Staring at her father, it looked as if the years hadn't been that kind to him and it was difficult to associate this almost sixty-year-old, slightly overweight man with the christening photographs of him holding Jenny high in the air that she'd found in the loft.

She hadn't been able to help loving those snapshots of a happier time as tangible proof that she did indeed have a father. The man in those photographs had appeared taller, had a shock of blond curls and a huge smile. Timothy had lost all but a skirting of hair and what was left was grey. The deep furrows in his brow and around his eyes spoke of a habit of worrying.

'You don't like what you see, do you?'

Timothy's comment startled her and she realised that she must have been staring hard at him during her appraisal.

'I'm afraid I feel completely detached at the moment. After all, I don't know you, do I?'

The words weren't quite true, her mind was in turmoil and her inner child kept threatening to resurface.

'Do you think you would be willing to *get* to know me?'

'To be honest, I don't see why I should.' That petulant inner child was stamping her feet.

'I suppose I've given up that right, but I'm still your father.'

'I think they refer to it as "birth father".' Oops, now the inner teenager was getting involved.

'That's a bit harsh, love.' The furrows on his brow were growing deeper.

'Is it? Wasn't it harsh to leave Mum and me struggling to pay the bills? Wasn't it harsh to leave me to the ridicule of my classmates at school, because I didn't have a dad? Harsh to leave me to my own insecurities about not being good enough for my own father?'

Jenny was alarmed to see a tear appear at the corner of Timothy's eye. She wasn't normally this forthright or hard, but the events of the last week had made her wary and suspicious.

'I guess I deserved all that.'

They sat in silence for a while. Jenny began to worry at a loose thread on her cardigan.

'Will you at least give me the chance to explain everything?'

She huffed out a long breath and forced a smile. 'Strange, I knew that other man wasn't my father. I didn't give him a chance, because it just didn't feel right.'

'Could it ... does it feel right with me?'

'Strangely, yes. I mean I can't pretend I'm not upset and angry – and you can understand how I feel after that man pretended to be you – but, yes, it feels much better.' She tested a smile. It didn't feel natural.

The waitress bustled over and they didn't say anything to each other until she had disappeared with their order.

'Everything seems so different here. Sowden has grown so big over the years.'

Jenny let him talk. He was obviously as nervous as she was. She observed his face and his mannerisms. Yes, this was her father. She fought down a spark of anger over the fact that he could have abandoned her for so long. His story better be good.

Cups, a jug of milk and a teapot were put in front of them by the waitress and Jenny served it out, asking her father how he took his tea, whilst lamenting the fact that she should damned well know how her own father liked his drinks. Considering she drank so much of the beverage, it was strange that she didn't feel she could face this particular brew. Her stomach was churning.

She thought maybe she should wait for Carver before starting to question Timothy, but she couldn't keep quiet any longer; her curiosity was bristling. 'Come on then, Dad. I'm going to get straight to the point. Where have you been all this time and why? And what is your connection to Michael Rodgers?'

Timothy grasped his teacup and looked in danger of snapping off the handle, he was gripping it so tightly. He took a large slurp of much too hot tea that made him choke. His face went puce. The tea must have been scalding. Jenny offered him her napkin.

She kept her eyes trained on his, refusing to look away. It was time for him to be honest. Time for him to face the music, if they were to stand any chance of salvaging some sort of ongoing relationship or even a civil parting.

'I knew you would want some answers today. Any explanations I come up with sound so hollow, but here goes.' He sat up straighter and returned her stare. 'Jenny, love, I more than … know Mike. He's been my partner for the last twenty-five years.'

'Business partner?'

'Yes … and no. We have run businesses together and … we … we've also been living together … as a couple.'

It was Jenny's turn to go red. She felt her emotions swirling across her face as she tried to decide how to react. She slurped her too hot tea and ended up choking just as he had. Timothy stood up and patted her on the back. She wasn't in any way homophobic, but this was her dad. It felt weird to contemplate him with another man, he'd been married to her mother for goodness' sake.

'You mean that you ran away to be with Carver's father … as … lovers?'

'In a nutshell, yes, although it was much more complicated than that. You have to understand that even twenty-five years ago society's views on a man living with another man were very different, especially if those men already had wives and children.'

'I appreciate that, but why all the secrecy with us? Did Mum know?'

Timothy nodded. 'Or, at least she did … eventually. I don't

think she believed it when Mike's wife first told her of her own suspicions. It led to them falling out.'

So that was why the two abandoned wives hadn't seemed friendly. Jenny felt her heart plummet. 'I don't understand why Mum couldn't tell me. Why wouldn't she explain what happened and why it happened?'

'How do you think she felt? And don't for one moment imagine I was oblivious to all that. Being rejected for another woman would be bad enough, but for another man? I know it devastated her, but I couldn't continue living a lie. I tried for so long. Michael and I fell in love. We were both married with children, so for a long time, we attempted to carry on as normal at home and met in secret whenever we could.'

Jenny was aware that her mouth was set in a severe line, so she made an effort to rearrange her features. She needed him to talk freely, not to clam up because of her disapproval. 'I don't quite know what to say.'

'I never stopped loving your mum or you ... it's just I loved Michael more, and then ... other things happened that made it impossible to carry on as we were.' He looked into his teacup, as emotions battled across his face.

'Other things? Has Carver's dad explained all this to him?'

'Carver? I thought Mike's son was called Damien?'

'He's not gone by that name for years. He's called Carver.'

'Okay, right, well I don't think Mike has explained anything to him yet. They've had one meeting so far and I think it was rather strained, frosty even.'

'Understandably, in my view. Well, I'm not sure how he'll react to this news.'

'It may be better if we are both around when Michael explains to ... Carver, but we can only take things as they come, people react in different ways. Michael and I were discussing that this morning in the car on the way from the airport.'

'So where have you been all of this time?'

'We've been living in Spain. But there is much more to our story than just falling in love.'

Spain, so that explained the accented tones, but how did this simple explanation account for someone bothering to impersonate her father? As he had hinted, it couldn't be that straightforward.

The café door opened. Jenny's legs turned to jelly as Carver and his dad entered through the door. They looked so alike it was unreal, even walking in a similar way. It was a relief to see Carver. He would support her through this. She longed already for him to take her hand, for some physical contact between them. She needed to feel the warmth of him, but she couldn't shake the thought that it was somehow weird that she and Carver were having a relationship if their fathers were too. Incestuous almost, except she and Carver shared no blood, thankfully.

She knew enough about Carver's moods by now to see that he was tense and controlled. His body was stiff in a checked shirt and jeans, his trademark boots rumpling the hems of the trousers.

How would he react to the news about their fathers being lovers? It wasn't one of the scenarios they had put on their brainstorming list. Or would he already have guessed, or been told on the way to the café? She began to feel really sick, even more so when Carver smiled broadly when he caught sight of her.

Michael introduced Carver to Timothy, pausing over his name, because he must have spent all of these years referring to his son as Damien. Timothy introduced Jenny to Michael, calling her *my lovely daughter*. Despite her mixed feelings, a lump came to Jenny's throat at the sound of pride in Timothy's voice.

They moved to a bigger table. Jenny and Carver sat on

273

chairs at one side. There was a period of confusion whilst more tea and some cakes were ordered. Carver briefly squeezed her hand, but didn't do anything to show the fathers that they were intimate with each other.

It was strangely uncomfortable watching her dad and Michael sitting together on the sofa opposite, their legs very close, their postures mirrored. She noticed that they wore identical signet rings on their wedding ring fingers. They began bickering like an old married couple, which was, of course, in effect what they were. Jenny wanted to ask whether they had been officially married, but she supposed it hardly mattered if the two men had been together for over twenty-five years and she was pretty sure her mother had never been divorced. Then again, would she have told Jenny if she was? She had many questions, but did she really want to know the answers?

A large pot of tea and a selection of cakes arrived. The waitress coming to the table silenced the group until she had unloaded her tray.

Carver appeared to have lost his tongue. His face was as sullen as in the early days of Jenny knowing him. She resigned herself to the fact that she would have to be spokesperson. She let Michael Rodgers pour the tea and then began.

'We asked you both here today because there have been some strange goings on which we believe may be connected to you two.'

'What sort of strange things? I know someone has been impersonating Tim?' Michael Rodgers appeared to be the more dominant of the pairing. Jenny wished again that she had a sign that Carver was aware of the relationship between their two fathers.

'Yes, someone claiming to be Timothy Simpson made contact with me last week.'

'Well, it wasn't me, I was still in Spain.'

'I know that now. I didn't then. As I said, someone

pretending to be you contacted me and I've met him twice already and spoken to him several times on the telephone. I haven't challenged him about his identity yet and I'm supposed to meet him again on Wednesday evening.'

The two men opposite looked thoughtful. Jenny was certain they knew something more, but would they tell Carver and her their secrets?

'If I'd had a photograph of you, Dad, I might have smelt a rat much sooner. But Mum had hidden all of the pictures of you away in the loft.' She waited while her words sank in. 'Why would anyone pretend to be you? What is there to gain?' As promised, she tried not to reveal too much to begin with. She was curious what the dads would say; she could almost feel Carver's curiosity bristling next to her.

Timothy looked at Michael, who nodded encouragement. 'There's an obvious explanation. When we lived in Borteen we both worked in normal jobs. I was a car mechanic and Tim worked at the auction house in Sowden, but we also had a business venture on the side. We used to buy clocks and watches at auctions.'

Carver chipped in. 'Why on earth would you do that?'

'It was a shared interest. They often go very cheaply at auction, especially if they're damaged. We used to restore them, or rather Tim did, and then we'd sell them on again, hopefully, but not always, at a profit.'

Jenny and Carver exchanged another look, as if reinforcing to each other not to volunteer information. It was crucial to wait for their dads to tell them their story.

'I have noticed that there are quite a few clocks in my mother's house.'

Carver voiced a question next. 'So what have clocks got to do with someone pretending to be Jenny's father, you two going away twenty-five years ago and hiding away all of this time?'

275

'We were not hiding. We have a house in the hills of Spain.'

'How do the locals react to you two?'

Jenny let out a breath. Carver did know.

'In our village, they just accept us as an eccentric couple. We don't exactly walk around holding hands all the time, we've been together too long for that.'

Michael playfully nudged Timothy. Jenny wondered if she imagined her father's strained expression.

'So, carry on, why the sudden departure from England?' Carver's tone was now icy and impatient.

'Things got a little tricky.'

'With the relationship or the business?'

'Both, actually.'

Jenny was feeling uneasy. 'But how can things ever get tricky over buying and selling clocks?'

The two older men looked at each other and seemed to collectively let out a breath. Michael squeezed Timothy's arm, before they turned to face their children.

'We bought one lot at auction. It was a Victorian clock in a tall wooden case. Nothing particularly remarkable.'

It was difficult for Jenny to keep a straight face and she dared not look at Carver, not yet.

'We had a look at the clock when the auction house held their viewing day and we thought, if we got it for the right price and polished it up, we could make a small profit. You see we knew, one day, we might want or even ... have to ... go away together and we were trying to save up funds for our ... escape.'

Timothy chipped in. 'We were adamant we wouldn't take money out of what we were earning for our families, so this was an alternative way. Although it was proving torturously slow to put money aside.'

Michael ran a weary hand over his face. 'But it seems

there was more to this clock than we realised. The auction was quite straightforward, but a man rushed in at the last minute and protested that the lot had gone to sale without him being there, without his permission. He came up to us in the car park when we were taking the clock home and he said that he'd double the price we paid to buy it from us then and there.'

'Why didn't we accept his offer?' Timothy said wistfully.

'Well, with hindsight, we should have done.'

Carver was getting fidgety next to Jenny. 'What happened?' he prompted.

'We refused to sell. I didn't like the guy's tone or manner and became stubborn about the whole thing. There was no way I was going to let him have the clock. We'd bid for it and bought it legitimately, everything above board. If he'd wanted it, he should have been at the auction in time for the bidding.'

Timothy took up the story. 'We didn't realise the guy had followed us. He tailed us to our usual meeting place and ... well, let's just say he saw enough to know that we were lovers. He must have followed us both home too, because he was aware we had wives and children, plus our home addresses.'

'He tried to blackmail us into giving him the clock. He made no attempt to offer us money again,' said Michael.

'We couldn't understand what was going on. It was surreal and threatening.'

'I was scared he'd tell your mum, Carver.'

'I still don't understand. Why didn't you just give him the damned clock?' Jenny was getting exasperated. The solution sounded so simple to her. Was it possible that her whole life had been changed by ... a clock?

'With hindsight, everything looks straightforward, I'm afraid. I was angry. I mean we'd bought the clock legitimately. We were desperately trying to scrape together enough to be able to tell our wives about our relationship and set up home together.'

'In those days, we didn't imagine moving far from our children, from you. We were naïve … stupid.'

'So what changed?' Carver's eyes held flames of anger, his words delivered staccato.

'I was polishing the disputed clock and, by accident, found a secret compartment. The drawer only opened if you rubbed a certain part of the clock case.'

Jenny sat forward on her chair. 'And … what was in this … compartment?' It was what she'd wondered ever since she'd found the secret catch on the clock and revealed the large drawer.

'Money and jewellery.'

All four of them fell silent. Jenny chanced a look at Carver. His face was thunderous and that was an understatement. She wished she hadn't eaten a cream cake. Half of the cake sat uncomfortably in her emotional, swirling stomach and the other half was stuck in her throat.

'I know what you're thinking. We should have gone to the police or at least back to the auction house to say what we'd found – but we didn't. You must understand that we were petrified of having our secret lives exposed, of our home lives falling apart … before we were ready.'

Timothy had gone quite red. 'The man said the clock had been sold without his permission. He didn't say anything about the contents, so neither did we.'

'So, then what?' asked Jenny.

'We discussed and discussed it, and eventually decided to bury the clock and scarper with the money. It felt like our one chance, you see. Knowing it was probably only a matter of time before the threatening man revealed our secret, we left in a hurry the next day, using some of the cash to finance our journey. We hitchhiked to Dover and got a ferry across to France and then hitched down to Spain. We paid for new documents with different names and gave cash for the rent on the first apartment we stayed in. We've been in Spain ever since, but in the early days we moved around a lot.'

The two men sat back and glanced at each other. They looked relieved to have finally told their story.

'Exactly how much money are we talking about?' asked Carver through gritted teeth.

'A lot,' answered Michael.

Jenny began mentally working out how much would fit in the compartment in the clock.

'How much?' Carver pushed for an answer.

'It was stacked with fifty pound notes. Around one hundred thousand pounds' worth.'

'Not a vast amount,' commented Carver.

'Remember it was worth more twenty-five years ago.'

'What about the jewellery?' asked Jenny.

'We buried that on your grandmother's land,' Michael answered, looking at his son.

'At Tree Tops?' said Carver.

'It wasn't called that then.'

Jenny looked at Carver and he nodded.

'We found the clock. The one you buried.'

Two pairs of eyes immediately fixed onto her face from across the table. Timothy went red once again.

'How on earth? We had to take up paving slabs to bury it. Had to wait until your mum had taken you to see your grandmother.'

'I've had a conservatory built at the back of Mum's house. The builder found the box you buried.'

'Well, who would have thought it. We imagined it would never be found.' Michael slurped more tea, unable to resist grasping Timothy's knee.

279

Did they both look furtive and sheepish, or was she just over-analysing?

'Thing is, love, the guy who was after us then has found us again.' Timothy's face was even redder.

'After all this time?' Jenny could feel the cogs whirring in her brain.

'Well, I think it was because we were stupid. We began collecting clocks at auction again. Anyway, he set thugs on us in Spain. We both got beaten up last month.' Michael rubbed a reddened patch on the side of his jaw.

'We were given a warning message to return what we'd "taken", or else.' Timothy drew brackets in the air as he said the word taken.

'Right, that settles it, we go to the police right now.' Carver's voice barely concealed his anger.

Michael put his cup back on his saucer with a rattle. 'There's just the small matter of the large amount of cash we took and spent that wasn't ours!'

Carver's voice had a thread of steel. 'I still can't get my head around the fact that you left your families with no explanation. I've spent my whole life thinking it was all my fault.'

Michael tried to clasp Carver's arm, but he shook him off. 'Of course it wasn't your fault, son. I've spent my life with regrets and guilt, but at the end of the day I had to be true to myself, and Tim. We believed that a shock revelation, by us or this man, would have been more harmful than just disappearing, but who knows if we were right.'

'And now it seems you've put Jenny and me in danger too.'

'We've no reason to believe he would harm you.'

'Yes, right … someone has been in my house, someone has been digging in the forest, in Jenny's garden too … who knows what someone with a grudge is capable of.' Carver pushed his chair back with a screech from the legs grating on the wooden floor. He stood, towering over the table. 'Look, I can't deal with all this right now. I'm starting to feel very angry, so I'm going to take a walk.'

He looked briefly at Jenny and then strode for the door. Jenny was uncertain whether to follow him or stay put. She decided to see if she could gain any more information from the dads, as the whole thing was as clear as mud so far.

'I hear what you two are saying about the past, but I can't even begin to understand or excuse it. There has been strange activity at Carver's house and mine and that man tried to make out he was my dad. Do we have a name? He knows about us. What does he want exactly? Does he believe you still have his clock? Is the clock valuable? Rare? Or is it just about the money and jewellery? Was the jewellery valuable?'

The barrage of questions poured out of her. The dads looked at each other. She still had a strange feeling about all this.

'At the time the cash gave us our ticket out of here and we took it. I don't think the clock is valuable. It's more a link to the past. He can't let go.'

'So did *he* put the money and jewels in the clock? And … and … how did it end up being sold? And why wait this long before trying to get it back? It makes no sense, anyone would know the things would be long gone by now.'

'We don't know, love. But he wants his money and jewellery back, has threatened us and … you.'

'Threatened me? Don't you think you should have told me about that?'

'We thought it was an empty threat, we never imagined he'd make contact with you. We don't know his name, not his real one anyway. All those years before he called himself Robert McBrae, but we never thought that was actually his name.'

Jenny was now feeling very cross. The imposter had used the name Robert at the archives that day, so it was more than likely the same man. Jenny was mentally trying to decide if that much money could possibly have been concealed in the secret compartment in the clock and why this man had suddenly reappeared after all of this time.

'Did you tell this Robert's men about burying the jewellery at Tree Tops?'

'I might have mentioned it ...' said Timothy.

Michael looked at him sharply.

She noticed that both Timothy and Michael were getting more and more uncomfortable. Both were straightening their clothes and shifting on their seats. She had the distinct impression they weren't telling her the full story, or even the truth. It seemed pointless to push any more when they weren't ready to tell the whole tale.

She made a decision. 'I think I'd better go and find Carver. Can I have your mobile number, Dad?'

Timothy scribbled a number on a serviette and handed it to her. 'I realise this all sounds awful, a sorry tale. And believe me, we are both sorry ... very sorry about everything.'

'I need to think all this over. I'll be in touch very soon.'

'Just take care.' The thought of the unknown man after his money, jewellery, clock and possibly revenge hung in the air between them.

# Chapter Thirty-One

Jenny left the café, her thoughts confused. She had the feeling that she was staring at the tip of an iceberg and that there was so much more to the story of the fathers to be revealed. There were questions she hadn't asked and questions she had asked which hadn't been fully answered, but it felt more important to find Carver right now. They would have to arrange to see their fathers again very soon.

She glanced nervously around her as she walked through the streets of Sowden, half expecting to see the man who had impersonated her father lurking in the shadows. She decided to call him Robert, it was easier than 'The Imposter'. It was feeling more and more likely that Robert was the aggrieved man who wanted his money and things back. But why would he have waited twenty-five years? The money wouldn't be worth as much now. And why would he imagine Timothy and Michael had kept the clock and jewellery for all of this time?

Instinctively she knew where Carver would be, or at least she hoped so.

She crept down the steps to the cathedral crypt and, at first, she didn't think he was there. Maybe she'd got it wrong.

As her eyes began to adjust to the dim light, she saw Carver, sitting so still in a corner that he looked like a statue in the gloom of the underground room.

He looked up as she approached. He had hollow eyes, red rimmed from obvious crying. He reached up a hand to her; she took it and sank down onto the stone bench beside him.

'What a story.'

'I know. Not quite as fantastical as some of the options on our list, but not far off!'

She leaned her head so that it touched the side of his, she hoped in a gesture of empathy.

He squeezed her hand and rested their joined palms against his warm leg. It seemed inappropriate to feel pleased in such circumstances, but nevertheless, she did.

'What now?'

'Can you give me a lift home? I came from Borteen in my father's car.'

She pressed his hand. 'Come on, let's get out of here. I need to fill you in about what else was said after you left and discuss what didn't add up.'

Jenny could hear that Carver's breathing was a little laboured and she prayed that he had his inhaler with him. Their fathers' revelations had been a shock for both of them. As if in answer he stopped at the top of the crypt steps and took out his inhaler.

'They weren't exactly honest and forthcoming with us, were they?' began Carver as they walked to the car park. 'I don't think we know what actually happened back then, do you?'

She noticed he was glancing around him, as she had done. They were both unnerved by the thought of a predator watching them.

'No, it was as if they were reciting a practiced script and that hurts. The trouble is ... it makes you doubt the information they did volunteer, doesn't it? Do you believe this thing about buying clocks ... about that clock we found?'

'I don't know what to think. It all sounds too simplistic and, I don't know ... like a *cover-up*. But, then again, we did find those auction receipts and the box of clocks and watches in your loft, so the part about buying and selling clocks and watches must be true.'

'Isn't there always a grain of truth in a lie? I think we



284

need to do some research about the prices these clocks fetch at auction and look more closely at the receipts we do have. For one thing, do we have a receipt for the clock they buried? I guess I'm looking for evidence to validate the story we've been fed.'

'You'll have to do the internet research. You might have gathered that I'm not very PC literate. In fact, I don't own many electronic gadgets full stop.'

'Was your wife into computers?' Jenny very rarely asked questions about Bliss and felt scared she might upset him as soon as she had asked.

'She had to use them at work. She was a librarian, but when she got home, she liked the old-fashioned ways. We don't even have a television. I used to spend my evenings whittling wood and she would read. Sometimes she read poetry aloud, or else I would drum and she would sing to her guitar.'

Jenny noted that once again he'd spoken to begin with as if Bliss was still alive. It must be difficult to adjust to being a widower.

'It sounds idyllic.'

'In many ways, it was.' Carver went quiet for a moment and Jenny could tell he was mourning the loss of Bliss yet again.

They reached her car and she smiled at Carver trying to slot his long legs and body into her tiny vehicle. Her mind returned to their fathers as soon as she turned out of the car park.

'I think it might be helpful to go over what we actually know to be true. To summarise the information for ourselves and decide what we think is true or false and where there might be gaps.'

He nodded. 'Sounds good. I'll start. So, as far as I understood it, our dads were saving to run away together when they happened upon a stash of cash and some jewellery hidden in a clock they'd bought at an auction.'

'That about sums it up. Sounds strange, though. I mean what would you do if the same happened to you?' Jenny turned on the indicator and turned right out onto the main road, unable to resist the urge to check if any other cars were following her. She was getting paranoid, but maybe with just cause.

'I'd go straight back to the auction house, or the police, and tell them what I'd found. I mean, finding one hundred thousand isn't like finding a tenner on the street. But then I'm staunchly honest and not in a desperate situation.'

She felt pleased with his response. 'True. We didn't ask them what sort of jewellery they found. The other gem of information was that "someone" tried to buy the clock back and our fathers refused after this "someone" caught them in an … erm … incriminating clinch?'

'I wonder if our mothers ever suspected? Or was it a complete shock when their husbands disappeared?'

'Dad said something about your mother going to see mine because she suspected something, but I guess we will never know exactly what was said. One thing I do remember though was that our mothers were at the police station at the same time, for the same reason, and yet they didn't seem to talk to each other. Dad thought they'd fallen out about your mum's comments.'

'You remember that day much better than I do.'

'A woman, see!' She turned briefly to wink at him and then looked back at the road. 'All I know is that my mum was terribly hurt by her husband leaving her. She forbade me to ever speak of it. I think that did more damage to my state of mind growing up than anything else.'

'My mum wasn't very receptive to discussions about Dad, either. I mean she did discuss it, sort of, if I raised it, but was always happy to change the subject, or talk about him being abducted by aliens.' He fell silent for a moment. 'How are we going to play this from here?'

'We need to do what research into the background we can, then I think we'll have to meet our dads again, question them further and take things from there. See if we can gradually put the whole truth together, because I have a canny feeling we only know a grain of the real story so far. One thing is niggling me ... they said they found the money and left the next day, but before that Dad said he had to wait until Mum went out to bury the clock.'

'And they had to bury the jewels too. I see what you mean, they couldn't have left that quickly ...'

'Also, I don't imagine it would be that easy to spend so many fifty pound notes or to swap them into Spanish currency ... because it was before the euro.'

'True.'

She pretended not to notice how he gripped the door handle of her car as they went around the twisty bends of Pink Moor. She would like to have known whereabouts the fatal accident that had killed Bliss had taken place, not solely from curiosity, but so that she could take extra care when she reached the fateful bend, so as not to unnerve Carver, but it wasn't the sort of thing you asked of a bereaved man.

It was fully dark when she pulled into the layby on the edge of the woods.

'Thanks, Jenny. I need to process all that was said today, but it would be helpful to talk it through again too. I'd rather you stayed with me here at Tree Tops until this situation is clearer and we know that this *Robert* isn't truly a threat to us. I won't sleep thinking about you on your own.'

'That's very kind, but ...' She was about to refuse, to try to be strong, but then she felt a shift in her mind. 'Okay, I feel safe here with you. I'd be grateful to stay, just until we know what's really going on. I'll pop home and pack a bag with a few days' stuff.'

'Right decision, I think. Now, I've arranged to collect some wood I've been promised by the churchwarden to use for carving the nativity figures. Pain to do it now, but he's been away and rang to say he's finally sorted the logs. I wouldn't go, but if I don't crack on the nativity scene is going to be minus shepherds. Come with me and then we can collect your stuff on the way back.'

'No, you go and get the wood. I'll pop back home and pack my bag, maybe get us something for tea from my freezer? Could you collect me about eight?'

'That sounds perfect.' He planted a kiss on her cheek and opened the car door. 'But please ... be careful? Is your phone charged?'

'Yes, Dad.' The words were out of her mouth before she'd realised their inappropriateness.

He smiled anyway and squeezed her arm in farewell. 'I'll see you later then.'

It only hit her as she drove away how dazed she felt. She'd been concerned for Carver's wellbeing, but now the full effect of finding out why her childhood had abruptly changed hit her full force.

A clock of all things! But was this the real story? Was it even plausible? Jenny had a horrible feeling they'd just been fed a lie. It might have grains of truth somewhere, but deep down her gut feeling was that it was a fabrication and didn't really explain the impersonation or the disappearance of the two men all those years ago, the consequences of which she and Carver had been living with ever since.

# Chapter Thirty-Two

She parked in her drive, grateful to switch off the engine. Resting her head on her arms above the steering wheel, she forced herself to breathe deeply and let out some shuddering breaths.

*Pull yourself together, girl. You are not a jelly. You are a strong woman used to looking out for herself.*

It was another of her mother's well-worn maxims.

Jenny laughed aloud as she went straight into the kitchen, filled and switched on the kettle. Her mother would never be completely dead whilst Jenny was repeating her sayings and following her rituals.

She opened the drawer to get out a spoon and noticed the list of goals she'd made what felt like an age away, but in truth it was only a few weeks. She read the points she had written aloud to the empty kitchen.

*Home – Make Mum's house my own. Decorate in my style. Buy lamps. Order conservatory?*

Well, she'd gone a fair way towards making the house her own. She'd got the conservatory and had decorated most rooms. Better buy some more lamps. She smiled.

*Job – What do I want to do? Do I really want to clean for a living?*

Her job at the archives was great, suited her down to the ground and allowed her to indulge her family history hobby too.

*Interests – Join family history group, rambling club, craft group?*

Hmmm, she hadn't done as well on her interests or increasing her social life. She sighed and then sighed again when she read the last item.

*Man – Too complicated – avoid (especially Carver Rodgers).*

Totally failed on avoiding men, in particular Carver Rodgers. She was about to pack to go and stay with him at Tree Tops for goodness' sake … almost moving in. She smiled again. Lost cause, Jenny Simpson.

She turned her mind to what she needed to take with her to Tree Tops. She grabbed her mug of tea and went upstairs to pack her bag.

All of her jewellery was arranged in lines across the bed, her jewellery box discarded empty on the bedside chair.

To begin with she didn't quite register what she was seeing. She sipped her tea as her mind tried to process the scene. She hadn't left her jewellery like this, would not have left it out like this.

Her eyes widened as the truth dawned and ice crept over her skin.

Someone had been in her house.

Had she had burglars? But no, if it had been thieves, her jewellery wouldn't still be here, surely?

Robert?

Was he still here?

Now what?

Her mobile phone was downstairs in her bag. *Stupid, girl.* She stood still and listened.

All was quiet inside the house.

She put her mug of tea on her bedside table with shaking fingers.

Adrenaline took over; she launched herself onto the landing and down the stairs. *Be as quick as you can*, she told herself.

Her handbag was no longer on the kitchen bench where she'd left it.

She reeled around looking for the bag and there he was,

the man who had pretended to be her father, wearing the same camel coloured coat. Robert was smiling, but with an expression that looked sinister.

'Jenny, love.'

'Don't you "love" me!' she yelled, running for the back door. It was locked and the key was no longer in the lock where she normally left it. She pulled ineffectually at the handle.

Turning, she faced him. 'What do you want?' Her eyes scanned around for something to use to break the window, something to use as a weapon. The frying pan, maybe?

'Now, that's no way to speak to your father.'

'But you aren't my father, are you?'

'Come into the lounge. I want to ask you something.'

There didn't seem to be a choice. Jenny walked past him into the lounge, thinking it would buy her time and maybe allow her to escape, or to reach her phone. She had no way of knowing what this man was capable of.

On the coffee table was the clock that had been buried in the garden, its secret compartment gaping open.

She turned cold from head to foot.

'Please sit,' he said as if it was his home and not hers.

She sat on the edge of a chair. Her eyes fixed on the man, whilst her mind darted around trying to decide what to do.

'Now, Jenny. This clock, where did you get it from?'

'I f-found it.'

'Found it?' His eyebrows raised questioningly.

'In the garden.' It felt like sitting in front of a severe headmaster.

'And, when you … *found* it in the garden, was there anything inside this drawer?'

She'd never been a very good liar and whereas she contemplated denying all knowledge of the drawer to begin with, it seemed pointless. 'No, nothing.'

'Are you absolutely sure about that?'

'Yes.'

'No jewellery?'

'Jewellery?'

Suddenly it all became clear. It wasn't the money he was looking for at all. Bliss's jewellery box going missing, her own jewellery strewn across the bed, holes dug in the garden and at Tree Tops. As she and Carver had suspected, there was more to this saga than their fathers had told them ... something to do with ... the jewellery?

'You see, your father made a promise twenty-five years ago and now I want what's due to me.'

'Twenty-five years is almost a lifetime. Why on earth have you left it so long?'

'Almost a life sentence, actually. Small matter of having been in prison for most of those years.'

Jenny's mind was working overtime about what sort of crime he could have committed to end up in prison for that length of time and how her father was connected to such a thing.

'Oh,' was the only sound that would come out of her mouth. Tiredness crept over her and she felt like a deflated balloon. She was scared, yes, but overwhelmingly disappointed that her father had lied this badly to her, or rather omitted this part of the story. A promise? Was her father involved in whatever crime Robert had committed?

'Right.' Robert came to the back of the chair she was sitting on. 'I need you to do something for me.'

'I'm not doing anything for you.'

That was when he took out a knife ...

# Chapter Thirty-Three

'I want you to make a phone call. As you've so rightly surmised, I'm not actually your dad, so I'm guessing you must have been in touch with your real father. Call him.'

The photographs of her real father were behind the man on the sideboard, but she decided not to say anything about that.

He put her mobile phone down in front of her on the table with a snap.

Jenny's hands shook as she picked it up. 'His number's in my bag – written on a serviette.'

He moved across the room to where he'd left her bag, the contents strewn across the chair cushion. The knife blade glinted in his hand as he rummaged around to find the serviette.

Jenny watched him, somehow detached, as if she was watching the scene from above, or on TV, her mind desperately searching for an escape plan.

He placed the rumpled serviette in front of her. 'Call.'

She selected the numbers with fingers that felt too large for the keys.

Timothy answered after several rings.

'Dad, it's Jenny.'

'Are you okay? Your voice sounds strange.'

'Yes ... no ... I don't know. Someone who knows you is here with me. Being threatened with a knife does tend to make your voice weird.'

She was aware of Robert – she still didn't know his real name – coming closer. He grabbed the phone from her and switched it to loud speaker. She heard Timothy Simpson's sharp intake of breath at the other end of the line as the menacing man spoke.

'Well, hello there, Timothy. Long time, no speak. It's time for you to make good on your promise to me, you and Michael blummin' Rodgers. I hope you and lover boy have had a good life living on your ill-gotten gains. Took a while to track you down once I got out of prison, but make no mistake, I've found you now, you and your daughter and Michael and his son. So what's it to be? I want to live out my life in comfort and so you need to pay up, give me what you promised to keep safe for me.'

'I hear you, Arthur.'

Jenny couldn't help blurting out, 'Arthur? I thought you said his name was Robert.'

'Arthur Monkston.' The man bowed in front of her, holding the knife in the air. 'So, Tim, the jewellery wasn't where you said it was. I had a look around Michael's son's ridiculous tree house and had a poke in your lovely daughter's garden and house, but surprise, surprise, nothing there, mate. And don't forget I've got your address in Spain, as you know very well following the *visit* from my friends out there. Surprising who you meet in prison.'

He reached out a finger and traced the curve of Jenny's cheek. She shuddered.

'Where's the stuff you promised to keep safe for me? Don't tell me you've spent the lot. Sold the jewels?'

'Arthur, you have to understand—'

'I understand nothing. I've done my time—'

'We were just meant to drive and carry stuff and you even blackmailed us into that. We didn't know you were going to use a gun ... collect some antiques you said, not steal some antiques and then nearly kill the owners.'

The prickles of fear were magnifying on Jenny's skin. She kept her eyes on the blade of the knife that Arthur was waving around as he spoke. It looked shiny and very sharp.

'I want what I'm due. You promised you'd keep it for

me … promised. And one more thing: absolutely no police, or your daughter gets hurt very badly.'

He waved the knife menacingly towards Jenny and she gulped down a scream, which came out as a whimper.

'I've been inside before remember, it holds no fears for me, so don't think I'll hesitate.'

'Did you … hear all that … Dad?'

'Yes … I heard.'

Jenny jumped, as Arthur suddenly grabbed her hand and squeezed very hard. She yelped in pain, just as he had intended. It was to stress his point to her father. But after all this time away, would he care enough about her to do as Arthur was asking? Had he even got what Arthur wanted? She glanced at her watch, but it was only seven o'clock. Carver wasn't due to pick her up until eight so she couldn't rely on him for rescue.

Arthur's voice was now louder and definitely more threatening. 'Be a pity for anything to happen to your children when you've only just reconnected with them. I've a couple of errands to run, then meet me in the clearing near Michael's son's house, the one where he and your daughter had their cosy *loved-up* bonfire. Be there in an hour and a half. And you'd better have something good for me, or else.'

He ended the call.

She decided to chance a question. 'Can I ring Carver?'

'I don't think so. No more calls.'

He slid her phone along the table away from her. It landed with a crash on the floor.

'Right, where are your car keys?'

'They were in my bag. I'll need shoes too.' She showed him her feet. She was wearing only socks.

'Get both. No smart moves. I'm watching you. I can always tell your dad I've hidden you away somewhere. He wouldn't know you were here … already dead.'

Arthur, she still wanted to call him Robert, waved the knife in the air and ran a finger slowly along her jawline again. It appeared to be his favourite scare tactic and it worked well. Ice-cold shivers followed the track of his fingers. When he moved away, Jenny got up quickly and went to retrieve her keys from the pile on the chair and shoes from the hallway, the man right behind her all the time. She couldn't see a chance to get safely away. Alarmingly, she began to cry.

'Stop snivelling, you're driving.'

He escorted her to the car, the knife behind her back, his arm linked in hers, so a passer-by would suspect nothing.

Her heart leaped; he'd have to let her get into the driver's side of the car while he went to the passenger side. If she was quick …

But he'd second-guessed her. He made her get into the passenger side of the car and shuffle over. She felt disappointed and defeated.

Arthur told her to drive out of Borteen along the Quarry Road. Jenny thought several times about trying something daring, like an emergency stop or causing an accident with the intention of getting help, but in the end, she wasn't brave enough to try.

He told her to turn into the long drive to the caravan site on the hillside above the quarry. He pointed to a run-down caravan right at the top of the site. She parked next to it, wondering what was coming next.

'Out of the car.'

It was a chance. She decided to take it. She jumped out of the car and ran, only to twist her ankle in a rabbit hole and fall crashing to the ground.

Arthur was over to her in an instant. 'Silly girl. You do realise you can't get away from me?'

He hauled her to her feet and half-dragged her to the caravan. The air inside was foul smelling, as if the windows hadn't been open for decades. He pushed her down on one of the bench seats. 'Sit still, or else I'll tie you up.'

Jenny could feel her ankle swelling painfully. She watched as Arthur packed a rucksack with clothes and various small black bags. When the rucksack was bulging and fastened, he put it by the door and came over to her. Again, he ran his finger along her jawline. She felt sick, revulsion making her skin crawl.

'Pity we haven't got longer ...' His suggestive leer made it obvious what he was thinking. Jenny started to shudder.

'Come on, I've some deals to do before we meet your dad. I'd better drive seeing as you've stupidly hurt your ankle. Up.'

He hauled her to her feet, then spun her round so that he could tie her hands behind her back with what felt like cable ties. Once he'd shoved her unceremoniously into the backseat of her car, he applied ties to her ankles too and pulled a rough bag over her head. She lay trembling on the seat, her twisted ankle throbbing.

Arthur drove fast. She could tell by the twists and turns that they were heading over Pink Moor towards Sowden.

She tried to envisage the route, but it was pretty difficult from where she was lying and she couldn't stop horrible possibilities invading her mind. Would he hurt her? Was he taking her somewhere to kill her and dump her body? Would she ever see Carver again? The thoughts just kept getting more terrible and before she knew it she had no idea geographically where they were.

Eventually, Arthur stopped her Mini.

'I'm going to be gone a little while, I've a few deals to do, but don't try anything stupid again. I will be watching the car.'

She heard him get his rucksack out of the boot and lock the Mini. What now? She would have liked to think she could wriggle the bag off her head and somehow escape from the car, or at least open the window so that she could scream, but not being able to see where Arthur was, or indeed where they were parked, made her hesitant. She could still see the glint of his knife in her mind's eye. What sort of man carried cable ties around with him on the off chance he might need to tie someone up?

Her ankle was still painful and realistically she didn't think she'd be able to run even if she managed to get out of the car. Breathing the stale air in the sack was making her hot and light headed. On balance, she decided she was better waiting for another opportunity to escape ... if there ever was one.

Sometime later she heard the car's central locking disengage and tried to sit up.

'Still here then? Good,' Arthur taunted.

'I think I'm okay to drive,' she mumbled through the sack.

He pulled the material off her head.

'What was that?'

'My ankle's fine now. I can drive if you like.' Anything was preferable to being trussed up like a turkey.

Arthur thought for a moment and then used the tip of the knife to sever the ties on her ankles. He didn't untie her hands until she was in the driving seat and he was in the car with the doors locked.

Her face, when she caught sight of it in the rear-view mirror, was red and her hair flattened. Her eyes looked so unlike her own, she was alarmed.

'Tree Tops, and don't try anything or you know the consequences.' He waved the knife around.

As she drove to Tree Tops, she was very aware of Arthur sitting next to her, the knife on his lap. He knew exactly where they were going, so there was no chance to deviate from the route. Her ankle hurt and she winced against the pain as she accelerated.

She parked in the now familiar layby. Carver's pick-up wasn't there. He was probably at her house wondering where she was.

As soon as they were out of the car, Arthur tied her wrists behind her back again with cable ties. The plastic dug painfully into her already sore flesh. He towed her through the trees with the confidence of someone who had been here many times. He still brandished the knife in his other hand, as if to remind her he was in charge. Her ankle throbbed as she walked.

By now she was pretty sure he would use the blade if he felt he needed to, or indeed if he wanted to.

When Carver parked outside Jenny's house, it was already ten minutes past the time they had agreed. The churchwarden had taken ages to select the wood for him to take away. He hoped Jenny wouldn't be annoyed that he was late.

He walked up the path, a strange prickle of apprehension between his shoulder blades. Her car wasn't in the drive. He went back over the conversation about him collecting her. They'd definitely agreed eight o'clock.

The front door was ajar. She must have left it open for him.

'Jenny?' He went into the hallway, closing the door behind him. The house was eerily quiet. The kitchen was empty, the kettle cold when he put his hand against it to check.

'Jenny?' He shouted louder. The lounge was deserted, but then he noticed the clock on the table, its secret compartment gaping wide open. Jenny's bag was on a chair, the contents strewn across the cushion. Her mobile phone was lying on the floor, the screen smashed.

Moving through the house more quickly now, he established she wasn't downstairs and sprinted up the staircase. He kept calling her name, although instinctively he knew she wouldn't reply. A half-drunk mug of tea was abandoned on the bedside table. Jewellery was strewn all over the bed. Well, that wasn't quite true, jewellery was arranged on the bed. It seemed odd.

He sat down on the edge of the mattress, running his fingers over a fine chain. Not burglars then, or this wouldn't still be here.

Where was she? What now? If it hadn't been for recent events, he might have thought she'd just popped round to see a neighbour, but he realised he was kidding himself to even think that.

Police?

He checked his phone. There was no point dialling Jenny's number, her phone was downstairs in pieces. There were two messages, both from his father.

Before he could listen to the messages, his mobile phone began to ring, making him jump. His father's name flashed up on the screen, formally identified as Michael John Rodgers; he hadn't been able to bring himself to refer to Michael as Dad in his contact list.

'Where have you been? We've been trying to get hold of you.'

He listened in disbelief as Michael told him about Jenny, a knife and arrangements for them to meet someone called Arthur Monkston, who was holding Jenny captive.

'We're in a taxi on the way to Tree Tops,' Michael said.

The surge of anger Carver felt was so strong, he almost couldn't reply.

Anger with his father and Jenny's for bringing this danger to her door.

Anger with this unknown Arthur Monkston.

Anger at himself for not keeping Jenny close, for not protecting her. For leaving her to go and get the stupid wood for the stupid nativity scene.

'I'm coming straight there.'

'Approach with caution. Arthur is dangerous. He's not long out of prison. You should know that he was convicted of aggravated burglary and two counts of grievous bodily harm, or was it attempted murder?'

Carver's hands shook at the thought of Jenny in the hands of such a dangerous man. He wanted to gather her up and keep her safe.

'What does he want? And no bullshit this time.'

'He wants the money and jewellery he asked us to keep for him for when he came out of prison.'

'Don't tell me, you haven't got either?'

'No, we haven't.'

Carver's knees threatened to buckle as he allowed himself a second of weakness, a momentary memory of his fear of scattering Jenny's ashes at the Wishing Tree too. But then he pulled himself together; there was still a chance he could save her.

'I'll meet you there. Keep Arthur talking.'

He hung up and retrieved Jenny's house keys from the pile around her bag, locking up the house as he left, all the while trying to think what to do for the best.

When he arrived at Tree Tops, he noticed that Jenny's car was in the layby, only this time it wasn't parked in her usual straight line, more dumped away from the kerb and facing in the opposite direction as if she'd approached from Sowden, not Borteen. Carver's heart was hammering. He took a couple of precautionary puffs of his inhaler, just in case and pushed it firmly deep into his pocket. He couldn't afford an asthma attack now.

Just as he couldn't go blundering noisily into the wood, it might be dangerous for Jenny.

He had an odd feeling. His mind felt razor-sharp and he hadn't been this clear-headed and decisive for ages ... well, since before Bliss died. His concern for Jenny had made him feel protective and somehow strong. He realised with clarity that his feelings for the spiky-haired blonde woman had magnified without him realising it. He was in no doubt that he was in love with Jenny.

He dialled Kieron's number, explained what had happened and gave his brother-in-law some very clear instructions and directions. He knew the man well enough to be sure he would do exactly as he asked.

Trying to portray an air of bravado to himself, he set off cautiously down the forest path, weaving through the trees. He turned back when he heard a vehicle pulling into the layby. A taxi.

Michael and Timothy looked somehow older as they got out and paid. Both pale, despite their Spanish tans, they greeted Carver quietly, both avoiding meeting his eyes.

Carver could feel an anger brewing inside him again, but vowed he would keep it under control. Now was not the time to sound off at these two men, whatever he was thinking. Jenny was the priority. She was too important.

When they reached the clearing where he normally did his wood carving, Jenny was sitting on one of his upturned log seats. Arthur, or at least he assumed that was who the man was, pulled Jenny to her feet, placing a knife strategically near her throat when he heard them approaching. There was a lantern torch on the ground near to them, so Jenny hadn't told the man about the floodlights, or else Arthur didn't want too much light. Carver saw Jenny swallow and try to recoil from the blade, but her hands were tied behind her back.

*He wouldn't hurt her really, would he?*

Carver tried to assess his chances of tackling the man and keeping Jenny safe. He decided that course of action was a last resort. He would have to listen to what Arthur wanted to say; besides, hopefully if Kieron played his part ...

302

# Chapter Thirty-Four

The tension in the clearing was building as Arthur, holding Jenny against him, faced Michael, Timothy and Carver.

Carver could stand the silence no longer. 'What's this all about? Don't be stupid, man, let Jenny go.'

'Ask your dad what this is about,' said Arthur, gripping Jenny even more tightly, so that her face contorted with pain.

Carver deliberately positioned himself away from Michael and Timothy, so that he could observe Arthur while he was speaking to the other two men. Jenny's face was pale. Carver checked that although her hands were tied behind her back, her legs were still free. That detail might be important later.

'Has he hurt you?' He directed his question at Jenny.

She almost imperceptibly shook her head.

Michael Rodgers spoke next. 'Son, this is the man who threatened to expose my affair with Tim all those years ago.'

'I gathered that,' said Carver. 'But something doesn't quite add up here. Why have you all come back now? Why after twenty-five years?'

'They promised to keep my nest egg safe until I came back,' growled Arthur.

'What do you mean by that? This is ... is getting exasperating. Will one of you tell the full story, for crying out loud? So that I can understand what the hell is going on here.'

Timothy stepped forward. 'It's my daughter with a knife at her throat. Let me take her place, Arthur. Your argument is with us, not with her, or Damie—Carver.'

'Ah, but how better to get you to take me seriously, eh? Lovely long, white throat your girl has. But, my goodness, you and Mike haven't aged well. At least they kept me fit in prison.'

Timothy began to talk out loud, walking from side to side, all the while his eyes fixed on the knife at Jenny's throat. 'Like we said earlier, Carver, we started to buy clocks and watches at auction and we were selling them on to make a profit. Saving to go away together.'

'Cut the crap, you can explain all this to your kids later. Have you brought me my ticket to a happy retirement?'

Carver was standing with his back against the trees. Arthur was getting increasingly agitated; he might yet have to rugby tackle him to save Jenny. He felt adrenaline pumping through his veins as he decided where would be the best part of the body to grab Arthur to deflect the blade away from her.

Michael held out a bag. 'Here … a down payment. We can get more, but not quickly.'

'Are you trying to fob me off?'

'No, no,' said Timothy, with panic in his voice.

'You promised to keep the money and jewellery safe for me. What happened to that corker of a diamond necklace? I can understand the cash being gone, but the jewellery wouldn't have been that easy to fence.'

'No idea. We haven't been back to dig it up. We just high-tailed it with the cash. We've not been back here till this week,' said Michael. 'Someone else must have found the necklace.'

'You must not have hidden it well enough.'

'We buried it in the forest. Who goes digging around amongst trees? We thought it would be safe.'

Carver had been watching carefully. He'd almost worked himself up to the point of acting, of tackling Arthur. There was still a risk to Jenny, but he reckoned he could pull the knife away from her.

Then, as he had hoped for all along, he felt Wilf's warm muzzle against his hand. He was careful not to show a reaction on his face to this, even though Arthur was looking at Michael and Timothy. Carver hoped that Kieron was in the background with the others. Wilf was silent and obedient. Carver was yet again grateful for the fact that he'd been well trained.

Jenny's face was paper-white. Carver feared she might faint. He wanted to rush over and grab that low-life scum by the neck and shake him, like the rat he was, but the knife loomed closer to Jenny's skin. Carver couldn't believe it hadn't nicked her yet and drawn blood, as Arthur continued to berate Timothy and Michael. Carver had never agreed with violence, but right now, he could easily imagine the pleasure he would get from sinking that knife into the man's chest again and again to rescue his precious Jenny.

'I was the one who ended up in prison on an aggravated burglary and attempted murder charge. What happened to you two? Get-away driver? Lookout? Waste of space more like. You two swanned off, I now know, to Spain. You got sangria and suntans, I got prison rations and lice.'

'You blackmailed us into coming with you that night. We didn't want any part in it. We took our chance. You can't tell me you wouldn't have done exactly the same if you'd heard those shots ring out that night. Besides, it was you holding the gun, not us. We weren't even in the house.'

Carver couldn't believe what he was hearing. He didn't know what had really happened in the past, only those involved could ever truly know that, but now he was certain that the dads hadn't given himself and Jenny a true account of events. The item on the list that he and Jenny had made about possible reasons for their fathers disappearing, which referred to crimes, seemed to have been correct. Sadly. Unbelievably.

Arthur was refusing to take the bag that Michael was trying to give to him. 'I want the full amount with interest, not a *down payment* as you call it. I want my money and jewellery, all of it. What did you do with it? And don't tell me it's all gone.' Arthur's tone was verging on hysterical. 'You knew I'd be out and want my due, you should have kept it safe. Or did you imagine I wouldn't find you?'

Timothy spread his hands in the air. 'Calm down, we can get you more money. The jewellery seems to have gone. For all we know, you sent one of your cronies to get it after I told him where it was buried. You're probably trying to get extra out of us after having sold the jewels already.'

'Seems to have gone! Gone where? You watch your tongue, mate. I happen to have your daughter here.'

Arthur carefully and deliberately grazed Jenny's neck with the blade and a trickle of blood ran down and soaked into the edge of her T-shirt. Her eyes were wide with horror and it was all Carver could do not to rush the man. He winced as the knife twitched closer to Jenny's neck again.

'There wasn't a building then, it was just a wood. We've searched and searched, but we can't find our box. Someone else must have dug it up.'

With sudden clarity, Carver realised it must have been Bliss. She'd said she'd found some jewellery one time when she'd been going through her metal detecting phase. It was no good voicing his suspicions aloud though, because he hadn't the faintest idea what she'd done with the jewellery she'd found.

'Maybe you'd better get a metal detector here right now, have another look. I'm not taking no for an answer. I've done my time. I want to retire in luxury.'

'You can help us search, Arthur. Just let Jen go.' Timothy's voice had gone up at least an octave in his panic.

'Do you think I was born yesterday?'

'No, of course not, but you surely don't want to go back inside again, do you? Let her go.'

In answer, Arthur pulled Jenny even closer, rearranging his arms and the knife. Despite these movements, Carver could tell the man was tiring; he'd been holding himself so tense in such an unnatural position for all of this time.

He willed Jenny to look at him. Eventually, she turned her eyes and he nodded at her, hoping against hope that she would understand something was about to happen. There was an almost imperceptible movement in her face as acknowledgement.

'Where have you already searched?' Arthur's attention was on Michael Rodgers off to the right.

Carver took a deep breath. It was time to act. Now or never. For one second, he thought he heard Bliss's voice urging him on. He grabbed Wilf's collar. He nodded at Jenny.

'Get him down, Wilf. Get him, boy.' Carver's cry rang out.

Jenny dug her elbow in Arthur's side.

Disorientated and off balance by Jenny's unexpected shove, Arthur screamed as Wilf leapt up and sank his teeth into the arm holding the knife. The blade fell to the ground. Jenny scrabbled away into the trees and Carver dived over to the other side of the clearing. He was sitting on Arthur's back, with Wilf growling inches from the man's face, by the time Kieron and several policemen emerged from the cover of the trees.

Carver waited until Arthur was safely handcuffed, told Kieron how to switch on the spotlights to illuminate the clearing and then went to find Jenny.

She had scrambled away into the undergrowth. Her hands were still tied behind her back. She had leaf mould under her fingernails and a briar had scratched a trail across her face, but she was safe, albeit white-faced and shaking.

He took out his penknife and when he managed to stop

his hands shaking sufficiently, he cut through the ties binding her hands and pulled her against his chest. She slumped against him, rubbing her wrists and moaning.

Wilf padded over to them. Jenny surprised Carver when she reached up and hugged the animal. The dog licked her face and for once she didn't pull away.

'Good boy. Well done.' Carver fondled the dog's ears.

He pulled Jenny to her feet. She winced.

'Has he hurt you, apart from this?' He lifted her chin to examine the nick in her skin, but it was superficial and already scabbing over.

'I hurt myself actually. I tried to run away and twisted my ankle in a hole. It's fine, just stiff and swollen.'

She put her hands up to Carver's face and pulled him close for a kiss. 'Thank you for saving me. There were a couple of times tonight when I thought I wasn't going to live until tomorrow.'

Carver couldn't answer, the lump in his throat was too big. He held her hand and led her back to the others. They watched Arthur being taken away in handcuffs, a makeshift bandage on the dog bite on his arm. Carver recognised the local policeman, PC Ogilvy, holding a plastic evidence bag containing the knife out in front of him as if it might bite him.

PC Ogilvy spoke loudly. 'I will need everyone here to come to the station in Sowden to make a statement. Please follow me.'

'You might like to look in the boot of my car. He's got the keys, but he put a backpack with some strange packages in it in my boot,' Jenny told Ogilvy.

The policeman holding Arthur spoke. 'Found these in his pockets.' He threw the keys over to PC Ogilvy.

Given what he'd heard during the last hour, Carver wondered what all of this would mean for their fathers, but he decided that was a secondary concern. He could hardly look at them. Jenny was all that mattered. He wondered if Timothy and Michael would make a run for it, but that didn't bother him either. They could do what they liked.

He put his arm around Jenny and she leaned against him as they walked back through the trees to the road. She was limping with her twisted sore ankle.

'They didn't come back for us at all, did they?' she whispered.

'I have to believe our fathers were curious about us, but, no, I think they came to retrieve the jewellery they talked about. They said they'd been beaten up in Spain. I bet Arthur's thugs threatened them, told them he wanted his ill-gotten gains back or else.'

'Or maybe they thought they'd get to the loot before Arthur did.'

'Who knows. I don't actually give a damn any more.'

'Nor me, my father disappeared twenty-five years ago.'

He saw that Jenny had tears running down her face. Carver felt like crying himself. He wasn't sure if it was with relief or regret. 'And so did mine. We've managed this long without them.'

'I know, but I always dreamed of a joyful reunion,' Jenny said wistfully.

'At least we both know that their disappearance had absolutely nothing to do with us, or even our mothers. We are all victims of crime here.'

'And of a forbidden passion. Tell me, Carver, does it make you feel odd about having a relationship with me, now we know our fathers are together as a couple?'

'I hadn't really thought about that aspect of all of this ... but you obviously have?'

'It just seems weird that we are attracted to each other and our fathers live together.'

'We don't have fathers, remember – not any more.'

# Chapter Thirty-Five

The policeman driving the car to take them to Sowden police station wasn't very keen to have Wilf in his vehicle, but Carver insisted. It was either that or he'd drive himself to Sowden, he declared. Wilf was, as far as he was concerned anyway, the hero of the evening and there was no way he was being left behind.

Jenny, Carver and Wilf got in the back of the car and Kieron in the front with the driver.

Jenny rested her head against Carver's shoulder and did not object when Wilf laid his big, shaggy head on her knee.

'He saved me ... Wilf saved me,' she said dreamily.

'I told you he was trained by a police dog handler. He knows when to be quiet and how to react when given the right commands.'

'Well, I'm very grateful.'

'Look at him. He knows that he's your new best friend.' Wilf was gazing up at her with adoring eyes. Jenny didn't answer, she just nuzzled closer to Carver. Carver sighed with relief and contentment, reaching out a hand to pat Wilf.

Their fathers were in a different police car for the journey to Sowden. Carver thought it just as well. He couldn't decide how he felt about his dad at the moment. It would almost have been better not to have his illusions shattered, to have clung on to the hazy image from his childhood. Better that Michael had remained a mysterious enigma, as he had been for so long.

Then again, maybe the whole point of their fathers going missing was to bring him and Jenny to this point ... as a couple. He sighed, hoping against hope that she felt the same as he did.

Carver was enjoying the warmth of Jenny against his body and was relieved that she was safe, but nevertheless, underneath the surface, he was a seething mass of rage. He'd done without a father up until this point in his life and then just as he'd had a tantalising glimpse of the man who had fathered him, the box he'd opened appeared to be like Pandora's box of mythology, full of irritants and pain.

Logically, he knew that they had to go to the police station to make statements, but all he really wanted to do was to maroon himself at Tree Tops and brood, or was that grieve?

The lovely woman resting against him had been through enough and not just today. She surely didn't need him to be in a foul mood on top of everything else. He'd allowed himself to begin to relax, to imagine his life could be normal again, but was he just kidding himself?

Kieron asked Jenny if she was okay and she stirred and sat up straighter.

'I'm tired. I think it's because all the adrenalin has gone after being terrified I was going to have my throat cut.'

Carver felt guilty that he hadn't thanked his brother-in-law for the rescue party. It was difficult to speak normally with the looming presence of the police officer driving the car, but he tried. 'Thanks, Kieron. You did everything I asked without question and it, thankfully, worked out.'

'I recognised the tone of your voice, mate. It said do this and do it now, no questions asked.' He laughed. 'I couldn't believe how Wilf understood exactly what I meant. He could easily have been a police dog. He was fantastic today. He just did exactly as he was told. I was so impressed.'

'I think he's too big to be a police dog. He was given most of the training though and I knew it would come in useful one day.'

Hours later, way past midnight, Nina came to collect them from Sowden police station. She was full of questions, but Kieron thankfully promised to explain all when they got home. By this point, they were all worn out and largely silent.

Statements made, there was nothing more to do, unless the police decided to take things any further.

Carver was just about to get into the car when Timothy and Michael came out onto the pavement. It was all he could do not to take a swing at his father. The surge of rage was incredibly powerful and his normally pacifist fist itched to lash out.

Jenny got back out of the car. Carver put his hand on Wilf's collar. The dog made a low growling noise in his throat.

It was a them and us situation, the dads on one side and their children on the other. Jenny remembered what Carver had said about Wilf only growling in certain situations.

'You lied,' said Carver.

'I think they call it being economical with the truth to protect the innocent,' said Timothy.

Jenny lunged forward and Carver thought she was about to hit her own father, just as he had been imagining attacking his. She drew back at the last moment.

'You didn't come back for me at all, did you?' She eyeballed Timothy.

Even in the eerie light of the street lamps, Carver could see sudden tears sparkling on her cheeks. The air temperature had dipped and when anyone spoke their breath formed a mist cloud, which hung in the air in front of them, almost like speech bubbles.

'That's not strictly true. There were many reasons why we came back.'

'Yes, like trying to find things to pay off Arthur before he had you killed, or else getting the loot before he could.' Carver almost spat out the words.

Michael was standing behind Timothy, shifting from foot to foot and avoiding Carver's eyes.

'What happens now, police-wise?' asked Jenny.

'The police need to decide whether we have any charges to answer, whether to re-open the original case. We've had to surrender our passports and been told not to leave the country for now. You have to believe we weren't involved in the violence, or even the crime. We were just sitting in a van outside, waiting to transport the things Arthur was taking from the house and we'd been blackmailed into doing even that, as he'd threatened to tell our families about *us*. The owners came back unexpectedly and Arthur got carried away.'

'So the story about the clock was complete twaddle?' asked Jenny.

'Not completely ... the clock *was* originally sold by accident. It should have been left in the storeroom at the auction house, where Arthur worked too, but somehow it got put in the sale and we bought it. I didn't suspect Arthur of dodgy dealings. He was just a colleague at work, but he was using the front of the auction house to move stolen goods around. I only found that out after he threatened us about the clock and blackmailed us. The deal was that we'd have a share of the money and his silence if we helped him with that one job, but it all went wrong. He made us promise to hide the clock, complete with the money and jewellery and he wouldn't mention us in the court case. He wanted something to come out of prison to ... a nest egg.'

'Shhh, Tim, don't say any more,' Michael said.

'It sounds as if you were at least involved in handling stolen goods from that crime and possibly others too. How can we trust anything you say now?' Carver could feel his rage growing again. He would have to walk away very soon or risk committing his own crime.

313

Jenny exchanged a look with Carver and then turned to her father. 'I think you've forfeited any right to … to any more of my time or energy. Mum was right to close the door on all of this.'

They got into Nina's car without another word, leaving Timothy and Michael on the pavement. Sadness enveloped the vehicle. Nina drove quietly and carefully over Pink Moor.

From the way Nina drove, Jenny felt she'd finally identified the corner where Carver's accident had happened. She made a mental note for future journeys across the moor.

She was so weary when Nina dropped them off in the layby near Tree Tops. Her car was still there, very badly parked she noted. Her car keys had been kept at the police station in case it was decided that it was necessary to do any forensic tests on her car. Arthur was locked in a police cell. Jenny hoped they would throw away the key. Horrid man.

It was dark here in the lane with no street lamps, but Carver produced a small torch attached to his house keys to illuminate the layby. A surge of emotion went through her as she looked at his face in the glow of light.

'Can I still stay with you tonight?'

'I'm not letting you out of my sight.'

'I never got around to packing that bag.'

'Doesn't matter, we'll manage. You can wear one of my T-shirts and you can share my toothbrush anytime.'

Wilf led the way through the trees. Carver unlocked the house for Jenny and went to switch off the spotlights still illuminating the carving clearing.

Jenny had the kettle on by the time he came into the house. Carver took the mugs out of her hands and put them on the work surface. He took her hands and looked carefully at her damaged wrists.

'At least the skin's not broken.' He kissed each wrist

314

gently. 'I'll make the drinks. You go and sit down. I'll bring some ice for that ankle.'

He brought a tea towel full of ice into the lounge and gave it to her.

'We'll never know the real truth about what happened twenty-five years ago, will we?' Jenny asked.

'I'm not sure it even matters any more.'

'No, but it would be nice to have closure on all of this. I doubt we'll get that now.'

Later they lay together in bed, touching, but only for comfort and warmth. The drawbridge to Tree Tops was raised and, for once, Wilf had been allowed to curl up at the bottom of the bed to sleep. Carver had said he wanted all of his precious beings close by him tonight.

Despite feeling safe here with Carver and Wilf, Jenny lay sleepless for a long while, going through the events of the evening. She especially went over what she'd said in her police statement to make sure she hadn't forgotten anything. The moment when Wilf had launched himself at Arthur was particularly vivid and set on an almost constant loop before her eyes for a while.

The next thing she was aware of was the dawn chorus. The birds were rather loud at Tree Tops due to the number and proximity of the trees.

Carver nuzzled into her neck in the dawn light. 'Mmm, morning, Bliss.'

She felt her body stiffen and then his body did the same when the realisation dawned of what he'd just said.

He sat up. 'I'm so sorry. I …'

'Look, it was bound to happen sooner or later. You were with Bliss a long time. Used to having her near …'

'But that felt so wrong to say her name to you, even if it was an accident.'

'Look, it's okay. You might have been dreaming about her.'

Somehow that thought didn't make it any better. She understood the slip, but she didn't at the same time. It made her feel strange, as if she was in the wrong bed. It was all she could do not to turn her back to him and hug herself in her sudden misery. She forced herself to lie still until his breathing deepened again.

Was that all she was? A Bliss substitute? Did he really care about her for her own sake? She questioned whether she was like Bliss in any way; was she just a reminder, a pale reminder, of his wife … his first love? The pain multiplied inside of her as she tortured herself with thoughts and questions. She moved a little away from him in the bed, not able to stand the warmth of him, just in case she had this relationship all wrong.

Eventually, she dozed from mental exhaustion rather than anything else and when she woke the next time, Carver wasn't there. His side of the bed felt ice-cold. A wave of concern and also wretchedness made her alert.

She pulled on her jeans and the sweatshirt he'd given her to use as a dressing gown and went down the stairs. He wasn't in the downstairs rooms either.

Wilf padded out of the kitchen when she opened the door and nuzzled her hand. The kettle was cold.

'Where's Carver, boy?'

The dog went to the front door, so Jenny put on her trainers, wincing at her still tender ankle. She noticed that her wrists had red lines around them and a couple of bruises from the ties that had bound her the previous evening. The dog waited patiently for her to be ready.

The air outside was crisp with frost. Wilf led her through the carving clearing and along a narrow path into the trees.

She could see a figure ahead. It was a scene reminiscent of her first sighting of Carver through the trees as he carved a tree trunk, but this time, he was kneeling at the base of a tree. He appeared to be talking out loud, but there didn't seem to be anyone else nearby. Was he *talking* to Bliss?

Jenny approached quietly, but then purposely snapped a twig with her foot, so that he would be aware she was there and not think she was sneaking up on him.

His head jerked up. His face looked stricken, but he quickly changed his expression to a smile.

'Is this the notorious Wishing Tree?' she asked.

'Yes. One and the same.'

'You came to *talk* to Bliss?' She looked into the branches at all of the offerings tied to the tree. There must have been so many hopes and dreams represented by these scraps of ribbon and charms.

'I find that the quietness here helps me to think.'

'Look, Carver, I want you to listen to me for a moment and not try to reply.'

He looked alarmed, his eyes widening, but he nodded as he slowly got to his feet and came over to her. The knees of his jogging bottoms were wet from kneeling on the ground.

'I care for you, maybe even love you, but I recognise that you're still grieving for Bliss. You can't rush grief, it's a process, not an event. You can't stick a relationship with me over all this emotion like a … a plaster. You need to be ready and I think you need more time.'

Despite her resolve, she took in a shuddering breath, tears not far away. 'How about if I promise to wait for you for a while? It will give you space to decide if you are actually ready for a relationship with me, because I need you to be sure and wholeheartedly involved.'

'I don't want you to go.' He caught her hands in his.

'I know, but I think I have to do this, for both our sakes. Take all the time you need and process this carefully. It is the only way to be fair to yourself … and to me.'

He pulled her close and she snuggled into the fleece he

was wearing. She breathed in the scent of him, just in case it was the last time she would get the chance, trying to imprint a deep memory to sustain her in difficult times. It was very hard to hold back the tears, but now that she'd said her piece, she needed to be strong and follow through. It was the right thing to do. She disentangled herself from his embrace and Carver didn't resist.

'Take care of you,' she said, not trusting herself to say more.

'Take care of you too.' He leaned in and kissed her gently on the lips, as if he was taking his own imprint memory of her. His beloved lips drew away, the silvered scarred part of his lips she loved best another memory to take with her.

She walked away, her heart breaking, as Wilf began to howl, just as if the dog had understood every word.

Jenny stumbled away. Wilf stayed with his master. She walked as quickly as she could back to Tree Tops. All she had there were her socks, a jacket and her house keys. Carver had returned those to her the previous evening. It wasn't until she reached the layby that she remembered she hadn't got the keys to her car.

Determined not to look back, knowing she couldn't ask him for a lift, she managed to hobble her way down the road, across the promenade and up the hill to home. Her ankle was terribly sore, but the sensation was something to focus on rather than the absolute grief she felt about what she'd just done, given up ... possibly forever.

As soon as she was through the front door of Priory Avenue, she slumped down onto the mat and sobbed. Her ankle was very swollen after the long walk and now her eyes were swollen from crying.

Cold, stiff and empty, she rose from the front door mat with renewed purpose. She went through to the kitchen, clear-mindedly searching a drawer for the meat tenderiser, which had been part of her kitchen utensil set and she'd never ever used on meat. She went into the lounge.

The clock lay on the table with the secret compartment open, where it had been left by Arthur the previous evening. It now felt the full focus of all of her pent-up frustration, anger and sadness.

The clock that changed her life.

The clock that had been responsible for her growing up with no father.

The clock that made her keep meeting up with Carver.

The clock that had made her fall in love.

She lifted it up and threw it onto the floor. The secret drawer detached in the fall. Then, she pulverised the clock case and face with the meat tenderiser. She kept hitting it and hitting it until there was nothing left but splinters of wood and shards of glass, until she couldn't see what she was doing through her tears, oblivious of numerous tiny wounds on her hands.

# Chapter Thirty-Six

Jenny couldn't believe how things had turned out. She'd been so sure that she and Carver were on the verge of a relationship and not just a casual one either. It had felt so right.

The absence of him in her life made her realise once again that she'd failed to build much of a social life for herself here in Borteen. Thank goodness she had the job she loved at the archives to at least anchor her existence and keep her sane.

She spent the next couple of days in a tearful limbo land, rousing herself to pretend to be okay while she was working at the archives and slobbing around when she was home, eating ice cream and watching inane television programmes to pass the time, trying not to think too much about anything.

Clearing up the mess from the destruction of the clock had taken ages. Splinters appeared to have lodged everywhere and she kept finding them, long after she thought she'd collected them all. It had felt better though when the cursed object was no longer in the house. Even better when her dustbin had been emptied that week and the council refuse lorry had driven away, taking its remains out of her life ... if not the memories, which were branded in her mind forever.

When she felt strong enough to talk about it, she rang Rosie in London. At least with Rosie she could be totally open and candid. She poured out the whole sorry tale, the dads, Arthur, the police and her split with Carver ... her bewilderment. By the end of it she was in tears and she could hear that Rosie was too. Her friend made her promise to come to London the following weekend.

'A change of scenery will do you good,' said Rosie.

She rallied her girlfriends. She bought the drinks at the wine bar for Pippa and Mandy on Friday evening and led a toast to singledom, as the other girls were both not in relationships either. She tried to drown her sorrows in wine ... it didn't work.

She skirted over why she was *back on the market* as Pippa had termed it, instead focussing on what social and hobby groups she could join in the area and where the best Christmas and New Year parties were being held this year. The smile on her face was a fragile veneer and what made it worse was the knowledge that Pippa and Mandy were both aware that she was wearing a mask to hide the depths of her pain.

On Saturday, she forced herself to shower and go down into Borteen. As she'd hoped, Buzz had drawn another labyrinth on the sand. There was a battered notice on the promenade advertising the spiralling walk, with a board declaring the proceeds today would go to a children's cancer charity.

Buzz smiled at her when she put a banknote into his pink bucket. She set off along the sandy winding path, trying not to remember the joy of the first time she had done this with Carver ... but, of course, failing.

Despite herself, she felt the tension unwind a little from her shoulders as she walked, but it returned again as she neared the end of the path; she hoped that Buzz might give her a message or a sign, as he had the first time she'd done this.

'Do you feel better for walking the path?' Buzz asked, his blue eyes seeming to pierce her soul.

'I'm not sure anything could make me feel better right now.' She sighed heavily.

Wordlessly, he took her hand and stared into her palm for a while. Her heart leaped in anticipation.

'Give things time. All will be well.'

She was disappointed. This message seemed almost a platitude, as if he hadn't got a sign for her at all, as if it was all a sham. Nevertheless, she thanked him before walking away.

Her next stop was the craft centre. As she entered Owl Corner Crafts, Mandy's face lit up.

'Hi. What have you been up to today?'

'I've just walked the beach labyrinth.'

'Isn't it weird how light it makes you feel?'

'Yes. I was very sceptical the first time I did it, but it certainly changes your mood.'

'That's my experience too. Now, what can I do for you? Did you come looking for anything in particular, or just a chat?'

Mandy helped her to choose some new pictures for her freshly painted walls. Not too modern, but different enough to stamp her individuality on the house and so that she could evict her father's paintings. She planned to donate the colourful Spanish oils to her mother's favourite charity shop. She didn't want them in her house any more, just as she wanted nothing to do with her father.

She paid for her purchases and Mandy agreed to deliver the paintings to her house later, as Jenny was on foot and not in her car.

'Have you made things up with Carver?' Mandy asked.

'No, I don't think that's going to happen. I haven't seen him at all lately.'

Mandy paused in wrapping the pictures in bubble wrap. 'That's a pity. I thought you two could be good together.'

Jenny found that she'd crossed her arms defensively across her body. 'That's what I thought too at first, but it seems not.'

'He's been through a lot. He probably needs more time. Don't give up on him yet.'

'Hmm, you're not the first person to say the same thing today.'

She checked on the time Mandy would bring her pictures round to the house and made her farewells.

Standing on the promenade staring out to sea, she began to think about her mother. The dreadful episode with her father had made her realise how much her mum had done for her as she was growing up. The feelings of gratitude made her go to buy flowers to put on her mother's grave.

Outside the church, there was a makeshift stable roof and inside a beautifully carved nativity scene. The wooden figures and animals were exquisite ... Carver's work, she realised. Despite everything she felt a stab of guilt. She'd agreed with Carver that she would provide cloaks to dress this Christmas scene.

Here was something she could do productively with her time in the evenings. She placed the flowers on her mother's grave, expressed her thanks and stood for a while in contemplation, then she went back to the nativity scene and took measurements for all of the figures that required clothing, using her hands and fingers as units of measurement. She wrote everything down in the little notebook she always carried in her handbag.

That evening she sorted through her material stash and for the next few days worked at the archives in the day and at night she sewed the garments to clothe the nativity scene. She had lots of off-cuts of material that were suitable, but did visit the fabric shop in Sowden for some trim and a length of cream woolly fabric.

It gave her great satisfaction to brighten up the nativity scene the following Thursday evening, when she went to dress the figures in their newly made clothes. It was dark, but she knew the church had floodlights to work by and couldn't help feeling excited as she gave Mary her blue dress and the sheep their woolly coats. Standing back, the jewelled colours of the kings' cloaks looked lovely. She felt a glow of pride and couldn't help wondering if Carver would see the nativity and realise who was responsible for the transformation.

Whenever she thought of him now, it was with the sorrow of regret and missed opportunity.

The main reason she was out on a dark night clothing nativity figures was that she was going ahead with her visit to Rosie in London the next day. She was getting a train from Sowden after work. Maybe her friend was right and a change of scene would help her to come to terms with everything that had happened.

As the train sped through darkened countryside on Friday evening, she began to wonder if she'd done the right thing. It was almost a year since she'd been in London. Part of her wanted to know if she could be comfortable living there again, with the hustle and bustle of the City. To use one of her mother's phrases – *The world is your oyster. You can be whoever you want to be.* She could return to an office job in the City if she wanted to. The other half of her felt like the proverbial country mouse, shrinking away from the thought of crowds, traffic and the faster pace of life.

Rosie was at the station to greet her, wearing her office *uniform*, her huge handbag hung over her arm. She enveloped Jenny in a sympathetic perfumed hug.

'You poor thing, you've been through so much. We are going to have fun.'

Why didn't that statement fill Jenny with joy? Her immediate reaction inside was *Oh, no.* She was filled with dread as to what her friend might mean by *we are going to have fun.*

They fought their way through the busy station, Rosie barging people out of the way with her handbag – so that's what it was for – Jenny following behind towing her overnight case. It was airless and dreadfully noisy. The steps to the tube station were precarious, especially as there was a stream of people coming the other way. Jenny's immediate impression was of the impatience and lack of politeness all around her. Her pulse began to throb in her temples.

The tube train was busy, packed with commuters, although this thinned out as they got closer to Rosie's address on the end of the tube line. Rosie kept up a constant chatter about work and mutual acquaintances in London, as if she feared Jenny would crumple into a sobbing heap if she didn't keep her mind occupied with trivia.

Jenny had forgotten just how small Rosie's flat was. It was basically two rooms, plus a minute bathroom. It was situated in a complex of apartments formed inside an old Victorian factory building. Jenny was almost embarrassed about the size of the case she had brought with her, as it took up far too much floor space. Rosie bustled around the lounge-dining-kitchen room, closing blinds and putting on lamps.

Jenny was to sleep on the bed-settee, so she just wheeled her case to one side of it for now. Rosie opened her tiny fridge and produced two microwave meals.

'You have a choice – chicken jalfrezi or rogan josh?'

'Chicken, please.'

Rosie microwaved the meals with the air of someone who did this a lot.

Jenny was glad to sit down at the table for two. The meal was edible, but not great.

'So, I want you to tell me everything that happened after that weekend I stayed with you again. Just so I can be clear about everything. I can't believe you've split with the dishy Carver. I really imagined wedding bells.'

'It's complicated.'

'Isn't it always with relationships?' Rosie glugged some wine into Jenny's glass, even though she'd said she would prefer water.

Jenny went through the whole tale again, step-by-step, sipping the wine despite her resolve. Strangely, with each telling it had become easier to feel more detached from the feelings associated with the kidnap and what she saw as the father betrayal. The clock story was still not fully explained to her satisfaction and probably never would be, but the emotions around losing Carver were as sharp as ever.

Rosie swirled her wine around her glass and eyeballed Jenny. 'So are you staying in Borteen, or coming back to the rat race?'

'That's one decision I have to make.'

'I could put out feelers for a job for you. There might even be something at Borden Glass.'

'Hang fire on that. Let's get this Christmas over with first.'

Rosie grinned. 'Sounds to me like you still have hopes things will come good in Borteen.'

'I am getting attached to the place, I must admit.'

'What about your dad? Have you heard anything from him?'

Jenny grasped the stem of the wine glass tighter. 'Not a word.'

'That's a bit mean.'

'Maybe. I don't expect to hear from him. He knows I was aware he hadn't really come back to Borteen for me. His motivations were more directed at saving his own skin, or retrieving more stolen goods to finance his Spanish lifestyle. I'm done with him. I've survived this long without a father, I don't need one.'

Rosie appeared to sense Jenny's mood was dipping and began to clear away the crockery. 'Right, early night, because tomorrow we are going shopping and Christmas window spotting. Then, in the evening, I thought we'd go to Hyde Park Winter Wonderland.'

'Sounds fantastic. You remembered I love the Christmas lights and the decorated shop windows. And I haven't been to the Hyde Park fair for a few years. How lovely.'

Rosie looked pleased that she'd lifted Jenny's mood and Jenny had to admit she did feel genuinely better at the prospect of the day ahead.

The next morning was a crisp winter day with lots of sunshine flooding onto the bed-settee where Jenny slept. It was a firm, but surprisingly comfortable bed. She sat up and made a resolution to have fun today; her troubles could wait until she was back in Borteen. Rosie had intended she should find distraction and a change of perspective in London and Jenny was going to embrace the trip wholeheartedly.

They had a lovely time, even though they were mainly window shopping. Jenny couldn't believe the inflated prices that she'd once not batted an eyelid to pay. The lights and the windows were stunning, she'd missed them. They made the string lights and Christmas tree in Borteen seem very tame. Even as she thought that though, Jenny had a surge of longing to be home. Borteen was now where she belonged.

Hyde Park Winter Wonderland was noisy and packed. The smells of hot dogs and candyfloss lingered in the cold air. The girls paid extra to go into a tent of ice sculptures, laughing at the depicted cartoon characters, admiring the skill of the ice carvers and emerging back into the fair with frozen fingers. Jenny couldn't help wondering if Carver would be as good at carving ice as he was wood. He was never far from her thoughts. She smiled at Rosie and said she'd had a great time, but the pangs of loss were as bad as ever.

All too soon it seemed, she was on her train back to Borteen on Sunday lunchtime, her head filled with Christmas lights, her phone full of photographs of lavishly decorated Christmas windows and the ice sculptures from the Winter Wonderland in Hyde Park.

She sent a text of grateful thanks to Rosie, as she watched the countryside zoom by. At least the trip had helped her to decide that she now belonged in Borteen, for better or for worse. It was fine to visit London, but her days of being part of the commuter rush were over.

Carver had regretted letting Jenny walk away. He had not been able to give her clear answers to her doubts, so he was unable to put up a logical argument for her to stay with him. He'd not even been able to gain the usual peace from marooning himself at Tree Tops with Wilf, or even from his carving. He'd lost the ability to read the grain of pieces of wood, so deep were his feelings of desolation. So much so, he was almost ashamed of the last few figures for the nativity scene, as they were so crudely carved. But he'd promised a nativity scene and he'd assembled it outside Borteen Church even if he didn't feel it was up to his usual standard of work.

His thoughts were tormented. Why was he denying himself a companion? Why had he allowed Jenny to doubt him? He'd seen her face crumple, even in the dawn light. He'd been responsible for extinguishing the light of love in that lovely girl's face. He was stupid and cruel. Cruel to both Jenny and himself. But then he couldn't deny he was still in love with his wife.

Wilf was his constant, loyal companion, regardless of his mood. The one emotion the dog couldn't cope with was when he became angry. Wilf would lower his tail and slope off into the shadows of another room, or into the trees if they were outside, if Carver began to shout his frustration to the four walls, or the sky.

After one such episode, Carver felt so guilty that he

hailed Wilf and attached his lead, before taking the dog for a long walk through Borteen and across the beach. Even though he'd gone on the walk to appease his feelings about upsetting the dog, he had to admit that he felt much better himself after a bracing run on the sand.

They skirted the promenade and Carver decided to go and see if his nativity scene figures were staying upright in the blustery wind. He hoped that the stable roof he'd erected would protect the figures from the worst of the wind and weather.

At first he thought he was seeing things when he realised that the kings were wearing brightly coloured cloaks. Mary now had a blue dress and even the sheep had fleece wrappings. He stared in wonder. A miracle? Or ... dare he hope it ... Jenny?

Maybe the world wasn't as dark as he imagined. Maybe it wasn't too late after all. He set off for home with a new spring in his step. He took a route that allowed him to go past the Wishing Tree. He needed to talk to Bliss.

# Chapter Thirty-Seven

Jenny was at work at the archives in Sowden on Monday. The tall thin windows framed the walkways around the building. As she went to fetch a volume of Borteen marriages, she thought for a second that she had seen Carver outside, standing by the wall.

The thought was so distracting that she began to look in the list of surnames beginning with 'S'. Her client had to remind her they were looking for a James Taylor.

It was over an hour later when they finally finished the Taylor family research session. Jenny went to put the volume of marriages away and couldn't resist looking outside again. The man was still there, perched on the low wall. Goodness, he must be icy cold by now. It was definitely Carver. Colour leaped to her face and her heart began to race.

'Sandra, I just need to pop outside for a moment.'

Her colleague nodded. 'I should think you do need to clear your head after that intense research session.'

Jenny smiled and shrugged on her coat. There wasn't time to share any more detail with Sandra. She took the stairs as fast as she dared; her ankle was still a little weak and sore after all the walking she'd done in London.

A blast of cold air hit her when she opened the doors. Carver didn't notice her approaching. He appeared almost in a trance. Frozen to the spot, perhaps?

'Carver?'

He jumped. When he looked at her, his eyes filled with emotion. To her horror, tears began to roll down his face unchecked.

'I'm an idiot, Jenny. I'm so, so sorry. Is it too late?'

'Too late for what exactly?' she asked calmly. She hoped

she understood what he meant, but she needed him to say the words himself. She sank down onto the wall next to him.

'Too late for us? You see, I've realised something.' He shifted round so that he was looking directly at her. 'If I love you, it doesn't take anything away from the special relationship Bliss and I shared. If I put the past in a special compartment, I can cope with it. But you have to be all right with the fact that I still love Bliss. And that … I always will.'

She paused as she searched his face, but she saw nothing but sincerity.

'Carver, I can't dispute that you loved Bliss … that you still love her. She was your wife, the woman you pledged to spend the rest of your life with. You can never erase that and why would you ever want to? It's a given, but … you have to be ready to let me in … emotionally … into a new phase of your life, for us to stand any chance of a future.'

'Would you still be interested in such a future? Even though I've made such a mess of things?'

She didn't hesitate. 'Yes.'

He smiled. 'Bliss gave me a gift last night.'

Jenny sat up straight, senses on alert. Uneasiness crept over her. He'd mentioned talking to Bliss before. Was he sound in mind?

'You're not making sense, Carver. How can Bliss give you a gift?'

He rummaged in his pocket and drew out a beautiful necklace that shone in the sunlight.

Alarmed, she looked around to see if anyone was near and had noticed.

'Put it away quickly, Carver. Is that what I think it is?'

He encased the necklace in his hand and nodded as he put it back into his pocket.

'It was hung high on a branch on the Wishing Tree when I went to speak to Bliss. Goodness knows how long it's hung there. I had to climb to reach it.' He showed her a long graze on his forearm. 'The moonlight made it twinkle in the bare branches. It's most definitely *the* necklace our fathers talked about, the one that caused us all this heartache and a big part of the reason why our fathers disappeared.'

'But could it have really hung there for all these years?'

'No, I think Bliss found it when she had that phase of metal detecting the year before she died. She must have hung it in the tree. So, if I'm right, it's been there for four years. She had very different views about the value of things and she loved to climb that tree.'

'But why wouldn't she have mentioned it to you?'

'I think she probably did. With hindsight, I'm sure I remember her saying she'd found a piece of jewellery. I was heavily involved in a big project in Sowden Cathedral at the time and I'm ashamed to say I barely listened.'

'Are they real diamonds? If they are, they're huge and must be worth a fortune.'

'I believe them to be real diamonds, yes. The necklace was filthy when I found it, but a quick scrub followed by a polish and it sparkled. It's why Arthur Monkston made such a fuss, why he and our fathers were searching the woods and your garden.'

Carver reached over and captured her hand in his.

'I told Bliss about you.'

Her breath caught in her throat, but she forced herself not to look at him, not yet. Her eyes would betray her.

'Did Bliss reply?'

'Difficult to say, but it was just after I'd said what was on my mind that I noticed the necklace. It felt like a clear sign.'

She looked at him then. She turned her palm and squeezed his hand. Somehow, she didn't need to know anything more. They had Bliss's blessing.

'What are you going to do with the necklace?'

'It has to go to the police, of course.'

A mischievous thought occurred to her. 'Could I wear it ... just once?'

He stared at her, the corners of his mouth twitching into a grin. 'Tonight?'

She smiled and felt the heavy emotions of the last few weeks falling away. 'We could have another bonfire.'

'Only if you bring marshmallows.'

'Done.'

She sorted out warm clothing, including two fleeces, and visited the supermarket for marshmallow supplies.

As she parked in the layby and made her way through the trees by the torch app on her phone, she reflected that the forest didn't feel scary any more. The huge trunks were more like friends now.

Wilf came bounding up to her. She was so pleased to see the dog, and kneeled down to hug his neck. Wilf rewarded her by rolling completely over on his back to demand a tummy rub. She obliged and then made her way through the trees with Wilf at her heels and joy in her heart.

Carver had already got the fire burning. He was meticulous about using stones to keep it in one place and building it in a certain way to allow the flames to draw air underneath. Living in a wooden house in a forest, he was very aware of the potential dangers of fire. A spade and a bucket of sand lay nearby for emergencies.

By the time she sat on the makeshift log seat right next to his, her nerves had been replaced by excitement. Even so, she couldn't help reliving for a moment the time when she had been Arthur's captive.

'Is it too creepy being here after what happened?' he asked, as if he read her thoughts.

'No, strangely, although I will admit I have just thought

about that time, but my overwhelming memories of being here are of you and the fire glow.'

'Have you heard any more about Arthur Monkston?'

'He's gone back to prison, after all he breached the terms of his parole.'

'And ... our dads?'

She held out her hands to warm them in the heat of the flames. 'I've not heard anything about whether they'll be charged with anything ... yet.'

'How do you feel about them now?'

Jenny unzipped one of her fleeces. It was hotter by the fire than she'd imagined. 'Indifferent about sums it up.'

'I know what you mean. I'm not sure I could ever trust anything my father says again. He did send me a text message, but I told him to leave it a while before getting in touch again.'

'I had a text message from mine too, but I haven't replied yet.'

'Are you going to?'

She stretched her legs in front of her. 'I guess I will eventually. I want to get to the truth and to do that I'll have to speak to him again.'

'Yes, it would be good to know the real story.' He stretched his legs out parallel with her own. She knew that couples in tune with each other mirrored their body language. Experimentally, she folded her legs back and Carver followed suit. She smiled.

'I smashed the clock, by the way.'

'Good. I bet that was cathartic.'

'I smashed it into little bits, but then I was worried the police might want it for evidence. It took ages to clear up. I watched it go down the road and out of sight in the dustbin lorry.'

He rubbed her shoulder.

She noticed he'd put on a subtle fresh smelling aftershave. The fact that she'd never known him wear much before made her wonder if he too thought that this could be a special evening.

She slipped her hand into his and he squeezed gently in response. They sat silently for a while, until Wilf insisted on pushing his way between them. The dog wouldn't listen to Carver's demand to move, so Jenny and he sat with their hands linked over the animal's neck.

'You dressed the nativity figures, didn't you?'

'I promised I would, so I did.'

'Thank you. The nativity looks great with the bright clothes and I love the idea of giving the sheep woolly coats.'

'I'm so pleased. I did wonder if you'd be upset, because I'd covered up your lovely carving.'

'Not at all. The fact you'd done it gave me hope that I hadn't blown things completely.'

She watched as he poked the twigs at the base of the fire. The fine hairs on the back of his hand were silver in the firelight. He had interesting hands. Sturdy with straight fingers, made even more powerful by the skill she knew lay in them to make something wonderful out of wood and to evoke sensations on her skin. She wanted to feel those hands on her body again. She was ready for 'overtures' or even a full opera. She smiled to herself.

Carver startled her out of her reverie.

'So, when do you want to wear the necklace?'

'Later.' She deliberately said the word with a suggestive tone. 'We need marshmallows first.'

He lifted, from beside his log seat, long thin branches that he had sharpened at one end. They each threaded some gooey sweets onto their sticks and held them to the flames. As soon as the outsides showed brown they turned them to toast the other side.

'Careful, don't try to eat them until they've cooled a little,' he said.

'Yum,' said Jenny as she licked the sticky marshmallow off her lips. Carver was doing the same. She wanted to kiss him to share the sweetness.

'Carver ...'

'See, I knew there was something on your mind.'

'I was only going to say ... do you think this saga is over?'

'I don't see how it can ever entirely be over. We know some of what happened to our dads and, I guess, some of the reasons why, but it's our history, the path our lives have taken up to now – and all for money and jewellery.'

'And love, I suppose. Our dads love each other, or at least I hope they do. PC Ogilvy told me in confidence that Arthur's rucksack contained bags of loose diamonds. I think he told me because he'd never seen any before.'

'Wow. So Arthur must have retrieved some more of his loot from somewhere.'

'He really didn't need to pursue our dads for the money and the necklace, did he?'

'I suppose he felt cheated when he found they hadn't kept to what he saw as a bargain.' Carver took her empty stick from her.

'People never give up the chance to get rich quick, do they?'

'No, although I've never seen the attraction myself. The things I love are mostly free of charge and I don't need much money to live on.'

'What do you love most in life, Carver?'

'The trees, the birds, working wood, watching a stream babble over rocks, being in the fresh air, walking on the beach – you.'

Jenny jumped. Had she imagined that last one? He'd spoken the word so quietly.

Wilf at last relinquished his position between them and

wandered over to the far side of the clearing, sniffing around the tree roots. They moved closer together.

'How about you – what do you love?'

'Trees, birds, tracing family trees, working with cloth and wool, watching the tide come in, walking in fresh air, being on the beach, sea glass – you.'

She held her breath and closed her eyes. When she opened them, Carver was kneeling on the ground in front of her. Slowly, he put his hands behind her shoulders and pulled her nose to nose with him.

'It's taken us a long time to voice that.'

'We both have reasons to be cautious.'

'But we both need to live life to the full too.'

He kissed her gently and she returned the kiss, pulling him closer.

When they broke apart, he stood up and damped down the fire, spreading the bucket of sand over the site to make sure it was safe. Jenny collected up their belongings. They made their way to Tree Tops, hand in hand. Wilf followed on their heels.

Carver pulled up the drawbridge as soon as they were inside the house. He looked down at the dog. 'Wilf, would you like a bone? Come on, there's a treat waiting for you in the kitchen.'

Jenny went into the lounge. The wood burner was roaring and a soft rug spread invitingly a little way from the heat. There was an open bottle of red wine, two glasses and the diamond necklace on the table.

She heard Carver close the kitchen door and walk along the hallway. Her eyes connected with his across the room.

'He'll make a terrible mess with that bone in the kitchen, but I don't care.' He picked up the necklace and held it up, so that it reflected the light of the flames. 'Do you want to put this on now?'

'Wait just a moment. I need to take off some layers.'

She began shrugging off her warm fleeces and had just put her hands under the hem of her jumper when Carver exclaimed.

'Wait. Stop.'

He said the words so sharply she was alarmed. Had he changed his mind? Had he realised all of this was a terrible mistake?

'Carver?'

'Whoa, hang fire a minute, Jenny.'

'Is everything all right?' Her voice sounded shaky.

'There are some things that just can't be said naked.'

She giggled, but his face was deadly serious, so she sat down and waited for him to speak. Had he actually blushed?

'I need to say something serious to you, but I will admit to being scared.'

'I'm not scary, am I?'

'Right now, you are the most terrifying woman in the world.'

'Why on earth would I be that?'

'Because I care about you, probably too much.'

'Is that possible?'

'Look, I need you to know that this isn't just about sex.' He looked embarrassed. 'I mean, I delight in making love to you, suspect I always will, but I wanted to declare my intentions before we get carried away.'

'Intentions? That does sound serious.'

'Jenny Simpson, I've nearly lost you forever several times in the last few months and yet, I believe I knew you were the woman for me from the first time you came to Tree Tops. You jolted me out of my self-imposed cave of grief and solitude. You made me want to live again, but I realise now, only if I can be with you?'

His serious declaration deserved a serious reply and

she spoke from the heart. 'Carver Rodgers, you are a very special man, moody at times, exasperating at others, but I don't think there is anyone else I want to walk into the future with, but you. If you are sure you want me?'

'I'm sure.'

She smiled and his own smile answered hers. She moved towards him with her arms outstretched. 'Right, now we've sorted out the rest of our lives, what was that about being naked and wearing diamonds?'

# Thank You

Dear Reader,

Thank you for reading my second novel published by Choc Lit. I do hope you enjoyed it. I still love Harry Dixon, the hero from my debut novel *The Girl on the Beach*, but Carver Rodgers is now competing for my affections. (Neither of them are as heroic as my husband, of course ;-))

When you are writing a novel, you get very attached to the story and characters. It feels very scary to launch your creation into the world, a bit like hoping your child will be popular in the school playground.

If you enjoyed this book, please leave a review for me on the retail site where you purchased it. Reviews help to increase the profile and sales of a book.

Details of how to contact me are at the end of my author profile.

Love Morton x

# About the Author

Morton S. Gray lives with her husband, sons and Lily, the tiny dog, in Worcestershire, UK. She has been reading and writing fiction for as long as she can remember, penning her first attempt at a novel aged fourteen, the plot of which closely resembled an Errol Flynn film. Life got in the way of writing for many years, until she won a short story competition and the spark for writing was well and truly reignited. She carries a notebook everywhere as inspiration strikes in the most unlikely places.

She studied creative writing with the Open College of the Arts and joined the Romantic Novelists' Association New Writers' Scheme in 2012. Previous 'incarnations' were in committee services, staff development and training. Morton has a Business Studies degree and is a fully qualified Clinical Hypnotherapist and Reiki Master. She has diplomas in Tuina Acupressure Massage and Energy Field Therapy.

She enjoys history, loves tracing family trees and discovering new crafts. Having a hunger for learning is a bonus for the research required for her books.

Her debut novel *The Girl on the Beach* won Choc Lit's Search for a Star competition.

*For more information and to contact Morton,*
*see the links below:*
www.twitter.com/MortonSGray
www.mortonsgray.com
www.facebook.com/morton.gray

# More Choc Lit

## From Morton S. Gray

## The Girl on the Beach

**Borteen Secrets series**

### Who is Harry Dixon?

When Ellie Golden meets Harry Dixon, she can't help but feel she recognises him from somewhere. But when she finally realises who he is, she can't believe it – because the man she met on the beach all those years before wasn't called Harry Dixon. And, what's more, that man is dead.

For a woman trying to outrun her troubled past and protect her son, Harry's presence is deeply unsettling – and even more disconcerting than coming face to face with a dead man, is the fact that Harry seems to have no recollection of ever having met Ellie before. At least that's what he says …

But perhaps Harry isn't the person Ellie should be worried about. Because there's a far more dangerous figure from the past lurking just outside of the new life she has built for herself, biding his time, just waiting to strike.

*Winner of Choc Lit's Search for a Star competition!*

Available in paperback from all good bookshops and online stores. Visit www.choc-lit.com for details.

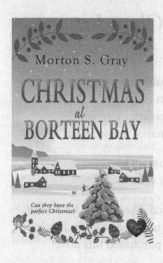

## Christmas at Borteen Bay

**Borteen Secrets series**

**Christmas has a way of bringing family secrets to the surface …**

Christmas is a bittersweet time for Pippa Freeman. There are good memories, of course – but some painful ones too.

Then her mother is implicated in a mysterious occurrence in their home town of Borteen, and Pippa wonders if she'll ever experience a happy Christmas again – especially when a family secret is revealed. But when police officer and old school friend Ethan Gibson offers his support, Pippa begins to realise that even though her life has been turned upside down, a happy and hopeful Christmas isn't impossible …

Available from all online stores. Visit www.choc-lit.com for details.

# *Introducing* Choc Lit

We're an independent publisher creating
a delicious selection of fiction.
*Where heroes are like chocolate – irresistible!*
Quality stories with a romance at the heart.

*See our selection here:*
www.choc-lit.com

We'd love to hear how you enjoyed *The Truth Lies Buried*.
Please visit **www.choc-lit.com** and give your feedback
or leave a review where you purchased this novel.

Choc Lit novels are selected by genuine readers like yourself.
We only publish stories our Choc Lit Tasting Panel want to
see in print. Our reviews and awards speak for themselves.

**Could you be a Star Selector and join our Tasting Panel?**
Would you like to play a role in choosing which novels we
decide to publish? Do you enjoy reading women's fiction?
Then you could be perfect for our Choc Lit Tasting Panel.

Visit here for more details…
www.choc-lit.com/join-the-choc-lit-tasting-panel

*Keep in touch:*
Sign up for our monthly newsletter Spread for all the latest
news and offers: www.spread.choc-lit.com. Follow us
on Twitter: @ChocLituk and Facebook: Choc Lit.

*Where heroes are like chocolate – irresistible!*